So the Path Does Not Die

D0927576

Pede Hollist

Langaa Research & Publishing CIG
Mankon, Bamenda

Publisher
Langaa RPCIG
Langaa Research & Publishing Common Initiative Group
P.O. Box 902 Mankon
Bamenda
North West Region
Cameroon
Langaagrp@gmail.com
www.langaa-rpcig.net

Distributed in and outside N. America by African Books Collective
orders@africanbookscollective.com
www.africanbookcollective.com

ISBN: 9956-727-37-7

© Pede Hollist 2012

Dedication

To the memory of my parents, Pede and Ruby, Snr.
To Josephine
Wife. Friend. Supporter. Thanks for enduring.

For the title and some of the ethnographic ethos, I am indebted to Michael Jackson's Allegories of the Wilderness: Ethics and Ambiguity in Kuranko Narratives.

Prologue

Far away and long ago, there was a village in which only women lived. It was called Musudugu. The women of this village could do everything as well as, if not better than, the men of neighboring villages. Envious, men tried many times to conquer Musudugu, but they failed because Musudugu's women defended their village with the bravery of patriots and because it was protected by the Virgin Girl, the daughter of Atala the Supreme. In return, the Virgin Girl asked the women to keep only one rule: darkness must never cover a man in Musudugu. If a woman gave birth to a boy, she could nurse him in Musudugu, but every mother knew he must be taken to his father the day he could stand up and pass water without soaking his feet. Women cried when the time came for their sons to leave. Those who could not bear the separation left Musudugu, but most returned after a few weeks, for Musudugu was a place of harmony, of singing and dancing, but most of all, of sharing and caring.

But a sweet taste in the mouth does not last forever. When Atala the Supreme wants to test a people, He does not send a stranger. He sends a kinsman. So it was for Musudugu the day Kumba Kargbo was born.

She was no ordinary child, for she forced her way out of her mother's belly, feet first! A few months after her birth, Kumba disappeared from her mother's yard, only to be found, hours later, sitting at the edge of the village, looking at the horizon. Before she even became fully a woman, she spoke of letting darkness cover a man in Musudugu. Troubled, the ruling council called a meeting of the entire village to question Kumba Kargbo.

"Why do you want to do that which is forbidden?" the council leader, a short, stout woman, demanded.

"To know what will happen." Kumba stood erect as she spoke.

"Which will be ruin to Musudugu!"

"How can one man bring ruin to all of us?" Kumba surveyed the gathering. "Have we not been victorious when they tried to conquer us?"

None of the women spoke, but Kumba could see from the look in their eyes that some agreed with her. "We must learn new ways," she continued. "When you plant a seed, does it stay a seed? No! It grows. And if you give it water and manure, does it not grow fast? Why do you want us to stay like seeds?"

Kumba's tone angered the council leader. She snatched the chewing stick from her mouth, sat upright, leaned forward, and addressed Kumba.

"Pah! A calf cannot stay a calf forever, but if it sucks greedily, it will tear away its mother's udder. Look around. See the order in Atala's creation. Each plant and animal has its place and follows its own path. Maize grows best in the rainy season but groundnut grows during the dry season because it does not need much water. When you do not follow the path, you will end up lost in the bush."

The council leader paused and looked around to make sure everyone was paying attention. Out of the corner of her eye, she spied a nursing boy reach for his mother's breast. The mother pushed away his hand. He wailed.

"Men are like elephant grass in a vegetable garden," the council leader's voice became shrill. "If you do not root it out, it will suck up all the water and sunlight and the seedlings will die."

"But how can we grow if we plant the same crop on the farm every year?"

"We know that we must plant new crops, but we begin with small patches. We leave the land fallow so that it can build itself up again. We know the thrill of a hunt and that one needs special eyes and hands to do the work of the blacksmith. We know the pleasure of being with a man and know all too well that one person cannot do *that* sweet work Atala meant for two."

The leader stopped, got off her stool, and walked away from Kumba. Her abrupt departure confused many. But just as the gathering began to disperse, the council leader spun around and addressed Kumba:

"No one is forced to live in Musudugu, to follow its ways like a slave. Every woman here is free to go and live in the world outside. But do you know why they all come back?" She paused, tightened the one-piece cloth *lappa* around her waist, and panned across the assembly. "Because they discover that life is not about killing the leopard, owning a hundred head of cattle, or being the best wrestler, praise singer, or drummer. Life is about seeing yourself as a part of others and being ready to share in their pain. When you understand that, then, and only then, are you ready for life here. Do not bring trouble for us because you feel trapped. Go live and learn in the world outside. You will find that knowledge is like a baobab tree. No one individual can embrace it. Villagers sit under their tree according to the shade it casts. Only a fool like you cuts down the baobab in her village and replaces it with the one from a neighboring village. If the tree does not die, the shade it casts changes and the village changes forever. I am done."

But Kumba was not done. She left to find out why darkness should not cover a man in Musudugu and why women should continue to follow the ways of the Virgin Girl. She traveled far and wide and for many years. She saw and did many wonderful things. At each new place, she sought the wisest men and women and asked her questions. Though no one could answer them, Kumba learned many things on her travels, and the more she learned the taller and bigger she grew, till her head was in the sky. It was *there* she met Atala the Supreme.

"Child, why are you here, so far from your kind?"

"I don't know, Father. I can't remember where I am from or who I am. I have much knowledge, yet I feel lost."

"That's because you have learned only the surface of things. You need knowledge of the self."

"How do I get that?"

"Journey into the self. True knowledge lies deep within the self."

"And then I'll be able to return home?"

Atala chuckled. "Not *return* home, but be *at* home."

v

"I don't understand."

"Home is not a place, like a village. To be at home means knowing one's self and sharing that self with others."

"But what about all the knowledge I have gathered? Is it not useful?"

"It is, but what you call knowledge are things of the senses, those things which you see, hear, smell, touch, and taste. They are like the tools of the farmer. When you own a hoe, seedlings, and a plot of land, does that make you a farmer? No! It is only in the understanding of weeding, planting, watering, and harvesting, in seeing one's hard work bear fruit and feed others that you become a farmer. Journey into the self. See what fruit it bears. Only then will you know who you are. That knowledge will be your true home."

Atala the Supreme pointed Kumba back to Musudugu, but when she got there, she was too big for it. Her feet trampled the homes, plants, animals and women of Musudugu. Those who did not perish underneath the weight of Kumba's enormity fled. By the time she realized what she had done, every woman had left. Musudugu was no more. Overcome by the destruction she had caused, Kumba cried and sang:

"*Waiyooooo, mal soey ar' tiyan*
Atalaaaaaa, ama feleh n'bara min keh n'na la
Waiyo N'Na, N'Na, N'Na, N'Na.".

(Waiyoooooo, my village has been destroyed
Atalaaaaaa, look what I have done to my mother Waiyo my mother, my mother, my mother.)

"Dance Offering to the Earth-Mother"

I will return home to her—many centuries have I wandered—
And I will make my offering at the feet of my lovely Mother:
I will rebuild her house, the holy places they raped and plundered,
And I will make it fine with black wood, bronzes and terra-cotta.

Max singing and tapping his foot to a highlife rhythm in Chinua
Achebe's *A Man of the People*

Chapter 1

Finaba Marah could tell from the length of Baramusu's stride, her erect shoulders and granite stare that her grandmother had come for serious business, so she sprang from under the tree where she had been sucking sugar cane, spat out the dry pulp, and ran toward her. She slid her hand into her grandmother's and skipped alongside to keep pace with the tall, sinewy woman who fed her *ogi* and thick slices of plantains fried in palm-oil when she was younger.

"How are you?"

Baramusu did not answer. She veered toward her daughter-in-law's mud-packed, palm-thatched house. Finaba knew trouble lay ahead. She spent considerable time around adults and had become adept at understanding their behavior. However, this afternoon, she did not need that experience to understand the reason for her grandmother's visit. Baramusu had come to talk about her.

As soon as they walked into the house, Finaba's mother, Nabou, ordered the child to go outside and play. Finaba left the house but did not go to play. She walked around to the back, sat underneath the open window, and listened to their conversation.

"We don't have to be excised, Baramusu," Nabou tightened her *lappa* and sat down next to the rickety wooden table on which lay the black second-hand Bible Finaba had been studying for her religious knowledge exam.

"*Allah dando*! It may be that you city women are proud to carry around that ugly *manhood* between your legs, but *here*, that is not our way." Nabou's city background, particularly that she was not a *musu ba*, an initiated woman, irked Baramusu, the most well-known *digba* in Koinadugu.

Her son, Amadu, had brought Nabou home as his wife after a visit to an uncle in Conakry. Tall, almost stately with her high cheekbones and round eyes, Nabou spoke Fulani fluently and

1

efficiently performed her wifely duties. But Baramusu resented that Amadu had not consulted her in choosing a bride, especially because she herself had started negotiations for a girl she was now convinced better understood her role as a wife. Aware of her mother-in-law's resentments, Nabou had learned to be firm when dealing with Baramusu.

"I don't want this for Finaba, not after what happened to Dimusu."

"The ancestors sent your first-born here and chose to take her away. Why do you blame me?"

"I don't, but Finaba must not miss school."

"*Si-kool?*" Baramusu glanced at the Bible. "Will *si-kool* teach her how to preserve our ways?"

"Don't you want Finaba to do more than cook and take care of a husband and children?"

"The family crumbles when women do not take care of their men and children." Baramusu stood up as if to emphasize the truth of her assertion. Nabou followed suit.

"*I* want my daughter to learn new ways, just like the sons of our village."

"Pssh! Sons who seek nothing but wealth for themselves and never come back? Old Mama Fatou's sons send money for her. Does the money feed and clean her? And yet you want to send our daughters away to follow footprints in the sand?"

Baramusu paused but continued to scowl. "Okay," she exhaled, "if you must send this child away, at least let her leave here a *musu ba*. Our ways will escort her among strangers."

"Finaba is just a child," Nabou's arms fell limply to her side, and she stared at the crusted earth of the soil.

"Stop fooling yourself." Baramusu pounced into Nabou's hesitation. "Have her breasts not come? You think the men have not noticed? Do you and Amadu want to become the foolish husband and wife who were so busy admiring their ripe fruit that they did not notice when it started to rot? People are already talking and soon her

2

age mates will shun her. Finaba is ready! The initiation will make her a woman—"

Nabou recovered her resolve. "Like it did to Dimusu?"

"Will you not let Dimusu rest in peace? Do you forget the great healer told us your children came to show us the path?"

"Yes, that the path we follow in cutting is wrong. That we must do things differently, learn new ways," Nabou held Baramusu's stare. "She who has never travelled thinks that her mother is the only good cook in the world."

"Yes, but if God dishes you rice in a basket, do not ask for soup. I am not against learning, but new ways are like strange food. Eat it in small doses. Otherwise, you will spend much time in the latrine."

Baramusu stomped towards the entrance as if to leave. Then she stopped, turned around and spoke softly to Nabou, like a weary parent to a recalcitrant child. "Our lives today are the harvest left to us by women like you who refused to see what is at their feet but instead looked to the horizon. The ways of white people bring only trouble. *Si-kool* turns our children's heads away from home. The path you and Amadu have chosen for this child will lead to nothing but trouble. A wise woman walks through the high grass where the elephant has already trod, so she does not get soaked with dew. So the path does not die, do not follow footprints in the sand."

"Those who leave footprints in the sand cannot expect followers. Finaba will *not* go to the initiation!"

Outside the window, Finaba ground her fists into the sun-baked earth. Now she will not belong, will not be able to dance and sing with the other initiates, will not have people in the village cheer and tell her that she is beautiful and brave. If her age mates ever allow her into their circle, she will always be the outsider, the one who will not be trusted, and the one never fully to understand what makes and binds women together.

****

3

"No one will like me, and no man will want to marry me, Baramusu," Finaba lamented as she escorted her grandmother out of their compound. Her face stern, as if pondering weightier matters, Baramusu neither answered nor acknowledged the complaint.

"My age mates will never trust me. I will be the one who does not belong, who is not a woman. Why is mama doing this to me?" She wiped the tears from her eyes.

"Do you know the story of Musudugu?" Baramusu stopped, faced her granddaughter, and waited for her answer.

"No." Finaba pouted, irritated and surprised at the sudden change in topic.

Baramusu walked over to the forest side of the path and eased herself onto the bulging arteries of a baobab tree.

"Come here and let me tell you." Finaba sat down beside her grandmother. "Your mother sends you to *si-kool* to learn the white man's stories, but she does not tell you ours, the ones that make us women." She shot a sliver of reddish brown saliva into the ground and cleared her throat. "Far away and long ago…," Baramusu began. Ten minutes later, when she came to Kumba Kargbo's lament, Baramusu stood up, extended her arms, pulled Finaba up, and started singing.

Waiyooooo, mal soey ar' tiyan
Atalaaaaaa, ama felah n'bara min keh n'na la
Waiyo N'Na, yo N'Na, yo N'Na

Grandmother and granddaughter sang and danced together as the Forest looked on. After several repetitions of their jig, Baramusu stopped, a little out of breath. She placed her hands on Finaba's shoulders and stared at the child.

"You are *not* a drifter and troublemaker like Kumba Kargbo. The knowledge and spirit of our people lie deep inside you. The night before you were born, the ancestors appeared to me and said they were sending one of their own to show our people the way because we had strayed from the path. I told your father and mother, and

4

they agreed we should call you Finaba, the storyteller."

"I am a *yeliba!*" Finaba glowed with pride.

"More than that. You must be a leader now. Show the way."

Hand in hand, grandmother and granddaughter strolled away from the baobab tree.

"Do you know why we tie rope all over the rice farm?" Baramusu asked.

"To scare away the birds that want to eat the rice crop," Finaba giggled, surprised Baramusu asked a question with such an obvious answer.

"Right and how do we do that?"

"By pulling the big ropes tied to the little ones. They make a loud noise that scares away the birds."

"And that is why we say life is like the bird-scaring rope. The big and little ropes work together to protect the farm from the birds."

Baramusu halted their stroll, stooped so that she breathed her words directly into her granddaughter's face. "Remember this: life is when people work together. Alone you are just an animal. So, do not cut the rope. Do you hear me? *Never* cut the rope!"

"Yes, Baramusu."

The grandmother reached into her bag and handed Finaba two stalks of sugar cane. The granddaughter beamed.

They reached the edge of the village, which was as far as Finaba was allowed to walk after sundown. Behind them, the huts and storage areas lay in the dim ambience of hurricane lamps and candles. Ahead, the Forest scowled at the two humans.

"Are you not afraid to walk alone in there?"

"No! I am afraid for you and the future of our village," Baramusu said and ruffled Finaba's hair. She then turned and disappeared into the forest. Moments later, Finaba thought she heard the Forest boom:

"REMEMBER: DO NOT CUT THE ROPE!"

"I will not," Finaba mumbled. Her resolve was tempered only by the sadness that she would never be able to join her age mates in the forest.

5

But a week later when Nabou had traveled out of the village, Finaba rippled with excitement when Baramusu grabbed her, covered her mouth, and led her into an edgy, early-morning forest, alive with trilling birds and crickets. Finaba knew her grandmother was taking her to the *fafei*, the initiation house, and she was happy. She was on the way to becoming a woman.

Deep into the forest, Baramusu broke the silence of their journey: "Do you know why initiation takes place in here?" She turned and faced Finaba who had been a half-step behind her.

"So that men and children will not know what women do?"

"No!" Baramusu reached into her bag and began to rub white kaolin over Finaba's face. "Like life, initiation is a journey into the unknown. *Here*, you come face to face with the unknown—about the initiation, the forest, and yourself. How you deal with them will tell you a lot about yourself and your age mates."

Baramusu untied Finaba's *lappa* and splattered heaping handfuls of the white kaolin all over her body. "*In here* and in life," she said as she dabbed Finaba's body, "you survive best when you can give strength to others and draw some from them when you need it. *That* is why no one is initiated alone. Life is when people work together. Alone, you are just an animal." Baramusu then wrapped Finaba in a white cotton *lappa*. "Soon you will die and a woman will be born."

Finaba smiled—her friends will now stop calling her a child—but it was a smile frayed by apprehension. She had heard that the initiation would be painful, but it was a price she was willing to pay.

6

Chapter 2

F irelight darkness. *Sorrowful chanting. Violent thrashing. Palm branches, strands of beads, earrings, anklets, headbands on the ground. Ghostly white bodies. A python devours the pale, writhing white bodies. Destruction! Girls descend into the cold, stinging water—DEATH OF AN AGE! Women rise into the warm air—BIRTH OF A NEW AGE. Weighted chest. Weighted thighs. Trembling, writhing thighs. Deafening, bitter, blue-red, all-consuming pain expressed into a spit-smeared cloth. Noises... shouts... screams...scrambling feet... toppling bodies. A voice... a man's voice. A smell... a father's smell. Wails throttle the air.*

****

The shouts, wails, and curses heaped on her, her father, and her family ascended into the air. Finaba had heard them in the leaves and had seen them arrayed in the moonlit sky when she and Amadu emerged from the forest; and now, as she lay on the bare metal table of a disinfectant-laden examination room in the chiefdom health clinic, they echoed in her head.

"There, the last one," the nurse grinned after giving her a tetanus shot. "You're going to be okay." An idling sob was Finaba's only response.

"It was just a small cut. In a few days, you won't even know you were touched," the nurse reassured Finaba, playfully tapped her just above the pubic area, disposed of the suturing materials, and left the room. But like an unruly student after a teacher's departure from the classroom, the pain ravaged her body. She looked to her right and then to her left, but she saw no one lying next to her from whom to draw strength, no one who could throw her a rope. "*Wayoyaaaaa...,*" she screamed. Her parents and the nurse crashed into the room.

The latter immediately examined Finaba, determined she was not in any danger, and gave her two Codeine tablets for the pain. Nabou

7

embraced her daughter. She felt the warm, pulsating body next to hers, and she recalled Dimusu's lifeless body in her hands. This time she wailed in happiness. Finaba also wailed, but her tears were for the friends who were not by her side, for the pain she could not share, and for the woman she would not become. Amadu, standing behind them, did not cry. He sniffed, coughed, and rubbed his eyes.

****

The grim-faced group of mothers and initiates had come to offer prayers, to cleanse Amadu's compound and the community, as they felt they must, as duty required. But when word of their impending visit first reached him, Amadu threatened to kill the first woman who dared to step foot in his compound. Aware of Amadu's threat, the women wisely stopped short of his compound, in a clearing far enough away so as not to provoke him but near enough for him to hear the purification rituals. They sat in a circle on the ground, waiting for the legendary Pa Yatta, the healer from whose house, it was said, you could hear several animated voices though no one had been seen going in. Various items sat in the center of their circle: a tray of cooked rice, rice flour, kola nuts, several gourds of palm wine, and a bottle of palm oil. Next to them lay a white cock, its head tucked under one of its wings, resigned to its impending death.

Every few minutes, the women's chanting rose to a crescendo and assailed the occupants of Amadu's house. Inside, no one spoke. Frightened by his threat, Nabou had summoned Amadu's brothers, two wiry men, to make sure he did not leave the house. They stood on either side of the log on which Amadu sat. Determined not to let him add the murder of a clansman to the desecration he had already committed, they eyed Amadu closely, their muscles taut with anticipation that he might break for the door. By it, Nabou sat on a small, hollowed-out log. She eyed the brothers, hoping they would be strong enough to stop Amadu if he made a move to carry out his murderous threat. She had experienced his strength in ways they had not, and she worried he might overpower them.

Finaba, in an adjacent hut, longed for the prayers to end. She wanted to do something but did not know what to do. She wanted to stand beside her father but knew that she should be sitting with the women. She understood that the women had to offer sacrifices to purify the village because no man should ever enter the *fafei*, but she also understood that her father had pulled her out of it because he did not want her to suffer Dimusu's fate. Finaba never fully understood what had happened to her older sister, but she had on more than one occasion heard Baramusu insist that the initiation had nothing to do with Dimusu's death.

****

It was a death that widened the divide between generations. Amadu and Nabou had come to learn their children were special because of Dimusu's menstrual troubles. Unusually, for a first period, the young girl bled continuously for eight days and was in constant pain. After the bleeding stopped, she was too weak to leave her bed for almost two weeks. By the time she started eating full meals and moving about again, her second period was only days away—and it was even worse than the first. Nabou, Baramusu, and the older women tried various herbs and treatments, but nothing helped. By the third day of her second cycle, Dimusu had become limp, almost lifeless. Everyone was sure she would die, but, miraculously, the bleeding stopped, and life crawled back into the young girl's body. Dreading what might happen at her next cycle, Baramusu and Nabou took her to see Pa Yatta.

After his preparatory rituals, the famed healer laid Dimusu on a mat, and with her mother and grandmother looking on, spread the palm of his hand on her stomach. The hand recoiled as if it had inadvertently touched hot coal.

"Go now and bring her sister!"

Baramusu was the first to recover. She dashed off to fetch Finaba.

"What is it?" Tears settled in Nabou's eyes.

9

"I am not certain. It happens once every three or four generations."

"What?"

"I will not be sure until I have touched her sister. You must wait." The healer swung around and walked to a dark corner of the room.

As she waited, Nabou sniffed, sobbed, and patted Dimusu's hand in succession. Pa Yatta busied himself, pushing aside talismans and amulets, pulling out calabashes, gourds, and dark brown and green bottles containing different herbs, roots, and potions. He mixed then drank and washed his hands with their contents. The odor of fermenting vegetation starched the air, obscured what little light was available, and plunged the room into a primeval gloom. Absorbed in his arts, Pa Yatta walked back and forth, chewing on a stick that dangled from the corner of his mouth. He pulled his sleeve up to his elbow, dipped his hand in a gourd here, a calabash there, and placed it on Dimusu's stomach. Again and again, his hand recoiled as if stung by fire. Each time, he shook his head, muttered to himself, and ambled to another part of the room to repeat the process with another combination of potions. Each shake of his head energized Nabou's sobbing.

By the time Baramusu arrived with Finaba, mother and daughter were in the midst of full-throated cries. In the room's dank atmosphere, Finaba immediately took up cause with her mother and sister and ratcheted herself into hysteria when Baramusu attempted to hand her over to Pa Yatta. It took the combined efforts of mother, grandmother, and healer to brace her for an examination. Pa Yatta dipped his hand into a calabash of slimy green gel, swished it around for a few seconds, and placed it on Finaba's stomach. The jolt knocked the old man back into a low stool laden with calabashes. Gels, oils, and distillates spewed onto the floor. The children cried; the women trembled.

"Your children are *Denkileni*," Pa Yatta pronounced several minutes later, after he had collected himself and restored the room to some semblance of order. He was sitting up against the wall, his left hand alternately rubbing and clasping his right shoulder, his head tilted forward and his eyes closed. Nabou and Baramusu sat opposite him, Dimusu and Finaba tucked between their legs, their eyes wide open, hearing and understanding only snatches of his words. "They have come to show the path. When they have fulfilled their purpose, they will be called home."

This revelation did not surprise Baramusu. She nodded and told Pa Yatta of the night the ancestors visited her, before Finaba was born. She was happy there were two of them. Nabou was less convinced. She had heard and seen her fair share of unfulfilled predictions and misdiagnoses, so she had an instinctive distrust of unsupported claims, even those made by legendary healers. "Is she a *Namfa*?"

"No," Pa Yatta snapped, sensing her resistance. He waited a few moments, collected himself, and, in a less impatient tone, added, "*Namfas* are restless and come alone, again and again. *Denkileni* come in pairs. One is born exactly fifteen moons after the other; they stay until their business is done, and then leave forever! *Denkileni* can die very young or they can live for a long time."

"How then is a Denkileni different from a normal child? What do these children come to do?"

"No one knows. All we know is that their work is for the good of all. They teach through the example of their lives."

"Can we not offer sacrifices to keep these children with us after their work is done?"

"No! Their time on this earth is fixed. They are not really your children. They will return to the ancestors where they belong once their work is completed."

So when Dimusu died after her initiation, Baramusu believed the child's death was a lesson to her people that they were straying from the old ways. Nabou and Amadu, however, saw Dimusu's death as a warning that initiation was harmful. It was a divide they would never close and one that, at different times, Finaba sought to understand, to bridge, but which mostly left her confused and uncertain.

Such was Finaba's state of mind as she listened to the women perform the purification rites. She laid her head on her knees, which she had pulled up close to her body with her arms. Suddenly a loud, mournful voice signaled a change in the proceedings. It sounded like Baramusu's, but Finaba was not sure and did not want to be sure.

"Almighty Father and Infinite Mother of the world," the voice entreated, "creator of all things, preserver of our laws and customs, consoler to the bereaved, caregiver to the sick, we come to ask your forgiveness for our foolishness. We come bent and broken so you can straighten and fix us. You do not desire the death of a sinner. You do not ask for the life of the one who desecrated the *fafei* because you are merciful. You want only that he turns away from his wickedness and walk in your righteousness. But if he willfully follows the path of the wicked, you must cast out the mucus from his eyes and the wax from his ears.

"Amadu, you foolish, swollen-headed man, for whom must the good be done? The one or the many? Which is wiser? To work for *me* and *mine* or work for *us* and *ours*? Almighty Father of the world, when a child says he is sorry, we forgive him even if he has broken the calabash. We have come as children to say we are sorry."

Inside his house, Amadu groaned, clenched his fists, and shuffled his feet. Finaba's uncles readied themselves in case Amadu made a dash for the door. For safekeeping, Nabou picked up Amadu's machete and deposited it outside the front door, well out of his reach. Then she stood in the middle of the doorway, providing another line of defense in case Amadu overpowered his brothers. Her eyes searched the canopy below which she believed the women were gathered. Her face and body contorted with anger at a society inviting the wrath of The Almighty on her family because she and Amadu chose to protect their child. A few feet in front of her, a line of fluffy yellow-feathered chicks followed their mother in lockstep. When she clucked they clucked; when she poked the crusted earth for food, the chicks followed suit. Nabou hissed, swung her hands and foot and sent the hen and her chicks fluttering.

12

"Atala," the Baramusu-like voice continued, "the seedlings of the baobab will surely grow big and broad and cast their shadow, for that is what baobabs do. We do not wish harm on one of your children, but if Amadu, Nabou and the child Finaba do not ask your forgiveness, and if they do not wash out the mucus and wax that has clogged their eyes and ears, may they never find peace. May they never know the comfort of home! May their insides wither so that no fruit may come from anything they touch and do, and may their ..."

Screams and shouts from the women obscured the praying voice. Feet kicked over the tray of rice, toppled the gourds of palm wine, and released the cock from death. It stood there dazed, transfixed by the stormy whirl of legs, *lappas*, and dust.

Moments later, some of the very women who knew of Amadu's wish to kill them ran into his house seeking refuge and screaming bloody murder. For several moments, Amadu and his brothers were too surprised to do anything but open their mouths and dart their heads from person to person, trying to make sense of the babbling filling the house.

The men were pleased that the purification ceremony had been aborted. But they did not have time to savor this victory of sorts. Only a terrifying danger could have driven these women to seek refuge in the wrath of Amadu's house. Duty and responsibility overcame personal gratification. The uncles grabbed their machetes and Amadu, not finding his, grabbed a log. They rushed out to confront the creature threatening to harm their women. And, lo, the sight they beheld stunned them frigid, for the creature was none other than Nabou--the mother of Finaba, the wife of Amadu, wielding his machete and chasing the women, sending them and the fluffy chicks running helter skelter.

****

At the urging of her uncles and some of the village elders, Finaba and her parents left the village that very afternoon, via a little used footpath behind Amadu's compound. They walked as fast as they could drag Finaba to catch a minibus on the main road. When they were seated in one, and it became evident they were traveling to some far-away place, Finaba asked where they were going and when they would be returning.

"Freetown," her father answered, "and I don't know if we will ever come back."

"I don't want to go there!"

Amadu ignored the sharpness in her voice. "As a child, you'd wake up early some mornings, well before it was light. I would tell you to go back to sleep. Do you remember what you would say to me?"

Finaba waited for her father to answer his own question.

"'But it hurts when I lie down for too long, Papa,'" he mimicked her drowsy voice and manner. Finaba was not amused. "You see, even a comfortable bed hurts when you stay in it for too long. We have to get up and leave Talaba. Staying will hurt all of us."

Finaba bowed her head. Only her heaving torso told of her sadness.

"Freetown is a big place. You will make many new friends and grow to be a princess." Amadu ruffled her hair, but his mind was already absorbed with thoughts of the uncertain future ahead of them.

Bang…bang…bang, the bus's undercarriage slammed into the potholes of a particularly bad section of the road. Unrestrained by either a seat belt or the protective hug of a parent's arm, Finaba rocked back and forth helplessly. She steadied herself by holding onto the handle-bar of the seat in front of her. She peered through the windshield and watched as darkness strangled the road and diminished the driver's ability to avoid the potholes. The jolts became more frequent and violent. Her anxiety deepened as the day darkened into night.

Chapter 3

It was, is, and would always be a place of refuge, of love and acceptance, of belonging. Such must have been the sentiments that compelled the people of Koya Chiefdom, through their ruler King Tom, to give land to the freed slaves to start the settlement that is today called Freetown. Nestled in a valley and draped by the dark-green, base-to-peak rainforest foliage of its surrounding hills, this capital city was the physical and psychic sanctuary to which Finaba and her parents had come to start their new life. They had brought with them nothing but a few hundred leones and the clothes on their backs.

They were to live with Amadu's uncle, Alhaji Umaru, a businessman who rose to prominence and became wealthy because he was the most reliable supplier of building materials to the national government as it readied Freetown to host the 1980 conference of the Organization of African Unity. Finaba and her parents arrived at Alhaji Umaru's compound at the same time as a black Mercedes 280 drove through the wrought-iron gates. Two sharp blasts from the car's horn commanded them to leap to the side and plaster themselves against the wall. The man in the car glared at the disheveled trio, accelerated, and left them coughing in a cloud of dust.

The man was one Christian Heddle, a. k. a. Pa Heddle, a short, pot-bellied, senior civil servant of twenty-five years in the national government. He had come to the home of Alhaji Umaru to conduct government business. Their business concluded, Alhaji Umaru recommended his nephew Amadu as a reliable, trustworthy worker to Pa Heddle. He hired Amadu on the spot as an all-purpose laborer and security guard for the building site of what he fondly called "only my second home." Alhaji Umaru also found Amadu night-time security work at the home of a Lebanese business partner. Nabou, now pregnant with another child, stayed at home and started a petty-trade business selling boiled eggs, oranges, cigarettes and mints with a cash gift she received from her uncle-in-law. From the business profits, she enrolled Finaba in school and cooked their meals.

Amadu was only a few weeks into his job when Mama Jinah, the woman who owned the rickety food stall opposite Pa Heddle's "only-my-second-home" building site, approached him. She offered him twenty leones for one or two of the eight-by-four wood planks lying around on the building site—the ones that they did not need. She explained she wanted to repair her stall but that going all the way to the wood depot across town was too much trouble for such a small job. Amadu obliged her. Later that afternoon, Mama Jinah sent him a plate of potato leaves served over brown rice. The next morning Amadu was still marveling at the delicious taste of the potato leaves cooked with *ogiri* and Maggi cubes when Mama Jinah showed up with another woman who lived down the road. The woman offered Amadu twenty-five leones, for two bags of cement, also that they did not need. Amadu obliged and a plate of rice and cassava leaves arrived later that afternoon.

Initially, Amadu felt guilty about selling his boss's property. But after Alhaji Umaru revealed that Pa Heddle regularly siphoned government material to build "only his second home," he and Mama Jinah pursued a brisk and mutually beneficial materials supply business. She acted as agent for customers; he provided the materials. Three short months after arriving in Freetown, Amadu could afford to rent a one-bedroom apartment style *adjoining* a short walk from Pa Heddle's building site and Finaba's school.

"*Here*, we can do whatever we want," Amadu explained to Finaba outside the front door of their new home. Finaba was sitting on his lap and Nabou by his side. "*Here*, you can choose your path, like them," he said and pointed across the street to a group of scraggy girls gathered around a street pump, splashing water on themselves. "No one will make you feel like an outsider because you're not an initiate. *Here,* you'll be the same as those girls. *Here*, you belong."

Freedom to choose one's path was the anodyne her parents used in times of difficulty—Nabou's pregnancy, Isa's birth, Amadu's run-

16

ins with his boss—and the mantra they instilled in Finaba when she complained that her schoolmates teased her. As a result, Finaba developed early a desire to be different. The memory of Baramusu's injunctions for her to be a leader dovetailed into a desire to become, first, a teacher, then a lawyer, and finally a dentist, especially one like the American dentist who treated her at the free dental clinic. Nabou had taken her there after Finaba had cried all night that her classmates called her *bon-tit musu, kak-tit musu*.

"*Clean you tit tree times every day,*" the dentist instructed in an American-accented Krio Finaba found highly amusing. "*And Mama,*" she turned to Nabou, "*make you no giveam too much sugar. Na dat dey spoil her tit. Make yu bring am back in tree mont',*" she held up three fingers. "*Then we go give am brace.*"

Nabou nodded.

"*Yu tit go white en straight and yu go become fine-fine gyal pikin,*" the American winked at Finaba.

But Freetown took away as quickly as it gave. A little less than a year after their arrival, Amadu died of tetanus poisoning. He had sliced his heel on a rusty corrugated iron sheet on the building site. Though on the day of the injury Mama Jinah urged him to go the hospital, he had refused, fearing that Pa Heddle would visit the site and not find him there. This had happened several times before, and Pa Heddle had assured Amadu that the next time he would be fired on the spot, no questions asked. To avoid losing his job and the additional income it generated, Amadu decided to wait until Pa Heddle's next visit to get permission to go to the hospital. He died waiting in the tool shed amid some wood planks and cement bags.

At Amadu's funeral, Pa Heddle told Nabou several times not to hesitate to ask for help. She took up his offer a few weeks later. On that first visit to his cool air-conditioned office, she told him that she had run out of money. She could not afford to pay Finaba's school fees, especially because she had the expenses of rent and formula for the infant that refused her breast milk. She knew few people in the city she could turn to for help. Alhaji Umaru had offered to take her as a wife, but she did not want that. Besides, she feared he would

17

insist the girls go through initiation, and that, for sure, she will not let happen. On that day, Pa Heddle gave her two hundred leones he borrowed from his office's petty cash. He gave her lesser amounts from the same source on subsequent visits.

One particular day, he found Nabou and Finaba sitting on the bench in front of his office. "I'll be back in five minutes," he acknowledged them but did not return until five hours later. Their forlorn sight tore into his heart. He emptied his wallet and the petty cash and handed Nabou twenty-five leones. A pittance. There and then, he proposed that Finaba should come and live with his family. "I have a daughter about her age. They will be friends, play and study together." Finaba scooted nearer to her mother, whose mouth remained half open but said nothing.

"It will be for a short while. Until you get back on your feet. You can see her and she can see you anytime."

Initially, Nabou was reluctant to part with Finaba, but she warmed to the idea in proportion to how life became frigid for her and her daughters. But she had to wait for Mrs. Heddle to warm up to the proposal, a tough sell for a mother managing an already large household.

"Why do you like taking on responsibilities you can't afford?" Mrs. Heddle slashed through her husband when he told her of his offer. "So that people will say you are a good man? Will you be at home to make sure she washes, eats, and has clothes to wear? Will you take care of her when she is sick? Do we have enough money to feed another mouth when we have to be saving to pay for Ade to go to England?"

"Farid and Farouk will help out with her school and upkeep."

"I'll believe that when I see their money."

"Okay, I'll let them give it directly to you."

That prospect wilted Mrs. Heddle's opposition. The following Sunday afternoon Farid and Farouk delivered their contributions through the front door. The next week, Nabou delivered Finaba to the Heddle home, through the back door.

"*Oona men am foh me, doya,*" Nabou implored and shoved Finaba toward her prospective foster parents, who sat in two straight-back chairs like royals receiving a lowly subject, this one a thin and forlorn girl in a second-hand blue and white floral dress. Its neckline hung loose and wide, revealing her collar bone. Head bowed, shoulders hunched, and fingers twiddling in front of her, Finaba absorbed their inspection like a candidate in a criminal line up.

The handing-over was short, without ceremony. Nabou turned to leave. Finaba squealed, rushed to her mother, and grabbed onto her *lappa*. Nabou hugged her daughter, wiped the tears streaming from her eyes, and pushed her back toward the Heddles. "Stop crying and remember to do as you are told," she instructed and left. Finaba swallowed her tears and sorrow. After allowing a few minutes for Finaba to compose herself, Mrs. Heddle summoned the household and introduced her.

"Where will she sleep?" Edna asked. She was nearest in age to Finaba and recognized the playmate potential.

"In the other bed in your room," Mrs. Heddle answered. Edna giggled and clapped her hands.

"What's her name again?" an adolescent male voice queried.

"Finaba."

"Fee…na…bar. Fi…na…bu. Fee… na… bra," voices mangled her name.

"Just call her Fina," Mrs. Heddle silenced the distortions. "And call *me* Aunty Matty, and him, she pointed to Pa Heddle, "Uncle Christian."

"Yes, Ma… Aunty Matty."

And that was how Finaba became Fina and the newest member in a household consisting of sixteen-year-old twin girls Taiwo & Kehinde; fifteen-year-old Ade, and twelve-year-old Edna, a year younger than Fina.

Aunty Matty and Pa Heddle did not treat Fina any differently than their own children. However, in a household of five children, competition for attention and resources was fierce, and, being the outsider, Fina was always at a disadvantage. When the household was not consumed by the twins' impending GCE O-Level examinations or their participation in the Miss Freetown Beauty Contest, then it was catering to Ade's running of the 100- and 200-meter sprints at the annual Western Area Secondary Schools Track & Field meeting, or it was celebrating the person receiving ten awards for scholastic achievement at a school's prize-giving ceremony. Fina learned quickly to appreciate the virtues of restraint and deference among children who were accustomed to having their needs and whims gratified.

Fina spent Saturday mornings ironing heaps of clothing with a shaky charcoal iron. The only good thing about this weekend chore was that Fina commanded the portable radio and listened, undisturbed, to Freetown's most popular disc jockey, Tamba the Groove King, a. k. a. TGK. Like most teenyboppers, Fina loved TGK's record selections and his dreamy, American-accented voice, which he acquired after a two-day visit to neighboring Liberia. As she ironed and imagined herself close dancing with Kemi Koker, a boy in the neighborhood on whom she had a secret crush, she did not notice that a glob of ash had fallen onto Ade's shirt—the very one he had earlier asked her to iron carefully because he planned to wear it later to the popular Saturday afternoon jump, a teenage get-together that featured live bands, alcohol, and prowling sugar daddies. Distracted by Kemi Koker's imagined hand racing down the small of her back, Fina made repeated passes of the iron over the ash before she noticed what had happened. The damage was not so much a burn as a deep grayish-black smear, which, with prompt and careful treatment, could have been washed off and the shirt restored to usable condition. However, Ade discovered the damage before Fina could fix it, and he vowed revenge. Later that day, Fina returned to her room to find one of her dresses ripped from hem to collar and the only photograph of her mother torn up into small pieces.

"She burned my best shirt, Mama. The blue poplin with the round collars," Ade narrated the next day after Mrs. Heddle demanded an explanation for his behavior."

"It was a mistake, Aunty Matty, I was—"

"That's a lie," Ade cut her off. "She was dancing and playing around."

"You're careless, Fina. It was the same carelessness that made you break my Tudor porcelain vase and put bleach on my indigo skirt. When are you going to make yourself useful in this house? And as for you, Ade, how many times do I have to tell you to control your temper. You have no right to cut up her things. Both of you get out of my sight!"

Out of his mother's view, Ade stuck his tongue out at Fina, mimicked her overbite, and strode off. That night, Fina cradled the fragments of her mother's photograph to her chest and sobbed—for herself, her father, her mother, Baramusu, and Talaba. The crying proved therapeutic, for she woke up the next morning determined to avoid Ade and people of his kind.

But avoiding Ade only delayed the inevitable. He was a mere cog in a design which had been mapped out much earlier and which continued to unfold in the long summer holiday of her second year at the Heddles. She had turned fifteen and was shaping up to be a beautiful young lady. Aunty Matty and Pa Heddle had gone to work and the other children had gone about their individual business. Fina had overslept. When she woke up, Edna was not in the room, so Fina decided to enjoy the room by herself. She walked over to the window and looked through the finely woven silk window curtain into the back yard. In it, she could see Ade and his friends picking mangos by hurling stones to snap the dangling orange-yellow fruits from their stem. Of course, the easier, more sensible option would have been for one of them to climb the trees and pick the fruits or to take up Ali, the houseboy's offer to climb up the trip and pick the mangos of their choice. But, boys being boys, they avoided the easier options and turned mango picking into a competitive event. The first to fell three ripe mangos would be crowned the most accurate shot.

Volleys of the stone pebbles streaked toward the dangling fruits. Some of the pebbles thumped against branches and fell back to the ground; others whizzed through the leaves and landed on and around the one-bedroom living quarters in which Ali lived with his wife and son, Chernor. Every once in a while, one of the boys would shout gleefully, "*Ar ghet am*," dash underneath the tree to retrieve a mango that had fallen or, in a feat of agility, catch a mango before it hit the ground. The person would hardly have emerged from underneath the tree before another volley of pebbles zoomed upward. Two of the boys quickly felled three mangos and retired to the shade of a nearby tree to eat their spoils and to tease Ade and the other boy. Neither had even one mango to his name. Tired and frustrated but determined to prove themselves, Ade and his partner in incompetence picked up the pace of their throws with larger stones on even more wayward trajectories. It was at the height of this assault on the mangos that four-year-old Chernor appeared from the back of his family's quarters. "Vroom, vroom," he revved his car made of wire and navigated the jutting rocks and bulging tree roots. From the bedroom window, Fina could see what Ade and his friends could not: Chernor's path led directly into the zone where the fruitless stones fell.

"Get back, get back," Fina shouted through the window, but her warnings arrived late. Thump! One of the heavier stones smacked Chernor's forehead, just above his left eye.

"Aaaah! *Papa, dem don bos mi yaye o!*" He pranced around in pain before he ran off to find his father, holding his crimson fingers over a large gash.

That evening, Chernor, his head bandaged, accompanied his father Ali to report the incident to Pa. Heddle. He was sitting in his favorite chair by his Grundig radio and record player, pained by indigestion from hastily eating a heaping plate of rice and cassava leaves and by his indignation at having to answer to a civil service boss he described as "an illiterate nincompoop." From the dining room table where they were eating, Fina and Edna watched the encounter.

Ali complained he had offered to climb the trees to pick the mangos for Ade and his friends. He had warned Ade not to throw stones but they had ignored him. Now Ade had busted Chernor's head and almost killed the only son that God gave him.

Pa Heddle scratched his underarm and squirmed. He had to put up with an illiterate at work and now at home. He sighed, reached into his pocket, and handed Ali some crisp leone notes and promised to discipline Ade.

"*Tenki sa*," Ali pocketed the notes, his face awash with happiness at his master's generosity. Pa Heddle's face contorted from a sharp twinge of his worsening indigestion. Ali saw the pained look. He felt empathy for this master who had always been fair to him.

"If you weren't such a good man to me," he explained his forbearance, "I would have gone to the police."

Pa Heddle shot up like a junior employee caught sampling his boss's comfortable leather chair. He reached into his back pocket and, after a brief tussle, pulled out a wallet from which he yanked out several more leone notes. "Here. This is your salary for this month. *This* for next month and *this* to buy medicines for your boy and pay his doctor." He thrust a bunch of notes into the breast pocket of the stunned Ali. "Since you've started talking about killing and involving the police, I don't want you to work here anymore. I want you out of my compound by the time I return from work tomorrow."

Pa Heddle put the wallet back in his pocket and marched out of the living room. Ali looked at Fina, who looked at Edna, who looked at Chernor who stared at the bowls of food on the table and licked his lips.

The next day Fina stood on the verandah and watched as an *omolanke* carted away the sum of Ali's family belongings: a mix of second-hand clothing, two grass-stuffed mattresses, a rusted spring bedstead, miscellaneous pots and pans, and a battery-operated radio. Ade and his friends stopped their football game long enough to let pass the *omolanke* which also carried Chernor with his bandaged head. As soon as the couple walked past them, Ade and his friends resumed their game. Fina walked to her room, fell on the bed, and sobbed.

****

23

Months later, Fina bathed in delight and excitement. Kemi Koker, the boy she had a secret crush on and a sixth-form senior set to attend college the next year, had invited her to his birthday party, the first she would be attending alone. Fina was delirious with anticipation.

But she relished more the "oohs" and "ahs" when Aunty Matty unveiled the red dress with the big bow she would be wearing and glowed with pride as all that week leading up to the Friday night party, she was the center of attention in the house.

Aunty Matty gave instructions.

"Kehinde," she said to one of the twins, "you will go with Fina to buy shoes to match her dress."

"Taiwo, you will help her curl her hair. No lipstick."

"Mammy Nursey, you will make sure she has food to eat before she leaves for the party."

On the eve of the party, Fina heard Aunty Matty and Pa Heddle argue over who should take her to the party and bring her home. Although a little scared that the argument might mean she would not go to the party, she did not particularly mind that. She was pleased they were arguing over her. But by the morning of the party the matter of her transportation had been settled.

"Christian, on your way to choir practice, drop Fina off. The party is in the big white house next to the Chinese Embassy. One of us will pick you up at midnight, sharp."

That afternoon, Mammy Nursey, after she had prepared Fina's food, strolled down to *Omole* Corner to mellow out on a few tots of the locally distilled gin. On her way to piano lessons, Edna admired Fina who, with Taiwo and Kehinde's help, was dressed a full ten minutes before Pa Heddle's expected arrival at six-thirty.

"Don't get up until you hear Daddy's car," Taiwo instructed. "I am going next door to get my history book."

"You mean you're going to see Samfa," Fina snorted.

****

Pa Heddle's late arrival that Friday night around 9:30 p.m. touched off the same routine as on any normal weekday arrival. Whoever was in the house at the moment he walked in first notified Mammy Nursey. She checked the food to make sure it was warm to eat. Second, the person notified Aunty Matty to join him for dinner. These responsibilities fell to Edna who had minutes earlier returned from her piano lessons.

Dinner for Aunty Matty and Pa Heddle always started in disagreement. No matter how promptly she came down to join him, he never waited for her before he began eating. She never failed to comment on his inconsiderate behavior, and his retort was always the same. "Matty, I haven't eaten all day. You come home, snack on something and then keep me waiting by taking your sweet time to come down."

But this evening of Fina's party started differently.

"I wasn't able to drop off Fina," Pa Heddle announced.

"What do you mean?"

"The president wanted a feasibility report. I got busy. I did not go to choir practice."

"So you couldn't even send a driver or call me?"

"Do you understand what it means to work with people who don't know what the hell they are doing?"

"*Ha bo,* Christian, *yusef,* how could you disappoint the child like that?" Aunty Matty stood up in disgust, flung her napkin on to the table, and stormed out of the dining room. Pa Heddle hobbled after her.

The conversation did not make sense to Edna. She had been up to their bedroom and had not seen Fina. If she had not gone to the party, where was she? Tears welling in her eyes, Edna dashed in and out of every room in the house, looking for Fina. She was nowhere to be found. Frightened that her playmate might have run away, Edna rushed into the bedroom where her parents had taken their argument.

"Fina's gone!" The revelation touched off a flurry of activity: phone calls to the house where the party was held, in case Fina had somehow made her own way there; other calls to aunts and uncles she might have gone to; interviews with Kehinde, Taiwo, and Mammy Nursey to determine who had last seen Fina. They considered that she might have gone to her mother, but they wanted to exhaust other options before they went down that path. What a scandal it would be if she wasn't there.

"I knew this was going to happen?" Aunty Matty kept repeating. "This was why I did not want her here in the first place."

"Yeah, but you have never turned down the money you get every month."

Although well past the end of her workday, Mammy Nursey was dispatched to scour the neighborhood, in case Fina was just wandering around. But she returned with the same disturbing result: Fina was nowhere to be found

By eleven, concern had graduated to alarm and desperation. Someone had to be blamed. For Pa Heddle, that person was Aunty Matty. Why did she have to saddle him, a deputy permanent secretary, with driving a child to a party? Was he supposed to tell the president to wait?

For Aunty Matty, the matter was simple. Christian was a coward. He did not have the balls to send a government car to pick up Fina like other senior civil servants routinely did for their children. Yet she wondered how nobody knew of Fina's whereabouts.

"TAAAAAI," she bellowed. Her voice echoed throughout the house. Taiwo appeared promptly from around the corner, as if she had been expecting the summons.

"What did you say you did after Fina got dressed?"

"I went to get my history book."

"From where?"

"Next door."

"You mean you went to see that Samfa boy? If you get pregnant, you will not live in this house. Don't think you will disgrace us with an illegitimate child."

Pa Heddle overheard the exchange. "You went to see who?" he waddled over to mother and daughter.

"Esther, sir. I went to get my book from her," Taiwo said.

"She's lying. She went to see that Samfa boy. His parents don't come home until after from their store till after eight."

"*Samfa*! *Samfa*? You cheap, worthless thing." Pa Heddle whipped off his belt and reached for Taiwo.

"I only went to get my book, sir." Taiwo retreated.

Whack! The belt caught her on the back of her neck, but the momentum carried the tip around her neck to her throat. She gagged and bolted from the room into the hallway, knocking Fina backward as she came around the corner.

Belt in hand, Pa Heddle chased after Taiwo but bumped into Fina. "And where the hell have *you* been?" He grabbed Fina by the hem of her red dress and dragged her into the sitting-room.

"In my room, Uncle Christian."

"Didn't you hear us calling you, you ungrateful thing! We have been worried sick. This is how you behave after all we've done for you?"

"No, Uncle, I was—"

The belt slammed full across Fina's back and cut off her explanation. All over the cowering girl's body, Pa Heddle worked the belt with the fury of a race car piston. He whipped the ingratitude he saw in her back; the indignities he felt he suffered at the hands of the nincompoop minister he served; the nepotism he felt had usurped twenty-five years of loyal service; and the naked bodies of Taiwo and Samfa threatening to saddle him with a bastard.

"Christian, Christian, leave the child alone! You'll kill her!" Aunty Matty inserted herself between Fina and her husband's belt. After a brief tussle, she slapped away the hand that had been holding Fina's dress. The big red bow hung like a dislodged letter on a plaza marquee. The seam around Fina's waist was ripped open, exposing her bare belly.

"Why didn't you answer when we called you?" Pa Heddle panted.

Fina did not move and did not answer. She scowled and stared back at Pa Heddle.

27

"You want to challenge me?" Pa Heddle tightened his grip on the part of the belt folded around his hand and advanced on Fina.

"Go to your room, now," Aunty Matty ordered and shoved Fina away from her advancing husband.

Fina did not go to her room. She walked along the hallway to the windowless second-story bathroom, shut the door, and lay down on the tiled floor beside the commode. She pulled her knees into her chest and curled her shoulders and head into them, fetus-like. She bathed in the darkness, comforted by the sound of the water dripping into the cistern.

A cool breeze pried its way through the three slits in the wall that allowed fresh air into the bathroom. Fina floated back and forth, existing both then and now, so she did not hear the door open or see the light from the hallway flood the bathroom. All she remembered was a hand gliding into and gently squeezing hers. She did not raise her head or ask any questions. She knew it was Edna who had curled around her. For a long time they lay there together in the darkness, wordless, hand-in-hand on the cool, tiled bathroom floor.

"Where were you? Why didn't you answer when we called?" Edna asked later when they had made their way up to their bedroom.

"When I realized your dad wasn't going to pick me up, I came upstairs, crawled under the bed and cried myself to sleep. I woke up and went downstairs when I heard your mom shout out Taiwo's name."

****

His was a culture in which adults did not admit they were wrong much less apologize, so Pa Heddle made amends the only way he knew how. He gave her additional money to buy lunch at school, paid her compliments, offered her encouragement, bought her comic books and literary classics from the CMS Bookstore, declared Mammy Nursey should now do all the ironing, and limited the household chores she had to do. He also agreed that she and the giggly, nubile friends that frequented the house could go to the

Saturday afternoon jumps. She welcomed the changes because she understood they were the efforts of someone trying to make up for something he had done wrong. And the young girl learned: endure the pain, sacrifice a little of the body and much will be gained.

****

With time, Fina might have forgiven, if not forgotten, the belting she got had she not run into Mama Jinah. It was during one of Fina's rare visits to her mother. After admiring how Fina had grown into a beautiful young woman, Mama Jinah inquired, "Are they treating you well?" Fina mumbled something incoherent. It was the cue Mama Jinah wanted.

"Wicked man," she declared. "If it wasn't for him, your father would be alive today." Fina's eyes popped open and her ears perked up.

"Jinah, don't poison her mind," Nabou cautioned from the pantry area where she was serving food. "She has to live in his house."

Mama Jinah ignored Nabou. "Your father was a good man, very helpful. If that wicked Pa you're staying with had not threatened to sack him, he would have gone to the hospital and would be alive today."

Later when Nabou returned from seeing Mama Jinah off, Fina asked, "Is that what really happened?"

"Don't listen to her. She has more stories to tell than a *yeliba*." Nabou caressed Fina's cheek and smiled. "You have truly grown."

"I want to come home, Mama," Fina pouted.

"To this?" Nabou pointed around the sparsely furnished room and sat down.

"Yes! Look at what he did to me!" Fina extended her arm, pulled the strap off her shoulder to expose the blotches and welts.

"You must have done something bad." Nabou stood up and walked over to the kitchen.

"He's wicked, just like Mama Jinah says."

29

"You have food to eat, a bed to sleep in, and light to read by. That's what is important. Stay there for now. Finish school! Go to college! After that you can do whatever you want."

"*Why?*"

"Dimusu!" Nabou snapped. "She died to show us that the cutting is wrong. Now you must show that a woman can drive her own car and build her own house. That is your path."

"But—"

"No buts. I was taken out of school to marry your father..." At that moment, Isa, Fina's little sister, bounced back into the room, fleeing from a barking dog, and knocked over the end table, spilling Fina's drink. Isa stopped, scanned her mother and, like a mouse at the scent of an approaching cat, scurried into the bedroom. "Do it for *her*." Nabou pointed to the room into which Isa had disappeared. Nabou picked up the table and wiped the floor. "What is a little pain for the gain to come, hmm?"

Fina could not have replied to her mother even if she knew what to say, for Isa bounced out of the bedroom and sprung onto her lap and began pulling Fina's earrings and playing with her face.

Fina returned to the Heddles that night, renewed in her determination to endure so she could set an example for Isa. She tried to remember something tangible about her father, his face, his walk, a mannerism but nothing came, except the tears that settled in her eyes. She did not wipe them away. She wanted them to come. She wanted the pain of her father's death to overwhelm her, to knock her down. Mammy Jinah's words metastasized into an inchoate resentment of the Heddles, even her playmate, Edna.

****

That may have been the reason why, even though she knew it was wrong, she accepted the crisp leone notes, perfumes, and make-up kits Pa Heddle delivered stealthily, and why she said nothing when his eyes wandered over the bodies of her giggly, nubile friends. Soon she and her friends visited his office on Friday afternoons. Giggly

30

requests for money tendered by these nubile bodies were promptly and amply granted. Fina and her friends assured themselves of money for entrance fees, drinks, and taxi-cabs to Saturday afternoon jumps and nightclubs.

But then one of the nubile bodies—purposeful and unaccompanied—visited Pa Heddle in the office. Lunches graduated into dinners with alcoholic drinks. Fina wanted the trysts to stop, but resentment combined with gifts of fashionable clothes and money compelled her silence and enabled the trysts, until one of the nubile bodies discovered her stomach was ready to swell. They made the swelling disappear but not before rumors floated into the Heddle household to sully her friendship with Edna and make life uncomfortable.

Relief came only when the young Fula girl, now a beautiful musu, was admitted to Crowther College (a. k. a. CC), the citadel of Sierra Leonean learning, a place where she would get an education and one day go on to the land of the smiling dentist.

Chapter 4

Although only ten miles separated her from them, Fina felt as if she had traveled a world away from the Heddle household on her first day as an enrolled student on the CC campus. Like most first-year students, she was happy not to be accountable to anyone for her comings and goings. But she had other reasons for being delighted with her campus home. Although neither Aunty Matty nor the girls had ever accused or confronted her about facilitating Pa Heddle's affair, Fina felt guilty enough to find accusation in every stare, comment, and conversation that mentioned his name. Besides, Edna had grown cold in a way that made Fina certain she knew of those things that happened that ought not to have happened. The Heddle home had become a prison. CC provided liberation.

Her sense of freedom and her adoption of the campus as her home was a product of both its location and its culture. It was perched atop the mountains overlooking Freetown. CC students fondly and ironically referred to their campus as Mount Olympus. Their tuition, board and lodge paid by government and European scholarships, many, literally and figuratively, breathed a rarefied air and, unlike the majority of their compatriots, lived lives free of responsibility. CC students walked with a swagger and developed an expectation, if not a sense of entitlement, to which Fina was unaccustomed but which she quickly got used to and sometimes even displayed.

Fina was a beautiful Fulamusu the day she stepped foot on the CC campus. Hers was not the kind that stunned and made one stop, look, and go "wow"! Her beauty was courteous. It invited one to contemplate, even study, it like a work of art: the bronze skin tone, highlighted by charcoal-black, braided hair and slender, elegant neck; the smooth, broad forehead, the thick contoured eyelashes that shaded her lowered brown eyes, the pointed nose, and the fleshy round lips. A slight overbite was her only quirkiness.

Thus endowed, Fina was never far from admirers and never short of invitations to parties and other campus events. Indeed, during her first year, Fina had such an active social life that she visited her mother only once and the Heddles twice. It was on the second visit that she found out Edna had left for America. The news was both a shock and a disappointment—Edna had been the only Heddle she had been close to and was the third to leave home to study abroad, though she was the first to go to America. Not that Fina ever expected she would be sent to America. That had never been part of any conversation she had heard. She had always known that her path to America involved surmounting Mount Olympus. But still it hurt that Edna had not breathed a word to her. Her spirits rose only with the prospect of spending the long summer vacation with a group of friends on campus to study and retake her end-of-year exams.

****

Fina and her roommate, Memuna, started their second year with a whirlwind of parties. It was from one of them that Memuna acquired a boyfriend, Simeon, a young man who claimed he belonged to one of Sierra Leone's traditional ruling families. They had taken to sending Fina into "exile," a campus euphemism for frequent and prolonged use of a room for sex by one roommate that forced the other roommate to spend extended periods either in nearby dorm rooms or in the library. The exile wreaked havoc on Fina's study schedule. She protested the inconvenience. Memuna promised they would curtail their love-making to "just one round."

Fina had taken to staying out late enough, especially on weekends, to give Memuna and Simeon time for at least two "rounds" and to ensure she would not be barred from entering her room. So it was late one Saturday night that she walked toward her room, the last door of the hallway. A few steps from it, Fina heard Simeon's angry voice.

"You want to disrespect me?" Palms smack flesh. Push, shove. "You want to challenge me!" Fists crunch bones. Pant, grunt. "You want to be a man?" Bones bang walls. Sniffles and cries.

Fina reached for the doorknob but stopped, recalling a lesson she learned as a little girl: "Mama," she told Nabou one morning back in Talaba, "Uncle shouted and hit Aunty last night. Why was he beating her?"

"Those were not your aunt and uncle," Nabou barked. "Those were Old Papa Wind and his one-legged wife searching for their long-lost daughter, Wohu. At night, they travel around the world, calling out her name:

"'Wohu…., Wohu…' old Mama Wind cries out.

"'Wohu, Wohu,' old Papa Wind bellows. When you hear screams at night, cover your ears and do not go outside. If you do, they will think you are their daughter and take you away from me."

Fina remembered this story, pulled her hand back from the doorknob, and walked away, but not before she heard Memuna's sobbing punctuated by more slaps and blows. She walked around the campus feeling guilty for not doing something—banging on the door, calling out Memuna's name—to stop the beating. But, a few hours later, she felt a little less guilty when she opened the dorm room door and the hallway light revealed Memuna and Simeon in a naked embrace on the cot-size bed.

But this portrait of reconciliation brought her neither peace of mind nor sleep. Try as she might to rationalize her inaction, she kept returning to the conclusion that she and her mother were as much a part of the violence of the night as was the sleeping couple. She pulled the cover over her shoulder and turned her back to the lovers as if to distance herself from them—a vain attempt at internal exile.

Fina woke up precipitously to whispers and quiet movements. Memuna and Simeon were getting dressed. Still facing the wall, she remained in that position until they left the room. As soon as they closed the door behind them, Fina breathed a sigh of relief, turned, and examined the room. Only the taped wallpaper between the overhanging bookshelves and the desk hinted of the previous night's fight.

"Is everything okay?" Fina asked when Memuna returned later that day.

"Yes… why are you asking?"

"Can't I ask how my roommate is doing?"

"I'm fine. It's just our inorganic chemistry class that's giving me a headache." She sighed, sat down on her chair, and began to study.

But Memuna was not fine, and signs of more fights became visible. A chair leg mysteriously broke. Their only thermos flask shattered. Memuna started wearing dark glasses because, she explained, she was suffering from conjunctivitis. But Fina could see the bruises and the swelling. When, one day, Memuna showed up with a tooth missing and another chipped, Fina confronted Simeon.

"Why don't you take care of those teeth of yours before you start worrying about others?" Simeon hissed dismissively and turned to leave. Then, as if something had just occurred to him, he stopped, and faced Fina. "Come and talk to me when your men stop beating their wives." Minutes later, Fina was still rooted to the same spot.

That same night, Memuna accosted her. "Who do you think you are? You think because you were raised in a Krio household so you have become one of them? Talk about not knowing where one comes from and taking on airs and graces." The remark cooled their friendship and also removed Fina's rose-tinted glasses. She began to see, for the first time, the ethnic divisions on the campus and realized that their roots stretched to every corner of the country from which students hailed.

The divide reared itself again the next week during the inter-hall football competition. Milton Margai Hall had ended Lightfoot Boston Hall's long reign as campus football champions with a 5–1 drubbing. In celebration, Margai Hall supporters danced and sang to the beat of a *Milo* drum band. Fina and Kemi were standing in the dirt-packed parking lot next to the field when the jubilant crowd of Margai Hall supporters noticed them. Songs—bawdy, satiric, joyous, and nonsensical—had always been the lifeblood of campus celebrations, and no event could lay claim to campus lore without a particular song being attached to it.

Fair game and subject matter of these sometimes biting songs were the participating athletes, faculty, hall and event officials, and actual incidents on the field. So when the crowd noticed Fina and Kemi, both expected that he, as captain of the defeated team, would soon become the object of much good-natured ribbing and, perhaps, some caustic humor. But by some strange alchemical turn, fueled perhaps by the socio-economic climate in the capital city at the time and a latent resentment of her beauty, the crowd made Fina the subject of their singing:

Fulamusu eh, bo doya tehl mi tayme
Ar mi noh no, ar yerri nohmoh tek-tek-tek, tek-tek.

"Hey, Fula woman, please tell me the time
Sorry, I don't know how to tell the time. I hear only the tick-tock of the watch."

"*Yehba*," the crowd chorused. As if cued by the *yehba*, the drumming intensified, and the crowd exploded into a feverish round of foot stomping that raised the red dust of the un-tarred parking lot. The orgy ended in more "*yehbas*" and other high-spirited exclamations. When the drumming slowed, the crowd caught its collective breath, coughed out the dust, and started singing again, faster and louder.

Fina could have dealt with the mockery of those among her people who wore watches but couldn't tell the time, with the mimicking of the infelicities of Fulas speaking Krio, and even with the mistaken idea that most Fula women were illiterate. What upset her were the focus and venom of the crowd. Disrespect, even hatred, and a sense of superiority lurked amid the dancing and merriment. She saw them in the eyes that looked straight at her; in the fingers and tongues that pointed at her; in the bodies that danced and rolled around next to her; in the backsides that shimmied in her face; and in the sharp arrows of "*Fina bontit, Fina kak tit*" that pierced her ears. The orgy continued behind her until she and Kemi disappeared into her hall room.

Fina knew she could not hold Kemi responsible for the crowd's behavior, but she expected him to be empathetic if not sympathetic. After all, she had been targeted because the crowed associated her with him. At the very least, he owed her a comforting hug. However, once inside the room, Kemi dropped onto her bed, yawned, and closed his eyes. Then, about thirty minutes later, after the crowd had cleared, he leaped up from the bed, said goodbye, and left. Fina confronted him about his indifference and the crowd's behavior.

"Come on, it was just a song," Kemi protested.

"Yeah that stereotypes and insults Fulas."

"But aren't they true?" he chuckled.

"So, when they're talking about my teeth, it's just a song for you?"

"Come on, Fina, they were having a little fun."

"That's how it starts. Fun then unprovoked beatings. Isn't that what has been happening in Freetown the past few days?"

She was referring to the spate of beatings of ethnic Fulas that had been taking place in the capital city.

"People are angry because the price of petrol and everything else has gone up."

"Then they should beat up the government officials responsible. Why pick on Fulas?"

"Because the government says illegal Fulas and Nigerians are taking work away from Sierra Leoneans."

"Yeah, but crowds don't stop to ask for immigration papers. If you look like a Fula, they beat you up. I'm scared even here, in this so-called citadel of learning."

"Come on, nothing is going to happen to you *here*."

"That's easy for you to say," Fina scoffed. "If I feel scared up *here*, can you imagine how Mama and Isa feel right in the middle of the East End?"

Fina leaned her back against the wall and stared into space. Kemi, seated on a chair, tapped his thumb on her study table.

"I'm going to see them, right now." Fina jumped up from the bed and walked over to the wardrobe from which she pulled out a couple of dresses.

"Now?"

"Yes, now! If something happens to them while I sit here, I will never be able to live with myself."

"Are you coming back tonight?"

Fina shook her head. "I'll come back when I feel they're safe."

"But you can't go now, alone…"

"I can't stay here either."

Fina saw Kemi's struggle and saved him from further distress: "Don't worry. You don't have to come with me."

She dressed, picked up a bag, and left the room without saying goodbye.

During the taxi ride home, Fina raged at the city that made her people foreigners in their own country and at Kemi's indifference. Tears stung her eyes, but she knew feeling sorry for herself would achieve nothing. She simply had to work hard and earn enough money to insulate her family from the discrimination and hostility she was now witnessing. The imperative to focus on her academic work, to graduate with a first- or second-division degree, to be an example to her sister and other Fula women, took center stage that night.

After her return to campus, Kemi Koker dumped her for another, younger student. Having fallen out of love with Kemi herself, Fina was thankful he had spared her the awkwardness of doing what she had wanted to do for almost a year. But her relief was short lived when Memuna explained why he had left her.

"He says his family will never allow him to marry a woman like you," Memuna reported, the trace of a smile around her lips.

****

Fina's cool relationship with Memuna and break up with Kemi created the space for her to concentrate on her academic work. And it began to pay off. Dr. Samuel Prescott, an American zoology professor who insisted his students call him Sam, handed back her assignment with the comments like "Excellently formatted!" "Intelligent!" "Keep it up and greatness will be at your doorstep." His encouragement renewed Fina's determination to earn a first- or second-division bachelor's degree and, through Dr. Prescott's help, to one day study in America.

But Fina had not reckoned on the department's UK-educated professors. They decided that "Uncle Sam," as they dubbed him, was an academic lightweight who was too easy on the students. He gave them multiple-choice exams instead of twenty-page reports, allowed them to make up missed tests instead of penalizing them, and awarded grades in the 80s and 90s when scores in the 40s were the norm. Some of Uncle Sam's colleagues were prepared to tolerate the occasional high score, but all of them were scandalized when every single one of the students in all three of Uncle Sam's classes passed their finals with a score in the 90s. "A hundred percent pass rate shows no respect for the learning curve and is, in fact, downright disgraceful," a Leeds University educated professor complained. Coupled with reports that he often responded to students' questions with, "What do you think?" and admitted that he did not know the answer to others, the UK-educated professors acted. Uncle Sam's contract was not renewed. "Better that the department remains short-staffed than pass students who can't learn what they've been taught," one professor was heard to have remarked.

The news of Uncle Sam's firing left Fina with the disappointment and emptiness of waking up just before the climax of an early morning dream. She faltered. Her assignment and test scores dropped accordingly. Not graduating now seemed inevitable, and her organic chemistry course featured prominently in that outcome. Desperate to avert failure, she sought help from Professor Thompson Ghenahan, a.k.a. TompeOrganic, who taught the course.

He was an old-school academic—tough, uncompromising, and known for including in his exams topics he had never taught in class. Campus lore told of a group of students who, studiously avoiding any suggestion of unfairness, brought this practice to his attention. "Did Newton have notes on falling apples to help form his hypothesis? Anticipate, prepare, or fail!" Ghenahan was said to have replied. Since then, generations of students taking organic chemistry had spent the run-up to TompeOrganic's chemistry exam studying a ten-year collection of his dog-eared notes, lectures, and exam questions, anticipating the unexpected, but, invariably, failing. Fina decided to go directly to TompeOrganic for help.

"Good morning, Miss Marah," he greeted her and pointed to a chair. Fina perched on the edge of the chair, head bowed, hands tucked between her knees.

"Dr. Ghenahan, I need help, sir."

"You've just realized that?" He swiveled to his left, then to the right, as if figuring out where he had placed something.

Fina continued as if she did not hear him. "I just can't seem to understand reaction mechanism, especially as it applies to aldehydes and ketones, sir. I don't even know the difference between them."

"That's what happens when you spend more time going to parties than studying."

"No sir. I have—"

"You think we lecturers don't know what goes on, Miss Marah? I help people who help themselves." He scrambled from his desk to the blackboard behind Fina, picked up a piece of chalk, and sat back in his seat.

Fina pushed her chair to the side wall, exposing the blackboard, her head still bowed and her hands clasped between her knees. In this attitude, she absorbed TompeOrganic's five-minute rant about the virtues of regular studying. "I don't know how some of you even qualified to enter this college." He stared pointedly at Fina and then stepped to the blackboard. "Now," he began scribbling on the board, "an aldehyde like ethanol will have a hydrogen atom attached to the carbonyl group."

41

Fifteen minutes and hundreds of jerky movements later, he sat down in a self-satisfied glow, reached onto a shelf above his head, and pulled off a textbook with sheaves of paper tucked among its pages. "Here." He thrust it into Fina's hand, along with the dust he blew from the textbook. They both coughed. "Come back tomorrow at the same time."

Fina did not go back. Instead, she went to see Dr. Davis-Kamanga. Unlike TompeOrganic, D.K., as he was popularly known, was approachable and helpful but unreliable. He agreed to help but failed to keep their first two appointments. He made the next six but was late for all of them. Some of the sessions ran for longer than the hour Fina had planned, while others lasted only long enough for him to arrive, provide a minute or two of explanation, and announce he had something important to take care of. Nonetheless, by their fifth meeting, Fina felt the organic fog begin to lift. However, the clarity that ensued also allowed her to see his amorous advances form like rain clouds on the horizon. To thwart them, Fina started wearing loose clothes, avoided making eye contact, kept the desk and other physical impediments between them, and tossed deferential "sirs" and "doctors" in his direction. But her efforts were no more effective than throwing dead fleas at a charging male rhinoceros that has picked up the scent of a female in heat. After a ninth session, loaded with questions about boyfriends and with eyes that roved and probed, Fina did not return for the tenth.

By the second term of their final year, Fina and Memuna realized that they were not going to pass organic chemistry. Failure seemed ready to define them better than ethnicity, class, and upbringing. It repaired their friendship, somewhat. But only divine intervention could save them from failure.

"Talk to Kizzy," Memuna proposed a more earthly intervention.

Short, very short, tight-muscled, balding, and unremittingly black, Hezekiah Mendelssohn Bacchus, a.k.a. Kizzy, was the senior lab technician of the Faculty of Natural Sciences at CC, and in his sixth year of an ill-defined Master of Science program. When he was serious, his face had what appeared to be a sneer. One became sure it

42

was a sneer when he smiled. The consequence of this gaffe by the Almighty was that just at the times when Kizzy felt he was being friendly and positive, he appeared cynical and superior. Therefore, people tended to keep him at a distance. Over time, Kizzy had developed a misanthropic disposition to match his sneering smile.

"Even if he doesn't have the questions, he might be able tell us which topics to study. Just give him some attention."

"*You* give him some attention then," Fina bristled.

"Krio boys are not my type. Besides, everyone knows he likes you. Just make friends with him so he can help us."

"No way! He'll want me to be his girlfriend."

"Rubbish. We've got to do something. Otherwise we are going to be back here next year. Forget about studying in America."

Memuna rose from her bed and stood beside Fina's study table, which was littered with opened books and sheets of handwritten paper. "He'll be so happy you're paying attention to him that he'll settle for whatever you want."

"But I don't want a relationship with him."

"Then you'll have one with failure." Memuna stalked out and slammed the door.

Fina did not like the idea of cheating and liked even less the price—to be or be known as Kizzy's boyfriend—she would have to pay. However, a dismal score of twenty-three out of a possible one hundred points in her practice exam along with Vivarin-induced sleepless nights changed her attitude.

"You're my only hope," she said, smiled at Kizzy and pivoted on her heels in the dimly lit chemistry lab. Kizzy pounced on her request, for a fee. Fina was relieved that he preferred a business arrangement, so she quickly shelved the smiles. With final exams three short weeks away, they agreed to meet in the lab every night.

Kizzy prepared as best he could for their tutoring sessions. He dredged up an assortment of dusty, outdated books, diagrammed and wrote formulas on the blackboard and on sheets of paper, and even gesticulated like his boss TompeOrganic. Unfortunately, Kizzy's grasp of his subject matter was as tenuous as kite paper. Then the

43

sight of Fina stretching her body to expel the stiffness from sitting in the same position; their accidental touching and brushing; the whiff of her breath, hot and stale, engorged his mind and anatomy to the point that even the little he knew came out in convoluted gibberish. By the end of the first week, the late evenings in the dimly lit lab with its pungent scent of ether had displaced the teacher in Kizzy and brought out the lecher. Fina sensed this new dimension in their encounters, but anxiety about not graduating persuaded her to continue seeking Kizzy's help until a few days before the final exam when her inability to understand the material and fatigue pushed her over the edge.

"I give up. I'm going to fail!" she wailed two nights before the final, swiped the teaching notes off their work table, and stormed out of the lab.

The prospect of losing the woman he never had and an income he had never earned drove Kizzy to desperation. The next morning he told Fina to pick up some questions from his flat after 9 o'clock that night. Although Fina briefly considered taking Memuna with her, she reasoned that since she alone was enduring the pain, she alone would enjoy the gain.

****

Around 8:00 p.m., she slipped out of her room, dressed in a white silk blouse and cotton *lappa*, cut across the steep tarred road that separated the two women's halls of residence, and emerged into the clearing that served as a parking lot. At opposite corners, farthest away from the residence, sat two cars. Within them, she could see the faint outlines of people. No doubt some of the cars contained students and their sugar daddies on nocturnal trysts.

Fina avoided the cars and the scattered islands of illumination created by the twenty-watt bulbs that shone from the open verandah doors of the hall rooms. She could see some of her peers hunched over their books in the countdown to final exams. Reproached by these portraits of diligence, she scurried out of the parking lot and

44

emerged onto a dark stretch of the steep road that snaked its way into the faculty residence area.

Clouds raced toward the sea, warning of an impending storm. The wind howled, and crickets and cicadas chirped an antediluvian chorus as Fina pounded her way up the hill into the night. The iron railing that marked the edge of the road and the dots of light from the city in the valley below were the only signs that she had not embarked on a primeval odyssey.

The wind picked up, spraying her with leaves and knocking her off balance. Raindrops pelted her arms. She considered returning to the safety of her room but dismissed the idea as summarily as it had formed. She was sure and determined to get to Kizzy's flat before it started to rain heavily. Besides she knew the gain from her trip far outweighed the discomfort of a wet blouse or soaked hair. She was sure she could beat the coming storm.

But she could not beat the beam of the headlights that illuminated her forlorn path. With the inadequate response that comes when someone is caught with a hand in the proverbial jar, Fina hurled herself over the iron railing on her left. Her small frame dropped to the ground, assisted by a gust of wind. She landed with her feet on a granite boulder, but her rubber slippers, coated with a thin layer of moisture, provided no traction. She twisted her right ankle, slid down the boulder, and settled on the damp earth in the posture of a hurdler, her left leg extended and the right one bent at the knee with her toes pointing backward.

She sat like that for a few minutes. Then slowly she straightened her right leg, and, with the steadiness of an acupuncturist, nestled her upper body into the shrubs at the base of the boulder. The pain from the thorns was sharp but sweet. Soreness, burning, and pain surged through her, enraging her muscles, bones, and parts of her anatomy she had long forgotten existed. The world spun out of control...

****

Fina opened her eyes to a black void, yet it was a blackness in which she could see. Standing over her was Amadu, her father, dressed in a blue cotton gown with a matching Moroccan fez, his praying beads rolled around his wrist as if he was ready to pray. His smile beamed a purity and majesty that made Fina shudder. She wished she had known him better.

"Finaba, what path is this that you have taken?"

"It is the path si-kool cut for her," said a voice Fina recognized. Her heart skipped a beat when she turned to her other side and saw Baramusu, sitting on a cane bed. She was wearing an indigo tie-dyed camisole with a matching head wrap.

"She is on the path you carved for her the night you snatched her from the fafei," Baramusu added, whisking her chewing stick to and fro in her mouth.

"I have to pass the exam, Papa. I have to."

"But why do you want to take the easy way?"

"You ask now that you see the rotten fruit you and Nabou have sown," said Baramusu, who took the chewing stick from her mouth and spat.

"It's the only way father."

"No! The only way is to submit to Allah's will. Come with me. Let us follow in His path."

"Pssh! Your deed has brought nothing but suffering for you and your family. Finaba, come with me. Follow the path of our people. Do not cut the rope."

"No!" Amadu shouted as Finaba reached for her grandmother's outstretched hand and stood up.

****

The reproach from her left ankle brought Fina's visions to a tail-hook stop. She swiveled her head from right to left, but the black void had disappeared and with it Amadu and Baramusu. Back in the wretched night, she could hear the approaching storm. She again considered going back to her dorm room, but the thought of another year at CC, another round of TompeOrganic, Kizzy, the Heddle household, and, worse, teaching in some dingy, poorly equipped school, banished that idea. Earning a degree was the only way she could see herself ever going to America.

So, like someone who accepts that mishaps are a test of character, she removed the thorns from her arms, back, and neck, brushed off the blades of grass from her cotton *lappa*, and clawed her way up the embankment to the road. She hobbled to her destination. The wind, the rain, and her ankle combined in opposition to her efforts. Self-pity was her companion. Why had life been so hard for her and her family? She recalled Baramusu's curse the afternoon the women had prayed outside their compound. Maybe it explained the problems that had beset her family. Okay, but what about other Fulas, the ones being attacked and beaten up in the city? Why were they being blamed for shortages of petrol and food, for high prices? Why were Fulas, born and bred in Sierra Leone, being rounded up, locked up, and treated as if they were foreigners? What crime had Fulas committed?

Absorbed by these thoughts, Fina was surprised when she found herself, dripping wet, standing in front of Kizzy's flat. She raised her hand to knock on the front door, but the image of her father exhorting her to choose another path robbed her of the will to follow through. She turned to leave, but the elements conspired against her. Thunder bragged with the shameless abandon of a tyrant, and lightning, his consort, shrieked into the cavernous night. Wind cowered trees and bushes and whisked away empty cans, bottles, twigs—anything not rooted or bolted down. A branch shot past Fina and crashed into the wall next to the door. The impact, it seemed, triggered the door open to reveal Kizzy, his eyes bulging in excitement at the sight of Fina shivering on his doorstep, her wet blouse revealing her breasts in their intoxicating fullness.

Yet Kizzy was also disappointed. He had half hoped she wouldn't take up his invitation. Now she had shown she was no better than all the other female students who slept with lecturers and married men, whether for exams, money, or pleasure. He had no final exam questions for her. Never did. That was just a pretext to get her to come to his flat. Well, she'd get what he did have! He scowled and gritted his teeth. His nostrils expanded and contracted. A vein in his neck convulsed like a worm that had had salt thrown on it. Fina's resolve to earn the degree that would be a passport to America dissolved in the heat emanating from his body. She took a step backwards. Kizzy noticed the retreat, grabbed her arm, dragged her into the flat, and back heeled the door shut, muffling the noise of the storm.

Fina yanked her arm free and tried to step around him, but he drove his fingers into the folds of her hair, and yanked her to a stop. Fina felt her neck cracking. Kizzy pushed her down to her knees. She wanted to scream but remembered that at night no one answered a cry for help. So, she pleaded instead.

"Kizzy I'm sorry, okay?"

He yanked her head sharply to the right, incensed and excited at the same time.

"Ouch! Please, Kizzy, I beg you."

But Kizzy ignored her pleas and extended his fingers further into the folds of her hair, like a laborer strengthening his grip just before hoisting a heavy load. Fina's neck craned so far to the right that her head stood almost at a right angle to her body. A numbness descended into her arms, which floated limply by her side. Her awkward position dictated compliance, and she could not put up any resistance as his other hand pulled her head to the bulge of his shorts.

****

Fina only remembered she had scrambled to the door and hobbled out of the flat toward the campus. The return trip on her swollen ankle was agonizing, but her pace slackened only when the light bulbs from the student rooms came into view. Brimming with bile, she limped through the mountain-top campus and down into the city. Such was her physical and psychological state that the furies, *djins*, *ghommids*, and other inhabitants of the night thought she was one of their own and did not bother her as they sought ways to cause havoc. Fina stopped only when she arrived at her mother's *adjoining*. She banged on the door until Nabou opened it. Then, without even

48

so much as a greeting or explanation, she walked straight to the bedroom and collapsed into a long, deep sleep.

"I'm not... I'm not a Jezebel," Fina proclaimed and woke up with a start. She sat upright in a fog of semi-consciousness and waited until it cleared into recognition of her mother and sister standing by the bedside, watching her apprehensively. They could tell from the bruises on her face and eyes that something bad had happened. They asked her what had happened, if she was going back to college, to the Heddles, about her belongings, if they should call the police, if she wanted to eat. "I just want to be here with you," she answered. In fact, Fina wanted nothing more to do with Mount Olympus; she wanted nothing to do with the Kizzys, Memunas, the Kemi Kokers, and Heddles of the world.

When Memuna showed up with one suitcase and two large boxes of her belongings after the college had closed down for the summer, Fina offered an initial greeting followed by a thank you and then clammed up. Soon after Memuna left with the same explanation of Fina's disappearance that had been circulating on the campus. The pressure of final exams had become too much for her; she'd gone bonkers and quit!

Fina didn't care that her silence left the insanity narrative as the story of her college experience. She had more pressing concerns. Any day, she expected Kizzy and the police to come and whisk her off to jail. For months, each swing of the compound gate, footstep, or strange voice sent her blood racing and her heart pounding.

She later told her mother she had earned her degree and explained the night of her bruised, harried, and unexpected appearance as the result of a fall, exam pressure, and exhaustion. Grateful for Fina's help with the young Isa's homework and in the kitchen, and hopeful that a soon-to-be, government-paid worker would ease her financial burdens, Nabou accepted the explanation even though her motherly instincts told her otherwise.

By the fourth month of her return home, Fina realized Kizzy had not reported the campus incident. She ventured into the city. It seemed everyone she knew had come out to greet her. Their questions and the prospect of meeting Kizzy or one of the Heddle adults filled her with such anxiety that she decided leaving Sierra Leone was her only sensible course. She was not sure how she was going to achieve that, but she was sure of her destination: the land of the American dentist!

Fina's certainty had none of the eagerness of the opportunist or the resignation of the fatalist. She was quietly determined, aware that while each decision closed some paths, it also opened others, and she had come to understand that the trick in life was not to become complacent in one's situation but to seek out its opportunities. This outlook enabled her to gorge herself on the manicured Americana of the books, magazines and photographs of the U.S. embassy's reading room.

From one of its chairs, she would watch visa applicants—serious, grim-faced, and apprehensive—walk into the embassy's consular section. A few came out smiling, skipping as they showed off their visa-stamped passports to waiting friends and relatives. Together, they inspected the visa and beamed like miners after a big diamond find. Many, many others, not so lucky, came out crestfallen and disappeared into the teeming city. Some stormed out, belligerent, invoking the wrath of their ancestors, heaping curses upon and calling damnation on the consul and America. Fina often visualized herself walking into the consular section but never the outcome of her many dream visits.

Her frequent trips to the reading room soon put her on a first-name basis with one of its librarians, and he told her that an American church mission in diamond-rich Koidu was looking for someone to work in its health clinic. Fina saw the door of opportunity open and stepped through. Armed with the librarian's letter of introduction, she traveled to Koidu for an interview. She was hired on the spot.

The church mission was certainly not America, but it was far enough removed from Freetown for Fina not to worry about running into people she knew. The job also came with perks: a two-room apartment, a salary twice what she would have earned as a non-degreed teacher in Freetown, and regular interaction with Americans that created a sense of the independence and freedom for which she yearned. Her stay at the Koidu mission fueled even more her determination to live in America. Yet her excitement came tinged with a sense of betrayal of a sister primed for the kind of guidance her mother could not provide. Only the help she gave to the patients of the clinic assuaged her guilt.

Chapter 5

Fina worked with American Meredith Frank, the gentle and soft-spoken office manager of the church mission. Temperamentally, Meredith was the perfect friend, for beyond the requirements of the job, she made no demands on Fina. In her conversation, outlook and demeanor, Meredith displayed nothing of the class-consciousness and superiority Fina had felt in the Heddle household and at CC; nothing of the self-satisfied arrogance she had noticed in some of Meredith's compatriots. In fact, Meredith seemed timid, even uncomfortable, about being American, preferring, for instance, loose cotton dresses and head ties to jeans and other clothing that emphasized her difference from the locals. She spoke a near-perfect Krio that surprised everyone until she revealed that she had grown up in Freetown.

She was the younger of two daughters of missionary parents who began their work in Sierra Leone when she was eight. She and her sister lived in Freetown until she was sixteen when her mother's health problems forced the family to return to America. Unlike her older sister who had never liked Sierra Leone, Meredith was never able to fit back in the country of her birth. "I felt out of place," she told Fina the very first time they spent an evening together after work. "Kids in my high school thought I was weird; in college, my peers talked about making money, living in big houses, and driving fancy cars. All *I* ever wanted was to come back here, stroll along Lumley Beach, and dig my toes into its wet sand."

Meredith paused. Fina adjusted her position as if to say you have my full attention. Like a storyteller satisfied that she had piqued her audience's interest, Meredith continued. "I was accepted to Crowther College, you know, but my parents objected. 'You're too young, standards at the university have fallen, the country is lawless, not what it used to be,' my father argued, but I never stopped dreaming of returning. And the first opportunity I got? Here I am. I'm

American by birth and passport, but, you know, deep inside, Sierra Leone is my home." Meredith sighed.

"Let's switch passports because all *I* want to do is get the hell out of here!" Meredith's eyes flew wide open. She stared at her new friend, waiting for an explanation.

Fina hesitated, uncertain whether or not to tell her story. But it demanded telling, for she could already hear the *yeliba*, distant and separate from her body, telling of the afternoon Baramusu had come to talk to her mother about the initiation.

That exchange of stories turned a tepid work acquaintance into an enthusiastic friendship. From then on, they spent most evenings together, eating rice with a variety of *plassas*—cassava leaves and other leafy greens cooked in palm oil with onions, peppers, and either meat or fish—followed by a dessert of seasonal fruits.

Meredith traveled to Freetown twice a month to collect supplies for the mission clinic, take care of its administrative business, or meet arriving medical specialists who had come to volunteer their expertise. Trips to Freetown stressed her. Something always seemed to go wrong. If the heat and humidity did not drain her energy, then cascading rain converted the poorly drained roads, pavements, parking lots and market areas into seamless sheets of water and brought life to a standstill. When weather was not the problem, machines were. The mission van overheated and stranded them in the middle of nowhere or overladen lorries broke their axles in the middle of the road and created torturous delays and detours. When the machine deity permitted an incident-free ride to Freetown, it was sure to exert penance in other ways—the generators that supplied electricity to Freetown broke down, were under repair, or lacked fuel. This meant rationed or no electricity, which compromised temperature-sensitive supplies and made useless entire caches of medicines.

But, most often, people caused Meredith the most stress. Freetown was damnably overcrowded—with inhabitants that pressed and bumped against her and hawkers that tried to take advantage of her, not realizing how well she understood and spoke Krio. But it was the corrupt shenanigans of the customs officers that sent her blood boiling.

She usually returned to Koidu exhausted, her desire to continue in her present work and remain in Sierra Leone drained from her like the sweet dregs of palm wine from a gourd. On her way to her apartment in the mission compound, she would tap on Fina's door, knowing she would have readied some rice and hot stew for her. While Fina watched and listened, Meredith would eat and rant about her tribulations in Freetown and the various problems besetting her adopted homeland.

"Save yourself a lot of aggravation and give them something," Fina suggested one evening after Meredith had complained bitterly about customs officers who demanded bribes.

"Never!" The response came with the ferocity of a marching band member playing his one and only note on the cymbals.

"Just being realistic."

"Bribery is wrong! It's that simple, Fina," Meredith insisted. "*You* should be encouraging me to do the right thing, not providing me a cop out. Corruption is ruining this country!"

Meredith exhaled, closed her eyes, and almost immediately fell asleep. Fina did not. She had heard the reprimand, seen the passion, understood Meredith's patriotic fervor, and they had bothered her. She knew she should feel outraged. Indeed, she wanted to be as outraged as Meredith. Try as she might, she could not. The screams on her initiation night, the jolts of the minivan ride to Freetown, the image of her mother's grief on the day of her father's untimely death, and the wormlike vein of the feral man on that stormy night bubbled to the surface. She appreciated Meredith's stand against corruption and her love for Sierra Leone, but that did not lessen her desire to go to America. It did, however, inspire her decision never to involve herself in any corrupt practices and always to do the right thing.

The first test of that resolve came a short week later on the day she met powerful and handsome Mandingo diamond merchant, Sidibe Kakay. In his brand-new Land Rover, he had personally driven his mud- and diarrhea-stained foreman, Kurubalie, to the clinic for medical attention. He would spare no expense for this long-time, trusted employee who started with Sidibe Kakay's deceased father. Unusual for a man in his position, Sidibe Kakay stayed with Kurubalie until the doctor examined him. The latter explained that so long as Kurubalie and others continue to work in the stagnant pools of human and animal wastes around the mines, they will get a lot of infections. He also said that Kurubalie's blood pressure was high and that he was showing signs of early arthritis.

"*E too ole foh mine wok,*" Meredith explained after the doctor had left. "*Giveam orda wok foh du,*" Meredith recommended a different line of work for the aging miner. Then she gave Sidibe Kakay a course of antibiotics, anti-diarrhea, pain and high blood pressure medications. "*Bring am bak nex week.*" She smiled and disappeared behind closed doors.

After Sidibe Kakay had helped Kurubalie into the Land Rover, he came back into the clinic, sidled up to the table where Fina worked and asked for large quantities of all the medications prescribed for Kurubalie. "So that I can give them to my workers when they're sick," he explained. Then he slid a four-inch high wad of leone bills onto the front edge of the table. "Just between us," he winked at Fina.

"Keep your money." Fina ignored the wad of notes and left Sidibe Kakay standing in open-mouth surprise. Until that moment Sidibe Kakay had not taken any particular notice of Fina. Women usually had to force themselves into his space to get his attention and, even more, had to fight to hold it. Fina's summary rejection, particularly her seeming indifference to his wealth and prominence, energized his competitive drive. In an instant Fina became the huge diamond Sidibe Kakay simply had to have. That she was educated and beautiful made acquiring her as his wife or concubine all the more alluring.

And he undertook the campaign to win her in the only way he knew how—by sending emissaries with gifts and promises to set her up in her own house and business. She would have enough money to go wherever she wanted and do whatever she wanted.

Sidibe Kakay assumed Fina's initial rebuffs were part of the customary courtship game women played: pretending not to be interested in a suitor for a while before eventually accepting his attentions. But after two months and several gift-bearing emissaries bore no results, he realized he had to give Fina some direct, personal attention. Having to chase her mildly excited him, but it also irritated him. He was a busy man. He did not want to devote too much time to wooing Fina, so he decided to use his fail-safe technique: the glitter bath.

Sidibe Kakay developed this seduction technique by accident. Like all good diamond dealers, he kept a large supply of small but uncut stones at home and took a briefcase full of them whenever he traveled. Individually, the stones were not worth much. As a collection, they could fetch a handsome price. Whenever Sidibe Kakay encountered a stubborn woman he wanted, as wife or mistress, he would send his Mercedes to bring the woman to his office or hotel room and open the briefcase of uncut diamonds among which he would have liberally sprinkled polished stones. He would instruct the woman to look, touch, and hold the stones, in that order. Usually, she complied, sometimes even asking questions. Then he would tell her that if she agreed to have him, she would have access to diamonds like the ones in his briefcase. Most women did not need more than a hint of that possibility for him to have his way with them. Others, made of sterner stuff, recognized the briefcase was bait and resisted. Sidibe Kakay would leave such women alone with the briefcase. By the time he returned, many were marinating in the bedazzling fictions created by their own minds. Soon, he was having his way with them. But once a Mauritanian woman had refused to touch or even to look at the diamonds. She was unmoved. When she told him she wanted to leave after being alone with the cache for an hour, Sidibe Kakay acted impulsively. He scooped a handful of the cut and uncut diamonds and let them roll off his fingers onto her arms and chest. The woman quivered as the cool stones rolled over the exposed parts of her skin. Her face and neck flushed red. Sidibe Kakay cupped another handful, lathered her face, and tucked some over the neckline of the loose blouse she wore. The stones rolled over her breasts and down to her waistline. A couple settled on her thighs. The woman swooned, whimpered. Soon after, Sidibe Kakay had his way with her. That incident established the fail-safe glitter bath. Sidibe Kakay had needed to use it only occasionally, for very stubborn women and when time was an important consideration. He found searching under tables and chairs to retrieve his stones too time-consuming and beneath his dignity.

****

When he arrived at Fina's apartment to give her personal attention, Sidibe Kakay spent fifteen minutes pleading with Fina to let him in. By the time she agreed, he was already angry, so he sat down and dispensed with niceties. He set the briefcase on top of the small wooden center table, snapped the lock open, and turned it toward Fina. He had included many more shiny, cut stones than normal. Fina's heart skipped several beats. She was looking at diamonds for the first time in her life. They were not as attractive as the ones she had seen in magazines, but it took only a recall of H. Rider Haggard's *King Solomon's Mines,* a book she had read in the Heddle household, for her imagination to transform the briefcase into a sparkling and overflowing treasure chest.

Sidibe Kakay scooped a handful of stones and released them through his fingers on a bedazzled Fina. The stone droplets landed and bounced off her face, neck and torso. Some settled in the folds of her clothes, others rolled onto the wooden frame of the sofa, and a few tap danced on the linoleum floor. Sidibe Kakay released another handful. Fina shifted her head to the side and scooted as if she wanted to get up, but Sidibe Kakay blocked her. He released another handful. Fina's body radiated with warmth, and her hand instinctively reached out and caught a couple of the stone droplets. Diamonds! The magical stones, the ones that turned paupers into the wealthy and dreams into realities; the ones people killed and died for. Fina's chest heaved, and she swooned.

Had Sidibe Kakay been less angry and impatient, he would have recognized that he was just one or two more handfuls away from another successful glitter bath, but unused as he was to exerting himself for anything, he felt he had expended too much time and energy on this sapling of a woman.

"These will give you anything you want."

Fina did not answer.

"They will take you anywhere, England, America."

Again, Fina did not answer.

"You will be my wife here or anywhere you want to live."

It might have been the imperative of "will." It might have been the idea of being his wife. Either way, his statement stung Fina out of her reverie with the same acrid revulsion as vinegar on the palate.

"I don't want to be your wife, here or anywhere."

"Okay, my woman."

"Or your woman either."

"You would rather be a messenger and clerk for these whites?" Sidibe Kakay pointed in the direction of the main building. Again Fina did not answer. "I see," he nodded, "you're too good to be my wife or to take my money?" He chuckled. "I've dealt with your type before. You think our business is dirty."

"Isn't it?"

"If it is, then everyone in Kono is dirty, including your mission people."

Fina's face registered a mix of incomprehension and disbelief.

"Yes, your people," Sidibe Kakay insisted. "They hide behind their clinics, churches, and schools, but let me tell you, they are all here for diamonds. Everyone in Kono is a trader. Some of us are just better at it than others."

"Maybe, but that does not make the way you trade right."

Sidibe Kakay stood up and motioned for Fina to do the same. A couple of stones caught in the creases of her dress fell to the floor. She picked them up and handed them to him, along with the two in her hand. Sidibe Kakay dropped them in his briefcase. He then lifted the cushions from the sofa and picked up a couple more stones that

59

had settled in the grooves where back, seat, and armrest met. He handed the cushions to Fina, tilted the sofa backward and looked underneath. He set it back down, walked around it, and picked up a few more stones. He straightened up and kneaded his back with his fists for a few seconds, grimacing with pain. "Everything we do in this world is a trade for gain," he said as he returned to scanning the floor. "The whites in your mission understand that. That is what their black book says. Trade the things of this world for better ones up there." He pointed to the ceiling. "The diamond business is about trading for gain. We trade to get better than what we give. When you understand that and are ready to trade this," he sneered dismissively at the apartment, "come to me." He picked up the briefcase and left.

Sidibe Kakay's offer might have been a serious temptation for Fina, but she recalled that her school friends' visits to Pa Heddle's office and her tutoring sessions with Kizzy Bacchus had started innocently enough only to mushroom into trouble. Besides, she could not imagine being one of Sidibe Kakay's trophies, for that was how she came to view his wives after she befriended one of them weeks later when she visited the clinic.

She had been sitting at the reception desk when a black Mercedes pulled up to the front entrance. The driver got out, walked round to the passenger side, opened the car door, and waited respectfully. A young woman, in her late teens, dressed in a *gara temle* and *lappa,* stepped out of the car. Her hair was neatly threaded into a pear-shaped cone at the back. She looked elegant in the two-piece blouse and wrap-around skirt combination as she high-heeled her way to the waiting room. An older woman, probably in late thirties, also wearing the same two-piece *temple* and *lappa* combination but of a much shabbier and ungainly variety, stepped out of the other side of the car, carrying a baby. In flip-flops, she followed her Madame into the clinic.

Inside, they waited without conversation for the nurse. The young woman seemed on edge, alternately tapping her feet on the marble floor, fiddling with her manicured nails, sighing, inhaling, exhaling, and shooting exasperated glances at the older woman every time the bundle she held erupted in a cry.

Fina introduced herself and discovered that the young woman was Sidibe Kakay's third and latest wife, Aziza. Her baby girl was sickly. Over the next three visits, Fina pieced together Aziza's story. She had been married to Sidibe Kakay for three years. She was in her late teens. The baby was her second child. Sidibe Kakay believed the baby was sickly because Aziza did not have pure Mandingo blood. He had therefore insisted they get a Mandingo woman from his village to nurse the child, believing that if she was breastfed by a true Mandingo woman, the child would become strong, and they would not have to bring her to the clinic so often.

Aziza was not unhappy. Oh, no! Sidibe Kakay provided everything she wanted: cars and drivers to take her everywhere, money to spend as she chose, a house and servants to do her bidding, and a cloth material business to keep her out of mischief. She had to cook, but that was only because Sidibe Kakay preferred the food that *she* prepared. He also liked it that she was young and tight when they slept together. He spent a lot more time and money on her than on his other wives which made them jealous. For peace and family harmony, Aziza encouraged him to spend more time with the other wives. Then they would not wish evil on her. No! No! She definitely was not unhappy.

Fina did not want to be Sidibe Kakay's trophy, so she continued to refuse his gifts and sent discouraging replies through his emissaries, a couple of whom worked at the mission. They could not believe Fina turned up her nose at a diamond merchant, and their incredulity increased her self-esteem. Inwardly, Fina thanked Meredith.

Fina's burgeoning confidence and sense of purpose contrasted with Meredith's growing frustration and disillusionment. She became short with her co-workers and now more frequently and uncharacteristically laced her responses with insults about them and their country. She was at her worst the nights and days immediately following a trip to Freetown, so much so that Fina sought to lessen the stress of these trips by organizing a bath and food to await Meredith's return. She also put the mission workers on standby to inventory and store the supplies so Meredith could sleep in the next day.

Such were the plans Fina had in place the evening Meredith entered her apartment, flushed red and almost swooning with excitement. While she was at the Queen Elizabeth II Quay waiting for a ship to dock, she had met Chip Monroe from the US Embassy. By the time the ship docked, offloading had to be postponed to the next morning. Chip invited her to dinner at Mammy Yoko Hotel and afterward they strolled barefoot along a moonlit Lumley beach. Chip was charming, witty, and kind. And he was coming to visit her in Koidu.

"Should I wear European or African clothes? Would you help me choose? What type of food should we eat? African, European, American or all three? Would you come to meet him? You have to, Fina. I never thought I would *ever* meet someone like him."

Fina was curious to meet the man who had reduced the usually sedate Meredith to girlish excitement. And she understood why that same weekend. Chip Munroe was near perfect. He was neither too tall nor too short, neither thin nor fat, neither pale nor sunburned. He was manly without being overly muscular, polite without being timid. His white shirt, knee-length khaki shorts, matching socks, and crepe soles made for a pleasing compromise between the scruffy, dashiki-and-sandals-wearing foreign backpackers and the stuffy, be-suited foreign bureaucrats.

"You must be Fina." He smiled and laid his hands over hers like a priest on a supplicant.

The consummate diplomat, Chip Munroe did not try to dominate their conversation or impress them with his knowledge. He did not talk dismissively of local politics and politicians and took no hard line position on any issue, neither agreeing with Meredith when she expressed her frustration over the pervasiveness of corruption in Sierra Leone, nor disagreeing with her when she condemned America's unbridled capitalism and gunboat diplomacy. He listened

62

and talked only in questions. Where were you born? When did you leave your village? Who are the Heddles? What did you study at Crowther College? Chip Munroe made people talk about themselves. He seemed as attracted to Meredith as she was to him, and soon became a fixture in her life.

Chip's early visits to Koidu ended with Meredith and Fina walking him to his guest house on Main Road. Later Meredith became his sole escort. Once, as they approached the guest house at which Chip lodged, Sidibe Kakay's Mercedes pulled up next to them. He rolled down the window and greeted Meredith. She introduced him to Chip, and they exchanged pleasantries. Sidibe Kakay offered to give them a ride but Meredith declined, explaining they were enjoying their walk.

"Okay, but talk to your friend, please," he replied. "It could be worth a few stones." He winked, smiled and drove off, leaving them coughing in a cloud of dust. Chip's questions followed immediately. "Who is he? What does he do? Which friend is he talking about? Does he mean diamonds?"

"Oh, he wants me to match make between him and Fina. I suppose he would pay me with diamonds if things worked out," Meredith explained as they approached the front door of the guest house.

"And will you?"

"No, I won't," Meredith stopped and stared at Chip

"What?"

"He already has three wives."

"Is that a problem for Fina?"

"Of course! You think she'd want to be wife number four?"

"I don't know. Have you asked her or do you presume to know what she wants? Fina might have no objections, and don't you want a handful of diamonds?"

"Even if Fina wants to marry him, I'll not be party to putting another woman in a position I would not want to be in."

"Isn't that cultural arrogance?"

63

"If you lived with these women and heard their stories as I have, you would understand that you're just talking diplomatic correctness."

"Okay, can we talk about something else?" Chip took her arm and insisted on walking her back to the mission.

But his accusation that she presumed to know how Fina felt stayed with Meredith, so a few days later she told Fina about Sidibe Kakay's request.

"I can't see myself as wife number one let alone number four," Fina responded with even more indignation than Meredith had imagined. "He has offered to pay for me to go to America, to give me anything I want. Do you know why I haven't taken him up? Because people like Ade believe they are entitled to have whatever they want."

"Who?"

"Sidibe Kakay."

"Okay, I thought I heard you say Ade."

Fina hesitated. "Him too. They are all the same. Tell him to keep his diamonds."

Meredith looked at Fina, perplexed.

****

Over several months, Fina realized that Chip and Meredith were moving in a direction that certainly did not include her and decided to focus her attention on achieving her own heart's desire. She started by taking passport-size pictures for her visa application. The next and more difficult step was to muster the courage to ask Meredith to help her secure a visa through Chip. But the thought that such a request would make Meredith think badly of her and confirm her opinion that all Sierra Leoneans were corrupt made Fina decide not to ask for her help. So Fina was in the midst of a mild, self-induced depression when Meredith told her that she and Chip had decided to get married.

"I'll be leaving at the end of the month. Chip will join me in three months at the end of his tour of duty."

And before Fina could digest the consequences of Meredith's impending departure, the time had arrived for her to leave. The goodbye happened in two stages. First, Fina organized a surprise send-off party on Meredith's last day of work. Patients she had served at the clinic and students she had taught at the school arrived in droves to say goodbye. A few gave her either sewn *dockets* and *lappas* or pieces of tie-dye and batik material. Most, poor and of little means, offered her hugs and kisses. Among the well-wishers were Aziza and Sidibe Kakay. Fina saw Sidibe Kakay pull Meredith aside for a brief, whispered conversation and press a small manila envelope into Meredith's hand. He did not even glance in Fina's direction as he and Aziza left. Surprise and the volume of visitors had kept Meredith occupied, but as the well-wishers dwindled to a trickle, the sight of each receding back made her cry.

The second stage of the goodbye took place at dawn on the morning of the departure. Meredith wanted a quiet exit, so Chip had arrived the previous night and loaded her suitcases into the van while she and Fina reminisced in the living room. They talked until they both fell asleep in their chairs.

Meredith's plan to depart before sunrise left no time for conversation when Chip woke them the next morning. Fina watched the pair scurry around the apartment like ghosts eager to return to their underworld before they were trapped in the world of the blinding sun. She and Meredith hugged each other perfunctorily, like two people suspicious the other was contagious. Meredith boarded the van. The engine burst into life, drowning out the crowing cocks and twittering birds. The park and headlights came on, and the van moved off. Ten yards later, it stopped and reversed.

"Can I have a picture of you?" Meredith asked.

"I don't have any."

"What about those passport pictures you took not long ago. Something to have as a keepsake... *please.*"

Fina ran across to her apartment and, a few minutes later, handed Meredith two passport-size photographs. "One for your wallet and one for your bedroom. Remember me, okay."

This time the van took off and disappeared.

****

Fina was in the middle of a full blown depression when Sidibe Kakay showed up at her apartment one night, almost four months after Meredith left. She had not heard from either Meredith or Chip. Sidibe Kakay threw a manila envelope on her coffee table.

"Look in there."

Fina was too depressed to argue. She lifted the flap and reached inside and pulled out a Sierra Leone passport, a huge wad of twenty dollar bills, and a British Caledonian Airways envelope. She raised her eyes from the items and looked at Sidibe Kakay for an explanation.

"Open the passport."

She opened it and saw her name and photograph.

"Turn the page."

She turned several empty pages before she came to one with a visa stamped on it. Her brow furrowed in incomprehension, but her heart raced with excitement. She guessed at the players, but she did not understand the game.

"Do you know what your friends traded for that?" Fina looked confused.

"*Our* diamonds, cut and uncut. I wanted to say no, to tell them that this would not change your mind. But I am a trader. The passport, ticket, and money I give to you for free."

Sidibe Kakay smiled cynically at the growing shock on Fina's face. "You are a good woman but do not be deceived by the surface of things. Understand that everything in life is a trade."

Chapter 6

From her visits to the U.S. embassy reading room and from stories she had heard, Fina knew enough about America not to be too apprehensive about what to expect. But turbulent weather over the Atlantic in the last two hours as the air ship approached the American coastline made for a gut-wrenching ride. Passengers were required to remain seated with their seatbelts securely fastened, and many turned off their reading lights. Claustrophobia seized the air ship. It banked violently to the left and right. Some passengers groaned. One or two even vomited. The smell of vomit and body odor tinged with urine and shit seemed to pour through the air vents. The deploying landing grated. Fina, like many others, closed her eyes, frightened that her journey was going to end in disaster. She prayed. She wanted to go back home. She did not want to come to America.

"Ladies and Gentlemen, welcome to John F. Kennedy International airport. Local time is 1:35 p.m.," the upbeat voice of an air hostess burst through Fina's incubus. The relief was momentary. She scrambled to fill out the customs and immigration cards that threatened jail and financial penalties for giving false information. As she disembarked and made her way through the winding passageways toward immigration control, stories she had heard of redneck officers named Bubba interrogating, searching, detaining, and sending Africans back home for wearing multi-colored tie-dyes and cornrows tortured her. In fact, that's why she had worn a simple black dress and permed her hair. She opened her passport, checked her visa—it was still there. Though Sidibe Kakay had claimed Meredith and Chip had approached him, Meredith had never confirmed this, not even as she agreed to pick up and accommodate Fina till she got settled in the U.S. Fear that the visa might after all be a fake and that the trip was Sidibe Kakay's cruel joke on her for rejecting him ransacked Fina. She broke out in deep breaths and had a crushing urge to pee.

Fina was still desperate to pee when the blonde female immigration officer summoned her to the counter. She tip-toed toward the counter, put her passport into the waiting hand of the officer, and mumbled the *Sura Fatiha*, the Moslem prayer, for the first time in years.

The immigration officer opened the passport, gave the photograph and then Fina a cursory glance, and turned to the visa page. Fina could hear her heartbeat, felt sweat rolling down her back, and knew that she was in imminent danger of peeing on herself if she did not soon find a bathroom.

"Welcome to America and have a pleasant stay," the officer pushed the passport onto the counter and looked in the direction of the next person in line. Fina was shocked and hesitated long enough for the officer to look back at her and nod in the direction of baggage claim. With nothing to declare, Fina sailed through customs. No one stopped her to inspect her suitcases. In fact, she could tell from the way the two male customs officers standing around the inspection tables stared at her that they were more interested in inspecting *her* for contraband than her suitcases.

Relief and a bouncy exhilaration bathed Fina as she rounded the corner from customs and walked towards the international reception area. She could not pin down how she was feeling, but she knew it had something to do with America, its courteous and hassle-free immigration and customs processes, the clean, halogen-lighted, and spacious place that was the arrival hall of the international terminal. Relief mixed with happiness coursed through her veins. Was this freedom—the irrepressible urge to shout, strip, and dance naked? But she didn't. Instead she broke into tears. She wasn't quite sure why or for whom, but Nabou and Isa, Amadu and Dimusu, Baramusu, Kumba Kargbo, the women of Musudugu, and the village of Talaba all came to mind—even the Heddles, Kemi Koker, and Memuna.

"It is okay, Fina." Meredith put an arm around the shoulder of her Koidu buddy. She and Chip had watched Fina as she had emerged from the customs area, looked around, and then started to cry.

"America can be pretty overwhelming eh?" Chip picked up her suitcases.

****

They never spoke of how Fina got her visa, but even as a greenhorn to America, Fina could tell Meredith and Chip were doing well, and she felt she partly understood how that came to be. They lived in a 7000-square foot Georgian house in Westchester, New York, drove two Lincoln Town Cars, and owned two ice cream franchises. Since Meredith was expecting their first child in two weeks and had taken a leave from managing one of the ice cream franchises, Fina spent her first week in America almost exclusively with Meredith. Though they reminisced about Koidu and Sierra Leone, and both were clearly pleased to see each other, the question of whether Fina planned to overstay her three-month long visa dampened the visit like rain through a summer excursion.

"Because of his former work, it would be best if you leave here as soon as possible and live on your own," Meredith broached the issue on the third day after her arrival. They were sitting at a table by the bay window overlooking the pristine lawn of the five-acre estate.

For a fraction of a second, Fina itched to ask if Chip had considered his job when he cut the deal with Sidibe Kakay, but so much was unclear in her mind. Suppose it had been Meredith who pressured Chip into the deal? Suppose, the whole story had been made up by Sidibe Kakay? Anyway, what did it matter? She herself had used the passport, grateful if not indifferent to how it was obtained, and had taken Sidibe Kakay's ticket and money. She held her peace.

With Meredith's help Fina enrolled in an associate degree program in business management at County Community College. Through a friend of a friend of Meredith's neighbor, she secured a minimum wage job at Juanita's Twenty-Four Seven Child Care & Learning Academy, working the overnight shift. With a steady income she could now afford to pay her rent. She had used the money Sidibe Kakay gave her to pay her school fees, rent an apartment, and pay six months in advance.

Less than two months after her arrival, Fina was essentially independent, on the American path to success, going to school during the day and working at night. Free at last! And the night shift job at Juanita's worked well with her schedule. After a full day of classes and study at the library, she could count on at least five hours of sleep every night—that is, until seven-year-old hyperactive and developmentally delayed Billy Bob registered. He was not a bad kid, but he lacked the ability to clearly explain his needs. He also had loads of energy, and the night shift did not have enough activities or children his age to help him release it. Fina coped with Billy Bob by not contesting anything he wanted or did. She simply outlasted him. While he roamed the building, opening, overturning, or defacing everything he touched, Fina fed and readied the other kids for bed. Then she would simply wait for Billy Bob to pass out, which often meant finding him flopped out in some death-defying position wherever exhaustion overcame him. There were a few days when Billy Bob stayed awake all night, but he was usually out soon after midnight.

However, eight months into her routine, Fina discovered that the money she was earning was not enough to cover her rent, utilities, transportation, and food. Sending money home to Nabou and paying her college tuition became impossible. She either had to get another job or give up one of the two obligations. She was not ready to give up either. So she took a second job as a check-out clerk in a grocery store. Her income increased but so also did her stress level. Without a car, getting from home to school, from school to job, and from one job to the other became a chess match of fitting unreliable bus schedules with shifting work schedules and factoring in distance, fatigue, and weather conditions between destinations. If she was late in arriving for her overnight shift at Juanita's, the co-worker she relieved, a.k.a. Crosspatch, gave her a tongue-lashing or cold stare. Over time, chronic fatigue set in just as Billy Bob's hyperactivity worsened.

One night, after a particularly frustrating and exhausting day, Fina arrived for her shift forty-five minutes late. Crosspatch, bag and coat in hand and halfway out the door, informed her that Billy Bob had run her ragged. She had no choice but to restrain him in one of the play rooms. Fina was too tired to express her disapproval. Her better judgment urged her to go and see exactly what Crosspatch meant by restrain, but fatigue disguised as common sense argued that she should first attend to the other kids. Billy Bob would be easier to deal with by himself.

So when the pain from a blow that landed on her shoulder woke her up, Fina swung around to confront Billy Bob.

"What are you doing, boy?"

"No, what the fuck are *you* doing, African?" Juanita the owner of the Academy spoke through clenched teeth. As was her practice, she had come in early to catch up on paper work and prepare for the early-birds when she discovered Billy Bob. Crosspatch had covered his mouth with masking tape and tied him to a chair with a skipping rope. He smelled of shit and urine. Fearful the early-birds might come in and discover Billy Bob and that calling out for Fina might wake one of the sleeping children, Juanita untied the boy, cleaned and dressed him in his back-up clothes, and laid him on one of the inflatable sleeping beds. Billy Bob immediately flopped into deep sleep. By then, Juanita had worked herself into a titanic rage, the force of which Fina had felt as the blow on her shoulder.

"If that's how you people treat your kids, that's not how we do it here. Pack your bags and leave now! And don't come back asking for pay either. Pray he is too dumb to tell his mother or your African ass could be sitting in jail for a long time."

"But I—"

"Don't wanna hear nothing! We don't tie up our kids like animals. Do you know what will happen to this place if this gets out? This is how I make a living. This is how you repay me for helping your sorry ass? Just pack your bags and go, now, *now!* Crazy bitch."

A pallid hue hung over the rest of Fina's day. The clean, halogen-lighted and spacious place had suddenly become dim. Fina had expected and prepared for her first racial incident, but she had thought it would come from Bubba the redneck. She never expected it would come from Juanita, black Juanita, who now seemed to pop into view behind every black face she saw on the college campus. Africans treated their kids like animals? This was a surprise to her. Even Baramusu who put her through the pain loved her, gave her fried plantains and sugar cane. When Fina eventually fell asleep that night, she dreamed of Baramusu and the dim ambience of hurricane lamps and candles in the huts of Talaba. But.

Dreams of Talaba gave way the next morning to the reality of finding a job. And that proved more difficult than she had anticipated, especially because she did not want any kind of work that involved children or dealing with Juanita types. Inertia mixed with fear and self-doubt had also set in. She toyed with the idea of asking Meredith and Chip for help but could not bring herself to pick up the phone and call them. She thought of calling Edna, whose phone number she had secured, but was too scared to revive ghosts from the past. She walked into stores to ask for work but stopped short of asking, suddenly conscious she might sound too African. She picked up application forms to fill out but did not fill them, or, if she did, never turned them in. Identifying her place of birth now became fraught with anxiety.

But the first past due rent notice galvanized Fina into action. Though she did not have an active social life, she had befriended a few Sierra Leoneans in the New York area. It was to one of them that she turned. He, Sangallay, a thirty year resident of the U.S., arranged for her to get a position as a customer-care representative for Be Assured, a nationwide insurance company. But the position would require her to move to the Washington Metropolitan Area. It was not a difficult decision to make. Many Sierra Leoneans she knew lived there, and it was an epicenter of immigrant activity. At the end of her lease a few months later, she moved.

A couple of months after Fina settled down in her new job and one-bedroom apartment in Langley Park, Maryland, she contacted Edna. The step-sister lived in San Diego, California, so they talked on the phone. Far away from home, their reconnection provided a cultural comfort zone they both understood and needed. Initially the calls comprised polite salutations and inquiries about each other's work and health. If the conversation drifted to talk of home, it was never about back home. That would take them to a past neither wanted to give voice or form. So they talked, complained really, about their present American home, about work, but especially about men—how difficult it was to find BMWs (black men working); but how they frequently attracted SUVs (serially unemployed villains); and how they weren't really into white men, but given the lack of BMWs, they would settle for dirty dishwater to lubricate their rusting engines.

Laughter, shared values and experiences are the wellspring of friendship, so the two women who years earlier as pubescent girls had folded into each other on the cold, tiled bathroom floor, skipped right back into a friendship after a few phone calls. Soon they began talking about a reunion. With a decent-paying job, a rekindled friendship with Edna, a home within a vibrant community of Africans, and the Billy Bob incident consigned by time into a learning experience, Fina enrolled in a Langley Park area community college. The clean, halogen-lighted place brightened up again.

"I've got a surprise for you," Fina announced to Edna a few seconds into one of their now regular bi-monthly phone conversations.

"What a coincidence. I have one for you too, but you go first."

"Okay. I've decided to come and visit you. We have to talk about what happened."

"You know, I've been toying with the same idea."

"Good! Then it's settled. I'm not sure exactly when, but I'm planning on coming either Labor Day or Thanksgiving. Now, what's the surprise you have to tell me?

"I'm engaged," Edna giggled.

73

"Wow, congratulations! You never even mentioned a boyfriend before and now you're getting married? When did all this happen?"

"It happened so fast. I wasn't sure how serious we were at first, so I decided not to say anything. Then last week, he proposed. I'll tell you about him, how we met, later. Right now, I want you to be my maid-of-honor."

"Sure, sure. When is the wedding? If it's going to happen this year, then I'll just wait till the wedding to come over."

"No, we're planning for next summer."

"Okay then. I guess I'll have to make two trips. So who is he? You got yourself some African American hunk, eh?"

"Nooo… not African American but a hunk from home. He's a little older than me, but he's mature and treats me with respect. Guys my age are not serious."

"I hear you, especially these control-freak educated Africans."

"Well, Mendel is not like that."

"That's a Sierra Leonean name?"

"Yeaaah. Hezekiah Mendelssohn Bacchus, but he says most people know him as Kizzy. Do you know him? He said he was a lab technician or something at CC."

Though inclined to the sciences, Fina enjoyed reading, and it was through the literature classics she had read at the Heddle household that she now processed Edna's revelation. It had the element of shock the suitors must have felt at the moment Odysseus revealed his true identity; it had the irony Ezeulu and Umuaro must have realized to learn that Oduche, the son of the Chief Priest of Ulu, had imprisoned the sacred Royal Python; but it was the realization that she could not escape what had been ordained by the Ancestors and Baramusu that reverberated through her. She felt puny and inconsequential; now she understood the deep distress of the Greek woman, Jocasta.

"Fina… Fina…, are you there?"

"Yes… yes… I'm here. I got distracted for a minute."

"His name is Kizzy. Do you know him?"

"Er… um…kinda. Er… did he say he knew me?"

74

"He said he'd heard your name and may have seen you."

"Me too."

"Well, he's really nice, a gentleman."

Fina coughed and gagged for the next twenty minutes as Edna extoled Kizzy's virtues and described their wedding plans. But she heard nothing. Her mind was already working on how to get out of her commitments.

She contracted chicken-pox two weeks before Edna and Kizzy's wedding, came down with the flu for the christening of their first child, and experienced severe diarrhea, coupled with life-threatening dehydration, for that of their second. After the wedding, Edna had forced Kizzy to talk with Fina, but through their combined subterfuge, they had avoided meeting each other, until Kizzy's work transferred him to Richmond, Virginia. But the evasive tactics continued, especially on Kizzy's side. Twice when Edna and her kids visited Fina, his job prevented him from accompanying them. It also somehow kept him away from home the one or two times Fina visited them in Richmond.

Fina wanted to tell Edna about her past with Kizzy, but she could never summon the courage to do so, and, as time passed, she grew less inclined to conjure up ghosts of a bygone past. Besides, since Edna had never said anything to her, she assumed that Kizzy, too, had found putting their past behind them, like an old grudge, a prudent way to move forward.

Chapter 7

Amanzinga Al-Quarta was proud of her African heritage. She did not learn about Africa—Olduvai Gorge, Egypt, Cleopatra, and Nubia—only during Black History Month. She did not wear *Kente* cloth and kaftans only to attend African art shows, festivals, and Sunday church services. She did not celebrate Kwanzaa only to assert her difference or make a political statement. She did not plan a-once-in-a-lifetime pilgrimage to the Motherland to discover her roots. No! Amanzinga was *not* an occasional African. She was an African for all seasons, the first expression of her rebirth occurred the day she announced she wanted to be called Amanzinga, not Laquandrista, the name her mother, Quanda, and her father, Larista, had fashioned for her in the headiness of their young, all-consuming and eternal love.

Before her rebirth, Laquandrista was, for her age, a big girl, so much bigger than boys her age that her classmates called her "Amazon woman." For months, Laquandrista suffered through the taunting mill until, late one night, she stumbled on a PBS television documentary about puberty rites among the Ashanti of Ghana. The narrator had explained that the Ashanti publicly celebrated the bodily growth of their girls and emphasized that men did not actively participate in such celebrations. One excerpt showed a group of young Ashanti girls talking happily about attaining puberty. Another showed young boys scurrying off when they heard the songs and drums of an approaching group of female celebrants. The next morning, Laquandrista, who normally cowered and found the nearest exit when her classmates teased her, smacked the jaw of a boy who called her a gorilla. The blow sent him reeling into a metal pole that supported the roof of a walkway. Later that day in the principal's office, Amanzinga saw the bump over the boy's right eyebrow. She was pleased at her work.

Even though this assertion of self resulted in their being summoned to her school for a meeting with the school principal and counselor, Quanda and Larista were pleased that their daughter had fought back. But phrases such as "channel her aggression... inappropriate behavior... hyperactive and slow... ADD... medications and suspension" charged the conversation. Yet, later that night, in a rare assertion of his African heritage, Larista taught his daughter the little he knew about Africa's famed and death-defying Queen Nzinga Mbande. "If dem kids talk mean 'bout Africa, tell 'em you're proud of your African roots. You 'ear me? Queen Nzinga was a big 'n strong African woman. You're a big 'n strong gal. Tell 'em you're proud to be like her. You 'ear wha' am sayin'?"

The following morning in school, Laquandrista felt unrestrained in getting back at anyone who called her a name. She swatted the backs of heads, pinched arms, and shoved into walls and polls those who called her "Amazon woman." In the bus ride home that day, she declared she wanted to be called Queen Nzinga. Her classmates obliged for a day or two but then stopped. It was no fun calling someone a name if that person named what she wanted to be called. So, at the risk of her awesome and certain retaliatory strikes, they started calling her 'Amanzinga.' Ironically, Laquandrista liked the name and it stuck. She told her parents she wanted to be called Amanzinga. They were not happy but obliged her because they wanted to build her self-esteem—a youthful fad that would soon pass, they figured. But to their dismay, more than a name, an entire lifestyle took hold of their daughter.

Amanzinga devoted herself to Africana—reading books, visiting museums, attending lectures, and participating in cultural events. She discovered a wealth of information about black people that she used to flavor her conversations, accessorize her clothes, nuance her habits, and culture her life. Disapproving of her obsession with things African, Quanda and Larista stopped calling her Amanzinga. But shortly after her first semester of college, she retaliated by officially changing her name to Amanzinga Al-Quarta. Quanda compromised by calling her "Aman," but Larista held firm. When he addressed her with substitutes like Miss, Lady, or Poo, Aman refused to answer. Very soon he did not even bother to talk to her and communication between them all but ceased. What small hope remained of reconciliation disappeared completely when, a few months later, Larista left Quanda for a younger woman.

With a resistant father gone, a mother halfway won, and a sibling Shantea too busy with her own life to be concerned about her sister's, Aman indulged her love for Africa. She seized every opportunity to befriend Africans, which was exactly what happened with Fina.

Aman was the district manager of Be Assured, the insurance company where Fina worked. As part of her work, Aman often called the customer-care representatives in the branch offices to discuss difficult cases. It was during one such call that she complimented Fina on her clear-headed thinking and decisiveness. Aman parlayed a polite phone acquaintance into what eventually became a friendship by inviting Fina to lunch.

Fina was agitated and twenty minutes late when she finally stepped into the atrium of the food court of the local mall. All manner of people criss-crossed its wide, marble floors. Fina looked around for Aman, but nobody approached her or appeared to be waiting. It had occurred to her to call Aman to exchange details on what they would be wearing, but then she wasn't overly concerned that they might miss each other. Now here she was late and not sure whom she was looking for, though she figured that with Aman's educated speech and polite phone manners, she was probably looking for an elegant and sophisticated woman, the kind that often appeared in the glossy pages of *Ebony* and *Essence*. However her image of Aman was severely challenged as all manner, shapes, sizes, and complexions of African American womanhood walked past her. She decided to find a place that would give her the widest view of the food court.

Since the table offering this view was occupied by two black women engaged in an animated conversation, Fina sat at the vacant one next to them. Its view of the food court was slightly obscured by a wide support column, but it would have to do. If she paid attention, she would see someone approaching the food court and would either make eye contact or get up and introduce herself.

She glanced over at the women in the table next to hers. The amply built one with her back to Fina wore an African print dress and sported a buzz-cut, angled slightly forward and to the left to create the peak-of-a-cap effect. Must be a sista who thinks wearing African designs and materials makes her African, Fina mused. The other woman, facing Fina, captured the essence of elegance. Tall and slender, she wore a light gray, two-piece pant suit with long sleeves, peak lapels, and a two-button, double breasted jacket. Her hair was pulled into a French knot, and she wore Anafili glasses. Every bit the way Fina imagined Aman would look. Fina was about to introduce herself, when the women's conversation spilled over to her.

"You hear wha' happen to Chalandra?" the tall, slender woman asked. "Her husband left her for a woman twenty years his junior— one of them African girls. She flung them big-ass hips in front of the brother and, poo! Next thing you know, she's living in a mansion with a fat rock on her finger."

Suddenly conscious of her own buttocks, Fina shifted. The tall, slender woman detected the movement and raised her head. Their eyes met. They studied each other for a moment, each appreciating the tasteful elegance of the other.

"Brothers not only running off and marryin' white women, dey now runnin' off with Kunte Kinte's sisters!" The slender woman broke into a smile. Her eyes searched Fina's for affirmation. Fina managed a cross between a smile and a snarl, and then turned her head away, though she could still hear the conversation.

"So what happened to Chalandra?" the amply built woman asked.

"She now lives with her three kids in an old rinky-dink house."

"You mean she just let Tyrie walk away?"

"What could she do? This girl from Africa had his nose open so wide a train could go through it. Now I hear he wanna leave his job and go live in dem jungle communes in the Amazon."

"You mean the Congo."

80

"Whatever. It's all trees, animals, and *juju* witchdoctor stuff, ain't it? Lemme tell you, that African girl put that *juju* on Tyrie and mess up his head."

"You're so bad," the amply built woman laughed. "That's no way to talk about sisters."

"What? You think dem African girls don't use nasty stuff to mess up a brotha's head?"

"Like what?"

"Girl," the slender woman leaned forward conspiratorially, "I hear they sit butt naked over a pot and wash their selves, mix up the water with herbs and animal insides and put the stuff in a brotha's drink. One drink and poof! He lose his head and be acting all crazy like Tyrie."

"Brothers don't need African *juju* to do stupid things. Why would these girls do that anyway?"

"'Cos if they get married to a brotha, they can live and work here and don't have to go back to Africa."

"Oh, stop it. Do you really believe in *juju*?"

"I see how Tyrie is all messed up since he been with that girl from Zambezi."

"Zimbabwe. Ever heard of L-O-V-E, love? Besides, how come this stuff doesn't work on white people?"

"Who says it don't? You don't see it 'cos Kunte Kinte's sisters go for brothas. They have to. When they go for their green card, black marrying black don't raise no red flags like black marrying white."

"What about the men then? Don't they have to use *juju* to marry sisters?"

"Kunte Kinte don't need that *juju* mess. He got that big stick. He work magic with it and sistas go crazy!"

They paused, looked solemn for a moment, and then broke out into raucous laughter that engulfed the atrium. Stern, piercing, and offended gazes turned in their direction.

Fina cringed. Juanitas, she thought. She hated the loud talking and laughing but even more the ignorant remarks, especially from the woman she believed was Aman. To think she was moments away

81

from introducing herself and starting a friendship. Fina wondered how she could have so severely misread Aman. She sounded so sophisticated on the phone and knew so much about Africa. Now she had been replaced by this black woman with 'GAME'—ghetto attitude to manipulate the environment.

She stood up to leave, just as the two women embraced in goodbye. Fina's heart raced. Her palms sweated. It was too late. This ignorant woman was going to introduce herself. Should she confront Aman? That carried risks. After all, Aman was her supervisor and could make work difficult, if she did not decide to fire her. Yet Fina knew they could not be friends. She decided to be blunt. But to her surprise the tall, slender woman she had assumed to be Aman walked away with an elegant sway, and the amply built woman with the angled buzz cut stepped forward smiling, her hand outstretched.

"Hi, I'm Aman. You must be Fina. Forgive me. I had my back to you and didn't notice you until I stood up. Have you been waiting long?"

"Uh, not really. You and your friend seemed to be having so much fun I didn't want to interrupt you."

"Oh, Tamika. Isn't she a trip? Please forgive her foolish talk. Not all of us think like she does."

****

Fina and Aman became friends quicker than either would have predicted. The friendship began over a dinner of rice and cassava leaves in Fina's one-bedroom apartment. A sofa and love seat, a coffee table, a 14-inch pedestal oscillating fan, a 13-inch black and white TV with a V-shaped antenna sitting on top of it, and three 5 x 7 framed photographs on the mantle overhanging the faux fireplace made up the furnishings. Behind the love seat a door led to the bedroom. The friends sat at a round dinner table in the small dining area between the kitchen and living room. Fina had spent most of the meal asking if Aman liked the food.

"Tasty but spicy," Aman gasped after each inquiry and swallowed some of the ice-cold water she had requested after the very first spoonful. "This sure is hot, Honey."

"Really? And because of you, I did not put as much pepper as I usually do."

"You should just call this pepper soup," Aman surrendered after her sixth spoonful. She gulped down a full glass of water.

"Oh no. We have one that's actually named pepper soup. You ought to try it."

"No thanks. This one is hot enough."

Fina smiled.

"Let me get you some sweet-tasting ginger beer. Sit over there and cool down," Fina pointed Aman to the sofa directly across from the oscillating fan and walked to the kitchen.

"This beautiful woman must be your mother," Aman pulled the first framed photograph off the mantle, examined it and replaced it. By then Fina had placed a one gallon plastic jug and two glasses on the coffee table.

"And this one is of your mother and probably a sister." Aman inflected her voice and turned her statement into a question.

"Yes," Fina replied and sat down.

Fina was in the midst of telling about her sister and mom and how she longed to see them when the cordless phone on the coffee table rang. Fina picked it up to answer. Aman grabbed a copy of *Jet* magazine to read.

"Lord have mercy, Mama o, Mama o…," Fina dropped the phone and broke into a gut wrenching wail, flailing her arms, and running up and down the living room. Her sister Isa had called with the news that their mother had died, suddenly, unexpectedly— probably a heart attack the doctors had said but no one knew for sure. She was to be buried the next day.

****

83

"*Niya nehba behteh pass fawey fambul,*" Fina said to Aman two weeks later. They had just returned to Fina's apartment after wiring $1000 to Isa to pay her rent and pay off Nabou's debtors.

"What does that mean?"

"That it's better to have good neighbors and friends like you than faraway relatives."

Aman blushed. "But daarng, you Muslims bury real fast."

"It's our tradition. What is there to do with the body when the soul is gone, especially in hot weather where it will rot quickly?"

"But quick burials don't leave any time for family like you to say goodbye."

"No, we do that forty days later at the *sara*. Sort of like your memorial service. Friends and relatives come together, eat, and talk about the person."

"Okay, so you'll be able to go home for the sarah to say a proper goodbye to your mother.

"*Sara,*" Fina corrected.

"Sa-ra," Aman repeated. "That will give you closure. We need closure in order to move forward, you know."

Fina did not answer. She looked down at the floor.

"Oh, don't worry about your job. I'll take care of that."

"Thanks," Fina mumbled without looking directly at Aman.

"In fact," Aman's eyes popped out, "if you don't mind, I'd like to go with you." She sat upright and pushed her chest forward. "I've always wanted to visit Africa," Aman continued. "This would be such a great opportunity for me."

Fina smiled.

"I'd have you to show me around and I'll be participating in a real... er... sarah, Sa-ra. Oh, gosh. It would be so wonderful to go back to Mother Africa, the place where my people came from."

"I can't, Aman. If I go home, I won't be able to return."

"I'm sorry." Aman walked over, sat beside Fina, and put an arm around her shoulders.

84

It had to have been a combination of sympathy for her friend's predicament and her own desire to visit Africa. Either way, Aman felt compelled to help Fina.

"So what can we do to fix this?"

"Find me a BMW to fall in love with."

"How will a car help you?"

"No, dummy, a black man working."

"Child, I need one for myself." They laughed.

But it became an unstated mission for them to find Fina a man she could fall in love with and marry. If in the process, Aman met someone she liked to marry that would be a welcome by product. So they went on blind dates and dinner dates; they trolled night clubs and strip clubs; attended football games and church services, filled out and religiously checked profiles and preferences for "Men Wanted" and "Women Wanted" ads. Yet, Fina could not bring herself to like any of the men she met let alone consider marrying then. But then, quite unexpectedly, at the funeral of Big Mama, Aman's grandmother, she met and liked Aman's relative, Jemal, a self-described businessman and entrepreneur.

"He's cute. Introduce us," Fina said.

Almost from the moment she introduced them, Aman regretted her decision. Fina seemed too eager to like Jemal. He struck her as sleek, if not cagey. Aman's regret soon blossomed into resentment and finally settled into intense loathing for Jemal as she saw Fina's relationship with him degenerate from broken appointments, to animated public disagreements, angry phone conversations, and suspicious bruises and welts that appeared on her face and arms. Aman told Fina she was heading for trouble and should break off the relationship. But Fina would not listen. In fact, a couple of days after Aman's sister Shantea warned Fina Jemal was a veteran abuser of women and drugs, Fina moved in with Jemal. A few weeks later, she announced that they had gotten married—a quiet, civil affair.

In that civil marriage, Fina came face-to face with the stark reality of her ignorance and stubbornness, for soon after, Jemal took to disappearing, initially for a couple of nights, then for a week, and once or twice for a month or more. When he was at home, he was often high and looking for higher highs, forcing Fina to participate in his drug use and his drug-induced sexual fantasies. When she protested or refused, he punched and kicked her.

She knew she should leave him. She wanted to leave him. But she also knew there was no gain without pain. So she stayed, paying for Jemal's drug rehab programs, encouraging him to attend church and counseling sessions, reading books on spirituality to him, absorbing his mental and physical abuse, covering her shame with lies and convoluted explanations to Aman and her co-workers about her bruises, and waiting, painfully, for the day when she would go for her final interview to get her green card. But two short weeks before that interview, Jemal disappeared, again. Fina and Aman searched frantically for him. On the eve of the interview, they found him strung out in a local crack house. They took him home.

On the morning of the interview, Fina woke up at five a.m. and gave Jemal a hour-long bubble bath, scrubbing and plying him with coffee, black no sugar, to bring him to a level of alertness befitting the serious business ahead of them. She succeeded. But perhaps too much. Jemal threatened not to go to the interview unless Fina gave him five hundred dollars. Fina promised to give him the money after the interview. Then, to her surprise, Jemal fell to his knees, declared that he truly loved her. A few bad deals and the treachery of friends he trusted had ruined him financially. That was the reason for his drug use. He promised to be a changed man.

The sight of Jemal on his knees rattled Fina, but she maintained her composure with the discipline of yogi in meditation. "Let's talk about this after the interview," Fina coaxed, mindful that any hint of rejection might trigger a revolt but also determined to crush it if it so much as threatened her impending liberation. So, just before they left the apartment, Fina made a quick detour to the kitchen and slipped a meat cleaver into her handbag. On the drive to the immigration office, Jemal repeated his love for Fina. She pulled the handbag close to her.

By the time they arrived at the immigration office, Jemal was considerably calmer. As he was about to step out of the car, Fina grabbed him with one hand. Her other hand was in her handbag. "Look," she began, "this is serious business and my future depends on you." She paused for a moment. Then from somewhere beginning deep inside her stomach, she heard herself say, "But I swear to God, if you screw this up, I will kill you." With the meat cleaver, she sliced the air horizontally in front of Jemal's throat. He jerked back from the glinting blade. "No fucking up. You get me?" She put the meat cleaver back in her handbag, got out of the car, straightened her skirt, and walked around to the front passenger side. Like an escort to a Hollywood celebrity, she extended her arm out to Jemal. He stepped out of the car with alacrity and grabbed on to her. The interview was short, sweet and flawless.

But the rest of the day wasn't. In the car, Jemal grabbed the meat cleaver from Fina's handbag and forced her to take out all the money she had in her bank account. As soon as she handed the money to him, he threw the meat cleaver into the backseat, hopped out of the car and disappeared—until around 2 a.m. the next morning when he climbed into their bed and choked Fina in a frenzied sexual high. When he finally released her from his death grip and flopped over in sleep, she packed a bag and rushed out of the house to Aman. She had wanted to call the police, but Fina had refused. The gain had been worth the pain.

****

Though Jemal effectively disappeared from Fina's life after the choking incident and she sought and got a court-ordered divorce decree because he could not be found, it would be months before either she or Aman would discuss men. But inevitably they came up, indirectly. Aman had called Fina one day in the office.

"You want to go with me to a talk tonight?"

"About what?"

"African names."

"No."

"Come on, we'll be on a college campus. Bound to be some BMWs there."

Fina smiled. "Don't have anything decent to wear."

"It's not a cocktail party for Christ's sake. Put on one of those nice African dresses you have."

"Okay, but after this one, can we go easy on these talks about black issues? When does it start?"

"Eight."

"Better pick me up at seven, then."

Aman chuckled. "Trying to tell me something?"

"No, just wanna make sure we get there on time."

****

"That speaker, Baryour, is very intelligent," Aman said as they drove home after the presentation on African names.

"Bayo, Bayo," Fina corrected with native-speaker entitlement.

"He's right, you know, names do have mystical power. Don't underestimate a name."

"Puleeze. I saw how you hung around him. He's kinda young for you, isn't he?"

Aman ignored Fina's remark. She had, in fact, followed the speaker to his car and got his business card when Fina went to the bathroom. "Names define and shape who we become," she said.

"They don't affect how I feel about myself."

"Perhaps not for you, but they are important to me, us African Americans."

"But what matters is how you see yourself, not what others name you. Anyway, what's with these names you people give yourselves? Turkquinatria? Shaqrillia? Yours is easy though. I don't pull up mucous saying it, A-man-zin-ga," Fina said, giggling. Aman concentrated on the road in injured silence. Feeling guilty about her swipe and hoping Aman would feel better if she talked about herself, Fina asked,

"What does your name mean?"

"It's a compound name. Nzinga, from Queen Nzinga Mbande—"

"Who?"

"Queen Nzinga. You never heard of her?"

"No, should I have?"

"*Yeeessss*! She's one of Africa's most famous women. You don't know very much about your culture, do you?"

"No. I just lived it."

Fina's answer silenced Aman. They drove the rest of the way home without speaking. Fortunately, the pursuit of personal happiness and the American dream sufficiently occupied them to sideline cultural and personality differences. Over time, as Aman and Fina supported each other through work-related problems and failed relationships, they became friends who learned to accept their differences when they could not delight in them.

After the lecture on Yoruba names, Aman started dating the speaker, Bayo Karumwi, a doctoral student in mechanical engineering. Their relationship developed quickly. Initially, Aman made an effort to include Fina in dinners at restaurants and trips to the movies, but over time, she decided to give them their space. She would accept their invitations only to events which involved a lot of people. With lots of time alone, Fina dedicated herself to fulfilling the American dream. She set aside finishing her associate degree in business management and worked relentlessly: five days a week from 8:00 a.m. to 5:00 p.m. at Be Assured, then 6:00 p.m. to 9:00 p.m. as a telemarketer, selling a variety of products and services. On occasional Saturdays, she pulled a 9:00 a.m. to 3:00 p.m. shift. Her schedule was grueling, but the money she earned enabled her to buy a new car and then put a down payment on a townhouse. Her visitors nearly always commented on its upscale décor and neighborhood.

"Yeah, so upscale that twice now the security people have asked me if I live here," she told Aman. "And women here cross to the other side of the road when they see me coming. Then when I meet them at the gym, they overcompensate. 'Thank you,' 'Excuse me,' they say, even though *they* are the ones holding open the door for me, or it's *their* scheduled time on the fitness machines. Politeness gone amuck!"

"Welcome to America," Aman answered.

But most of the time, Fina accepted compliments about her neighborhood and tasteful furnishings with grace, though she did not really care about either. She was certainly happy to own a piece of America, and she understood the townhouse was an investment, but once she had got over the euphoria of a new purchase, she found herself unsatisfied, unfulfilled, the same way she felt after dinner at some exclusive restaurant. Invariably, she returned home after these dinners and, no matter how late, microwaved some frozen palm-oil based soup and ate until she felt satiated. Wholeness, fullness, completeness—what she sought and what the green card, townhouse, and car had failed to deliver.

Periodically, her mind wandered back home—to Baramusu's injunction never to cut the rope, to her father's desecration of the *fafei,* and to Isa who had barely completed secondary school. Invariably, these thoughts led to resolutions—to return home and to set up Isa in business—which involved larger sums of money. The realization depressed her, and the only way she could fulfill them all was by earning more money. Fina decided she would not only ask for a raise but she would also drive over to Wal-Mart to see about getting more part-time, weekend work. She was on her way to take a shower before going job hunting when the doorbell rang. It was Aman with an invitation to a party that same Saturday night.

Chapter 8

Fina did not want to go to the party. The invitation was offered at short notice, and she did not like the idea of being a third-string invitee. "Who's throwing the party and what's it for?"

"A doctor friend of Bayo's friend. For his parents. They're visiting from Trinidad."

"Can't be much of a doctor if he has to ask his friends to invite people to his party!"

"What do you care about his ability to make friends? Let's go and spend a couple of hours, have some fun."

Fina agreed to go, but mostly because she figured that when she started working weekends at Wal-Mart, she would not have any time for parties. She decided she'd enjoy this one. And she did.

At the party, the string of calypso tunes whose lyrics she knew by heart transported her back to her teenage years in the Heddle household. On Saturday afternoons when Pa Heddle came home reeking of beer and cigarettes, the house would be quiet. The older children and Aunty Matty were usually out. After eating a huge plate of *foo-foo* and bitter-leaf soup, Pa Heddle would pull out his vinyl records, play them loudly, sing off-key even more loudly, and loudly gulp more bottles of Star Beer, belching and farting to his heart's content.

He owned a variety of records—LPs of Tommy Dorsey, Glenn Miller, and Frank Sinatra; the symphonies of Beethoven, Mozart, and Strauss; hymns and anthems of King's College Choir, Cambridge. He played the hymns and symphonies exclusively on Sundays, believing they were appropriate for meditation and reflection. But on Saturday afternoons, the highlife of Ghana's Dr. K. Gyasi and His Noble Kings, the folksy tunes of Sierra Leone's S. E. Rogers (Rogie), and the Caribbean calypsos of the Mighty Sparrow and Lord Kitchener were his favorites. Sometimes when he played these records, he not only sang but also danced.

Fina and Edna did not usually have Saturday afternoon engagements and amused themselves by spying on this usually sober and stern father who on Saturdays turned into a belly-waddling, pelvic-thrusting dancer. Over time and by dint of repetition, they learned the lyrics, and, out of his sight in the hallway, they imitated his pelvic thrusts as the calypsos of The Mighty Sparrow and Lord Kitchener blared in the parlor. When Pa Heddle finally fell into a drunken sleep and the record player stopped, they would steal money from his wallet to buy cold soft drinks and roasted peanuts. Then, taking care not to wake him, they'd restart the records. Back in the hallway, in between crunching peanuts and sipping Fanta orange drinks, they would pretend they were dancing with boys from their class and break into conspiratorial giggles when one of them gyrated or shook her hips in a way the other considered shocking.

It was in this recaptured state of delight that Fina danced with the host of the party, Cameron Dexter Priddy, a.k.a. Cammy, as The Mighty Sparrow sang the infectious calypso classic, "May-May:"

Darling don't bite me, don't do that honey

I never had a man who ever did that to me,

Ah ya-ya-ya-ya, doo-doo darling, look me pores raise up,

You're making me feel so sweet, STOP! Sparrow STOP!

Fina rolled her buttocks in a slow, grinding circular motion, and her shapely gluteus sneaked out of her tight-fitting shorts as she feigned ecstasy, caressing her sides, pursing her lips and singing: "You're making me feel sooooo sweet, STOP! Sparrow, STOP!" Her dancing and the catchy melody were contagious, and Cammy responded with pulsating pelvic thrusts and undulations behind her buttocks as they acted out the salacious lyrics.

When Aman saw how much Fina was enjoying herself, she abandoned their plan to spend only two or three hours at the party. The mix of hip-hop, rhythm and blues, and top-20 hits that had been playing earlier to accommodate the tastes of the non-Caribbean guests gave way to a steady stream of soca, reggae, and calypso. But far from sounding the death knell for the non-Caribbeans at the party, the music gave the revelers a second wind and blunted the

92

sharp edges of culture and physical differences. Bodies—old and young, male and female, black and white, light and dark skinned, limber and stiff—contorted and gyrated to that universal logic of music that transcends culture.

Among the non-dancers were a few couples locked in embraces that telegraphed their intentions for later, more private accommodations. At the bar stood dark-colored liquor bottles, inviting guests to partake of their mysterious contents. Next to them lay two or three trays with an assortment of leftover finger foods. Between and during records, sweaty, drunk, and enamored guests made forays to the bar and returned with a drink in one hand and snacks in the other.

One such couple was Fina and Cammy. A Trinidadian in his mid-thirties, Cammy was one of those people who seemed to walk on water. His six-foot four-inch, body-builder frame and dreadlocks always sparked people's interest when they learned that he was a surgeon. In fact, Cammy was distinguishing himself as a gifted urologist when he met Fina, and his latest scientific paper, *Robotics, Renal Carcinoma and Surgery*, given at the annual conference of the American Association of Urology was the talk of the conference. It had put his career on a trajectory that led only to the stars.

At the moment, though, his trajectory with Fina led only to the bar, so they could refresh themselves after a long calypso medley. He trailed her like a randy dog, knowing only that he wanted more of her. More of what? interposed the rational man in him. Her beauty, her dancing, her knowledge of calypso lyrics, her sensuality, of course, the enchanted Cammy replied, not really convinced they were good reasons but not caring either. Fina compelled his attention, as well as that of another man following her.

"Ya sure got some good moves, sista," he said as Cammy served her the cold glass of 7-Up she requested and poured himself an old coaster—brandy and ginger ale.

"Meet Leroy McKinney, my neighbor," Cammy explained to Fina, who did not particularly like either the implication or tone of McKinney's comment.

"Thank you," she stepped around him to stave off further conversation.

"You have an accent. From the Islands?"

"Yes, I do have an accent, and, no, I'm *not* from the Islands. I'm from Sierra Leone, West Africa. Are you from Louisiana?"

"Me!?" Leroy asked, puzzled.

"Yes… *you* have an accent too, a southern drawl."

"No ma'am. Born and raised in da Branx, Nu Yark City."

"I guess you have a Bronx, New York, accent then."

"Guess I do, but I didn't mean it bad when I asked 'bout your accent. You don't look like no African."

Cammy squirmed.

"Oh? How does an African look?"

"Well, I mean you look different. More American, like a sista. Know wha' am sayin'?"

"No, I don't. You mean African like half-naked with dried-up prunes for breasts, carrying a load on my head and a child on my back?"

"I'm sure that wasn't what he meant," Cammy intervened, deftly guiding Fina away from Leroy, who was confounded that his compliments had been rebuffed.

"What's with the attitude, sista?" Leroy demanded of her back. "Brotha wants you to lay some moves on him. Know wha' am sayin'. You, me, get jungle wild."

Fina turned, glared and was about to respond, but Cammy pushed her toward the balcony. Leroy, now marinating in the possibility of a confrontation, added, "Oooh, I like it when a sista gets rough!"

"Hey, Leroy, cool it man," Cammy admonished as he closed the sliding balcony door behind him.

"Can you believe him?"

"Just ignore him. He's a little drunk and was probably just impressed by your dancing. I hope you don't get mad, but, like him, I was wondering how a woman from the land of the Lion Mountains, of Pedro da Sintra and Bai Bureh knew the words and tunes of so

94

many calypso songs."

Fina gazed at Cammy in astonishment. He had definitely kindled her interest—a handsome doctor, one who could dance, was easygoing and, most impressively, knowledgeable about Sierra Leone! "Lion Mountains, Pedro da Sintra and Bai Bureh! You have more than a passing interest in my country."

"I have family in Sierra Leone."

"Really! How so?"

"Well, sort of. When malaria killed the white boys, the British sent Trinidadians and other Caribbean folks over there to be governors and civil servants. They figured blacks could better withstand the mosquitoes and climate."

"I see."

"One of my great-granduncles was a governor of Freetown. We could be long-lost cousins."

"I doubt it." Fina smiled broadly. "I'm from Mande stock. My people come from the Guinea highlands that stretch into northeastern Sierra Leone."

"But many of the slaves were recaptured Mande people, you know. They resettled around Freetown after the slave trade was abolished. We *really* might be related."

Fina smiled. She knew there was only the remotest chance they might be related, but she was enjoying their banter.

"Well, if we are long-lost relatives, you'd better tell me what your intentions are for bringing me out to this balcony."

"Hmmm! Maybe ah should rethink dis 'hole we are related thing." Whenever he became excited and especially when he became angry, Cammy unconsciously reverted to a more informal Trinidadian English. He stared into the starry night as if doing some mental calculations. Then he banged his head with the base of his palm and looked at her. "Ah make a mistake. There's only a slim chance we related. In fact," he added with a sly chuckle, "Ah sure we not related atall."

"I guess that means there are no obstacles to carrying out your intentions then. What were they, by the way?" Fina cooed.

Months later, when they had become inseparable, some of those who were at the party that night said Fina and Cammy fell in love the instant they met. Others said the love came during their tête-à-tête on the balcony. They may have been right, for as they had talked that night, the universe contracted around them. Cammy felt as if he could reach in the air and shower Fina's head with little stars. She felt as if she could grab the moon, cut it in two, and place it over his head like a halo. Indeed, they both felt as if they had become the center of the universe. The music from the speakers sounded no louder than the whir of a tiny electric pump, and reminders from Aman that it was almost 6:00 a.m. irritated Fina like the whine of a hungry mosquito.

And in what better country could two immigrants start a romance than in America, the land where people learn from birth that their dreams and hopes are not wild imaginings but the blueprints of their tomorrows?

Chapter 9

Fina and Cammy transitioned into a loving relationship without the usual hiccups. There were no awkward first dates, no current relationships that had to be ended and no traumatic past loves or lovers that left either jaded about the opposite sex. Neither had family traditions, religious beliefs, ethnic or racial ideologies that restrained their headlong plunge into a full-fledged relationship. They simply absorbed each other. They spent all their non-working nights and days together, either at his or her place, coordinating their schedules or planning things to do. Weekends involved attending socials or traveling—her all-time favorite travel scene being the first time she beheld the night-lit New York skyline as it suddenly appeared in majestic focus from the Brooklyn Bridge with Cole Porter's "Night and Day" playing softly in the background.

As a result of her relationship with Cammy, Fina never followed through on the job at Wal-Mart, and she consigned completing the associate degree in business management and funding Isa to start her own business to a list of future tasks. On the nights when Cammy got called away to an emergency, she experienced some disquiet about the standstill in pursuing her dreams. But she chose to settle down with the more satisfying thought that she had a right to some personal happiness, to indulge herself with this man who made her feel alive and valuable. He drove her to and picked her up from her late evening telemarketing job and agreed with her ideas about how to help Isa but had enough sense not to sully her dreams and offend her dignity with crass offers of financial help even though he could afford to. Frequently, she came home to piping-hot curried chicken and rice he had prepared, just for her. One day he surprised her with West African *Jollof* rice and goat stew. He had prepared it, he explained, after watching her cook it for him just once. The goat was a Caribbean touch, "to inflect the food, man," he said. And his rendition tasted good too! What *Salone* man would cook for me after he worked a fifteen-hour shift, Fina mused.

Their evenings together were simple. After he picked her up and they ate dinner, they would cuddle, watch television, playfully disagree about the topic du jour, compromise, and seal the compromise by making love, beginning in front of the television and ending in odd places that provided fodder for their countless phone conversations the next day.

Thus they were one evening, cuddled together, discussing how they could outdo their previous night's bedroom antics, when a television report captured their attention. It was about an American court granting asylum to a Togolese woman who feared her daughters would be forced to undergo female genital mutilation if she was deported to her homeland.

"Outrageous and criminal," Cammy exclaimed after the report ended. "FGM should be banned and those who force children through it jailed." He looked to Fina for support.

"Making judgments about something you know little about," Fina replied, her tone trapped between being playful and being combative.

Cammy heard only the combative part. "What? Are you saying it's okay to mutilate little girls?"

"No, I'm just saying you don't know anything about the people or cultures that practice circumcision." Fina un-cuddled herself from Cammy, shifted far enough away to look directly at him.

"Ah don'n need to know 'bout culture," Cammy shot back, sensing Fina's resolve. "All ah know is that FGM is wrong."

"Well, I guess it's wrong if *you* say 'it's wrong'," Fina mocked. She got up from the sofa and walked toward the bedroom.

"Why are you defending the indefensible?" Cammy's irritation gained pace like water rushing to a precipice.

"I'm not. I just don't want you passing judgments and making decisions for women in Africa," Fina shouted back and disappeared into the bedroom.

Cammy scooted to the edge of the sofa but did not get up. He took a deep breath and waited. Several minutes later, Fina emerged from the bedroom, looking fresh and radiant. She did not say anything as she walked past him into the kitchen. She pulled out a packet of sliced bread, a jar of mayonnaise, and a packet of Oscar Meyer cold cuts from the fridge. She scooped some mayonnaise and lathered it on the bread in two quick swaths.

Cammy resumed the conversation in a tone of studied self-control. "Tell me something. Why are you getting so defensive about FGM?"

"I'm not defensive. What's it to you anyway? You just said you didn't need to know anything about the culture or the people who practiced it."

"That's because FGM is not about culture. It's about medicine—about whether the mutilation is necessary. You forget what I do for a living? FGM can cause serious medical problems."

"Yeah, but I don't hear you getting indignant at those who practice male circumcision. What's the difference? Why don't you try to stop that?" Fina returned to making her sandwich. From the packet of cold cuts, she pulled out slices of ham and laid them on the cutting board. Cammy observed her preparations from the sofa.

"Come on now, you're not seriously comparing male circumcision to FGM?"

"Yes, I am. And why do you keep calling it FGM? It's circumcision."

"Circumcision, mutilation. It's all the same to me, Fina."

"No, it's not! How you label something affects how you think about it. 'Mutilate' makes you think violence, suggests something negative. It forces you to see the practice only one way." Fina laid some ham, lettuce, American cheese, and tomatoes on the bottom slice of the bread, sprinkled some salt and pepper on it, and capped the sandwich with the second slice. Fina did not know why, but she had a visceral dislike of sandwiches with ingredients protruding from the edges of the bread, so she picked up the knife and trimmed off the protrusions. Bits of meat, lettuce, cheese, and tomatoes lay discarded on the cutting board and the big ugly sandwich was transformed into a small, contoured piece of art, beautiful to behold, layered like a sectional drawing. Cammy watched as she cut the sandwich into two and laid the halves on a side plate. For a brief moment he considered making a grab for them, but a glance at Fina and the knife in her hand dissuaded him.

"You have it backward," he said. "It's the forcing and the cutting that lead to the word mutilation."

"But that's not the word the people use to describe what they do. So that means they don't see the act the way you do."

"Well, they must be blind. Mutilate works fine for me, 'cos they're disfiguring."

"So do you and your patients call what you do at the hospital male genital mutilation—MGM, like the movie studio?"

"Don't make light of something serious. Like I said, it doesn't matter what I call it. The practice is wrong and should be banned."

Fina opened the fridge and pulled out a carton of orange juice. She poured herself a glass, returned the cartoon to the fridge, and set the glass next to the sandwich. She picked up the side plate in one hand and the glass in the other and stood directly in front of him.

"All right," she began, "so why don't you object to MGM?"

"You're not serious. It's not the same. The medical complications—"

"Do you want to ban circumcision because it violates children's rights or because it causes medical complications?"

"Both."

"Ok, then start right here in America! Fight for the rights of innocent Jewish and American boys who are forced into circumcision because their parents and grandparents believe it's required by their religion or tradition."

Fina paused, as if waiting for Cammy to make a decision. He was not sure how to respond, and he sensed that answering the question or speaking at that particular moment would weaken his argument. He also realized that he had not thought as deeply about the topic as Fina obviously had, and he glimpsed a steely, battle-hardened persona underneath her pliant exterior. Surprised and suddenly aroused, he wanted to make love to her right there and then. That would surely stop the argument!

Indeed, the argument did stop that night, but only because Cammy was called to the hospital. The misunderstanding, however, did not. In fact, it mushroomed. The subject had exposed a troubling side of the other person. It was in this more chastened emotional state of mind that the topic next came up. Fina had suggested they discuss it over brunch. "At least in public it won't become a shouting match," she reasoned.

****

They were seated in a corner table in the cafeteria of Memorial Hospital where Cammy had just finished surgery. Fina poked at the gigantic salad in front of her and occasionally took a bite from it. Cammy gobbled his chicken fried rice.

"Cammy," Fina took a deep breath after they had gone back and forth several times. "Instead of being up in arms about female circumcision in far-away Africa, why don't you do something about male circumcision here?"

Cammy felt his heart racing. With his knife, he swiped the last bits of his food onto his fork and shoved it into his mouth. He swirled the crushed ice in his drink, poked at it with a straw, and sucked. He was rewarded with air and a few fragments of ice. He frowned, determined he would speak to the manager of the cafeteria about soft drinks that were eighty percent ice.

"Well, the reality is," Cammy began, determined to put up a more vigorous defense of his views, "the risks and consequences of FG... uh... er... circumcision, as you want to call it, are far less for males than females."

"You know, it's the double standards and hypocrisy that make me mad. You respect the rights of adults in America and Europe to practice circumcision in the name of religion and personal freedom, but it doesn't cross your mind that Africans are entitled to the same respect."

101

Fina poked at the bits and pieces of her salad, put a forkful in her mouth, and immediately spat everything back onto the plate. She pushed her plate to the side, leaned back on her chair, and took two deep breaths. She wanted to tell Cammy that ever since their first conversation on the subject, she hadn't been able to ride the high tide of pleasure in their lovemaking; that now her pleasure trickled along and ebbed but never rose and crashed like when they first met; that now it fluttered like a moth around a light bulb, unable to settle; that now it was weak, tinsel-like, and no longer the massive explosions that thrilled and reduced her to pulp.

For his part, Cammy was irritated that Fina seemed to have an answer for everything and was forcing him to retreat. Although he sensed there was more at stake for her, he felt he had to hold his own. Early quarrels are defining moments in any relationship, he reasoned. If he backed down now, he could set their relationship on a course he might not be able to reverse. He did not want to be either the real or the perceived loser in this their first real disagreement, so he felt he had to respond—not to say anything mean-spirited that would escalate the quarrel, but something that would let Fina know that he, too, was firm in his convictions.

"FGM kills a woman's sexuality," he began. "You don't care about that? How can a man enjoy himself if his woman does not?"

"That's what it boils down to for you men, isn't it?" Fina chuckled. "The ones who support circumcision do so to control women's sexuality. The ones who oppose it do so because they want the woman to be able to give them pleasure."

Cammy became immediately angry. "Ah doh'n mean it like that, but ah doh'n see much wrong with it either."

"Understand this, Cammy. Most circumcised women do not end up psychological basket cases unable to enjoy sex, okay!"

"That's not my understanding. How would they know what they're missing, anyway?"

"Oho. Did you know research now shows that circumcised males lose about fifty percent of their sensitivity with the removal of their foreskin? You know what that means don't you?"

102

Cammy looked puzzled but Fina continued. "It means you're no different from a circumcised woman. "You're the doctor. Do you accept the medical evidence?"

"Yuh being silly. Ah talking medical facts and yuh talkin' 'bout sensitivity. Yuh jus' a blind lover of tradition. Ah tell you this. Holding onto the past is like walking on a treadmill. You may be in motion but yuh going nowhere fast. Ah shut my mouth now."

Cammy slid to the edge of his seat and picked up his tray, as if physically to enforce his decision to end the conversation. Fina remained seated, watching him.

"Cammy, I want to make a difference," she said with quiet insistence. "Instead of arguing, you should be doing something about circumcision here and I should be *doing* something about it back home."

"What yuh saying, Fina?"

"I want to go back home and open up a center for girls and women who have suffered because of this operation."

Cammy pushed the tray to the side, turned so he was looking straight at Fina, and grabbed her hands.

"What about us, Fina? We've got something here. You know it." Cammy looked at his watch and then back at Fina. "Ah got to go. Let's talk some more tonight and figure out something, awright?" He planted a kiss on her forehead.

****

Fina liked both his idea and his tone. For the rest of the day, she rehearsed what she would say. She would begin by explaining a village girl's longing to know about the secrets of womanhood, to become a woman, and to walk in rhythm with other women. Then, she would share the description her cousin, an initiate, entrusted to her about some of the wonders of womanhood. After that, she would tell him about Dimusu and explain the paradox of loving a grandmother who put her through the pain and loving the pain that made her a woman, of accepting the loss that sometimes comes with

103

the cutting. Next she would justify her respect for the rights of those who would put their daughters through the cutting. After that, she would share her desire to return home, to talk to Baramusu about the rope, the path, and the night of her initiation. But most of all, she would explain how much it would mean to her to have him by her side as they set up a center dedicated to preventing others from meeting Dimusu's fate. Finally, she would tell him, if he had not already guessed it, that she, too had been through initiation, of sorts.

When they entered her townhouse after a quiet dinner, Fina went to her bedroom, supposedly to change but in reality to rehearse one more time the order and points she wanted to make. However, when she returned to the living room, Cammy was slouched on the sofa, beer in hand, and already engrossed in a basketball game. She strode over to the TV, turned it off, put her hands on her hips and announced, "I went through circumcision you know."

Cammy stood up, like a soldier at attention when a superior officer walks into a room. His instincts had been right all along. Fina's defense of FGM had too much passion for it to have been just a matter of principle. His pride in his perspicacity was tempered only by a burgeoning recognition that his other senses had let him down. He hadn't noticed anything. He had assumed…thought… believed she was all there, yet she had just said she was circumcised. Had she been faking? She couldn't have been! He'd heard her and seen her many times. But *that's* the goal of faking, to make the other person think the fake is real. His heart pounded. He stared at Fina's dress to see if he could see through it. He wanted to lay her down on the coffee table and to examine her. His lips parted, but the words stuck in his throat.

"Well," Fina broke into his thoughts, "aren't you going to ask me if I really have orgasms?" Cammy opened his mouth, but Fina cut him off. "Don't bother and don't you dare feel sorry for me. I've heard the 'you-don't-know-what-you're-missing' argument. The circumcised, the blind, the deaf, the dumb, and the gay? Yeah, we all know our lives are not as meaningful, satisfying, or as pleasurable as you normals."

And with that she strode back into her bedroom. A few minutes later Cammy climbed into the bed and cradled her from behind. "Ah jus' want you to know ah love you, Fina. Let's not allow anything, anyone, to come between us." The last thing Fina remembered before she fell asleep was Cammy's light snoring and her realization that he was a tender man she wanted to love forever. So, the next evening when he proposed marriage, she agreed.

Later that same night, his chest heaving, his hands roaming, his mast bobbing, Cammy edged his tongue to her ear and whispered, "Ah wan' see the front. Lemme turn on the light."

"No!" Fina arrested his arm as it reached toward the lamp by the bed. "No, Cammy," she said more gently but maintained her vice-like grip on his arm, "I like it when it's dark."

He had backed off then, confident that in time he would see her, like his patients on the operating table, exposed, inert, fully at his mercy. But as a doctor who daily saw the naked body, he was surprised at the strength of her aversion to his desire. During weekend days, she studiously limited contacts with him to places where they would have no opportunity to make love, so the battle of the lights became part of their lovemaking ritual.

Sometimes he cajoled. At other times he sneered. He even secretly installed a clap-activated lamp in his bedroom and once, as Fina relaxed expectantly, he pulled back and clapped. Light engulfed the room, but Fina's reaction would have been the envy of any U.S. Navy Top Gun. Before he could see the object of his subterfuge, she had ejected herself from between his legs and from the bed.

"You bastard!" she shouted.

"Come on Fina, ah fed up with all this foolishness! A man can't see his wife?"

"I'm not your wife. And *your* need to see gives you the right to play games when I say I don't want to do something? What do you want to see so?"

"You! Ah want to see de front!"

"No, you want to examine me, like I was one of your patients."

"Maybe ah do. Wha' wrong with that?"

105

"Look, I'm just not ready for that yet. I don't want to become an object for you to study. This is our bedroom, not your operating table. I just can't do it, Cammy. Maybe it's cultural, but I just can't."

"Don' come with this culture business again. You think your shit don't stink?"

"Ooookay, let's stop right now. What you don't understand, you mock and insult. I just don't like the idea of you examining me."

"We're getting married! What more do you want?"

"Oh so marriage means I turned over myself to you? Let's just say I don't feel comfortable with you."

"What happen to you? First, everythin' awright. Now everythin' not!"

"Hey, sex should come naturally. You shouldn't sneak around installing clappers, and we shouldn't be debating. Let it come to you. Maybe on our wedding night."

And so with the prospect of an end date, Cammy was forced to let the issue go.

****

But leaving things unresolved was not Cammy's style. The next day at work, Fina received a call from a coordinator from Wedplan, a company that specialized in upscale weddings. "Dr. Priddy asked me to call you," the voice on the other end of the phone explained. "Have you decided on a date?"

"Er...I'm busy right now. Let me call you back in two or three days?"

"Well... er...okay, but if you want a summer wedding, we have to start planning right now."

That night at Fina's townhouse, the evening started with some tension. Fina claimed that he was moving too fast and that they should figure things out together. Cammy argued that the plans would move more smoothly if one person made the decisions and consulted the other as need be. But they navigated their irritations and settled on a July wedding. Cammy ordered some food, and it was

106

in the midst of their meal that he proposed Fina move in at once. He was lonely in his newly completed, seven bedroom home with the Olympic-size swimming pool.

"No, Cammy, let's wait till we get married before I move into your palace."

"It's not a palace. It's *our* home."

"Let me at least pay for some of the furnishings. I won't be a complete charity case."

"Oh, don't feel that way," he sidled up and hugged her. "It's done then. You take care of the furnishings and anything else you want. We won't sleep there together until we marry. How about that?"

"Well, now that you mention waiting until we get married, maybe we ought to suspend activities altogether till our wedding night." She got up, twirled her skirt, raised it just enough to expose her underwear. Then she ran into her bedroom.

Cammy sprang from the sofa and gave chase but lost his footing on the area rug and slammed his shin into the edge of the coffee table. He limped into the bedroom, cursing.

Chapter 10

Ever since she received her very first pay check in America, Fina had sent money to help her mother and sister—$100 one month, $200 the next, and sometimes $50 if money was tight. Every three months, she had shipped to them a container full of canned goods, household products, and assorted clothing (new, used, and donated). This state of affairs pleased everyone. The shipments assuaged her conscience. Along with the remittances, they had enabled her mother, when she was alive, to buy a few creature comforts—a new mattress, a larger fridge, and a radio-fan-light combination that stored power for when the electricity was turned off, which was almost every day. Isa got ten percent of whatever money Fina sent and used it to live a comparatively comfortable life. After their mother died, Fina was on the verge of scaling back the size and frequency of her support when two things happened in quick succession. The civil war in the country worsened, causing the mining company at which Isa worked to shut down its operations. This left Isa without a job. She was also a new mother. Far from scaling back, Fina's level of support increased, for she had, in fact, inherited another family: newborn Sarata, her niece and godchild, and Hassan, Isa's live-in boyfriend. Fina accepted her extended responsibilities in part because she felt the situation would be temporary. The war would soon end and Hassan, just graduated from Crowther College, would soon find a job.

Neither happened. In fact, nine months after Sarata was born, Isa revealed that she had given birth to a second child. Fina was incensed.

"Do you know about condoms?" she demanded.

"The ones they sell here are not good, Ms. Fina. They break easily and Hassan is really b… b…"

"I don't care if he is as big as an elephant's, Isa. Buy big and strong condoms with the money I send or let him wear a dozen of the useless ones, gad dammit! I don't want to hear about another child. Do you hear me?"

"Yes, Ms. Fina. We will do it less."

"*O bo*," Fina slammed the phone down.

Then the civil war that had engulfed Sierra Leone reached Fina in America. The beachhead arrived one morning with another frantic phone call from Isa. Marauding rebels had invaded Freetown. She, Hassan, and their kids either had to escape or be killed. They needed money, fast! Fina spent the next two days glued to the telephone, making calls to friends across America and Europe. Eventually, she learned that a New York–based, Senegalese businessman had an informal, money-transfer system that could get dollars to her sister. Fina swallowed her indignation at the exorbitant $30 per $100 transfer fee and took a leap of faith.

Many phone calls and five days later, Isa and her family set sail on a barge bound for Conakry, the capital of neighboring Guinea, two days north by sea from Freetown. Fina was elated and relieved, but these feelings soon changed to fear and guilt when BBC World News reported that an overloaded, barely seaworthy barge loaded with starving and dehydrated refugees was drifting helplessly off the West African coast. The reports feared for the lives of the thousands believed to be on board because none of the countries on the coast had the resources to mount a rescue. A British naval task force with such capabilities was three sailing days away. Guilt consumed Fina. "No, I won't let you fly in those Russian-made propeller planes whose engines stall and whose air conditioning spray hot water!" she had curtly dismissed Isa's stated preference to travel by air. Now her desire to save money had sent them to a watery death. Fina's sense that in their Atlantic grave they would be among kin was her only consolation.

Early one morning, almost two weeks after reports of the hapless barge first surfaced, Isa called. They were alive, barely, and refugees in Guinea. Fina was relieved beyond measure. But they were penniless and needed money for everything—housing, food, clothing, entertainment, and applications fees to be processed as immigrants and then refugees. And that was how Isa, Hassan, and their children came to occupy the same level of obligation as Fina's mortgage, car note, and wedding expenses.

At first, she accepted the increased financial obligation with zeal, buoyed by the twin mantras that she should not cut the rope and that life is about working together with other people. She ate out less, hardly bought new clothes, got rid of her cable television, and stopped protesting when Cammy offered to pay for dinner or for a trip. She made a conspicuous attempt to save money, and thus was able to accommodate her increased financial obligations without having to ask Cammy for help.

But time and circumstances soon turned the obligation she had taken up with such alacrity into a penance. The deteriorating situation in the capital Freetown foreclosed the chances that Isa and her family would soon return home and relieve her of their expenses. Finding work to support themselves in Guinea seemed about as likely for Isa and Hassan as the Sahara returning to its once green state. Meanwhile, the costs associated with buying the furnishings for their house loomed large, real and daunting like a freshly washed baby to a first-time mother.

Cammy argued that he should absorb all the expenses but Fina would not hear of it. She insisted on honoring her commitment— foolish pride. Her insistence blocked the sunlight and sucked the oxygen out of the world. A three-course dinner became guilt-ridden overeating. Friends expressing concerns about their pets amounted to depraved indifference for the plight of displaced persons and refugees. Invitations from Cammy to attend this or that function revealed his unbridled self-indulgence. Her conversations gravitated toward and settled irretrievably on the war and its consequences: drugged-up child soldiers who, on a dare, hacked off the limbs of innocent civilians; rebel leaders who killed for pleasure; the endless red tape involved in bringing a refugee to America; the frustrations of trying to convince barely competent speakers of English at her local Catholic Charities office that Sierra Leone was, indeed, a country and that *her* citizens also wanted, nay deserved, to come to America like the Cubans and Haitians.

"You're allowing your sister and this war to dominate your life, our life," Cammy interjected when she paused from one of her rants. "You're not much fun to be around anymore," he whined as he nibbled at her ear and reached under her blouse.

"Isa is my sister, my only family, Cammy," Fina retorted, extracting herself from his probing hands and staring at him in disbelief. "What I own is hers. What she owns is mine. That's our tradition."

"Don't want to sound harsh, but you're getting the short end of that tradition. Besides, you're encouraging her to be lazy. She and her boyfriend are young and able. They need to find work, Fina. Let them start the tradition of self-support."

"Good gad, Cammy. They are refugees. Do you have any idea what that means? You think they're happy to sit at home and wait for me to send them money? And let's not talk of the plentiful jobs in Conakry. Sometimes, I can't believe what comes out of your mouth."

"I'm okay with you helping your sister, but all I see is them taking advantage of you."

Fina folded her arms across her chest. Cammy walked over to the fridge and pulled out a beer.

"I'm willing to give them a loan, but they will have to pay me back."

"No thank you," Fina responded coolly.

"Look, it would be like unemployment insurance kicking in until they start working again."

"Don't worry about it. Isa is my problem, and I'll handle it."

Fina decided that she would never again ask Cammy for help or money, especially for her sister. She redoubled her efforts at finding part time work, any work. A few days later, she applied for a home equity loan.

****

Cammy was not happy when, several days later, she told him what she had done.

"How would you feel if I had done something like that without telling you? I can just hear you now: 'You did it because you want to show me you're the man.'"

"But I—"

"No buts, Fina. You should have told me. Ah goin' home."

"Please don't be mad at me."

"I'm not mad. Just disappointed. Ah see you tomorrow."

The next evening, Fina arrived home to a sumptuous dinner of shrimp served in a fragrant coconut stew that Cammy had prepared. Not only was she hungry after a stressful day at work and at the Catholic Charities office trying to understand the steps involved in sponsoring a refugee, she had also been worrying all day about how to make up to Cammy for her impulsive behavior. Certain she did not have the words to explain how badly she felt at that moment, she snuggled close to him and laid her head on his shoulder.

I wish there was something I could do to make you happy. When Cammy pulled away from her and sat up as if he was thinking of a request, Fina realized she must have uttered what she had been thinking.

"Well, actually, I... but...er... never mind," he sighed and fell back by her side.

"Go ahead, ask. At this point, there's literally nothing I won't do for you."

Cammy declined to make his request, but Fina urged him to. He hesitated and made so many false starts that Fina became anxious that he wanted to back out of the wedding.

"Have you ever considered braces?"

Fina adjusted her position on the sofa as if it might lead to an adjustment of her hearing and subsequently the question. The first dentist she visited in the States had recommended braces and a tooth-whitening regime, but Fina had simply not returned and never again stepped foot into another dentist's office.

"What's wrong with my teeth?"

113

"Nothing...well...um... you do have a slight overbite that could easily—"

"I was born with it. I don't have a problem with it, or the discoloration. They are part of who I am. If you don't like them, well tough! If you're going to be embarrassed by them, then let's call off the wedding."

"See, ah take up yuh offer, and yuh blow your top. Forget ah ever mention it."

Fina felt foolish for having made an offer she could not fulfill. She also felt disappointed that Cammy felt strongly enough about her overbite to voice it as a request. They did not argue that night, but each was sufficiently irritated by the other to welcome Fina's announcement that she was tired and wanted to go to bed. They never again discussed her teeth, but Fina became self-conscious about them, circumscribing her smile and brushing them with greater diligence, though she would most certainly have rejected both observations if someone had made them to her.

But as the wedding day approached, a cloud descended on her happiness. Aside from the not-so-pleasant side of Cammy that she was seeing and disliking, his thriving practice, her dwindling resources, and the intractable refugee situation of her sister's family had all relegated her aspirations to return home and open a center for abused and runaway girls into a footnote in this new life she was composing with Cammy.

Six weeks before the wedding, the cloud partially lifted when Fina found out she was pregnant. She was apprehensive about how Cammy would react, so she had prepared and fed him his favorite *Jollof* rice and stew before telling him the news.

Cammy jumped up, pulled her up from the sofa, scooped her into his arms, and plastered adoring kisses all over her face and head. When he set her back down, laughingly claiming she was already too heavy, they immediately fell into planning.

"If he's a boy, we'll call him Donovan after my brother."

"Oh no, he's definitely going to be called Amadu after my father."

114

"What 'bout if it's a girl?"

"Then she'll be called Dimusu. It means first-born daughter."

"And Celeste, after my mom."

"Okay then, she'll be Dimusu-Celeste. I like that. It speaks to her dual heritage."

"Don' you want to know its sex?" Cammy became excited.

"Nooooo! Let's wait till it's born."

"Why?"

"I like the suspense."

Chapter 11

*F*irelight darkness. *Sorrowful chanting. Violent thrashing. Palm branches, strands of beads, earrings, anklets, headbands on the ground. Ghostly white bodies. A python devours the pale, writhing white bodies. Destruction! Girls descend into the cold, stinging water—DEATH OF AN AGE! Women rise into the warm air—BIRTH OF A NEW AGE. Weighted chest. Weighted thighs. Trembling, writhing thighs. Deafening, bitter, blue-red, all-consuming pain expressed into a spit-smeared cloth. Noises…shouts…screams…scrambling feet…toppling bodies. A voice… a man's voice. A smell…a father's smell. Wails throttle the night air.*

Fina heard them and woke up, twenty plus years removed from the scene of her aborted initiation deep in the forest. She sat upright and breathed a sigh of relief as she recognized the lavender-themed master bedroom of her townhouse in a quiet suburb of Gaithersburg, Maryland. It was a warm July Saturday morning—her wedding day.

The dream left Fina feeling so jaded that when the phone rang, she ignored it. Here she was, just a few hours away from beginning a new life, taking a path that would bring her the happiness that had eluded her for so many years, and her past had chosen this particular morning to reassert itself. Fina leaned back against the headboard, her elbows tucked between her upper body and thighs, her fingers interlocked, and her thumbs pressed against her puckered lips. She was determined that before she got out of bed, she would put the circumstances of her initiation and youth into perspective, mold and revise them if necessary, so she could leave the past in the past and concentrate on the future, the promising new frontier that life with her soon-to-be-husband represented.

She pulled open the blinds, and the July morning sauntered through the window with the gaiety of a girl in a bright summer dress, but her grandmother's words and the initiation night hung in the background like dark ominous clouds. Fina reminded herself that she was not alone. Edna and her children were in the adjacent bedroom, and several of her friends would soon be arriving to prepare some bean cake *akara* and other West African finger foods for the reception. Yet, the dream of the initiation night had revived the sense of incompleteness she had felt most of her life. Its timing left her apprehensive about the future.

"Ding-dong, ding-dong," the doorbell chimed to break into her thoughts. Fina was glad her friends were arriving earlier than she expected. As she walked to the door, she decided she would set aside the past, particularly Baramusu's injunctions, and focus on the present. She unlocked the door and peeped around it. Cammy beamed at her.

"Fulani princess, you awright?" he asked, noticing the frown on Fina's face. He planted a kiss on her forehead and tried to edge through the narrow opening. Fina barred his way.

"I'm fine, Cammy," she replied. "We're not supposed to see each other until we get to church. It can bring bad luck, you know," she joked.

"Please stop your superstitious talk."

"Excuuusse me. I forgot you Trinis are all scientists. Don't get me started."

"Awright, awright, but can't I come in? Little Cammy wants to play. The Wedplan people won't be here till ten."

"Stop it, Cammy," Fina smiled. "Little Cammy will have to wait."

"Damn!" Cammy hissed. "Okay. Ah gonna be able to see you, right?" Cammy winked.

"Who?"

"You know… little Fina!"

"That's why you came here?" Fina asked in half-hearted indignation when she caught his meaning. "Go away!"

"Oh, you promised nuh!"

"Well, I always keep my promises. Now shoo!"

"Okay, ah goin', but you neva pick up the phone when ah call. Everything all right?"

"Okay, I guess. I had this dream about my initiation, and I've had this weird feeling since I woke up."

"You're just anxious, that's all," Cammy threaded his fingers through the crack in the door and ran them down Fina's face to her lips. She nibbled at his fingers and rubbed the side of her face on the palm of his hand.

"Forget the past," Cammy gently pinched her cheek with his fingers. "Look to the future, to *tonight*." He thrust his pelvis twice at the door behind which Fina stood.

"You're right," she said, yet she could not shake off the melancholy brought on by her dream and early morning ruminations. "Cammy, don't get mad, okay. I'm happy we're getting married, but a part of me feels sad, like I'm abandoning my home."

"Why?"

"Because the marriage and the baby make going back home very difficult if not impossible."

"Fina, let's not do this, not today. You have to live your life, and you have to move forward. Don't they say life is a series of beginnings and endings? You have to leave some things behind because there's something new and better ahead—me! I've got to let go of some things because I've got something better too—*you!*" He smiled.

"I understand that, Cammy. It's just that…"

Cammy's brooding countenance made Fina stop herself. She recalled her earlier resolve to leave the past in the past and that their previous attempts to discuss these subjects always ended in disagreement. The sound of a television set coming on and the flushing of a toilet reminded Fina that Edna and her kids were in the townhouse, that she belonged to them and Cammy here and now, that she was *not* alone, and that a dream, however much it reflected her fears, was not reality.

"Even if I wanted to let little Cammy in to play," Fina changed the subject, "Edna and her kids are up now. But he'd better be ready to play all night," she winked.

"He ready right now. Will little Fina show up?"

"Be careful what you wish for. But you've got to go, Cammy. We shouldn't be together like this."

"Okay, okay, but I've some not-so-good news."

"Cammy, please don't start. I thought you were okay with the pregnancy."

"I'm fine with that, Princess. It's the hospital board. It wants to hear a full cost-benefit analysis about the robot this Wednesday."

"So?" Fina raised her eyebrows, puzzled.

"They say it will cost too much, it's not been tested enough, and will lead to lawsuits—you know the same ol' administrative talk."

"Aren't these things true?"

"This thing is a no-brainer! The robot can perform microscopic surgery. It will remove all cancerous tissue and leave nothing behind. Humans can't do that, yet these stupid people don't want to buy one. A robot will never call in sick or take days off. Jus' plug it in, turn it on, give it the information it needs, and, boom! It will do the job, every single day, without so much as a beep. Get it?"

"Yes, Mr. Funny man, but it also sounds like you're saying doctors aren't necessary."

"Not atall, not atall. Robots will help us conquer diseases. Who benefits? Patients. They get the best care possible and at lower prices."

"But what has all this got to do with me?"

"Oh yes, the board wants to hear the presentation the Wednesday after our wedding. We can fly back in the morning. I do my thing, and we continue our honeymoon as soon as I finish."

"Okay, but I think I'll just wait for you at the hotel."

"You mean it? Oh, thank you, thank you," Cammy feigned gratitude. "Yuh my Cleopatra! I could swim the Nile, climb Kilimanjaro, and cross the Namib Desert just to be wit' you, Princess."

"You'd better take a compass, 'cos if you ever make it out of the Namib Desert, you'll find yourself in the Atlantic, a long way from me. Now go away. We'll sort out the honeymoon and your meeting later tonight," she said, winking at him again and closing the door.

Considerably more relaxed than earlier in the morning and beginning to feel the jitters of a bride just hours away from her wedding, Fina was in the kitchen amid a throng of boisterous women when the phone rang. She plucked it from the set hanging on the wall behind her. The maneuver was awkward, and she felt a pain that began in her stomach and radiated to her neck .

"You have an international collect call," said the computerized female voice. The pain mad Fina grimace, but she was pleased to find out the caller was her sister, Isa.

"It's me, Miss Fina," she announced. "How are you? I called to wish you all the best for your wedding."

Fina stood up from the table and felt another sharp sting in her stomach. She took a couple of deep breaths to recover from the pain that now coursed through her body. She excused herself from the kitchen, walked into her sitting room, and sat on the sofa.

"Miss Fina, Miss Fina…," Isa sounded panicky.

"I'm here. How are you? Are the kids well? How about Hassan?"

"They are well. *I* am the one feeling tired, and my mouth tastes bitter."

"Sounds like malaria. Have you been taking your Daraprim?"

"Yes, but they don't work that well on Guinea mosquitoes. They are worse than the mosquitoes in Sierra Leone."

"Well, you should take Mefloquine. It's supposed to be the best."

"That medicine is not good. It makes people crazy, especially white people. You remember the American Peace Corps who promised to help me to get a visa? Well, last week, he took off all his clothes in the middle of the market and chased after the women. They say it was the Mefloquine."

Fina chuckled. "Isn't there some other medicine that works? What about the local roots?"

"I don't know where to get them, and I don't know what they call them in French."

"Then find somebody who will give you the French or local names? How difficult can that be in a French-speaking country? Don't mess around with malaria. It kills, Isa."

"Sometimes, I feel we should go back to Freetown. Life here is too hard."

"*Ibi-ibi. Marrade dey na ya? Yawo dey na ya?*" Several voices called out from outside the front door.

"*Marrade de, yawo de,*" other voices responded emphatically. Fina rose from the sofa and walked toward her bedroom. She signaled Edna to answer the door.

"*Ibi-ibi,*" the voices chanted again. Through the slightly open bedroom door, Fina could see a gaggle of high-spirited women enter the townhouse. Among them were a couple of faces she did not recognize, but they were leading the charge to make merry with the bride-to-be.

"Is there a bride in this house, where is she?" one of the women asked.

"Come on out," a second instructed.

"You'll have plenty of time for bedroom gymnastics tonight," a third quipped.

Fina poked her head out of the bedroom and covered the mouthpiece. "Talking to Isa. I'll be out soon."

"I hope that Trini fellow is not in there," one woman said.

The bedroom door closed, Fina resumed her conversation with Isa. "I don't want to hear talk of going back to Freetown. At least in Conakry, no one is trying to cut off your hand, rape or kill you. Let's talk about how you can get the medicine for malaria."

"Some of my friends say that Fansidar taken together with a Chinese medicine called Artesunate breaks the fever in two days. But the tablets are very expensive."

"How much?"

"I don't know."

"That's the kind of thing you should know, Isa. How can I help if I don't know how much money to send?"

"About two thousand francs."

"In dollars, Isa, dollars!"

"About ten dollars, Miss Fina."

"Oh, well, that's not too expensive. I'll add ten dollars to the money I usually send on the fifteenth. When you go to pick up the money from Western Union, be sure it's three hundred and ten dollars."

"Miss Fina, Conakry is just like Freetown. One day, the price for the medicine is two thousand francs. The next, the price goes up to five thousand."

"Okay, I'll send fifteen dollars just in case the price goes up. If the money is still not enough, then buy less medicine."

"Miss Fina, I...eh—"

"What is it? Talk fast. These calls are expensive."

"The landlord has raised the rent again. We must begin paying two hundred at the end of this month."

"What? He can't do that! Didn't he just raise the rent two months ago?"

"He says we can go and live elsewhere if we don't like it."

"He's taking advantage of you.So, this means an additional thirty dollars every month, right?"

"Yes, Miss Fina."

"Damn! Start looking around for a cheaper place. For now, you'll have to cut corners, okay? I can't afford to keep sending money like this. Is there anything else?

"Er... yes.... I want to learn..."

The loud music and singing from beyond the bedroom prevented Fina from hearing the rest of the sentence, so she walked to the window furthest from the door before asking Isa to repeat her request.

"Computers, Miss Fina."

"How much will that cost?"

"Twenty thousand francs."

"Dollars, Isa, dollars!"

"About one hundred."

"For the whole course?"

"No. For one month."

"And how long does the course last?"

"One year."

"What? Twelve hundred bucks!? Do they give you the computer after the course is over?"

Isa did not respond.

"I can't afford that, Isa. For now, I'll send an extra forty-five dollars for the malaria medicine and the rent."

"I understand, Miss Fina. I know things are hard in America. That is why I am trying to learn computers so I can get a job."

"Are you and the children eating and sleeping well?"

"Yes, we eat rice with palm oil and cayenne pepper. Sometimes we don't have money for meat or fish."

Fina sighed, unable to respond. Her legs wobbled. Here she was just hours away from a lavish wedding reception with a sumptuous meal costing thousands of dollars while her sister, the only blood relative she knew, ate rice and palm oil. She would simply have to find a way to pay for the course and give Isa something to feel good about.

"*Take courage, ya,*" she said. "God will help you. And get all the information about the computer course."

"Yes, Miss Fina."

"Okay, bye-bye."

Fina hung up and fell backwards onto her bed.

****

"Excuse me bride-to-be, can you please tell us what you're doing in there?" a voice queried from just outside the bedroom door.

"Fina, get off the phone!" another commanded.

"Tell Isa to call another day."

The bedroom door burst open. Loud music, the smell of hot cooking oil, and a throng of women spilled into the bedroom. They yanked Fina onto her feet and pushed her into the sitting room, dancing and singing:

"*Yawo mammy don ansa yehs-o, don ansa yehs-o, don ansa yehs-o.*"

"*Ibi-ibi, yawo de na ya?*"

"*Yawo de.*"

Amid all the merriment Fina noticed a white couple standing by the door, wearing sheepish grins. They were the people from Wedplan. They had come to help her get dressed.

Chapter 12

Fina and Cammy were well-known in the Caribbean and African communities in the Washington Metropolitan Area. They were an immigrant couple that had made it. Word of their impending wedding spread quickly. Many in both communities planned to attend, invited or not, related or not, far or near. Guests coming from outside the Washington area flew in and stayed three nights at a Sheraton or Hyatt—not at somebody's house, certainly not at somebody's apartment, and never in some dingy, Indian-owned motel. They rented luxury cars and expressed surprise if the couple had not registered at Williams-Sonoma or Neiman Marcus. Then they mentioned that despite this incomprehensible omission, they had, in fact, bought the fashionable Hermes Damier water goblet or the Kvandrant juice glasses.

Those guests who lived in the area and did not have the expense of airfares and hotel rooms wore new *agbadas* and designer label suits and dresses. If they could not afford them, they bought them anyway. A fashionable wedding in this hub of immigrants was like an open house, an occasion for all to construct a public image so others could see how America was treating them. Fina and Cammy's declaration of love was easily 400 guests and $40,000 loud.

The guests arrived in a procession of reds, yellows, and pinks; a march of bold patterns and refracted light from the precious and semi-precious jewelry and the glinting Lurex strands of African fabrics. Indigo kaftans with appliqué trim, grand flowing *bubas and iros* of silk, lace, and voile arrived early in voluminous swirls like the dry Harmattan breeze of the Sahara. Tie-dyed batiks of flowing silk over sheer black tights and Finai-beaded necklaces trotted in on stilettos. Accessories included bone jewelry beads, chokers, pendants, necklaces, amulets, and bracelets of various sizes and designs.

Dockets and *lappas*—blouses combined with a one-piece wraparound of knee, calf or ankle length skirt—were the dress of choice. A Ghanaian hand-woven silk *Kente* came first. Behind it strolled a Lagos print *docket* with ruffled taffeta sleeves; its *lappa* had a high, right-side pleat that exposed a smooth, bronze thigh. Woven *lappas* combined sometimes with embroidered blouses of lace or silk crepe; at other times, they combined with blouses of the same woven fabric or of indigo *Adire* cloth from Nigeria. More *dockets*—the halter-neck, the strapless, the sleeveless, the backless—and *lappas* arrived. The sleeves of some *dockets* were short, some long, some plain and others exaggerated. Some *lappas* hugged small and medium hips that frolicked slightly, provocatively; others restrained mountainous mounds of protoplasm that shifted in independent majesty behind their bearers.

The bold designs and ankle-length print *kabaslots* entered the church slowly, with matching shawls hung over a shoulder here, over an arm there, and matching head ties, some wrapped from back to front, some tilted slightly to one side and forward. Hand-woven wool slippers stepped gingerly. A cloth wrapped Sarong sauntered in, followed by a simple black dress, trimmed at the hem with rows of small colorful beads and accessorized with a Moroccan fez of *Aso Oke* fabric with a gold tassel. To its right strode the thick weave and rough texture of a brown, waist-length, hand-woven *ronko*. The parade was punctuated by black and blue two- and three-piece suits, often but not always accompanied by elegant designer dresses. It was an international cast of characters, a gathering of tribes, to rival any United Nations General Assembly.

Women and daughters walked into the church to secure "good" near-to-the-altar and by-the-aisle seats. Men stayed outside to talk to old friends they hadn't seen in years. Nearby, their sons ran around and tugged at each other's newly bought suits and *agbadas*. Occasionally, their rough play provoked a "Tunde, stop it" or "Denzel, be careful" from concerned fathers.

Most of the men gathered in front of the church knew each other well. But among them were guests from Florida, Texas, and California. As the crowd of men grew and the conversation became animated, newcomers did not bother to greet each person individually. Instead, they simply said *"Man dem,"* the shorthand salutation of endearment signifying brotherhood and respect. It tacitly recognized those addressed as belonging to a community of men who, by their very presence in America, had succeeded in making something of their lives.

"Man dem," the crowd responded, after which followed more personal exchanges if the newcomer recognized or was recognized by someone. If not, he would simply join the periphery of the group. This Saturday, these were the *man dem* who had come to support their sister marrying this man from the Caribbean. *Man dem* believed Caribbean men were high- handed, so they had come to let this man know that if he mistreated their sister, she had people who would take matters into their own hands. So *man dem* walked with a certain edge. Their voices reflected a boldness fortified by their numbers and a visceral understanding of their right to assemble peacefully in America.

Their numbers grew. Their talk became louder, and soon, enough of them had assembled to block the entrance to the church, a kind of nuptial defensive line. This was *their* wedding. Anybody who wanted to get into the church would just have to walk around them.

Man dem talked about many things: their jobs, families, neighborhoods and cities. They argued about basketball, the statistical world of American sports, the hooliganish world of British soccer, the racism of American domestic life, and the double standards of American foreign policy. However, they became most animated when they discussed the number one topic of immigrant conversation: back home.

"All I know is, man, the gov'ment will have a real tough time rebuilding that country," Kizzy pronounced. He was one of those immigrants who found himself, came to value his individuality, potential and freedom, in America. He loved, adored, and was awed by his adopted country. His was not a half-hearted love or a love of the convenience, coziness, and economic opportunities America provided. It was an utter love, the grateful Cuban-exile kind that puzzled and sometimes even frightened the natives.

129

Brought up in meager circumstances and having lived most of his life cutting corners, Kizzy was overwhelmed by America's bounty, the sheer breadth and scale of American life. But it was American ingenuity that Kizzy admired the most, an indelible sense of which had been scorched into his mind the very first night he arrived in America. He learned from a TV newscast that Tampa was the lightning capital of the world. The newcomer had visions of a Tampa city skyline draped by jagged bolts of lightning. Although he could never quite fathom the value of the designation, the assertion had quite literally bolted him into a superlative mode of discourse. So even though many others in the crowd were better qualified to talk about Sierra Leonean issues, he was the central focus among the *man dem* gathered in front of the church. The combination of his deep-blue blackness and the extravagance of his claims transfixing some in admiring belief, others in amused disbelief.

"Hey man, right now, t'ings are real bad back 'ome. Nothing works. The gov'ment don't have no army and no money. The country is fucked up, man!"

Some in the audience nodded in agreement. Feeding on their endorsement, Kizzy continued. "I didn't see one good road in the 'hole gad dam country, man. Let's not talk 'bout education. The schools and university don't have no teachers, no books, no equipment. What kinda university is that, man?"

It was a rhetorical question, and Kizzy neither expected nor wanted anyone to answer, so when he saw the young man who had identified himself as a graduate student straighten up and inhale as if he was about to respond, Kizzy plunged right back into his exposition.

"Look 'ere, the war has made t'ings worse. There ain't never gonna be jobs if y'all go back 'ome. And even if y'all get work and get paid reg'lar, y'all never gonna be able to clothe and feed y'all's family. Not even to buy a freakin' hamburger for y' all's kids. What kinda life is that? Am gonna stay right here in good ol' US of A. Ain't never goin' back."

Kizzy paused, but this time the taller, graduate student pounced into the pause.

"I got a damn good education at CC. Even with all the things you say it doesn't have, I am holding my own in the US classes I sit in right now."

Nods and grunts of agreement rose from the group.

"So instead of going back to help your country," the graduate student continued, "you're going to stay here and gladly, put up with insults, racism and ignorant Americans, right? And if we all did that, who is going to build the roads so that you and your family can drive in comfort and stuff your faces with hamburgers, man? That's trading dignity for comfort!"

"Don't go there, bro," Kizzy warned. "I was talking general. You wanna make this personal?"

Man dem felt their collars tighten like a one-size-too-small shirt on a hot Saturday afternoon.

"Wha' 'appen?" boomed a voice. "Leh we pass," the voice continued. "We is the boys-from-back-home. Our boy getting married to de African gyal. Leh wi pass, nuh!"

The owner of the voice was Lincoln "Scraps" Ramjohn—all-purpose Trinidadian businessman, able to get you whatever you want, for a price. Scraps, as everyone called him, was a tall, broad-chested man. The scar that ran from the corner of his left eye all the way to the front cartilage of his nostril made him a fearsome figure. His reputation was founded on the story of how he got that scar.

The leader of a rival gang had challenged Scraps to a fight over territory. Both youths crouched and stalked each other like antelopes about to lock horns. Without warning, Scraps stood erect like quarried marble, screamed, and, with the jagged edge of a broken bottle he held in his hand, sliced his own face from just below his left eye to the middle of his left cheek. The act shocked everyone, particularly the rival gang leader, who looked first to his crew and then to Scraps' pack for guidance. But nobody knew what to do, for even among these impulsive youths who made the rules as they went along, Scraps' self-mutilation was madness they had never seen before. The thought that he might be moments away from fighting a complete lunatic had just begun to form in the challenger's mind when Scraps stepped forward, screamed again, and, this time, continued the mutilation from his left cheek all the way to his left nostril. Blood streamed down his face, but Scraps didn't groan or flinch. Instead, he laughed and edged forward. The rival leader had seen enough. He scampered, his crew following in his wake. From that day, Scraps became the undisputed leader of the neighborhood. By the time Scraps' street gang had graduated into its current all-purpose business, people generally understood that you messed with Lincoln Scraps Ramjohn only if you had the courage to mutilate yourself like he had.

But being a tough guy is a local phenomenon. The group of Africans blocking Scraps' way did not know the story of his scar and were not particularly intimidated by it. Scraps stared at the assembled Africans and, as he had done many times before, puffed his cheek to expand the scar, adjusted his tie, straightened out his hands, and shook them, twice, sharply, as if trying to shake the sleeves of his shirt past the cuff of his jacket. Then he waited. One step back, to his right and his left, were members of his crew—Insect, Meow, Foxy, Froggy, Mad-Dog, and Mumbly—dressed in various shades of blue and black double-breasted suits with gaudy colored shirts and ties. Like Moses and the Israelites at the Red Sea, Scraps and his men waited for *man dem* to part.

But this sea of *man dem* was simply not about to, especially not to someone calling their Fina "African gyal." This was *their* wedding. Nobody answered or blinked. Instead, *man dem* took their hands out of their pockets and made subtle adjustments to their stance. Scraps and the-boys-from-back-home noticed the adjustments spelling resistance and moved forward. The two groups of men eyed each other.

"Yuh neva hear me? Ah said leh we pass," Scraps repeated.

"Look 'ere, man," said Kizzy, his mind occupied by the image of his kids stuffing their mouths with bread and butter because they could not find hamburgers anywhere in Freetown. "Deere's a pass," he motioned a path that led around *man dem*. Kizzy's retort summoned a few chuckles from *man dem*, but the boys-from-back-home were not amused.

"Who you is?" Scraps peered at Kizzy.

"If is war y'all want, make we start it nuh!" The invitation came from Mad-Dog, stepping forward to support his boss. This was not a welcome development. Mad-Dog had not earned his nickname because he was soft and cuddly. Once he got into a fight, he was not the type even Scraps could order to stop. With Mad-Dog inserting himself into the situation, Scraps realized that events were about to take a turn for the worse. He did not wish for Cammy's wedding to be the setting of a fight, but then again, he had not earned his reputation because he was a pretty boy who shied away from one. And he certainly was not about to now, especially not from these Africans draped in curtains and bed sheets they called clothes.

"Dem Africans tink we stupid," Mumbly added.

"Pimp. Pimp. PIIIIMMMPPPP." The gaggle of men turned to see two stretch limousines stop beside the curb opposite them. The door of the leading limo opened, and Cammy and his best men stepped out. He was dressed in his tuxedo. Scraps recognized his boyhood friend and approached the car. The two men embraced warmly.

"Who they is?" Scraps began, spinning Cammy around so that both of them faced *man dem*. "Wha' happen to dem? We trying to geh ina di church an' dey getting on bad enough."

It was now the turn of the boys-from-back home to chuckle and give each other high fives. *Man dem* were not amused. A wisp of a smile crossed Cammy's face. He did not particularly care for Fina's people, and it was fun to have some of Scraps' irreverence around, but he did not want to openly offend his soon-to-be-wife's compatriots, so he dislodged himself from Scraps' embrace and approached *man dem*. The folds of *agbadas* parted for Cammy and his best men but closed again quickly to bar Scraps and the boys-from-back-home from passing. Mad-Dog, following close on the heels of his boss, threw an elbow into Kizzy's midriff. A scuffle broke out when Kizzy tried to retaliate.

"Wha' is this man?" It was Kizzy, his mind now consumed by an image of his children hobbling with distended bellies around Freetown, begging for hamburgers from a maniacal Scraps who threw pieces of bread on the ground and stamped on them as Kizzy's children stooped to pick them up.

"These are the kinds of people you call friends?"

Cammy did not hear Kizzy's words, but he heard the sneering and disgust in his tone. He spun around and walked back into the gauntlet of *agbadas*. He stared at the black faces and brightly colored robes, but saw no one that looked familiar.

"Let's be cool. "These are my boys-from-back-home. Let them pass, please."

"The problem is," Kizzy said, summoning his finest Trinidadian accent, "dees yuh boys-from-back-home don't know how to behave, mon."

Had the remark been devoid of mockery, Cammy might have played the gracious host, ignored it, and smoothed over bruised egos, but he disliked the smugness he sometimes detected among many Africans. He became animated.

"If yuh so want to fight, why don't yuh go fight Foday Sankoh, the idiot rebel cutting off yuh people hands and messing up yuh country?" He spoke with the assurance of a groom on his wedding day. Deflated, *man dem* parted. Cammy and his best men, followed by Scraps and his men, passed into the church without incident. But tensions still hung in the air—as they might at any wedding.

Chapter 13

Fina glided to the front of the church in a high-necked, form-fitting, butter-cream silk and satin gown with puffy cap sleeves. Every bit the princess, she wore a beaded Nubian headpiece with a long veil that flowed into a ten-foot long lace train. She had chosen her bouquet of sunset-colored roses bound together with yellow tulle and golden colored ribbon because the florist had told her it symbolized a love that existed not in the exuberance of sunlight but in the majesty of sunset. The bouquet was the one element of her wedding paraphernalia to which Fina's soul responded. She had picked it herself. She had deferred to Cammy about almost everything else.

Since both her parents were dead, they could not attend her wedding. Isa, her sister, had been denied a visitor's visa. Fina had invited her foster parents only one month before the wedding to ensure they could not attend. Edna was the only person in attendance who qualified as family on her side. Therefore, Fina walked up the aisle alone, clutching her bouquet of sunset-colored roses to her bosom. The congregation burst forth into a rousing rendition of "Lead us Heavenly Father, Lead us."

Christianity was Fina's adopted religion, yet for the longest time, nothing in its liturgy could evoke in her the reverence and love she felt at the sound of Salatul Fajr, Islam's first call for prayers. But this Saturday as she walked up the aisle toward to the altar, the satisfaction of finally meeting a man she loved and who truly loved her, gave the hymn and the religion new meaning for her.

Thou didst tread this earth before us,
Thou didst feel its keenest woe;
Lone and dreary, faint and weary,
Through the desert thou didst go.

She and the Savior were one, trekkers who had survived harsh conditions to emerge joyfully into greener pastures. Tears welled

135

forth and fogged up the world around her, so much so that she became fully conscious of her situation only when she heard the pastor ask, "if anyone knows of any just cause or impediment why these two people should not be joined together in holy matrimony, let him now declare it or henceforth hold his peace."

"I got me a reason. We ain't divorced, that's why!" The declarer stood up from one of the pews, waving a crumpled piece of paper above his head. Glued to their seats, the congregation tracked the man and the paper as he stepped out into the aisle and swaggered toward the altar.

"She my wife. Says so right 'ere." The man wagged the paper first to Cammy and Fina at the altar and then to the congregation.

"Do you know him?" Cammy grunted into Fina's ear. She did not answer.

"What the heck is he talking about?"

Again, Fina did not answer. Instead, she picked up her gown and attempted to run from the altar. But the train of her dress lodged between the minister and Cammy. Both were busy looking at the man now high-stepping from pew to pew, wielding the warrant that supposedly justified his intrusion. Fina yanked frantically until one of her bridesmaids, now attentive to her responsibility, untangled the train and let her escape. Moments later, Cammy bolted after her. The minister, the man alleging bigamy, the dumbfounded bridesmaids and groomsmen, and the congregation looked helplessly around and at one another. Inertia gripped the congregation, but not Cammy's mother, Celeste Priddy.

Short and tending toward the plump side, she nevertheless had a tantalizing hour-glass figure that belied her nearly sixty years. She wore a dove gray classic style dress that accentuated her breasts, hips and ivory skin tone. She had a round baby-like face with small, succulent lips. She was the kind of woman you hugged even though you did not know her, in the same leap of faith way as you would extend a hand to stroke the fur of a stray kitten that happened to brush by your leg. But you approached Celeste Priddy as if she were a kitten to be stroked at your peril.

Like a vulture spotting entrails from afar, she immediately grasped the potential for the interruption to develop into a bloody scandal. She understood all too well how a spicy detail added here, a did-you-know inserted there, could transform a small embarrassment into a dishonor that stains and shames a family forever. She was not about to let that happen.

****

From the moment he had sat down in church, Scraps had dozed off, so he was in a light sleep when the man with the paper had jumped into the aisle. Mad-Dog and the crew did not wake their boss, in part because the man with the crumpled paper had stopped adjacent to their pews and addressed them, like a lawyer his jury.

"She my wife. A man's gotta right to git his wife, ain't he? 'Fore she can marry somebody else, she gotta divorce *me*."

"Uhu," Mumbly agreed. Then, realizing the approval might not please his boss, he tried to muffle it by coughing and clearing his throat. The noise jolted Scraps awake.

Emboldened by Mumbly, the man continued to make his case. "I ain't studyin' 'bout no Africa; over *there,* they be marrying three and four wives, doin' all dat *juju* mess. I ain't with origami!"

Scraps had seen and heard enough. "Shut your dam mout," he roared. The congregation let out a collective gasp.

"Foxy, hol' him. Leh we take him outside."

The man tried to run, but Foxy and Meow seized and bundled him out of the church. Scraps and the rest of the boys-from-back-home followed.

The congregation broke out in conversation. Some were concerned about Scraps' swearing in a house of God. Others were angry at the man who interrupted the wedding, their wedding— calculated wickedness, they said, believing he was probably some stoned, and good-for-nothing, former boyfriend looking to embarrass Fina because she had dumped him. Still others argued he had done the right thing. Marriage is a sacred covenant that should

137

not be desecrated by anybody, no matter how pretty she is! If Fina was married to one man, she could not marry a second. Kizzy was the most ardent proponent of this view.

"The way I see it," he offered to the man sitting in the pew in front of him, "what's done in the dark, must come to light."

"Nonsense!" Edna retorted. "Do you expect them to tell the whole world? Do you tell people about the white woman you first married?"

Kizzy, like everybody who heard Edna's comment, was taken aback by the disclosure.

"Hey, look, mine was real. Irreconcilably differences," he made his case to the listeners around him.

"Idle talk," Edna scoffed. "I'm going to find out what this is all about."

"At least I had nuff sense to get a divorce 'fore I got married again," Kizzy mumbled. "What's so hard 'bout dat? She could easily have got a no-fault divorce for twenty bucks!"

"Wait a minute," said the man sitting in the pew in front of Kizzy. "We don't know for sure she married him. He could be a jealous former lover who can't get over her."

"Jeez, man," Kizzy sneered, "what you talking 'bout. You saw the certificate. It's plain dumb not to make sure your jealous former lover ain't gonna show up on y'alls wedding day."

"How? America is a big place," the man in the pew in front of Kizzy queried. "That guy could have been in Alaska or Hawaii."

"She should've thought of that before she got married shouldn't she? Maybe if they'd had a small wedding, this would never have 'appened. But you know us black folk. As soon as we gat a little money, we go showin' off. Would the guy know 'bout the weddin' if he lived in Alaska? Am sure they were keeping in touch. Know what I mean?" Kizzy expatiated.

Chapter 14

In the vestry, Fina sat in front of the stained glass Lancet window and stared at the picture of Christ on the cross. The deep red and brown tones diffused the sunlight from outside and cast a somber hue over the vestry. Fina absorbed the pain of the man on the cross and felt helpless, drained. But not Cammy. He charged into the vestry—swollen, wide-eyed, on the verge of spontaneous combustion. "And what the fuck was that?"

"Don't talk to me like that!"

"How the hell ah suppose to talk to yuh? Some drunk yuh know ruin my wedding, embarrass me in front of my family and friends, and all yuh can say is 'Don't talk to me like that'? I deserve… no, yuh *owe* me an explanation, damn it."

"*You* deserve, *you're* embarrassed, it's *your wedding?* It's always about *you,* isn't it? What about *me?* Is this not *my* wedding too? Am I not embarrassed? Do you have any idea how I feel? Huh? Do you even care? Of course not."

Fina bowed her head. She felt like crying, but she was too numb to put forth the effort crying required. She sagged into the chair.

"You're right," Cammy began after pacing through the office for several minutes. "I'm sorry. I was angry, and I forgot about you. This is our problem."

Fina did not reply. Her chin was tucked into her chest.

"Well," Cammy continued, "are you married to him or not?"

Fina shook her head in denial without changing her posture. "I married him to get my green card, before I met you…"

"I see. Just a minor detail, right?"

"I got a divorce."

"Well, he doesn't seem to think so."

"Will you give me a chance? At the time of the divorce, I couldn't find him. Me and Aman searched for over a year. When he didn't respond, I was granted a divorce. I have the decree to prove it." She pulled out a piece of paper from her bosom.

"You brought the decree to church? You were expecting him?"

"No, I wasn't but after the dream I had this morning, I just had this feeling something bad might happen. Bringing the decree to church made me feel—"

"Feelings don't exist in a vacuum, Fina. Feelings have sources, causes. If you took the time to look, you can identify them."

"Will you stop your psychobabble? I felt something and I acted to ease those feelings, okay?"

"That's yuh problem. Yuh jus' act. Yuh don't think. Yuh not logical!"

Cammy paused, aware he was getting angrier and louder. He took a deep breath and started more calmly. "Did this guy ever threaten to harm you? Maybe he'd disrupted a party in the past or acted up when he didn't get his way, but feelings have their origins in real experiences, Fina. Please don't tell me you just had a feeling."

"All I know is, I brought the decree here because I wanted to be prepared, Cammy."

"Well, what good did it do? I never heard anything so stupid. How was a piece of paper going to stop him? Damn, Fina, what were you thinking? He's messed up our wedding."

Tension choked the vestry, petrifying them—Cammy by the side of the Lancet window and Fina in a chair in front of it.

****

After Fina and Cammy fled from the sanctuary, Celeste Priddy summoned her husband and two sisters. She directed one to the main entrance with clear instructions: "Tell them it's a misunderstanding. Do whatever it takes to keep them from leaving." She positioned her husband and the second sister at opposite ends of the hallway to prevent anyone from walking into the vestry. Outside, she listened and waited. At the first lull in their argument, she pounced into the room.

140

"Cameron, what's the problem? People are waiting you know." She put her hand around her son's shoulder and shot a fierce, you-treacherous-bitch glance at Fina.

"Ma, this wedding is over."

Fina yelped like an injured dog. This was the second time in her life that she had cried, and like a long, overdue rain, it was sudden and violent.

"*Waiyo, waiyo, waiyoya, waiyoya. Waiyo, mi mammy* Nabou ooooo," she wailed and collapsed to the floor.

Cammy and Celeste Priddy fell to their knees, coaxing and cajoling Fina. But just as it seemed they had succeeded in calming her, Fina would break out in another long, violent cry. They went through several cycles of crying and consoling. Frustrated, Cammy walked out of the vestry, but Celeste Priddy was made of sterner stuff. Like a desperate gambler unwilling to cut her losses, she ministered to Fina, nursing a thin hope that she could get Fina to stop her voodoo gibberish, pull herself together, and march back to the altar. It was the least this African girl could do after having brought disgraced on her family. Calculating she'd have a much easier time spinning an interruption than a cancellation, Celeste Priddy continued to tap Fina's cheeks gently, call her name, wipe her brow, and fan her face while the pastor fed her alternating sips of water and Bible verses about facing adversity.

****

After Bayo completed his Ph.D., he secured a job at Honeywell—an offer he could not refuse. In addition to a competitive salary, the company agreed to pick up the cost of filing for his green card and gave him a $5000 signing bonus. Though his lawyer had explained they could petition for his green card to be issued in the U.S., Bayo had declined taking that route. He had not seen his parents in seven years, his mother was ailing, and his father wanted him to represent their family in a bitter chieftaincy accession dispute that had left his village without a bona fide chief executive for

141

over ten months. He decided he would go home to receive his green card at the U.S. Embassy in Lagos. In part to assuage Aman's worry about stories she had heard of African students promising to return to their affianced American girlfriends but eventually leaving them high and dry, he had proposed to her. "But wait until I get back to the States before you tell anyone" he said after he had showed her the ring.

"What's the point of getting engaged if I can't tell people?" Aman cross-examined. "Why do you even bother to show me?"

He did not answer. Instead, he sat down next to her and put his arms around her shoulder. Aman loved when he held her close but she did not move close to him. "You've got to trust me," he gently patted her hair and pulled her close so that her head nestled against his shoulder. "I'm committed to you. I want to marry you. I just don't want anything to happen and then have you left holding the ring, in a manner of speaking."

"I'll go along with this only if I can tell Fina. She can keep a secret. She looks like she has many of her own anyway. Please, please."

Bayo agreed. As soon as Aman got to work the next day, she dragged Fina into the bathroom and tinkled the ring finger in Fina's face. "Don't tell anyone. I'm not going to be wearing it yet. Baryour wants us to keep it a secret until he returns next month."

But apart from a large parcel containing an *Aso Oke* outfit in red, green and gold taffeta with a matching head tie two meters long and one meter wide, Aman had not heard again from Bayo. She continued to hope that she would one day marry him, but by the day of Fina's wedding, that hope was fading fast. Nevertheless, she set aside her own disappointment and prepared to celebrate her friend's impending march into happiness. She had seen enough of Cammy to be convinced he loved Fina.

However, Quanda, her mother, was far from convinced Bayo loved her daughter, and she did not shrink from letting Aman know her mind as she helped her to dress for Fina's wedding.

"You know he ain't coming back, right?"

"I don't know that, Ma. It's not like him to behave like this. Something is wrong."

"He don't want you. That's what's wrong. Has he called you?"

"No."

"Has he wrote you?"

"No."

"You need to move on then. You can't just sit around waiting, buying stuff for a home you ain't going to make with him."

"But we're engaged, Ma."

"Engaged?"

"He asked me to marry him before he left."

"How come I don't know about it?"

"He wanted to keep it a secret."

"And you agreed? Why you let these men treat you like that. Now he's gone and got married, ain't he?"

"I don't know. His behavior doesn't make sense."

"No, *you* don't make sense. Lemme tell you, men always got something to hide. And you're so desperate to believe *your* man is different, you'll buy anything he sells. They're all the same. Just wanna control, lie next to a warm body, eat and drink, and talk big. You gotta take men like my arthritis, day-by-day because they can flare up anytime."

Aman wanted to tell her mother she had become cynical ever since her father left but decided against what would have been a non-productive escalation.

"I don't see a ring. Did he ask you to wait for that too?"

"I am not wearing it because—"

"He don't want people to know. He got something to hide, girl."

"Like what, Ma?"

"Another woman. Could be he just lying to you. But if he ain't hiding somethin', he do the engagement for everybody to know, and he be proud too."

"But why would he spend two thousand dollars on a ring, leave all the furniture in his apartment, line up a job just to run away?"

"Maybe he's in trouble with the police. Drugs or somethin'."

143

"Ma, Baryour is the last person who would get involved in drugs or with the police."

"Well, maybe an African woman's gotta hold of him over there, and he don' wanna come back."

Aman's heart skipped a beat. She recalled the conversation she had with someone at the number Bayo had given her to call if he wanted to talk to her.

****

"Hello, is Baryour there?"

"Who you wan' talk to please," a voice answered.

"Baryour."

"Who please?"

"Baryour!"

"I no know am."

"Hello, can i talk to Baryour?"

"He no be here please. T'ank you."

"Wait-a-minute. This is 234-576-3421, right?"

"Yes please. This is."

"Okay, well, can I talk to Mr. Baryour? I am calling from America."

"Oh, America!"

"Yes, America. Mr. Baryour Karumwi gave me this number to call him."

"O, I understand. You wan' talk to Mister Bayo?"

"Exactly! Mr. Baryour."

"He go for village."

"When is he going to be back?"

"I no know, America. Before two or t'ree week or one month he go come back," the voice said helpfully. "He go village for big bizness."

"Who are you?"

"I be Bolaji Alakija."

"Okay, Mr. Akija, are you related to Baryour?"

144

"You say?"

"Are you Baryour's brother?"

"Yes, I go be Mister Bayo's brother."

"You're going to marry one of his sisters?"

"No, no, Amerika," Bolaji giggled. "He go marry my sister. I go come stay for here."

Silence.

"Hello…hello…, America. You day there?"

"Yes, I'm here. Did you say Baryour is going to marry your sister?"

"Yes, what you wan' for tell am?"

"Tell am, what the fuck are you up to?"

"Your name?"

"Aman."

"You say?"

"Aman, gad damn it!"

"T'ank you, Aman Gadamett. I go tell am."

"Yeah, yeah."

Click.

****

"Ain't you the one say he was a prince?" Aman's mother recalled her to the present. "Maybe, he got himself a princess. You need to get over there and find out what he be doing 'stead of going to someone else's wedding."

"I don't have the money. And right now I don't even know where he is. I wouldn't even know where to start looking for him."

"Uhuh. Sounds like you're finding excuses not to go. You just need to get up from your behind and close this mess."

Aman left home feeling a little despondent, but her mood improved as she strutted towards the church entrance. Her attire, especially her *Aso Oke* head tie perched on her head like a papal mitre, had attracted envious glances and compliments as she walked towards the church. So, she initially interpreted the raised voices and stares of the men standing a short distance ahead of her as the admiring heckling most women say they hate but secretly love. That initial assumption changed when the voices crystallized into speech.

"Get your hands off me," the man waved off Scraps and his men. "Touch me again and I'll sue y'all back to rasta land."

"Shut up," Scraps raised his right fist as if to pummel Jemal. He crouched to protect himself.

"A woman coming, Scraps," Mad-Dog alerted his boss.

Scraps and his crew backed off enough for quick-eyed Aman to recognize her cousin.

"Jemal, what's going on? What are you doing here?"

Scraps barred Aman's way. "Who you is?" he growled.

"His cousin. And who is you? Is he in trouble?"

"Yeah. He come in 'ere and embarrass meh partner, talk a set a shit, and buss up di wedding. He say he and the African girl was together."

"Aman, I was just telling them that Fina is my—"

Jemal never finished his sentence, for Aman lunged at him, head first, knocking off her head tie in the process and sending a couple of the boys-from-back-home tumbling to the ground. Arms, legs, and ties flailed and fluttered. Fedoras, flat caps, sunglasses, and pens fell to the ground. Expletives assailed the heavens and profaned the hallowed church grounds.

To Kizzy, who had come out of the church a few minutes earlier for a smoke, the scene was utterly disgraceful, just the kind of behavior he expected from these un-brought-up Caribbean fellas. It wasn't enough that the wedding was screwed up, but now here were Priddy's friends making asses of themselves for the whole world to see, and in front of a church too.

Also witness to the unfolding tableau was Roland Trailborn who lived across the road from the church. Four weeks removed from heart surgery, he was following doctor's orders to begin light exercise by taking a leisurely stroll with his dog, Hans. The spectacle of black people fighting in front of him was just what he expected from these lowlifes. They had bought the church he had attended since childhood and had changed its name from the respectable "St Martins" to the outlandish "Flaming Church of God."

While Kizzy and Roland Trailborn passed judgment, Hans wagged his tail and salivated, his hunting instincts activated by the flailing arms and legs. He lunged at them and, to his surprise, bounded free from his master's grip. He growled, crouched and snarled as if ready to attack the men. But this sheltered, well-fed dog was truly all bark and no bite. Unfortunately for him, he had taken his playfulness to a group of men who were not particularly fond of dogs. Scraps' foot lashed out and connected with Hans's ribcage, booting him like a game-day football. The dog was as pained and surprised as was his master.

Water rising in his eyes, heat and rage for his dog, religion, culture, and country congesting his chest, Roland Trailborn rushed at Scraps and promptly collided with a left jab. Dazed, his head swung loose like a button hanging on a thread. Yet all his motions signaled an intention to make another charge at Scraps. Kizzy leapt into the fray, bear-hugged and tried to drag the dazed Trailborn away.

It was not that Kizzy cared for this white man he was saving from a certain drubbing. He just wanted to have the satisfaction of thwarting Scraps. But, a small man himself, Kizzy fast became tired and could no longer restrain the agitated Trailborn who had continued to lunge in Scraps' direction. Like a wrestler about to throw an opponent, Kizzy took two quick breaths, heaved and dropped Trailborn to the ground. He lay there, gulping for air, his fingers limply caressing Hans, who licked his master's face and whined.

Everyone assumed the gasping man just had the wind knocked out of him. Scraps' crew restrained their boss and huddled to determine their next play. A livid and head-tie less Aman chased Jemal down the tree-lined street. Kizzy smoothed out his rumpled suit with his hands and shot a contemptuous look at Cammy. He had noticed him standing in the doorway of the office building adjacent to the church at about the same time that Aman confronted Scraps and his men. Congregants trickled out of the church and looked at the scene, baffled and intrigued.

****

Back in the vestry, Fina's wailing finally subsided to a whimper. Celeste Priddy immediately set about putting the wedding back on track.

"Pastor, this has all been a terrible mistake. That man merely wanted to embarrass my daughter-in-law." She faked a smile. "Go see her divorce paper, signed by a judge. Tell the congregation the delay is temporary, and we will be continuing very soon."

The pastor hesitated. He stared at the disheveled and tear-stained bride, remembered the angry groom, and common sense told him this wedding had little chance of being continued, at least not this Saturday afternoon. But Celeste Priddy's you'd-better-get-going-look was not to be contradicted. Just as the pastor walked out, Cammy whipped past him in the hallway.

"Cammy," Celeste Priddy began, "help me sit Fina up. I told the pastor we will continue in a short while."

"We're doing nothing of the sort."

"But Cammy—"

"Ma, I'm not getting married today. Now, please leave us alone."

"But the pastor—"

"I don't care, Ma. I'm not walking back out there."

"But the reception—"

"Leave us alone, Ma. I don't want to talk to anybody except Fina."

Cammy's steely cold voice made Celeste Priddy cower. She closed the door without a word, a response as foreign to her nature as a polar bear rejecting salmon.

"Why didn't you tell me about this marriage, Fina?" Cammy began. "I could have hired a detective or one of those companies that search for people. *We* could have found him and saved ourselves this embarrassment. Why you had to keep this secret? Shit!"

"I wasn't thinking about it. Cammy, I... I..."

"But you talked to me this morning and you said nothing."

"That's because Baramusu was on my mind. And then I had this bad feeling. I brought the decree with me at the very last moment."

"You should have told me. I would have understood."

"Would you have? I wanted to but never found the right moment. Then I put it out of my mind."

"So when we filed for the license you lied?"

"Lie? Remember you filled out the form and checked off 'never been married.' I just signed it."

"So I turned in a fraudulent form?"

"No," she sighed. "I later changed it. I figured you'd never look at it again. And if you did, I'd explain then. The way the licensing thing happened spared me the need to say something." Fina paused and took a big breath. "Cammy, I should have told you. Up to now, I'm not sure why I didn't tell you. Maybe I was scared at how you'd react, what you'd think of me."

"Oh, now you want to blame me. *Ah* fill out the form. Yuh 'fraid of my reaction."

"I didn't mean it to sound like that. Listen to me, Cammy, and try to understand. I have had some bad experiences in my life, so I've become guarded with people. I find it hard to trust people. I—"

"Yuh hear yourself? Now, yuh can't trus' anyone. I doh'n hear yuh taking responsibility, Fina. I hear yuh blamin' others. That's the trouble with black folk. Always blaming other people for the mess we make."

"My gad, Cammy, do you hear yourself? You're *so* smug! What does this have to do with black people? I am talking about me, me! I'm not blaming others. I'm trying to explain why *I* acted the way *I* did."

"Damn, Fina! All this boils down to is that yuh don love me enough to trus' that ah understand whatever yuh tell me."

"Well, not all of us can look at our past without bowing our heads."

"But when yuh past affects me, yuh should at least let me decide if ah want to live with it or not!"

Cammy stormed out of the vestry just as Edna entered it. He banged her into the doorframe. He did not look back or apologize. Fina did not cry or even turn to look in his direction. Only her heaving chest gave any indication of her sorrow. It lay deep in her soul and reached back all the way to the women of Musudugu.

Chapter 15

"Oh, Fina, it's okay," Edna began, uncertain how to approach her foster sister, who now sat with her head bowed. Fina took a deep breath and exhaled, as if trying to expel the square-shaped sorrow that lodged in her throat.

"Everything will be all right," Edna pulled up a chair next to Fina and put one arm around her foster sister's shoulder. "It's okay," she consoled and rubbed Fina's back every time she sighed or took a deep breath.

"Why me?" Fina's voice cracked into life like an old vinyl record.

"What?" Edna raised her head, momentarily confused. She was not sure how long they had been sitting in silence.

"My parents are dead, Isa can't be here, and my wedding is ruined. What did I do to deserve this?"

"Nothing."

"Then why do these things happen to me?"

"Fina, don't do this. We all have a little run of bad luck sometimes."

"A little run? Mine is a marathon! It started years with Baramusu's curse!"

"What are you talking about?"

"Baramusu, my grandmother, she cursed me. I can hear her voice right now."

"Why would she do that?"

"Because my father took me away in the middle of my initiation."

"So you belong? You're a society girl."

"At least you understand it is about belonging unlike that idiot Cammy always stuck on mutilation. Yet I have been miserable ever since Baramusu cursed our family. I am a walking target. Someone's always gunning for me. Jemal is just the latest person to hit his mark."

151

Edna took a deep breath but said nothing. They remained silent for a while before Fina resumed the conversation.

"I love Baramusu, but looking back, she took advantage of my youthful desire to belong, to not be the odd one out. At your house, your parents, especially your mom, made me feel like the odd one out. And don't deny it. At CC, the so-called citadel of learning, I was the Fula girl. Had to endure all those stupid Fulamusu jokes and comments about our teeth. Yeah, some people tried to hide their real feelings, but every so often that sense of superiority and lack of respect would slip out. I didn't choose to be a Fula or a foster sister!"

"Oh, Fina, forget the past. It's just upsetting you."

"Why shouldn't I be upset about the past? Is it because I mentioned your mom that you want me to shut up? You're no different from white people who want to sweep slavery under the carpet. It happened in the past, so let's leave it there. That way you and them can be comfortable and get on with your lives. Well, you don't have to listen to me. Go away and be comfortable. *I'll* talk to myself. I'll listen to *me*."

"Oh, Fina…," Edna began, but she was too hurt to complete her sentence. Fina was too engrossed in self-pity to notice her body blows.

For another few minutes neither spoke. Then, in a softer, less accusatory tone, Fina began again. "After college, I wanted so badly to get out of Sierra Leone to come and live here, where it wouldn't matter what ethnic group I belonged to, whether I was a foster child, or that I was a woman."

She paused. Edna said nothing.

"Boy, did I get that one wrong! I just replaced the circles on my back with ones that say black, African, and foreign—no, no alien. Black and alien. Is this what life is all about? Running away from place to place trying to fit in, to belong?"

"Fina, you're really upset—"

"I'm not upset! I am sober, clearheaded, and I know my problem. It's my genes. I attract bad luck like pollen attracts insects."

"I don't know about that, Fina. I just know none of this is your fault."

"That's right, baby. You're a good person," Aman interjected. She had walked into the vestry a few moments before and had caught the tail end of the conversation between Edna and Fina. "And don't you let anybody tell you differently. I don't know what got into Jemal's head." She hugged Fina and in the process elbowed Edna off her chair.

"Why would he want to hurt me like this?" Fina looked up at Aman.

"It's okay," Aman coaxed.

"But why am I surprised. Baramusu said I should never cut the rope and that alone I was just an animal. Did I listen? No! I have spent most of my life living alone, cut off from or running away from my people. And, today, I just tried to cut the rope by trying to marry Cammy."

"Baby, you need to get some rest," Aman signaled to Edna to help her escort Fina home.

"Where's Cammy?" Fina asked. "He's cut the rope too, hasn't he?"

"Don't know about any rope, baby," Aman said. "Cammy wouldn't leave you here. He's probably out there with the paramedics and police."

"Police! Did he get into a fight with Jemal?" Fina eyes sparkled.

"No, baby. Jemal ran off before I could wring his bloody neck."

"So why are the police and paramedics here?"

"A white guy got beat up in front of the church. His wife called them."

"Was he a guest?"

"Don't know. All I can tell you is that the police sure got here in a hurry. Takes them forever to answer a call in my neighborhood. The paramedics said the guy was unconscious and had a weak pulse. The man's wife told the police she saw this short, really black guy throw her husband to the ground. I tried to tell the police that he was really trying to prevent a fight, but the island guys told the police the

153

short guy was a troublemaker and started the fight with the white man. It was my word against theirs. If the white guy dies, this brother could be charged with murder."

"Was he wearing a blue blazer with gray pants?" Edna asked, striving to control her rising alarm.

"Might have been, baby. Do you know him?"

"Sounds like my husband. Was he African?"

"I don't know. You'd best go and check."

Edna dropped Fina's arm and bolted from the room. Aman turned to Fina, grabbed her chin and raised her head with one hand and, with her other hand, wiped Fina's tear-marked face. "You okay, baby?"

"Of course I am. I get disgraced on my wedding day, one of my guests kills another, and the man I'm supposed to marry abandons me. I'm peachy, Aman, just peachy!"

"That's it. Let's go!" Aman dragged Fina out of the vestry, past Celeste Priddy and a gaggle of people asking questions like a pack of reporters on a breaking story.

****

The ambulance carrying the unconscious Roland Trailborn sped off in a wail of sirens. Cammy used the distraction to scamper into his limousine. He did not want to talk to anybody, and he certainly did not want the "oh-you-poor-thing" look or the "cheer-up-boy" pat. He lunged into the vehicle, collapsed into the seat, and ordered the chauffeur to drive off, anywhere. His head swirled, his heart pounded, his pulse raced. He sat upright, dug his elbows into his thighs, cupped his head in his hand, and stared at the floor. He ran his fingers across his chin and felt his throat. It was hot. He undid his collar, ripped the boutonniere off his chest, and threw it to the floor.

How was he to face his colleagues at work? What would they think? How would they see him, behave toward him, and he toward them? How about Paul Levine, David Lerner, and Nischat Patel, his medical school friends from London? This whole business must have

154

seemed so sordid to them. Cammy remembered their student days at Oxford and how they had laughed at the absurd things they heard often happened in America. Now they had witnessed one.

"Blimey," Patel would say in his heavy Indian accent. "The bloke was going to get hitched to a bloody bigamist!"

"Only in America," Levine would interject.

"It's probably his tribal instincts coming through all that education and sophistication," Lerner would offer in his deadpan delivery. Then they would burst out laughing. Cammy covered his ears with his hands to block out the voices laughing at him.

"Excuse me, Dr. Priddy." It was the chauffeur, and he was looking at Cammy through the rear view mirror. "Do you want me to pull over, sir?"

The question was enough to make Cammy pull himself together. He could not let his emotions get the better of him. He was a man of science, a surgeon no less. He studied pathologies, weighed his options and, with the right instruments, corrected them. After all, how many urologists can go into a bleeding man to remove a dislodged kidney, re-implant it in the groin, and have it back working perfectly the very first time they headed a surgical team? He just needed a little concentration to think though this current pathology and fix it. Cammy poured himself a glass of orange juice from the decanter, took several gulps, and settled into the leather seat.

He'd done nothing wrong. Fina was the one who had betrayed him, hid a previous marriage from him, and disgraced him in front of his family and friends. Then she had the temerity to develop an attitude, the nerve to blame him. Why had she kept such a vital piece of information from him? Could it be she did not love him enough to trust him? But how could that be?

Cammy refused to countenance this question. But doubt crept into his mind and reminded him of a few things. Unlike his previous girlfriends, Fina did not crave expensive things. In fact, she seemed oblivious to his accomplishments and money. Once when she accompanied him to the construction site of his home with the Silicon Valley ethos, she was more excited by a group of ducks in the

155

lake adjacent to the property than by the square footage of the house, the imported Turkish tile, the twenty-foot fireplace, or the sub-zero trash compactor. Sure, she smiled and said thank you when he bought her the Rolex watch and the top-of-the-line Hewlett Packard Pentium chip computer with the DSL modem and an obscene amount of hard drive, but he remembered that he was disappointed she seemed underwhelmed by these expressions of his love. He certainly could not hide his consternation when, a few weeks after he gave her the Rolex, he saw it lying on the vanity in her bedroom. Perhaps he really did not matter to her? But how could he not matter? She was moving into a quarter of a million dollar home and into his BMW 500 series wedding present; she was moving into the Priddy clan, and, frankly, into a level of Maryland society that she could not have reached by herself. Of course, he mattered. How could she not love him? There had to be some other reason why she kept the information from him. He paused, swirled the remaining juice in the glass, and swallowed it in one gulp.

Maybe she believed he would think less of her if he knew how she had got her card? This explanation appeared to make the most sense the more he thought about Fina's personality. That was it. She had not told him about her first marriage because she felt ashamed, embarrassed, especially when she knew how easily he had been able to get his. She wanted to appear perfect in his eyes. The secrecy? A misplaced act of love. The decree she took to church? A reflection of fear and worry. The attitude? A defense mechanism. Cammy remembered that she had even said she was not sure how he would react to the news. And, boy, had she been right. He suddenly felt guilty. Instead of supporting her, he had bailed out, repaid her love by abandoning her. "Driver, driver," he commanded, "take me back to the church!"

But no sooner had the car turned around than Cammy reconsidered. Why was he rushing to Fina? She had screwed up all by herself. He was not the one who got married and kept it a secret, and yet he was the one now rushing to appease her! Hell no. *She* should be the one apologizing to him. He became angry at himself for even considering making up with her. Whatever she felt she was gaining from holding onto her secret, let her enjoy it now, by herself.

"Let's not go to the church anymore. Just take me home," he instructed the chauffeur. Cammy snatched the phone from its resting place in the cabin and called the coordinator from Wedplan.

****

Like teammates after a devastating away-game defeat, Fina and Aman drove home in silence, each engrossed in her own analysis, trying to determine which decision, action, or path caused the scene that unfolded in the church.

"Why didn't you tell Cammy about Jemal?"

Fina did not answer, though she had heard the question. Several minutes passed.

"I wasn't sure how he'd react. Cammy doesn't have the background, the context, to understand why people like me do the things we do."

"What's there to understand?"

"He has lived a charmed, trouble-free life. He had an exceptional university experience and is an internationally known surgeon. Marriage to Jemal was a minor event I didn't think he needed to know about until the right time."

"You guys never talked about immigration?"

"Not really. I know only that he got his green card in record time. Somewhere in his narratives about all-expense-paid, trans-Atlantic trips to visit famous American teaching hospitals clamoring for his services and offering generous moving packages, he had asked if my papers were all right. To avoid a long explanation, I just said yes."

They grew silent, each trapped in a loop of regrets and what-ifs, sifting through endless possibilities to identify that one action that could have averted the afternoon's fiasco. Inside the car, the air was laden with discarded thoughts, colliding theories, unclear memories, and deep sighs. Outside the raised windows, life sped by like a silent movie.

157

They reached the sanctuary of Fina's townhouse in silence. Once inside, Fina flicked off her white crystal Ralph Lauren sling-back heels, threw away the sunset-colored roses she had unconsciously held onto, and tried to unzip her wedding gown as she headed straight for her bedroom. Deciding Fina was best left alone, Aman flopped onto the living room sofa, turned on the TV, sank back, and channel surfed. She had twice flicked through all the channels when she heard banging and slamming coming from Fina's bedroom. She rushed to the room to find Fina, wedding dress halfway off her body, throwing clothes into a huge suitcase on the bed.

"What are you doing?" she asked as Fina shuttled from a chest-of-drawers to the bed and dumped clothes into the suitcase.

"Packing!"

"Why?"

"I'm going back."

"Back where?"

"Home!"

"Home? Where? What home?"

"I have only one home and that's Sierra Leone!"

"Whatever for?"

"What kind of question is that? Haven't you heard people say there's no place like home? That's where I belong right now."

"In a war-torn country? You've got no one there, not even your sister."

"Yeah, but several million people still live, eat, and sleep in my war-torn country. If they can survive, so can I. I can also go to Isa in Guinea."

"Don't be ridiculous. Your sister is a refugee. All this is about Cammy."

Fina paused from her mechanical movements between the chest-of-drawers and the suitcase and tried to slide the wedding dress down her hips, but she could not. She stopped struggling with the dress and looked directly at Aman.

"I didn't say it wasn't. But can you think of a better time for me to go home?"

158

"Come on, child."

"Don't child me. I hate it when you talk Ebonics."

Aman flinched but decided this was not the right time to quarrel with Fina. "Hold up on the cheap shots, okay? I'm your friend. I understand how you feel, but you've not talked to Cammy, and you've got nowhere to go right now." Aman paused to see if her words were having any effect. Fina continued to fling clothes into the suitcase.

"You're much better than this hurt little girl I see turning on her friend and running away like a scared chicken," Aman said.

Fina did not respond. She walked to the closet, reached inside and tossed, in quick succession, assorted shoes, handbags, and boxes over her shoulders. Then, with a groan, she hurled out a suitcase. Thump! It hit the floor. Panting, Fina turned to Aman. "I may be hurt, but I'm not scared. Cammy's just shown me that he's not the right person for me."

"But you haven't even heard what he has to say."

"Leaving me like that says a lot more than I care to hear. We are through! I don't want *anything* to do with him. Do you hear me?"

"You can't just give up like that."

"I didn't give up. He left *me*, remember!"

Fina winced. Then, with her fingers, she poked the underside of her belly below her navel. Aman eyed her with concern, but as her mouth opened to form a question, Fina telegraphed she was okay with an aggressive return to her packing.

"You've got to tell him how you feel Fina. He'll understand."

"He can't. He doesn't know what it feels like to walk in tight-fitting shoes."

"He may surprise you."

"Trust me, I know my man. I bet you that right now he's worrying what his friends will say or think about him."

"And this was the man you were going to marry?"

"*Et tu*, Aman. Go ahead, twist the dagger! Make sure I bleed to death."

"I'm sorry. I didn't mean it to sound like that. Believe me, I understand how you feel, but why do you want to leave America?"

"Huh," Fina cackled. "The friendly superiority of Americans, even the enlightened black ones."

Anger lodged itself in Aman's throat. "I can't figure out you Africans. I don't know any one of you who has ever returned home… well, Bayo, so I guess I know one. What's so bad if I wonder why you'd want to go back, especially now? You're always complaining about how bad things are."

"Yeah, but that's because I love my country and want to see it become a better place. But why should *you* be surprised because an alien wants to go back home? H-O-M-E, mom and dad, the place you feel comfortable no matter whether you live in a mansion with climate control or a windowless hut sitting on the equator."

Another wave of pain surged through Fina's body. She stopped talking and, trying to seem casual, stretched out on the bed, closed her eyes, and braced herself as the pain radiated all over her body. She exhaled the pain in short, shallow plumes until it subsided. She lay on the bed for a couple more minutes, gathering strength. The pain worried her. Had circumstances been different, she would have called Cammy, and he would have diagnosed, prescribed, and reassured her that all was well. But now, she was on her own. She decided she would ride out the pain until Monday and then go and see her doctor. If it became unbearable, she'd go to the emergency room. The decision left her elated. It was swift and did not involve consulting or considering Cammy. She wondered if the mess of the wedding was some kind of divine intervention, Baramusu and the ancestors guiding her to the path from which she had strayed. She certainly felt a presence in the room—and then it cleared its throat.

"Better take off that wedding dress," the Aman presence instructed.

"Never really liked it anyway," Fina said breezily as she stood up, jiggled the dress down her body, and stepped out of it. "Damn thing felt like a straitjacket. I only took it because Cammy liked it. Good riddance!"

160

From underneath a pile of clothes, Fina picked out a shapeless, print cotton gown that, apart from the circle cut for the head and neck, could easily have been a large tablecloth. She slid the gown over her head and allowed it to drape her bra-less body.

"Aaah! This feels so much better." Then, in a more subdued tone, she faced Aman. "Home is a comfort zone. It's the place where the way you feel inside connects with the way things are outside. Can you see yourself living in a place where you don't have television, Coca-Cola, and McDonald's? Or for black folks, I guess I should say fried chicken and barbecue ribs, eh?"

Aman did not laugh, though she appreciated the return of Fina's sometimes pointed humor. "Look, Fina, you're talking to me, so save the comfort zone jive. There's a war going on in your country. What do you want to go back to? Rebels and child soldiers? What values do you have inside that connects you with them?"

"The real question is what do I connect with here, Aman? Not much. I thought I would find myself here and enjoy being free of what confines and defines."

"But you can call Cammy, sort out—"

"*That* I will not do. Never! I'm *not* going to beg him to marry me. If he wants me, he is gonna have to run right back *to me*, wherever I may be, the same way he ran away. So let's not talk about him anymore, okay?"

"Okay, let's forget about Cammy. You can get another job. Things—"

"Another job. Where?"

"There are plenty of jobs out there. Work at McDonald's if you have to. You can even switch to nursing, computers."

"You want me start a new career?"

"If that's what it takes. Sometimes we have to change paths to keep going forward."

"Forward to where? I need to get on the path to return home."

"And give up on your dream?"

"What dream? I only have nightmares. *Ar taya*, Aman, I'm tired. I live in permanent anxiety, continually second-guessing people's motives. Did she say that, do that, because I'm black, because I'm African? Was I hired, not hired, promoted, not promoted because I'm a woman, a foreigner?"

Fina paused, as if realizing something new. "And they want me to believe that hypertension is in our genes. Bullshit! Do you know what the most common disease really is among black women?" Aman looked nonplussed, so Fina told her, "Hypercrap. Hypertension, cramps, anxiety, and paranoia. Let the federal government study that!"

"You don't need to tell me this. I live it too."

"But wait, there's more. I own a townhouse in a well-to-do suburb. I have an endless supply of water and electricity and a crop of brand new television programs that keep me happy by showing me the lifestyles of the rich and famous."

Fina took a deep breath. Aman sat on the bed, realizing that it was best to let Fina rant. Every so often, she nodded or grunted in agreement, passed a tissue, or rubbed Fina's back and shoulder.

Chapter 16

ammy's house was jam-packed with concerned and curious family and friends. Their wedding had been cut short and the script thrown away. The oldest among them vaguely remembered hearing stories of aborted weddings, but they'd never actually witnessed one, so no one could offer sage advice.

The practical wondered what to do with their gifts. Give them to Cammy? No, they were presents meant for a couple. What would a single man do with boxes of wine glasses, serving dishes, silverware, and wall decorations except store them? Take them back and get a refund? That had some merit, but it also meant another round of shopping if the wedding got back on track; maybe a smaller ceremony would be arranged in a month or two. Wait and see? Yes, that was the sensible course. The presents would still be good in a week, a month, a year, or however long it took for them to get back to the altar. But first things first. Now was the time to give moral support.

But many wondered about the details—about the man who interrupted the wedding, the bride's past, the courtship leading up to the marriage, and Cammy's ignorance—that would emerge and be reconstructed to elevate the incident into lore. So they had driven in a convoy to Cammy's home, occupied every inch of the house and awaited his arrival, curious to find out what he had to say.

As Cammy walked into the house, the expressions of sympathy and empathy, the drippy looks of concern and pity he had run away from at the church beset him. He scuttled across the marble floors of the oversized family room toward his bedroom. But even as he scurried along, he knew he could not simply ignore everyone, so he swung around and headed to the sofa where his grandmother was sitting. He hugged and kissed her and the line of aunts who, in turn, whispered incoherent biblical passages into his ear. He did not kiss or hug his uncles. They said all that needed to be said with bone-crushing handshakes and cough-inducing pats.

Cammy merely nodded to the many indistinguishable faces in the room, but he was struck by a lanky, broad-shouldered, light-complexioned young man who seemed out of place in blue jeans and a polo shirt. The young man looked familiar, like a nephew or the son of a friend, but Cammy could not remember him. He decided not to agitate himself. He would find out about the young man through his mother.

A couple of Cammy's cousins standing near the young man mumbled greetings and asked if he was okay. He muttered something that must have reassured them, for he was able to continue making his way toward his bedroom. He had grabbed the door knob and was about to enter when he stopped and turned around.

"Folks, ah sorry 'bout what happened this afternoon. Ah waste your time."

A chorus of disapproving noises followed this remark. Cammy pressed on. "Right now, ah tired and want to rest. The caterers will serve food and drinks at the reception. So yuh all go eat and drink."

A jumble of questions and statements followed, out of which Cammy picked out a word or two about the fight and the dead white man. He raised his hand and quieted the house. "As far as ah know, the white man is not dead."

"Di polis arrest Scraps dem?" somebody said.

Cammy hesitated. Like an alert aide assisting a politician stumped by a reporter's question, Celeste Priddy stepped into her son's hesitation.

"Judge, that's my husband, got a call from Scraps and has gone down to the police station to see what he can do."

The question answered, Cammy spun around and disappeared into his room. He had barely settled into an armchair when his mother opened the door.

"You should have at least explained the interruption was a mistake," she said. "Folks still don't know what really happened."

164

"Ma, I don't care what people know. Tell them anything that will make you happy."

Celeste Priddy retreated, thankful for the opportunity to reconstruct the afternoon's event. "People are always looking for ways to bring you down…," her voice trailed away after she closed the bedroom door.

Cammy stretched out on his back on the bed and blew air through his lips. He had fallen into a light sleep when his mother's voice woke him up.

"Ma, I told you I—"

"Yes, I know, but you've been sleeping for over an hour and there's a young man waiting to talk to you. A matter of life and death, he says. Just give him a few minutes, dear."

Reluctantly, Cammy got up, brushed his creased clothes, and followed his mother. The living room was deserted. He felt betrayed. Even though he had given the invitation for the guests to go to the hotel to eat and drink, he had hoped they would not have taken up his offer of the free food. And now here was somebody else probably wanting to freeload. He walked into the study determined to deny whatever he was asked. But his resentment dissipated the moment he saw the young man. He reminded him so much of his brother, Donovan.

****

They were only a year apart and were very close, almost like twins. Donovan was a sparkling, well-rounded youth who played cricket and football for his school, sang tenor solo for his church and was the darling of the girls. Many mothers in their neighborhood nursed a hope he would be the boy their daughters would marry. Family and friends said he had a bright future ahead of him. Cammy admired his elder brother and was most proud the afternoon both of them put up a sixty-eight run, ninth wicket partnership to help their school win the inter-secondary schools cricket competition.

But Donovan took ill and died a few days before his sixteenth birthday. Complications of renal failure, the doctors said. This explanation seemed to satisfy his parents and the adults in the family. Cammy heard them say it was "God's will;" that "His ways were mysterious;" that "He had a right to take back his son." This easy acceptance of Donovan's death pained the grieving sibling and clarified nothing. Cammy wanted to understand how his brother, the one who was unbeatable when they wrestled or ran, could so quickly change from being strong and healthy to being sick and dead. And no one, not even the doctors, were able to help him. He could not understand why they did not give him the right medicines or do an operation to cure the kidney. The lack of answers, the easy way the adults accepted what had happened, angered the youth and played a major role in his decision to become a doctor and to specialize in surgery. So unlike most of his peers, Cammy knew early that he would become a doctor, devote himself to science, and use it to save people like Donovan. This early singleness of purpose served him well in his medical studies and career, though it often made him impatient with people who did not seem to know what they wanted. Whatever his task, Cammy quickly identified a goal and pursued it with a vengeance.

****

This particular Saturday, after the wedding fiasco, Cammy's goal was to quickly dispense with this young man and then figure out how he was going to restart his life.

"Sorry to bother you sir," the young man began, "but I have a return flight to catch."

"Then make this quick. Ah've had a bad day?"

"Yes, sir. I heard. Please accept my sympathy."

"Ah don't need your sympathy. Tell me what yuh want."

"It's really awkward for me—"

"For me too. Say wha' yuh want nah."

"Well… eh…I… believe you are my father!"

166

****

Kizzy waited patiently in the egg-white interrogation room. Aside from the chair on the opposite side of the table at which he sat, the room had no other furniture or fixture. Not a window and not even an outline to suggest the room once had a two-way mirror, the kind he saw in police dramas on television. In all his years in America, this was the first time he had stepped foot inside a police station. He hadn't really wanted to go there, but the detective seemed like a nice officer and had persuaded him that collecting their statements would go much faster at the station. There will be other officers, and he'll be out in no time. The suggestion and benefit seemed reasonable. Certain about his role and innocence in the incident, Kizzy had complied.

And initially, Kizzy felt confident that some kind of assault charge would be filed against Scraps, but he became worried as the detective pressed him on who had thrown the first punch. "I tried to stop the fight," he waved his hand in exasperation.

"I'll be right back," the detective sprang from his chair and left the interrogation room.

That had been thirty minutes earlier. It was now nearing 6:00 p.m., and Kizzy's apprehension had grown into alarm. He recalled news stories of police brutalizing minorities. They ratcheted up his anxiety.

"Mr. Bacchus, we have a problem," the detective noted when he reentered the room, followed by Edna. Kizzy was glad to see her.

"Mr. Trailborn's wife and all the island guys say *you* started the fight." The detective stroked his chin thoughtfully.

"That's a lie," Kizzy sprang up, jolting the table and startling the detective.

"You'd better calm down," he warned, sliding his right hand toward his holstered gun.

Like a berated poodle, Kizzy promptly sat down and paid attention.

"Sir, why would eight people tell lies on you?" the detective asked.

Kizzy glanced at Edna. She also wanted to know the answer.

"Because they're protecting their boss, and we got into it before the service started."

"But what about Mrs. Trailborn? She doesn't know them. What's her gripe against you?"

"Dunno, man. All I know is I didn't start no fight. Fina's friend," Kizzy spoke directly to Edna, "what's her name?"

"Aman."

"Yeah, her. She'll tell you I tried to save the white dude from getting beat."

"Okay, that makes two against eight."

"What about the man himself?" Edna interjected.

"He is in a coma, ma'am. If he dies, your husband's looking at manslaughter, especially if those island guys don't change their story. Truth is we have no real reason to believe they're lying. You should be thinking about getting a lawyer."

"But it was jus' the dude and his dog. I didn't see no wife."

"She saw everything from her bedroom window across the street, sir."

"Well, she didn't see me hit her husband first."

"Was there anyone else who might have seen what happened?"

"Cammy! Dr. Priddy, the dude suppos'd to be getting married. He saw everything!"

"Then I'll need to talk to him. If his story matches yours, that would at least make three against eight. Not great odds if Mr. Trailborn dies. Do you know how I can get in touch with this doctor?"

Edna stayed with Kizzy at the police station while the officers determined what should happen next. Finally around 8:00 p.m., they released Kizzy with instructions he should not leave the Washington Metropolitan Area. Kizzy and Edna agreed she would ask Fina to make sure Cammy told the police what he saw. However, the plan

168

left Kizzy feeling vulnerable, at the mercy of Fina and Cammy, the two people he'd least like to be beholden to.

Chapter 17

"I wish I could go back to my village and sit in the shade of the baobab tree. I want to hear the mosquito whine in my ear. Then, I'll slap at it, miss, and give myself an ear ache," Fina mused aloud. Aman gave her a what's-the-fun-in-that look and then sipped from her mug of chocolate. They were both seated on the loveseat in the living room of Fina's townhouse. She was considerably less agitated now. Night had finally drawn the curtain on a dramatic day.

"I want to smell *ogiri* and palm oil," Fina continued. "Feel mango juice drip down my fingers as I lick it off. I want to play on the farm, pull the bird-scaring rope, and watch the birds flitter away."

Aman continued to look puzzled.

"Aman, I wish I had been able to say goodbye to my mother and Baramusu, that's my grandmother. I want to be sure she loves me."

"I'm sure she loves you, baby."

"Most of all, I wish I had got to know my father more. I just have this image of a tall, light-complexioned, smiling man."

"Hm! So Cammy resembles your father?"

"Oh, please stop your psychoanalysis 101. For years, I have wanted to go back to the village to talk to the old folks who knew my father."

"Why?"

Fina hesitated for a moment. "Because my father snatched me from the initiation bush. That's taboo."

"You mean FGM?" Aman held her hand to her mouth.

"Circumcision, belonging, society. Not FGM, but my point is that my family has never been back to Talaba, and we have never made amends for my father's action. Now's a good time for me to go and set things straight, right?"

The thought revived her spirits. "I have to find my passport—"

"But didn't you say rebels burned down your village and killed nearly everyone. Who are you going to make amends with?"

"Don't know, but I have to try."

"And what if you can't find your grandmother? Have things really changed from when you were there? Will you cease being a... eh... what's the name of your people again?"

"Fula!"

"Yeah, them. Will you? Six months or a year after you return, you'll be just as disappointed about your country as you are now about America. The only thing you can be sure of is that you will be facing a different set of problems. It may be discrimination hurts less when it comes from a brother or sister, but what about all the daily inconveniences?"

"Millions of people live every day with inconveniences. Are they any less happy? My life here is much more convenient than it could ever be back home, yet I don't feel fulfilled. Something's missing."

"All I know is, if I don't have happiness, let me at least have comfort," Aman said.

"Pssh! What is comfort without happiness?"

"Makes unhappiness more livable!"

"Well it amplifies mine and makes life here unlivable."

Fina leaned back into the sofa as if exhausted. Aman chose that moment to take a bathroom break. When she returned, Fina was in the same position, with much the same demeanor. Aman walked into the kitchen to make some more chocolate. Several minutes later, she set a mug on the coffee table, tapped Fina's shoulder, and pointed to it. Fina reached for the mug and muttered a thank you. Both women sipped in silence and stared at the TV. There, life proceeded with unrelenting intensity and gaiety.

"I'm fed up, Aman. I want to go to Musudugu," Fina said, returning to her musings.

"Where?"

"It's a place... in... uh... where women lived happily, without men!"

172

"Happy? Seems like there'll be a whole lotta frustration, girl. You know what I mean?" Aman winked.

"This is not funny, Aman? I'm going home. Just watch me."

"Okay, relax. This is not the right time to be making big decisions. If you still feel the same way, tomorrow, next week, *I'll* help you pack. For now, let's go grab something to eat."

"I mean it, Aman. I'm going back."

"I believe you. But wait till things blow over. You may not feel this way tomorrow. Where do you want to go eat?"

"I don't want to go anywhere. My tummy doesn't feel good. You go ahead and order some Chinese food if you're hungry. Then we can watch Lifetime television. There's bound to be some movie about a ditched bride."

"No, I'd rather watch a movie about an African American woman waiting for her African prince to come and marry her."

"Oh, Aman, I'm sorry. I completely forgot about Bayo. Have you heard from him?"

"Nope! But he did send me this outfit." Aman pointed to her dress.

"Men are all the same, aren't they?"

"You see, we're in the same boat, girl. Maybe I should pack my bags and go to Africa with you? We'll go and find Bayo, beat the crap out of him, and then settle down in your Musu-what-you-call-it-place?"

"Do you still want to marry him?"

"I don't know, Fina. Right now, I'd like to *Bobbittize* him first."

"Bobbi what?"

"You know, Lorena Bobbitt, the woman who cut—"

"Oh, yeah, that's a good idea. We should do that. But before we leave, we'll do Cammy first. We'll tie him on one of his operating tables and leave the thing there for one of his robots to sew back on."

They laughed heartily and speculated about places the detached members of their estranged lovers could be reattached. Exhausted by laughter, they dozed off.

"'Give your strength to others and draw from theirs,'" Fina said when she awoke and put her elbow into Aman's side to rouse her. "That's what my grandmother told me on the night of my initiation. That's why we lie next to each other during initiation—to absorb each other's pain and to gather strength from those lying next to us. Today, when I needed Cammy's strength, he ran away. Maybe God is trying to tell me something."

The door bell sounded just as the clock chimed ten. Aman answered the summons and guided a dazed-looking Edna to a chair.

"You, okay," Fina sat upright.

"Kizzy could be charged with aggravated assault, even manslaughter," Edna began and told them all that had transpired at the police station. She ended by asking Aman if she had seen what happened.

"Already told you and one of the officers what I saw."

"You have to tell them that Kizzy is innocent!"

"Sure will, baby."

"Here," Edna whipped out a business card from her handbag and handed it to Aman. "That's the name of the detective in charge of the investigation. Please call him."

"Okay, honey. I'll do so first thing tomorrow morning."

"Where is Kizzy now?" Fina interjected, somehow finding enough empathy to forget her own troubles.

"He's gone to see one of his lawyer friends. Then he and the kids are driving back to Richmond tonight. I wanted to go with him, but I also wanted to see how you were doing."

"Oh, Edna, you didn't have to."

"Of course I did."

"Hey guys," Aman interrupted, "this is a good time for me to leave. She picked up her bag and walked toward the door. Fina made the obligatory pleas for Aman to stay a little longer. Aman offered the obligatory appreciations but declined. The parting ritual done, all three of them walked to the door, hugged and kissed goodbye.

"Fina, I'll call you tomorrow, honey, and we'll plot how to deal with these men, okay?"

Fina closed the door and both she and Edna collapsed onto the loveseat. The flickering light from the changing scenes on the TV cast their faces in kaleidoscopic relief. They sat like that for several minutes, and then Edna broke the respite. "Fina, Kizzy said Cammy also saw what happened."

The muscles tightened all over Fina's body, and the pain in her stomach returned with renewed severity. "Will you please talk to Cammy, ask him to tell the police what really happened? Right now, it's Kizzy's word against the man's wife and the guys from the islands."

"Oh, Edna, this is not a good time. I haven't talked to Cammy since this afternoon. I don't know what he saw."

"Kizzy said he saw the whole thing. He *has* to tell the police what he saw. I just want you to make sure."

"Edna, Cammy might not even want to talk to me."

"Please, Fina. If Cammy does not come forward, Kizzy could go to jail."

Fina did not respond, and Edna did not press her request. But the last thing Fina wanted was to have to make overtures of any kind to Cammy, especially on Kizzy's behalf, a man a part of her felt was getting his just deserts. If she approached Cammy, he will think she was using Kizzy's situation as a pretext to ask for forgiveness. If she refused to ask him and did not explain her reasons, Edna would not forgive her. Fina leaned back on the sofa and closed her eyes. Her muscles coiled into steel as she cocooned herself, determined that though Edna may be sitting next to her, she did not want her company. Resentment and anger took free reign of her body—and she welcomed them.

But a few minutes later the resentment melted away as Edna placed her warm body next to hers. Fina felt happy. Neither woman looked at the other or spoke, just as had happened many years before on the cold, tiled floor of bathroom in the Heddle home in Freetown. They had held hands and they had felt like sisters then. That was how they felt now.

Chapter 18

They say there is no greater love than that of a mother for her child. But fathers the world over know there's no sight more pleasing to their soul than that of a son on the brink of manhood. This sight was no less pleasing to the man who had only just been informed he belonged to the society called fatherhood. Cammy's membership came as both a shock and not a shock.

After Donovan died, Cammy sought to replace him, but no one seemed able to provide the kind of companionship he wanted. The harder he tried to replace his brother, the wider and more removed from his social circumstances his circle of friends became. Celeste Priddy tried to steer him to the "right" friends, but he gravitated to the idlers, particularly a ruffian named Scraps. And because he was a straight "A" student and rarely got into trouble, Celeste Priddy did not have poor school work and bad influence as excuses to separate him from his friends. In his last year of high school, she smelled cigarette smoke on his clothes and noticed the girls who stayed in the cars and never came into the house. And even though she had twice seen girls sneak out of their yard when Cammy was supposed to be at some school function, she agreed with her son's declaration that Anushka Mutari was a slut trying to trap him into marriage after she claimed he was the father of her baby. The morning after the girl's allegation, Celeste Priddy swung into action. Before anyone could independently confirm the pregnancy, the young woman had disappeared. Just over a year later, she returned, gaily dressed, and began attending nursing school.

He remembered that soon after Anushka Mutari reappeared, one of his classmates insinuated his family had paid Anushka to have an abortion. When Cammy told his mother what he had heard, she explained that she had persuaded Anushka's struggling parents to send her away till she gave birth and to put up the baby for adoption. The consequences of the unwanted pregnancy resolved, Cammy had not given much thought either to Anushka or the fate of the child. After his scholarship winning performance in the A-level exams, he traveled to England to study medicine.

Of course, Cammy knew he would have to do a blood test to make sure the young man's claim was genuine, but almost as soon as he revealed the identity of his birth mother, a part of him had immediately yielded to the idea of being a father. Glen Gibson, that was the young man's name, seemed to be about 20 or 21, which would be right, considering when Anushka disappeared, and Cammy could definitely see aspects of Donovan in him. His doctor's eye did notice a certain lack of vitality in the young man, but he felt sure that could be easily remedied with the proper diet and some vitamin B-12. He looked calmly, admiringly, at the young man, more pleased with his handiwork than concerned about what Glen Gibson might want.

Celeste Priddy was flabbergasted, not just at the sheer unreality of having this boy turn up, years later, on this of all days, but at the way her son had reacted, dumbstruck as if he had just been awarded an unexpected prize.

"How old are you?" she snapped.

"Twenty-one," Glen Gibson answered and flicked open a piece of paper. Celeste Priddy glanced at it and handed it over to Cammy. The birth certificate, named Anushka Mutari, 22, as the mother and Cameron Dexter Priddy, 17, as the father.

"I thought you said your name was Gibson?" Cammy finally spoke, adopting his mother's stern tone even though he felt differently.

"I took the name of my adoptive parents," the young man answered, intensely scratching near his right eyebrow with one hand and the middle of his back with the other. The scratching left the area around his eyebrow a bright pink. "I was renamed Glen Gibson. That's the name I have gone by. I grew up in Fort Lauderdale, Florida."

"Have you ever met your biological mother?" Celeste Priddy asked.

"Not in person, ma'am, but I have spoken to her on the phone. She was the one who told us you were living in the United States," he said and pointed to Cammy.

"Us?"

"Me and my adoptive parents. Do you accept that you are my father, sir?"

The question too clearly indicated that a demand would follow if he accepted, so Cammy backed away from answering even though he believed the evidence before his eyes.

"Ah didn't say that atall. We need to check this out. Do some blood tests." His words had a tone of finality that in turn motivated the young man to speak more forcefully.

"With all due respect, sir, I don't have time for tests. My kidneys are failing, and I am not an acceptable candidate for dialysis. My doctor says my only chance of beating this disease is through a transplant. I am already on the waiting list, but I stand a better chance to live if I have the operation now and a close relative donates a kidney. That's why I have come to you, sir."

Cammy wobbled. A sharp twinge shot from his right shoulder to his lower right side. His eyes burned as he choked back nausea.

The young man saw Cammy's inner struggle. "This is a matter of life and death for me, sir. I need a yes or no right now. If you are not willing to help, I can make better use of my time finding and asking other relatives."

Cammy coughed and choked.

****

It was dark, past 9:00 p.m., as Cammy pulled out of his garage. Judge Priddy, driving in, signaled for him to stop. Both wound down their car windows.

"Are you awright?" the father asked, his dirge-like baritone voice a combination of distress and disappointment tinged with love and determination. It was the question he had asked Cammy many times

179

after Donovan's death. Then and now, the question sliced a path straight through the son's heart.

"I've just come from the police," Judge Priddy informed him. "Scraps is in some trouble."

"Yeah, Ma told me."

"We're going to have to help him."

"Sure, Dad. You know I'll do anything for Scraps. I'll call Tulame, my lawyer friend."

"That's all good, but there's something you have to make sure you do for Scraps."

"Consider it done. But it will have to wait till I get back. I've got some important things to take care of right now. Ma will explain. I'll get Tulame to call you. He'll take care of everything."

"This is important. It will take only a moment."

"I know Dad, but I really can't talk right now."

Judge Priddy was not reassured, and Cammy could see that. "Dad, I need to talk to Fina."

"You should wait till tomorrow to talk to her. You can't undo in one day things that have taken years to set. If you love her and she loves you, everything will be awright. Give this whole thing sometime to blow over."

"I hear what you're saying Dad, but this isn't about me and Fina. Go on inside and Ma will tell you what's come up. You'll understand why I have to see her now."

"Give yourselves time to sort things out."

"Okay, Dad, "I'll see you later," Cammy shouted, feeling elated by the fatherly advice.

Judge Priddy looked pained as Cammy's car rolled forward.

****

When Cammy walked in, Fina's townhouse was as solemn as early morning communion in a Catholic church. After a polite three-way greeting, Edna announced she was going to bed and furtively reminded Fina to talk to Cammy about Kizzy.

180

"Have a seat," Fina invited flatly.

Cammy did not sit down. He stood up straight, his hands crossed in front of him like a wayward schoolboy standing contrite in front of his headmaster.

"Fina, I'm truly very, very sorry for what happened today," he began. "I'm so sorry for the way I behaved. I had no right to shout at you or to walk out on you. I am truly sorry."

Fina sat with her head slightly bowed, listening but peering at a spot on the carpet as if she half expected a script of her response to pop up from it. She disliked it when Cammy became formal and spoke with a British accent. He reminded her of a former college mate whom they used to call "Iambic Pentameter" because he spoke English like some English aristocrat reciting Milton. Now here was his Trinidadian counterpart claiming he was truly sorry. This was not the Cammy who had gyrated with her the night they first met! This was not the slightly mischievous, irreverent man with the sing-song accent she so loved. *Her* Cammy was trapped somewhere inside this John Bull Englishman.

Fina had been hoping for *her* Cammy to say or do something so that she would not have to end their relationship as she had planned. He hadn't even come close. She choked back the disappointment, said nothing, and continued to stare at the unhelpful carpet.

Realizing Fina was not about to respond, Cammy continued. "Fina, I don't know what came over me this afternoon. I should never have left you at the church. I'm really surprised at myself. I promise I will never, ever, again let my emotions get the better of me. I hope you will forgive me. You know I love you and will do anything for you."

He paused to see if Fina would step into the opportunity provided by his declarations. She didn't.

"I realize I have to earn your trust and respect again," he continued. "That was not me back there," he pointed in the direction of the church. "You know that, right? Please forgive me, darl... dear."

Fina winced. "I have already forgiven you, *dear*," she half mocked. "I understand how you must have felt." She flopped backward on the sofa, her eyes wide open, staring at the ceiling.

"Really," Cammy blurted, pleased but uneasy. Fina's words were not quite matching her actions.

"Yeah, I have forgiven you," she answered, still staring at the ceiling. "To spring my secret on *you* like that, on *your* wedding day, I can't really blame you. I blame myself."

"Nuh, nuh," Cammy said, uncomfortable with the direction Fina had turned his mea culpa. "Yuh can't blame yourself."

"But I should've told you about my first marriage. If I had, none of this would've happened. What you said in church today is true. I want to blame others for my mistakes." She sat upright and looked directly at Cammy.

"Nuh, Fina," Cammy fell to his knees, seized Fina's hand, leaned over the side of the loveseat, his face just inches away from hers. She felt the rush of his warm, mint-flavored breath and saw the sweat beads on his forehead.

"Dat don't give me de right to get vex, to leave yuh in di chorch. Is our problem. Ah run when ah shouldn't have."

"Cammy, I appreciate what you're trying to do, but I have to take responsibility for my actions. Too many times I've let others make decisions for me. I'm through with that. From now on, I will do what's right for me," she declared with the confidence of a Lloyd's insurance policyholder.

"Ah understand what yuh saying," he tendered. "We mus' put this behind us. Make a clean start."

"Exactly!"

"Oh, Fina, what would I do without yuh? Yuh so understanding. Ah don't deserve yuh atall." He took her hand and gently kissed it. Fina recoiled and then clutched her tummy.

"Ah said ah was sorry," Cammy blurted, unable to reconcile her retreat with her agreeableness.

"Okay, we have to take things slow. Ah can't undo what happened today," he conceded, recalling his dad's advice and the urgent matter he wanted to talk about. "Ah'll do whatever it takes to bil' up yuh trust."

Fina's grimace turned into a scowl. She clutched her stomach and doubled over. Almost in spite of herself, her head fell between Cammy's chin and neck. He quickly put his hand around her shoulder. They snuggled into each other like puppies seeking the warm teats of their mother.

It may have been a minute later. It may have been longer. Either way, the words entered his consciousness faintly, from afar, like the sound of a siren in a car with the windows rolled up and the air conditioning blasting on full. "Hm, hm," he mumbled. Then the meaning of her words dawned on him.

"What?" Cammy jerked away from Fina and stood up. She fell back into the loveseat and spoke into the ceiling, softly but firmly: "I'm going back home."

"Going where? Yuh kyant be serious." But no sooner had he uttered these words than he saw the steely calmness in her eyes. "Why yuh doing this Fina? Yuh punishing me?"

"Punishing you? You think the world revolves around you, don't you? I'm doing what's right for me. Don't you see we're different and expect different things the other can't deliver?"

"So the difference make yuh going back to the insanity in Sierra Leone?"

Fina sat upright, took two deep breaths, and stared at Cammy as if he had committed a treasonable offense. "Yes, I am. At least there I know what insanity looks like: rebels, poverty, starvation, disease, blackouts, and potholes." She wanted to add and assholes like you. Instead she said, "Back home, I know when, where, and who to expect insanity from. Here, I can't tell what form it will take. It may be a mugger at an ATM, a psycho at a McDonald's, a disgruntled co-worker, a scared kid with a gun in school, or a druggie at *your* wedding. Heck, the insanity can even come from the person you trust the most, the one standing next to you, can't it? Now tell me, which place is more insane?"

"Ah nuh even goin' to argue with yuh, Fina."

"Don't! Because you won't change my mind. I'm going back, and that's it!"

"But you're carrying meh... our child, yuh know. Don't I have a say 'bout where it grows up?"

Fina suddenly realized the untidiness of their situation. She had not really considered her pregnancy. A child. Another rope to keep her tethered. "You lost any rights you had when you walked off today."

"Lost?"

"Yes, L-O-S-T, lost. The first chance you had to stand by me, you ran off, Cammy." Then, her voice broke. "You *ran*, Cammy. You left me alone, gad dammit! You cut the rope and ran. Life is about working together."

Cammy clamped his fingers around his head and squeezed. "Ah was angry, Fina. Ah sorry. If it had been the other way around, what will you have done?"

"I would be mad but I would have stood by your side."

"So, yuh neva goin' to forgive me?"

"I have. But that doesn't mean we now understand each other. We're different, and I can't be happy here. I just can't. You won't understand no matter how hard I try to explain. I have to go back home."

"So yuh goin' to take my child away from me. Yuh put pepper na yuh mouth to blow *dutty* outta meh eye?"

"No!" Fina snapped, shocked by the image and its implication.

"Wha' yuh call what yuh doing?"

"I cut the rope and must mend it, Cammy. I've taken the wrong path."

"What rope? What path yuh talking 'bout? Ah tired with yuh mystical nonsense. Yuh talking 'bout meh child. Our child. Ah not going to let yuh walk away wit' meh child, yuh know. Ah not."

Fina had not moved from the loveseat. She folded her arms across her stomach and gently rocked herself back and forth. Cammy paced around the loveseat, muttering to himself and exhaling plumes of anger mixed with guilt and sadness. He had felt this way once before, many years ago, at Donovan's funeral.

****

Cammy remembered the mourners, all dressed up, wearing long faces, hugging and patting one another on the back, praying and singing, saying "Amen," "Lord have mercy," asserting Donovan was "a good boy," "a good son," but doing nothing. Get up! Do something! Bring my brother back, he screamed. But no one heard him because the screaming was all in his head.

"It was so sudden," his grandfather muttered, shaking his head as he turned and walk away. But Cammy knew Donovan's death was not sudden. Months before he died, he had stopped playing football during lunch. He went straight to bed after they came from school, daily complained he was tired when he woke up, and winced and poked at his sides. Cammy wanted to tell their parents, but Donovan had made him promise not to tell them. Then Donovan had fainted in school. The next day he was dead. Cammy's grief was deep, in contrast to how the explanation of Donavan's death was brief. As he had stared at his brother's grave that funeral day, his head had been full of the chant their octogenarian maid had taught them after she got word her son had died:

Wayiiiii,
Mi pikin day (die) today,
Aayiiiii, he don go 'ome to meet him Maker,
Goodbye, go wayi-wayi goodbye.

As it had done years ago to the boy, the chant now consumed the frazzled mind of the man. He bowed his head onto the dining-room table to which he had retreated, closed his eyes, and softly chanted to himself.

Fina remained in the loveseat, lost in her own thoughts, so she could not be certain for how long she had been sitting when

185

Cammy's forlorn chant registered itself on her conscious mind. She concentrated enough to hear the tune that broke through his slightly parted lips. It reminded her of the women's melancholy cries the night her father snatched her from the *fafei*. They were not ordinary cries, originating in the vocal chords and complemented by tears. They came from the soul, the source of awareness and understanding. Memories—firelight darkness, sorrowful chanting—suddenly consumed Fina in love-sorrow for Baramusu, the women, and the age-mates she lost that initiation night; for her father and mother whose lives changed forever after that night; and tonight for Cammy, slouched over the dining table like a spent boxer after a grueling bout. She absorbed his sorrow and her body shivered. Cupping her lower tummy to brace the cramps she felt, Fina carefully rose from the loveseat and lumbered over to Cammy. She parted his knees, inserted herself between his thighs, and encircled him in her arms, her head resting on his chest as if she was attempting a psychic meld. He yielded to the melding but continued his melancholy chant, his eyes closed. He had repeated himself several times before his mind registered that Fina was singing along with him, though her words sounded different. He stopped singing and listened.

Waiyooooo, mal soey ar' tiyan
Atalaaaaaa, ama feleh n'bara min keh n'na la
Waiyo N'Na, yo N'Na, yo N'Na.

"My grandmother taught me that song," Fina explained when she noticed he was listening to her. "The song comes from the story of Musudugu, a village in which only women lived."

"Tell it to me."

Fina got off her knees and, Cammy in tow, walked back over to the loveseat, where, holding hands, she told him the story of the women of Musudugu. "... and that's how their utopia was destroyed."

"So yuh saying our old maid's chant is the same as your grandmother's song?"

186

Fina shrugged her shoulders. "Has to be. What other explanation is there?"

"Makes sense. Our old maid always said she was African. We laughed at her."

"Cammy," Fina became suddenly serious, "I told you that I went through initiation right?" Cammy nodded. Fina took a deep breath. "Well, that's only half the story. You see, my parents did not want me to go through initiation, so when my father found out my grandmother had taken me to it, he did what no man is ever supposed to do. He walked into the *fafei*, that's the initiation bush, and snatched me. He took me directly to the dispensary where the nurse was able to sew me up because I had received only a partial cut."

"So, you're... do you have—"

"Gosh, Cammy! Having or not having is not the point." She released his hand and shifted away, turning her back to him to emphasize her displeasure.

"Okay, okay. Jus' talk to me. Ah listening," Cammy reached over and pulled her back to him. She did not resist but would not speak.

"Ah listening," Cammy encouraged. After a suitable delay, Fina resumed.

"That night as we ran away and the branches of the trees flagged our faces in rebuke, I realized my father truly loved me. He had risked the wrath of the village and the ancestors for me. I learned that day that love is about sacrifice. That's what I mean when I say I'll support Isa, and I want to go home to build a center for abused, orphaned, and ostracized girls. Cammy, are you capable of the kind of love that is sacrifice?"

He opened his mouth to answer, but Fina put a finger across his lips. She took another deep breath. "You see, as I lay in the dispensary, I could hear the cries of Baramusu and the other women, clear as if they were just outside the window. But it wasn't just that I could hear their cries. I also felt their pain and sense of loss. Nothing binds people together like shared pain and loss. Can you share in my pain? The pain that is love?"

187

Cammy stared at Fina. He was uncomfortable with Fina's psycho-mystical talk, but the day's mix of pain, loss, and love had been just enough for him not to be dismissive. He continued to listen.

"That song you sang earlier is about pain and loss. Unlike Kumba Kargbo, I don't want to be the cause of pain for you or anyone else." By now, Fina's voice had softened to a whisper. She massaged his hands, raised and kissed them, and looked into his eyes. "I want you to know that I appreciate that you came this evening, and I love you for it."

"Oh, Fina, I doh'n know wha' to say. I doh'n deserve you," Cammy exclaimed. Both sensed they were finally on a path toward understanding and renewal.

Chapter 19

For over an hour, Fina told Cammy the whole story of her marriage and divorce from Jemal. It was part explanation, confession, and expiation. When she stopped talking, she leaned back into the loveseat and closed her eyes, reviewing her account to see if she had left anything out.

"Fina, I have something to tell you too," Cammy broke into her thoughts, his head half-bowed, and his face suddenly serious. "But, honestly, I did not know about it. Well, I did but I had... let's say that—"

"Say it, Cammy," Fina cut him off and opened her eyes, apprehensive but eager to have in the open whatever it was he wanted to say. The stomach discomfort she had been feeling since Isa's phone call had evolved into a strident, ongoing pain.

Cammy took a deep breath. "I have a son," he exhaled and waited for Fina's reaction. When he did not get one, he raised his head to see Fina's face. The revelation that he had a son coincided with another sharp twinge in her stomach, so Fina had a pained look on her face. Cammy saw it and immediately concluded she must be thinking he had been cheating on her. "No, no," he began with a slight chuckle, like someone about to give a simpler, more acceptable explanation to the sinister one in the offing. "The son I am talking about is twenty-one years old."

Cammy had somehow expected this piece of information to put the episode in perspective, so he was taken aback by Fina's stunned look. He immediately launched into a rambling narrative filled with "thens," "but thens," and "so whens." Many minutes, false starts, and clarifications later, he ended, "So I don't know what to do. Should I? Do I have an obligation to make this kind of sacrifice?"

"Yes. Absolutely you do," Fina declared. It was now Cammy's turn to be pained. He knew Fina had a way of separating issues. He had counted on it, but he had hoped for a more gradual, give-and-take process to help *him* arrive at a decision. This flat, out-of-nowhere declaration, with no in-between, irritated him. It's easy to be decisive about someone else's kidney, he thought, but said, prudence getting the better of his impulse, "Yuh not worried 'bout what the transplant means for us, for our child, for our future?"

"Sure I am. You're certain he's your son, right?" she asked. Cammy nodded a yes.

"Then you've got to behave like a father. I just told you about mine. Real fathers sacrifice themselves for their kids. Just do it. You can deal with consequences later. It's the least you can do," Fina ended.

Cammy heard the indictment. "But I was young."

"So, does that make him any less your child? That's why you men should think with your big head. What do you want the boy to do now?"

"Well, I could talk to one of my friends to see if we can get him pushed up on the transplant waiting list."

"You know that's a long shot. Besides, he could die waiting. What will you say then?"

"No, no. I'll make sure he gets the best care."

But Fina was definite that donating his kidney was the right thing to do. "I wouldn't even be thinking about it," she said, bending over to stifle another twinge from her stomach but looking upward at Cammy. He noticed that Fina seemed uncomfortable, but he was too full of gratitude she had not dwelled on his secret like he had on hers to consider her discomfort came from any other source but him.

He wondered how in just a few hours he had moved from the height of self-righteous indignation to the depths of guilty humility. At the hospital, he had often witnessed these sudden plunges in fate and fortune. Patients he fully expected to recover had suddenly, inexplicably, died, and those he expected to die had just as inexplicably and stubbornly gone on to live full and long lives. But he had thought these changes in fortune were confined only to issues of life and death. It was hard for him to conceive, for instance, that he could become a poor man. He was set for life. His stocks and varied

190

portfolio assured he would be comfortable even if he stopped working today. Besides, he had mobile skills that could provide him with a living wage far above what most people earned wherever he lived, even in some remote corner of the Himalayas. Grateful that Fina had not pressed her advantage, Cammy only now understood all too clearly that one's present could begin unraveling from a stitch sewn years earlier.

The realization was sobering. The day had been full of sharp angles and awkward turns. But he had learned long ago from Donovan's death that the important thing was how one responded to changes rather than how loud one moaned about them. So he decided he would give his kidney to this newfound son, if the paternity and compatibility tests panned out. His gratitude that Fina never mentioned his keeping secrets from her also weighed heavily in his decision.

Cammy felt relieved. As he answered Fina's questions about the circumstances leading up to Glen's birth and adoption, and the specific details of the tests and operation, he felt excited, like the way he used to when they first met, before the problems in her country started. He felt happy that he and Fina were back on track. His father was not right after all. Immediate attention to a problem, before it worsened, was just as good a remedy as time. But it was when he spied Fina's dark brown areola through the wide sleeve of the gown lazily covering her outstretched body that he realized some of his excitement laid deep in his unfulfilled consummation. He recalled how her nipples contrasted against her light skin and how they would feel granular as she became aroused.

"Let's make sure *nuttin* like this ever happen again, okay?" he said to Fina.

"Okay," she answered softly, her head resting comfortably on top of his, as his white-shirted chest gently undulated.

"Yuh have other secrets I should know about?" he joked. She groaned a *no* into his hair. Then settling her head back, she closed her eyes and searched the deep darkness they ushered. No, she had no more secrets to tell. Moments later, still without lifting her head she asked, "Do you?"

"Not atall," he answered, looking down briefly at her hair and then staring into the television as if it were a portal into the past where he could find answers. The laugh track of some situation comedy rerun suddenly sounded loudly. "Not atall," Cammy repeated.

Suddenly excited, Fina pushed his head from her chest and proclaimed, "I do have something to ask, though." He wasn't alarmed. He pushed her arms aside, laid his head back on her bosom, and deftly glided his hand through the wide opening of her sleeve. As if by accident, he let his hand rest on the naked, warm side of her body. Fina felt the hand and noticed all his other subtle shifts and adjustments. She welcomed them.

"Kizzy told Edna you saw what happened at the church," Fina began.

Cammy nodded and gave Fina a blow-by-blow of the encounter.

"You've got to tell the police what you saw, Cammy."

"Of all yuh people, he's the one ah like least. He mocked my accent, yuh know. But I'll tell the police what I saw."

Cammy snuggled up to Fina. They stayed like that for a while.

"Cammy," Fina said, breathing ever so lightly, "you promise never to leave me like that again?"

"Yeah man," Cammy mumbled, his mouth full of her cotton gown. She let out a soft moan, arched her back, and convulsed into him. Cammy could not remember when she had been so responsive, and so he pushed and squeezed and pressed. From somewhere within the amorous fog, Fina felt consciously pleased. Her mind and her body had become one again, comfortable, known, like when one returns to the home of one's childhood. Each step into a room, pull of a drawer, peer out of a window, feel of a mattress, touch of a photograph produced a particular but familiar pleasure. Fina's body sang joyfully. She could feel the music rising to a crescendo, like the final act of an orchestral piece.

But like all such visits to the past, one eventually encounters the evidence of change, decay, and sees the places and things that revive the painful, long-suppressed memories. Fina's body must have reached that turning point, for her joyful pleasure changed to blinding, cramping waves.

"*Waiyo, waiyoya, waiyo,*" she erupted and collapsed backward.

"Wha' 'appen?" Cammy jumped to alertness and stared at Fina who lay supine on the loveseat.

"Something's wrong, something's wrong," she blurted and attempted to stand up as if the source of the problem lay underneath her. Cammy helped her up. Spots and smudges of blood mapped the space where she had been sitting.

Chapter 20

A man woke up earlier than usual for a Sunday morning. She sprang from her bed, put on a housecoat, walked downstairs and sat at the kitchen table. After her conversation with her mother before the wedding, she had reluctantly accepted that Bayo was not returning. She decided selling the furnishings she had kept in storage for the home they were going to make was the first step in remaking her life and self. She compiled a list. At first, she proposed prices well below cost. She just wanted to get rid of them. But as each item reminded her of a conversation or an experience with Bayo, she increased the prices. By the end of her second cup of coffee, each item had been revised two or three times and was selling well above cost.

It was that time of the morning when the sun had been up long enough to cast light but not long enough to make heat. That ambient light eased itself into the kitchen through the yellowed and frayed lace curtains. It caressed Aman's broad back as she continued working on her inventory, which had now grown to three full sheets and included mementos from former boyfriends she was determined to auction off along with an erstwhile fickle self.

Aman realized she had not heard any noise coming from upstairs. That pleased her, for if her mother was awake and about, she would want to offer more advice about dealing with Bayo. And no matter how well meaning, rebuke sat staunchly within such advice. Aman did not want either. The silence upstairs also meant her sister Shantea probably came home very late, probably was very drunk, and probably was very asleep. Aman wondered who Shantea had been out with. She seemed able to change boyfriends at will. Aman wished she had just a smidgen of her sister's toughness. Then, as if to convert such a wish into action, she added the engagement ring to the list followed by three exclamation marks. She was in the midst of savoring the emphatic way she had closed Bayo out of her life when the phone rang.

"Oh, hello, Cammy," her tone reflecting surprise. He had never called her before. "I'll be right there." Aman gulped down her coffee, showered, and changed after she learned from Cammy Fina had been hospitalized. She was walking down the stairs when she saw the outline of a person open the door of their screened front porch. Aman skipped the last two steps to the front door to prevent the person from pounding with the door knocker and waking her mom and Shantea.

"Who is it?" she asked.

"Adebayo," the voice said.

"Baryour? BARYOUR! Is that you?"

"Yes, it's me, Bayo. Have you forgotten me already?"

Aman turned the door knob back and forth, twisted and yanked several times.

"I think you need to unlock the door first."

"Duh," Aman slapped her forehead with the fleshy base part of her palm. "Hold on." She dashed into the kitchen. From a wooden holder fixed to the wall behind the fridge, she plucked a bunch of keys and sidled out of the kitchen. The sheets of paper containing her list of things to sell stared at her in disdain. Aman paused. She realized her excitement was running roughshod over her resolve. She inhaled, slowed down, inserted the key into the lock but did not unlock the door.

"What are you doing here, Bayo?"

"This is the welcome I get?"

"You're gone for over three months, don't even write, and expect a ticker-tape parade?"

Aman turned the knob, opened the door, and tried to walk past Bayo. "Fina's not well. I have to go and see her." Bayo barred her way.

"I was also not well. Didn't you get my letter?"

"No I didn't. Where were you, Baryour?"

"I'm here." Bayo stepped closer to Aman. "Whatever you're thinking, it's wrong. You don't know what I've been through."

"What *you've* been through? Do you know what it's been like for *me*? Please move out of my way." Aman shoved Bayo backwards. He held his ground.

"Do you *really* believe that I would leave you for three months without so much as calling or writing?"

Aman wished a little of the resolute woman of the early morning would step forward. But like a trespasser at the sight of a land owner, that woman did a U-turn at the advancing Bayo.

"Did you get married?"

"How did you know about that?"

"Does it matter? Have you come here to marry your second wife?"

"Not a bad idea, but for *you* to qualify as a second wife, I'd need to have a first wife, right? So I am here to marry and make you wife number one. I can have a second wife later."

Months of accumulated anxiety and doubt tumbled to the floor. "So, you're not married or engaged?"

"Well, yes and no."

"Don't mess with me, Baryour."

I'm engaged to you. That's the yes part. I am not engaged or married. That's the no..."

Aman fell into his arms. He clasped and lifted her. Warmth and delight rippled through their bodies until Aman gasped for air. Bayo let her down, removed his hands from around her, transferred them to her face, squared it, and moved to kiss her. Aman shifted her head to one side like a boxer avoiding a blow and pushed him back.

"But why would your brother-in-law say you were getting married if you weren't?" The accusation and anger she tried to muster limped out as disappointment and insecurity.

"I don't know. My folks did have a girl picked out, but I told them I had an American queen waiting for me. We never..." he stopped. "Sit down for a minute. I have something important to say."

He clasped her face and gently kissed her lips. Aman's heart melted. He guided her to the weather-beaten leather sofa with the sagging cushions stationed in the corner of the porch. After some awkward shifting to adjust to the cushions, they settled into the sofa. It had been the site of many late-night, amorous activities, made all the more memorable because of the participation of some bloodthirsty mosquitoes that had flown in through the gaping holes of the screen.

For a short while, neither talked, confronted, it seemed, by the view of the disheveled front lawn—the street lined with aging Buicks, Pontiacs, and pickup trucks; and, to their right, the oil-stained concrete driveway that led to the watermarked garage door that had not been opened in over a year. As if he did not like the meaning spelled out by the scene, Bayo grabbed Aman's hands and folded them into his own.

"Let's get married tomorrow," Bayo proposed. "I don't want to wait anymore."

"We can't, Baryour, you know that. Why are you in such a rush, anyway?"

Bayo hesitated. Aman pulled back and stared at him.

"I want us to go back to Nigeria right after we get married."

"What? I can't just leave Ma and go to somewhere I know no one."

"Nigeria is not just somewhere. It's home to 150 million living, breathing humans."

"Don't go there. Bayo. You go away for months, don't write, march back here, and announce you want me to go back to your country."

"Nigeria, Aman, *Nigeria*."

"It could be Bugugeria for all I care. We made a decision together! Now, all by your high and mighty self, you change it, and you want me to jump up with joy, pack up, and leave without so much as giving me a chance to think about it."

"I'm not making the decision for you," Bayo muttered, stung and taken aback by Aman's anger. He had not expected her to be

198

deliriously happy, but he had calculated that the joy of being married and going with him to the Africa she always fondly talked about would easily quell any anxieties she had.

"I am making a proposal. I value you."

"Yeah, right! By scraping the plans *we* made and replacing them with new ones you've come up with all by yourself. Yeah I can see how you value me."

"Gosh! Was I supposed to have called and asked for your opinion when the village that paid for me to come and study asks me to stay on to help?"

"Yes, *yes*! What's so hard about that? If you had called and told me, the whole thing would not seem so sudden. But you spring the change on me and expect me to just pick up and go to live in a strange country—"

"Yes, just like I came to live in this strange country."

Aman heard Bayo but continued to make her point.

"Did you ever think how your parents would feel about me after you rejected the woman they chose for you?" Aman paused. "This is *so* unfair." She stopped talking, shifted to one end of the sofa, and folded her arms across her stomach.

"My folks will treat you with respect and welcome you as part of the family."

"I can't do this, Bayo. I just can't," Aman stood up. "Who's going to look after Ma?"

"Look, Aman, I don't literally mean tomorrow. I thought you were the one who always wanted to go to Africa. Now you have the opportunity, and you start coming up with excuses why you can't."

"That's not fair. This is too sudden, and you just don't seem to understand that I would have liked to have been asked instead of being told."

"Admit it. The only reason why you're reacting this way is because you've never even remotely considered living in Nigeria. Doing the tourist thing maybe. You want to marry a Nigerian, and you assume he would only want to live here."

"That's not my point and you know it. This is about equal input. I want both of us to decide where we live, whether in Nigeria, America, or Mars!"

"No, *you* don't get it. Did we discuss living in America? No, you just assumed that to be a given. Did you consider, for even one moment, that Nigeria could be somewhere else we could live?"

Aman hesitated, sensing the logic of his claim, but replied, "Baryour, living in Nigeria didn't come up between us. What you want is for me to be doing cartwheels because I am grateful you want to marry me. Sorry, that's not going to happen."

Bayo opened his mouth to respond, but Aman did not give him a chance. "This is not about living or not living in Nigeria. It's about letting me take part in decisions that will affect the two of us. And let me tell you, even if you don't think leaving my mother behind with Shantea is a big deal, I know it is. Sure she works and seems independent, but she still hurts after dad left. Sometimes, I wake up at night and hear her talking to herself. At other times she's crying, and I have to go and talk to her. Shantea doesn't have time for that. She—"

"Wha' don't I have time for?" Shantea poked her head past the front door and looked into the porch. "Hmmm, if it ain't the African prince," she exclaimed.

"Hello, Tea," Bayo replied. "How are you?"

"Don't be worrying 'bout me. Where you been, African prince?"

"Look, Baryour," Aman interrupted, "we need to go and see Fina. We can talk more about *your* change of plans in the car." She pulled Bayo after her and bundled him out of the porch.

"Change of plans? You better not be messing with my sister, African prince," Shantea mocked.

****

"It's called a threatened miscarriage," Cammy explained over Fina's mutterings and movements on the hospital bed. It was around noon, the Sunday after the aborted Saturday wedding. Cammy sat in

200

a single imitation-leather recliner on one side of the bed. On the other side, Aman sat in a ladder-back, metal chair with a vinyl seat. Bayo, jetlagged, stretched out on the hospital pull-out guest sofa directly behind Aman. He vaguely followed Aman and Cammy's conversation. They talked in subdued tones. Whenever Fina moved or muttered, they paused to see if she was waking up. When she did not, they continued their conversation. The smell of disinfectant hung in the air.

"But the baby is okay now," Aman whispered in a half-question, half-statement.

"Oh yes," Cammy assured.

"And everything is okay with Fina, right? Internally, I mean."

"Yes, she's fine."

They had never before talked to each other without Fina. Both felt awkward. They fell silent for a while until Aman asked Cammy what caused threatened miscarriages.

"Difficult to pin down, but stress is the most common cause. We are doing some tests to make sure nothing else is going on."

"Look, she's waking up." Aman stood and picked up Fina's left hand. Cammy sprang up too. He eased one hand under Fina's limp right hand and caressed her hair. She looked beautiful. He wanted to take care of her, to make her well again, to erase all the misunderstanding and hurt so they could recapture the unfettered, uncomplicated joy of their early days.

Fina opened her eyes, recognized Aman and Cammy, and mumbled a parched, weary hello to them. She was relieved to see them, but her relief was short-lived, for she recognized she was in a hospital and remembered why. She closed her eyes to shut in the sadness threatening to erupt in tears.

Cammy and Aman thought she had gone back to sleep, so they sat down again. Fina would have kept her eyes closed considerably longer, except that she heard movements and light snoring. Curious, she opened her eyes, eased her head to the right of Aman, and saw Bayo on the sofa. A smile radiated over her face, and a cheerful feeling, akin to but not quite happiness, enveloped her body. She was

201

delighted for Aman and felt a kinship with Bayo, even though they had never been really close. She felt he would understand her in ways Cammy and Aman could not.

Aman, noticing Fina's movement, slapped Bayo on the leg and woke him up.

"When did you get back?" Fina's voice cracked into picnic gaiety. Cammy noticed.

"At the same time as the dew," Bayo answered. He saw the puzzled look on Fina's face and followed up with, "That means just this morning."

"I bet somebody's happy to see you," Fina looked first at Aman and then at Bayo. Neither looked amused.

"Okay, what's going on?" Fina asked.

"I want us to get married," Bayo blurted.

"Don't leave anything out," Aman said. "Tell her you not only want to get married, but you want me to pack up and leave for Nigeria right after."

"Why?" Cammy inquired. "I mean, why do you want to go back?" he addressed Bayo directly, more because he wanted to steer the conversation away from marriage than because he felt the idea was wrong.

"I'm waiting for the answer to that question myself," Aman said.

"It's not like you've given me much chance to explain," Bayo sat upright and moved to the edge of the sofa. They waited for his answer.

"Let's talk about something else," Cammy said. "She," he pointed at Fina, "doesn't need any of this heavy-duty, going-back-home talk."

"I'm fine. I want to hear about Nigeria. It will take my mind away from this." She caressed her tummy.

Reminded why they were in the hospital, the visitors showered Fina with hugs, kisses, words of encouragement, and inquiries about her health—appetizers to a main meal, for no sooner had the expressions of concern and empathy run their course than Fina asked Bayo to explain why he was in such a hurry to return immediately after they married. Cammy frowned.

"My sponsors, the villagers, want me to go back to help them. You could say they want to see some return on their investment."

"I thought you said you worked to pay your fees," Aman said.

"I did, but that was after I got here. They paid for my plane ticket, tuition, and room and board for the first year."

"How much, Baryour?"

"Five thousand. A lot of money for laborers, farmers, and petty traders."

"Pay the money back then."

"I could, but I don't want to. It would be wrong."

"Wrong?" Aman stared at Bayo in disbelief.

Bayo stared back and then exhaled his irritation. "Yes, wrong. My father and uncle gave their word I would go back to help. I have an obligation to them, Aman." His voice wavered between a plea and a declaration.

Aman heard only the declaration. "And what obligation do you have to me, to us?" The tone of her questions depressed the mood in the room like an unexpected power outage during a convivial nighttime gathering of friends.

Bayo stood up, paced around the room for a few moments, then turned and addressed Aman.

"Not everyone in my village thought sending me abroad was a good idea. America is like *Mammy Wata*, they said. She turns people's heads and makes them slaves to their desires."

Bayo paused to let the assertion sink in.

"Do you know what my father said in response to them?" Again, no one answered. "'A bird that does not leave its nest to find food for fear it might lose its way back home will surely starve to death. The food it finds from flying into the unknown is what gives it the nourishment and strength to find its way home.'"

Fina's eyes lit up. Cammy noticed.

"For a long time, I did not really understand what he meant," Bayo continued. "I do now." His voice had softened to a whisper.

Aman, Fina, and Cammy were fully aware that soliloquies often have peaks and valleys, so they waited for Bayo to continue.

"I *have* to give something back to those traders, farmers, and laborers. I *have* to return to the nest."

"Return to the nest," Aman echoed, her imitation starched with sarcasm. "Get off your highfalutin' horse Mr. Savior-of-his-people. If you knew you had a *'nest'* to *'return'* to, you shouldn't have started building one here. Darn, Baryour! Why are you doing this to me? What have I done to you to deserve this? This relationship has been nothing but a lie." Aman walked to the pull-out hospital sofa, sat down, and covered her face with her hands.

"You don't understand," Bayo rushed to the side of the sofa and knelt down. "Look at me," Bayo tried to lift up her head by the chin and twist her shoulders so she could face him.

"Leave me alone!" Aman rocked her head and shoulders free of his efforts.

Annoyed and perplexed, Bayo stood up, then turned and stared at Cammy and Fina.

"*Ha bo*, you men!" Fina groaned, pained both by her effort to get out of bed and what she regarded as Bayo's neon-bright idiocy.

"Don't think you should be getting out of bed," Cammy cautioned as he reached over to steady her.

"Don't touch me. You guys are thoughtless and inconsiderate," Fina grunted as her body and the intravenous drip caddy resisted her efforts to walk. Cammy and Bayo reached out to assist her. She rebuffed their efforts and hobbled over to Aman.

"Get back to bed, Fina," Aman jostled Cammy and Bayo aside, escorted and then settled Fina back into her bed. The women patted each other's hands and shot contemptuous glances at the men.

Cammy was the first to react. "Gonna be awright, Aman. Gonna be okay," he mumbled and massaged her shoulder. Cammy's display of empathy warmed Fina's heart. It reminded her that a compassionate man was cocooned inside the sometimes clinical doctor. If she could explode that shell and release the loving man, she felt there would be hope for him and a future for them.

Cammy on the path to resurrection, it was now Bayo's turn to make an overture to Aman.

204

"I'm leaving," he declared.

"Why?" Fina screeched.

"To go and save his people."

"See, she's all lip and—"

"She has a right to be upset. You don't decide to move to another country like *that*," Fina snapped her fingers and then immediately glanced at Aman. The stared at each other for a moment and smiled knowingly. A little hypocrisy was well worth seeing their men on the defensive.

"Fina, my plan was to go home, see my folks, and come back. But I nearly died. I guarantee that changes your priorities. I never thought I would feel this way, but things are bad back home. A few live like royalty. The rest make do with little or nothing. I want to do my little bit to change things. I can't just turn my back on my country."

"Yeah, but you want to turn your back on me."

"Code Blue, sixth floor," the public address system blared into the silence. The smell of disinfectant reasserted itself.

"So what's going on back home?" Fina asked but noticed Cammy's unease. "I'm sure Aman would understand if you'd taken the time to explain how difficult things are. Why don't you try now?"

Bayo wanted to begin his exposition, but it took their collective cajoling before Aman deigned to listen. She registered her displeasure by rolling her eyes and sighing through his narrative.

"Roads, cars, machines, hospitals, electricity, water. Where do I begin? There's so much that's run down, broken, and very little in place to maintain and repair. But if people like us go back and help, I don't think it will take much to turn things around."

"You should have written or called, Baryour," Aman intervened.

"I couldn't. I was in a coma. Look at me," Bayo thrust his thin body forward. "Can't you see I have lost a lot of weight? Less than five days after I regained consciousness, I am here, with you. My parents pleaded with me to wait until I got stronger, but I said no."

"You could have had a relative or friend call to let me know what was going on, Baryour. How hard is that?" Aman persisted.

205

"I was unconscious, Aman! Calling you was not on my mind. Get it? As soon as I regained consciousness, I tried calling but making international calls from a remote village is an ordeal. Judging from how you are reacting now, we would just have argued if I had got through."

"Sounds very convenient to me."

"Convenient? I left my parents living with Lassa fever, may even have been exposed to it myself, got on a plane to come back to you, and all I get is attitude."

Aman was about to fire off a rejoinder when Cammy cut in, his medical interest piqued. "Lassa fever, how so?"

"Our village is infested with rats. I noticed them the very day I got there. They're everywhere and some are as big as small dogs."

"Urr," the women squirmed in exaggerated terror.

"So you think the rats transmit the fever?" Cammy rubbed his chin.

"Yes. The local authorities say people are getting sick from eating food contaminated by their urine or droppings."

"Can it be spread from person to person?" Aman asked, barely stifling her concern.

"Yes, especially if you come into contact with the bodily fluids of an infected person. I'm afraid the virus can be passed out in semen up to three months after exposure."

They all thought the same thing, but no one spoke. Sensing their concern, Cammy added. "But it cannot be spread through casual contact. Bayo, you'd better get tested just to be on the safe side."

"Can he do the test here? I don't think my sister can wait three months," Fina tried to choke off a smile.

"He was going to have to wait a lot longer anyway. Now with this, he may not be getting any." Aman maintained a serious, concerned look.

"How soon after you got to your village did you get sick, and what were your symptoms?" Cammy continued his impromptu consultation.

"About four days after. I woke up one morning feeling pain in my back and chest. At first, I thought it was the straw mattress. Then I thought malaria, so I took an extra dose of Mefloqiune. I figured it would help. And that's about as much as I remember. My parents said that by evening my face was swollen. Next came diarrhea and vomiting."

"Have you noticed any personality changes since you fell ill?" The doctor in Cammy was now in full throttle.

"Yeah, he left here sane and came back crazy," Aman cracked.

"No, but I'm having difficulty hearing." Bayo ignored her.

"That's right, but don't go blaming African rats. He had that problem before he left America."

"Amaaan," Fina faked reproach.

"How's all this connected to Lassa fever?" Bayo continued to ignore Aman.

"It's sometimes associated with personality changes, hair loss and deafness. Know what, why don't you come with me, and let's see if we can get some blood work done?"

****

When Bayo and Cammy returned some hours later, it was late afternoon and Edna was in the room with Aman and Fina. Not waiting for questions, Cammy told them that the preliminary results indicated Bayo probably had a severe case of malaria and not Lassa fever. They would be certain after they got the results of more sophisticated tests.

"What about his deafness?" Aman asked.

Cammy smiled. "That seems to be fluid buildup in his ears."

"Nooooo, are you sure? I could have sworn it was due to some defect you men are born with." The women laughed. Bayo frowned and sat down on the pull-out sofa.

"*You're* in a good mood, Aman. I've put him on a course of antibiotics. The ear problem should clear up in a few days."

As an uneasy quiet took over the room, Cammy told Fina he had been cleared for the transplant.

"What's wrong?" Aman asked.

Fina gave her audience a Cammy-friendly version of Glen Gibson's story. It left the women admiring Cammy and exhorting the virtues of working as a couple in the face of character-testing events. These upbeat feelings, combined with Cammy's assenting nods that he would tell the police what he saw, inspired Edna. She invited the assembled group to her house for a Saturday night dinner and get-together. "Nothing fancy," she explained. "Something intimate, so we can get to know each other better and celebrate overcoming adversity."

Chapter 21

Six days later, exactly one-week after the aborted wedding, Edna greeted her guests with, "Welcome to my humble abode" accompanied by a curtsy. She was dressed in a contemporary three-piece *Kente*-cloth *buba*, *sokoto* pants, and hat, all of them embroidered in gold. She then introduced the newly arrived guests to the already arrived and walked them over to a cocktail table covered in a tie-dyed tablecloth. Joining them, Kizzy invited the newly arrived to try the Caribbean and African specialties—rice porridge laced with rum, freshly squeezed sorrel, and ginger beer. Against Edna's wishes, he had added bottled palm wine from Nigeria but, after one woman gagged on her first sip and described the drink to her husband as "gad-awful and chalky," Edna, unobserved by Kizzy, seized the palm wine bottles and stuffed them into the back of the pantry. Later, she accepted without comment Kizzy's self-satisfied observation that the guests drank all the palm wine and that *she* had been wrong to think no one would like it. Edna made a mental note to get rid of the bottles before he woke up the next day.

Once the guests were seated, hors d'oeuvres of black-eyed bean fritters served with a corn relish dip were passed around in hand-woven baskets lined with green, white, and blue linen. The tight vocals, intricate guitar work, and talking drums of King Sunny Ade's juju music; the aroma of fried plantains, sweet potatoes, and simmering collard greens; and the tonal accents emanating from clusters of conversation filled the air and enticed the senses.

The call to dinner came at 8:00 p.m. sharp. A medley of African foods surrounded the centerpiece, a wide galvanized bowl adorned with palm fronds and filled with papaya, pineapple, mango, coconut, oranges, bananas, persimmons, and sweet-and-sour sop.

Some guests ate exclusively from the whole snapper laid out on a brightly colored platter garnished with parsley sprigs and lemon wedges. "It is baked in banana leaves," Edna explained as she supervised their selections like a grandmother plying the neighborhood kids with food from her overfilled pantry. Other guests ate from the shingled rows of roasted pork loin coated with toasted cornmeal and cumin seeds. "Don't forget the mango, papaya, and lime salsa. It's supposed to go with the couscous. Try the rice seasoned with smoked fish and coconut milk," she suggested to some and directed others to the vegetables and crusty French bread. When it came to the desserts, she prodded the guests to try a little of the all-butter pound cake, the sweet potato pie baked with butterscotch liqueur, or the yam pie sweetened with sorghum molasses. Rice bread and rice *akara* cake chunks were the finger foods of choice throughout the evening.

The children had been packed off to bedrooms to amuse themselves on PlayStations and Nintendos. Although some of them did eat from the fare of the buffet, their cuisine was supplemented by hot dogs and pizzas. While the adults ate, the children asked Kizzy to play some of *their* music. A number of the youngsters had twisted, jerked, spun, and gyrated to a mix of hip hop and rap that thumped from the speakers.

Initially, the parents had been content to snigger at the "gymnastics" their children called dancing, but the base guitars harmonized with ancient rhythms deep within them and soon moms and dads, their joints creaking in resistance, imitated their children, to the bemusement of all. For a while, music bridged the generation gap, but Kizzy, who at one time supplemented his income by working as a D. J., gradually forced the children back into the bedrooms with a relay of maringa, calypso, salsa, and reggae that appealed to the older generations. For close to an hour, they danced, their bodies speaking a language that needed no translation.

Fina had been apprehensive about being in the same room and possibly even the same conversation as Kizzy. They had not made any special effort to avoid each other because the number of guests, the eating, and the dancing provided them with natural buffers. It was only after most of the guests had left and only family remained that they had to sit within the same conversation. Even then, Fina did not have much time to think about the past because the talk centered on the present and the future.

"I want to return home to train and give young girls skills that will make them independent," Fina had announced as her contribution to a discussion about returning home.

Cammy smiled to see the childlike excitement that had so enamored him in their early days return to Fina's eyes, but his smile creased into an ever-so-slight frown as he considered the implication of her dreams. Fina noticed the change. "Maybe not right now, but I have to do it. I *have* to do it," she added and stared at him.

"Each of us has a responsibility to do something, however small," Bayo affirmed.

Cammy looked at Aman to see if she would step in to oppose the direction of the conversation, but she seemed preoccupied.

"You guys are not being honest with yourselves," Cammy intervened, deciding he had to slow down this return-home bandwagon threatening to whisk Fina away from him. "You don't want to go back to help make things better. You want to go back to make yourselves rich."

"That's right, it's all about money," Kizzy began and then stopped, uncomfortable with the idea of being on the same side as Cammy.

"That's awfully cynical, isn't it?" Bayo half-queried, undecided whether he wanted to be polite or combative.

"Don't mean to sound negative," Cammy responded, "but you guys know change won't happen unless you join the system or start a new one. Either way, it means you'll be driving the fancy cars, living in the fancy houses with your servants, and sending your kids to study abroad."

"And what's wrong with living a good life if I bring some benefits to my country at the same time?" Bayo sat upright and stared at Cammy.

"Nothing, but then you should be upfront about your real motivations," Cammy replied unfazed, like a card player holding a royal flush while his opponents bluster and bluff.

211

"You all have what I call the diaspora complex. You think you're superior to people back home, and you see home as an opportunity for personal gain. But you cover up your real intentions with talk about development. Caribbean folks talk the same way."

"I don't see anything wrong with linking personal prosperity to improving the lives of others," Bayo retorted. "Whatever our motives, going back involves sacrifice. You'll agree with that much, right? When I return, I will have given up a good income and a whole lot more."

"Going back is not about money for me," Fina said. "The kind of work I want to do won't make me rich—not one bit. In fact, I will definitely be poorer than I am here. So let's lay that baby to rest. I want to go back because I want to feel as if I belong. I don't fit in here. At least back home, people will accept me as one of them."

"C'mon, Fina," Cammy groaned. "Are *your* people treated as equals in your country? Do women have the same rights as men? Is it fair that men can beat their wives and girlfriends and get away with it?"

"These are the very reasons why I must go back. If I'm not willing to stand up for women and work for change, who will? You? Besides, aren't there things you'd like to see changed in your country, or even here? Should we abandon our countries because they have problems? For me, going back is about finding where I belong. Cammy, I don't think you really understand how we feel."

"Sure ah do." Cammy became irritated that Fina had singled him out. "Ah felt the happiness of returning home, visiting the old haunts, sharing a drink and home-cooked food with old friends. But yuh know, as good as those visits felt, every one of them also confirmed that ah outgrown home, just like we outgrow our childhood clothes and toys. Sure, yuh remember how fond yuh were of them, and yuh might even keep some as mementos, but yuh would never wear them or start playing with them now, would yuh?"

"You never outgrow your home, not if it meant something to you," Fina replied. "It's the smell of the marketplace, the sound of

212

the church bells, or the call to prayers of the Muezzin. It's the world that you recognize and understand."

"These ideas are all in yuh head, Fina," Cammy chuckled. "Every time ah gone home, ah come back disappointed because what ah imagined or hoped for is not the way things really are. Know why?" No one answered. "Because back home is a memory, a canvas of good times stitched together to cope with present realities. All this talk of going back reflects our unwillingness to accept our new home."

From the expressions dawning on their faces, Cammy knew he had got them thinking. "Sorry to burst yuh bubble, but there is not and never has been a "back home" to go to. It's all in yuh heads, a fiction, like tradition and culture, which controls and keeps yuh tied to one country, one way of seeing and doing things. Ah want to be more than Trinidadian, American, or Nigerian—more than even a black man. I want to be bigger than one place and one culture!"

"You're dreamin', man," Kizzy reentered the conversation, his high spirits the result of the cocktail of spirits he had been downing steadily all evening. "So what are you if you're not Trinidadian, American, or black? I love America but there's a part of me back home!"

"There's no back home." Cammy could barely contain his disdain. "There's no past we can ever return to. Nigeria and Sierra Leone exist today, now! Each country is a real place with its own peculiar circumstances—good and bad." Cammy paused again to let his words sink in. "Look," he began moments later, "Ah suppose yuh have a right to be homesick, but yuh all spend way too much time moping about going back. Yuh can visit Sierra Leone, Nigeria, or Lesotho, even live there. Yuh just can't return to some ideal past in any of them. Yuh'll romantics. Back home talk is nothing but seeking refuge in nostalgia."

"Don't want to sound jealous or anything," Bayo noted "but I guess it's easier for a man with a six-figure income to deal with the set of circumstances here and now."

"What about me?" Aman spoke up for the first time. "*I* want to go to Africa... someday," she added.

Cammy again took the initiative. "It all depends, Aman. If going to Africa is about going back to your roots and becoming authentic, yuh no different from these two, and yuh'll be disappointed. That Africa is not available to you or them. Look at what is in front of you instead of some imaginary past, and you very well may enjoy and deal with the reality you meet."

"Well, *my* African past is not imaginary because last week I learned that I come from the Kru people in Liberia & Ivory Coast." Aman pulled out a sheet of paper from the handbag in which she had been fumbling.

"Oh yeah, how did you find out?" Fina asked. "Let me see."

"DNA analysis. A friend was doing hers and asked if I wanted to try. All you have to do is stick a cotton swab in your mouth and send it off to them. They do an analysis and in three weeks they tell you where you come from and who your ancestors are—for three hundred bucks."

"Dat don't make you no African," Kizzy snorted.

"That's uncalled for," Edna glared at her husband.

"It's about belonging, knowing that I have a past to own," Aman panned the entire room. "The very past which these two want to return to but which Cammy says does not exist. Even if I have no past to recover, at least I now know where it once existed."

"You should take this blood test too, Cammy. Maybe we are siblings after all," Fina smiled, recalling their conversation the night they first met.

"He don't need no test to know he gat white blood," Kizzy swirled the gold-colored liquid in his glass.

"Looks can be deceiving. I don't have any white blood in me," Cammy looked directly at Kizzy.

"Don't believe it."

"Believe it," Cammy smiled. "I am one hundred percent African. For a genetics refresher course, we had our DNA analyzed. Mine showed that I am from the Yoruba people in Nigeria. Let me see yours."

"You must come from *Osu* stock them," Kizzy poured some cognac into his glass.

Cammy took the result sheet from Aman. A palpable tension encircled the group. "See here. You're twenty-seven percent European," Cammy smiled.

Aman snatched the paper from Cammy. "I don't care about percentages. This points me to specific people, culture, and place. I belong somewhere. I am no longer defined just by my color."

"Yeah, that's wha' 'am talking 'bout, Kizzy slurred. "You can be a hundred percent African by genes and yet be a hundred percent European by ways."

"So does all this mean you're going to Nigeria?" Fina asked Aman to shift the focus from Cammy and Kizzy.

"I guess so. Even though I don't want to leave Ma by herself, she says I should go."

"That's great!" Fina exclaimed.

"Hey, folks, we have to be going," Cammy interrupted. "Fina needs her rest." He stood up, extended his hands to Fina and gently pulled her up.

"And you also have the surgery, right?" Edna asked. "When is it?"

"Next week."

"Thank you so much, Edna, Kizzy. I really enjoyed myself," Fina began, hugging and kissing Edna on the cheek and shaking hands with Kizzy. They searched each other's eyes for a few moments. Fina was surprised to find that she did not feel anything in particular. She knew they could never become friends, but she felt she could at least be cordial with him, for Edna's sake.

"I really enjoyed the music," she took the initiative. "What was the name of that singer whose CD got everybody dancing?"

"Youssou N'dour, from Senegal. Africa's number one singer."

"He's good. His music reminds me so much of home." Fina glanced at Cammy.

"Lemme burn it for you," Kizzy offered. Fina immediately began fumbling with her purse.

"Thanks! Here's some money."

"Come on, I don't need your money. This one's on me."

"It's just something to cover the cost of the CDs."

"They sell 'em by the dozens. You gat too 'mericanized," Kizzy teased.

"So, Cammy, you'll confirm that the Caribbean fellow attacked Mr. Trailborn, right?" Edna asked as Cammy and Fina walked to the door.

"Well... er... you know... er..." Cammy fumbled. Edna, Kizzy, and Fina stared at him in anxious disbelief.

"But you saw wha' 'appened!" Kizzy shot into Cammy's hesitation, alarm coursing through his veins and visions of jail flashing in his head. "Damn, wha' kinda man are you?" He looked from Cammy to Fina.

"The white man's goin' to recover. He'll tell the police what really happened."

"That's not the point, gad dammit." Kizzy became as rapidly angry as he became sober. "Suppose he don' recover? I could go to jail, man. All 'cause you don' wanna tell the truth. You hate me that much?"

"Cammy, you told me you'd seen everything," Fina interjected.

"Ah jus' can't say outright it was Scraps' fault."

Kizzy became incensed. "You bastard," he spat, like someone finally able to escape from a formal cocktail party to expel mucous from his throat.

"Don't call me a bastard," Cammy squared up and edged toward Kizzy.

"A lyin', no-good bastard. That's what you are and that's what I'll call you," Kizzy reasserted, standing his ground to the taller and stronger-looking Cammy.

"What's the matter with you guys?" Edna looked at Kizzy and Cammy in turn, unable to understand the source of the glaring animosity between them.

216

"Leh wi go, Fina. Ah doh'n like dealin' wit' ignorance atall." Cammy marched out into the spotlight created by the motion sensor lamp hanging over the garage door.

"Yeah, I'm ignorant, but you're a liar, wicked, evil!" Kizzy shouted after Cammy. "Your man is a liar!" he spewed as Fina walked past him.

She stopped and stared at him. She saw the flared nostrils, the gritted teeth, the heaving chest, and the bulging vein in his neck. She remembered.

She stifled a ferocious desire to bash Kizzy's face. "You should not be calling the person you're asking for help a liar."

"What help? Go and join your liar boyfriend. You deserve each other," Kizzy sneered, disdain and anger nourishing his words and countenance. Then, like someone who just remembered a vital piece of information, he walked past Fina and addressed Cammy, who was halfway into his car. "And your woman is a cheat too."

"Take that back," Cammy got back out of the car and lunged at Kizzy. "She's done nothing to you." Edna and Fina inserted themselves between the two men but Kizzy stepped around them.

"Let her tell you what she did when she was a student at CC, bro."

Cammy glared at him but saw only the quiet confidence of a man who knew he had the upper hand. He turned to Fina for some reassurance but saw only the same dejection and guilt he had seen at the altar the week before. His legs wobbled. His mouth dried up. He felt disgusted, empty, and powerless—the way he sometimes felt when he had tried everything to save a patient but had failed. The way he felt as the dirt thumped on Donovan's casket.

But now it was his heart that thumped with the anxiety that Fina had yet another secret he did not know about.

"Wha... wha... what's he talking about?" the words stumbled from his mouth. No one answered. Instead, Fina rushed toward the car. Cammy, Edna, and Kizzy stared at each other with the bewilderment of passengers beside their out-of-petrol *poda-poda* on an isolated stretch of forested roadway.

217

Cammy stomped after Fina. The car and house doors slammed one after the other with the authority of jailhouses on lockdown.

Chapter 22

Except for the one time when Fina said, "Take me home please," after Cammy took a turn toward his house, they drove to her townhouse in silence, each burdened with a load from the past they knew must now be unloaded, but each wondering if the other had the strength and understanding to accept and share its weight, its pain.

When they arrived, Fina dropped her keys on the dining table and walked straight into her bedroom. Cammy turned on one of the table lamps and sat on the loveseat. He recalled how shocked he had been when Fina began spotting the week before. Instinctively, he raised his leg but saw no signs of blood on the loveseat. He briefly wondered what chemicals had been used to clean the cushions but settled back, uncertain of how or what he was going to say. On the table across from him, he noticed for the first time the inscription at the bottom of the small lamp on the coffee. "Timing is everything," it read. Moments later, Fina emerged from her bedroom and sat down beside him.

"Cammy, I'm tired and I want to sleep, but what I have to say needs to be said."

"Go ahead," Cammy said. He braced himself by staring above her head into the distance.

"Many years ago, when I was a student and he was a lab assistant, Kizzy sexually assaulted me," Fina stated and bowed her head.

Cammy stared into the distance, his heaving chest the only sign of his agitated state. Visions of Kizzy assaulting Fina, mistrust and fear sacked his mind and occupied the townhouse with the élan of a conquering army.

"Yuh were dating *him?* Kizzy? Your sister's husband? And yuh neva breathed a word?"

219

"No, we were not dating at the time, and we've never dated. He did not even know Edna at that time. They met here, in America, many years later."

"But, this is the guy you say assaulted you, right? Does Edna know?" Fina shook her head. "Yuh didn't tell your sister before she got married to him?"

"Say what to her? 'Your husband-to-be assaulted me, so don't marry him?' What happened between us took place a long time ago, when we were younger. I wanted to leave that in the past."

"Yuh like making these decisions for others," Cammy chided and then paused. "How did it happen anyway?" he began after a short silence.

"I'd rather not relive that night."

"Come on, Fina. Yuh talkin' 'bout someone ah can't stand. At least give me de satisfaction of knowing that ah was right the whole time in dislikin' him."

"Cammy, this incident happened at a time when we did not report sexual assaults. I wouldn't have even known who to tell back then. And those I did tell would have said I got what I deserved. So I accepted my pain and learned to live with it. I told no one what happened because I knew I was partly responsible. I felt ashamed."

"Ashamed and responsible when *he* assaulted yuh?"

"No, for putting myself in the situation which led to the assault."

"Yuh know better than that Fina. It doesn't matter what the situation is. He raped yuh? Ah don't know, Fina, ah don't know."

"You don't know what?"

"Ah don't know what to think."

Fina shifted to the front edge of the sofa. "I'm sorry, Cammy. My past has come to haunt us again."

He neither agreed nor disagreed. He just sat there and stared. Fina did the same.

"Fina, don't apologize, because ah've got something to tell yuh, too."

Cammy also slid to the edge of the loveseat so that they were now facing each other. With both hands, he grabbed Fina by her shoulders to secure her attention. They stared at each other for several anxious moments. Cammy took a deep breath.

"Many years ago, I was involved in an accident in which a little girl was killed."

"What are you saying, Cammy?" Fina asked and then pushed his hands off her shoulder.

"Me, Scraps, and a cuppla friends got into an accident on our way home. We had been drinking, smoking some weed—"

"You were the driver?"

"Don't know. Don't remember getting into that car, let alone driving and hitting that girl."

Fina's eyes widened. "Were you or weren't you?"

Cammy became irritated. "The police say ah was driving. Ah swear ah doh'n remember, Fina."

"Could one of your friends have framed you?"

"Ah dunno," Cammy replied and then leaned back into the loveseat with a faraway look in his eyes. "We had gone for a beachlime."

"What's that?"

"Hanging out on the beach, eating, drinking, and listening to loud music. The last clear thing ah remember is us heading to the car to return home. The next thing ah know is ah sitting in the driver's seat and policemen are around me."

Cammy grabbed his head.

"My God, so you've lived all this time not knowing what really happened?"

Cammy nodded. "Sometimes ah wish ah jus' know one way or de other." He closed his eyes and took a deep breath.

"Oh, Cammy, I am sorry," Fina moved over to the loveseat and put his head on her shoulder. "But whose car were you driving? How old was the girl?"

"It was Scraps' car. She was eight or nine."

"Oh, my God," Fina exclaimed, a pained sadness enveloping her. Again, neither spoke for a while.

"Did you sometimes drive it?"

"What?"

"Scraps' car."

"Sometimes, but not regularly."

"And you can't remember if you were driving that night because you were—?"

"Drunk, stoned, or both," Cammy finished off the sentence Fina did not want to complete.

"And what does Scraps have to say?"

"That ah was the one driving."

"So how was the case settled?"

"Scraps and the others told the police the girl dashed in front of the car and that ah couldn't see because of the high grass on either side of the road. Based on their testimony as the only witnesses and the fact that the accident happened at night, no charges were filed. But now Scraps is claiming that my dad and his lawyer friend told him what to say and bribed him and the police to keep quiet about my condition. He's threatening to go public if ah don't tell the police that Kizzy attacked the white man. He wants to make sure he is not charged."

"So what are you going to do?"

Cammy did not answer.

"You've got to tell the police what's happening, Cammy."

"Ah can't do that, Fina. Bringing in the police will ruin my family's name and put me and my practice at risk."

"But Kizzy might go to jail."

"Don't tell me what ah already know, Fina. Kizzy could rot in jail for all ah care."

Cammy did not really feel the way his words sounded, but they hit Fina like an earthquake. She stood up, walked to her room, and closed the door. Cammy slept on the sofa that night, afraid that if he left, Fina might think he had abandoned her again.

In the hospital waiting room, Fina rolled her neck around to relieve the stiffness she felt from holding her head at an awkward angle to watch the wall-mounted television set. She stayed attentive as the infomercials rattled off a litany of cautions, cures, new and improved medicines, and common-sense advice about healthy living because she did not feel like talking to the room's other occupants, Nicholas and Anne Gibson, Glen's adoptive parents. As immediate family of the two transplant patients, Fina had exchanged words of hope and faith when they had first met. But then she had found herself the subject of their inquisitiveness.

"Sri Lanka ... that's near Kenya, right?" Nicholas said.

"No, Sierra Leone, West Africa."

"That's right, West Africa, where all the hurricanes come from," Anne clarified.

Fina did not reply, hoping her silence would discourage further conversation, but Anne was determined to rescue her husband from his initial gaffe. "Sira Loney. That's a former French colony, isn't it?"

"No, British."

"So what language do you speak there?"

"Many, but the lingua franca is Krio."

"Oh really, like the Creole in Haiti and Louisiana?"

"No, ours is an English-based Creole that has evolved into a language called Krio, with a K."

"Fascinating," Nicholas bounded back into the conversation. "Say something in Creole with a K."

For a moment Fina toyed with saying empty vessels make the most noise, but instead offered a harmless greeting and promptly asked to be excused. When she returned some fifteen minutes later, Celeste and Judge Priddy had arrived and were seated in the waiting room. Fina deliberately put two seats between herself and the Gibsons and studied the TV screen, which continued in its relentless bid to inform them into health.

Fina and the other occupants of the waiting room had become hypnotized by the somnolent narratives of the television set when an olive-skinned woman bustled in with the authority of a fire engine entering a busy intersection. Her over perfumed and buxom body commanded everyone's attention.

"Mrs. Priddy, Judge," the woman extended a handshake when they answered. Judge Priddy got up and shook her hand. Celeste

Priddy muttered something and offered her fingers, like royalty obliged to shake hands with commoners but aware of the potential for contamination.

"The woman turned to Nicholas and Anne. "You must be the Gibsons. I am so pleased to meet you."

The Gibsons stood up. "Anushka? So, glad to meet you too," Anne beamed and nudged her husband to follow suit.

Fina's heart raced as she examined Glen's biological mom! The woman, the girl, she quickly reminded herself, with whom Cammy had a child!

"We didn't think you'd make it." Nicholas' voice broke into Fina's unease.

"I asked my husband to call and let you know I would be flying through Caracas."

"We didn't get his call. We just assumed you wouldn't be coming," Anne Gibson chimed in. "But that doesn't matter now. We're glad you're here."

"Thank you. I'm so grateful you're allowing me to see him," Anushka gushed as she reached out, grabbed their hands, and pulled them into an embrace. After Anushka released the Gibsons, Judge Priddy introduced Fina.

"This is Cammy's fiancée."

"Congratulations! Then Glen is your son too." Anushka promptly yanked Fina into an exuberant embrace. Fina recoiled.

"Group hug," Anushka demanded, her chubby hands beckoning them all. Celeste Priddy raised her eyebrows at her husband but complied with Anushka. During the hug, Anushka launched into a prayer.

"Almighty father, we leave Cammy and Glen in your hands. Guide the surgeons so they may do your work and guide all of us here so we may follow the path you have planned for us. We sometimes want to go our own way because we think we are high and mighty or because we have money and we feel powerful, but twist our neck if you have to and point us in the right direction, so we may always be in your service. Lord in your Mercy, Amen."

The group exhaled but for only a moment, for as they broke towards their seats, Anushka commanded, "Lord's Prayer! Our father, who art in heaven…"

Prayers over, they finally sat down. Suffocating, insufferable, Fina raged within. Since Cammy's revelation, she had never given more than a passing thought to Anushka who had remained a disembodied figure from Cammy's past. Now she was this effervescent presence, and Fina did not like her. What had Cammy seen in her? She never had a chance to formulate an answer because Anushka conducted the conversation with questions about the hospital, the surgery, the surgeons, and the convalescence. Judge Priddy and the Gibsons supplied answers like witnesses in a court case. Then Anushka turned to Glen—oh, how his eyes were like hers. She was grateful for the picture they had sent of him. She had never really forgotten about him, and, in her mind all these years, had always called him Cammy. And, oh, Cammy! What a wonderful, selfless, father. To so easily, willingly, give a kidney to a son he had never even met! How considerate, loving, and thoughtful. Those were the qualities she must have seen in him many years ago as a young, foolish girl. Fina cringed. Judge and Celeste Priddy squirmed. Nicholas and Anne Gibson nodded.

Perhaps there was a sense that the only way to break Anushka's stranglehold on the group was for someone to steer the conversation in a different direction. The Gibsons did just that. They had twice vacationed in Trinidad, they said, visited Chaguaramas, traveled the Arima Blanchesuisse road, and loved the mossy green mountains that fell steeply into the ocean.

"We knew he'd one day want to know about his homeland, and we did not want it to be a strange place to him," Anne explained.

"Oh, you're wonderful people to have kept him connected to his roots."

"Glen loves good *roti* washed down with some *mauby*," Nicholas said.

"That'll tell you a place can neva change what's in the blood," Anushka smiled approvingly.

225

"I just found a nice lil' place downtown that makes a decent *pelau* and sells carnival CDs too," Judge Priddy put in. "Perhaps we can go there before you return home?"

Then the conversation turned to carnival, designer Peter Minshall, steelband and Limbo, moco jumbies and Cocoa-panyols. Fina felt alone, an intruder in this family gathering. Anne and Judge tried to include her, offering an explanation here and there and directing a question to her, but the joy of their common experience was all too evident. They had a place which connected them, a place to which they all belonged.

Fina shrunk in her seat in proportion to how she felt disconnected from the others. She concentrated on the TV, which was now showing moisturizer pads that made age lines disappear. She wished she had giant-size pads to smother away these annoying people.

****

Two weeks later, Cammy was at home, still recovering from the transplant, when Anushka came to say goodbye. She was returning to Trinidad the next day. Celeste and Judge Priddy, on their way out to join the Gibsons to sample some *roti* and *pelau*, had let her in. Glen was asleep in his bedroom. Cammy was resting on a La-Z-Boy, a black remote control in his hand. It was the first opportunity Cammy had had to talk to Anushka alone since their trysts some twenty-one years earlier.

"I just wanted to tell you that I'm sor—"

"Sorry for what? We were young and foolish. Things happened. My parents did what they thought best for me and them and so did yours. End of story. We are all children in the service of God. Look at the way things have worked out. He moves in mysterious ways, you know."

Cammy nodded in agreement, surprised at how easily she had put the past in perspective and let it go. So unlike Fina. They reminisced for about five minutes, and then Anushka rose to leave.

226

"I have a few other goodbye stops to make," she explained. She kissed Cammy on the cheek, wished him a full recovery, and walked toward the door. Halfway there, she spun around.

"There's something you need to know," she began. Cammy gulped spit and air. "Remember the accident you had?" Cammy gave a brusque assenting nod. "Well, when you were studying in England, Scraps told me Chaplin—remember him? He's dead now—was the one driving the car when it hit that little girl. He convinced them to put you in the driver's seat because you were too drunk or stoned to know what was happening. Since your father was a judge, they figured you stood a better chance of avoiding prosecution."

Anushka paused to give Cammy a chance to respond but continued when she realized he was too stunned to do so. "When I pressed Scraps for details, he quickly changed the subject and wouldn't talk anymore about it. I tried to confirm his story, but the others said they were too drunk to remember what happened."

For a long time after Anushka left, Cammy tried again to recall the events of that night, but he couldn't. Though he did not feel the innocence and vindication certainty afforded, he felt relieved that an alternative narrative to the accident existed. He wanted to share it— particularly with Fina, whom he realized he had not heard from for two days. He wanted her to see him in another storyline, as a different character, with a different past, and, therefore, with a different future. He wanted to step out of the limitations that the story of the accident had imposed on his life. But he also had practical questions for Fina. Should he tell his father? Should he confront Scraps? Fina was always good with these things. He picked up the phone and dialed.

When the recorded message said for the second time the number was no longer in service, Cammy sat up and checked to see if he had misdialed. He had not. Alone and not fully recovered, it took him several minutes to locate and dial Aman's number.

"She left yesterday to go back home," Aman told him. "No, for good, as far as I know. I'm sorry, she gave me the impression you knew and that you both thought it was for the best."

227

Chapter 23

It was a homecoming she needed to make, tethered as she was by the rope. This time, she walked through the front door of the house in which she grew up in Freetown; this time she stood erect in front of a stooping, graying man and woman and pressed a small envelope with cash into the woman's hands. They introduced her to a little boy and girl, replacements for their children who now lived in far-off places. The pubescent pair followed her around the house as she greeted the now bent-over, emaciated Mammy Nursey, coughing in the smoked-filled outdoor kitchen, a bottle of *omole* by her side; as she smiled and ran her fingers atop the Grundig radio and record player; as she pushed open the bathroom door and touched its cold, tiled floor; and as she looked under the bed where the girl in a red dress with a big bow had cried. The pubescent boy and girl wondered at this woman who took such pleasurable interest in the ordinary people and places of their lives.

She shared a drink of water with the graying man and woman, but that was all they could share without raising ghosts from the past. She made no apologies and received none. She rose, said goodbye, and walked out through the front door, her head held high, the graying man and woman staring at her straight, receding back.

Then she had rocked and bobbed in the minivan on the potholed road to Falaba and walked, with a guide, an overgrown footpath back to the place where the little hamlet of Talaba once stood. She looked around for the compound where it had all started. But all she could see was the scorched earth—charred pieces of timber and metal; crushed and rusted aluminum cans, cooking pots and pans; torn and bloodstained clothes, odd sandals and gaping shoes; a thinned and browned forest submitting to her gaze; a rice farm disfigured by craters and trenches, yielding a harvest of skeletons, overturned trucks, their wheels in the air, and other broken and rusted machines of war. The remnants of a place where homes once stood and lives flourished.

All of a sudden the place had come alive. In the craters, trenches, and burnt-out armored personnel carriers, she heard shrieks and saw her age-mates fighting each other, child soldiers fighting adult soldiers, men fighting women, brothers fighting sisters with bayonets, machetes, knives, blades, and jagged bottles. She heard buzzsaws and saw the trees and branches of the forest being cut by men eager for profit. She saw the crushed and impaled bodies of the villagers. Then there was noiselessness, like that in cemetery.

Her heart raced and her hopes soared when she saw a segment of rope. She stooped and pulled and pulled. But with each pull, the slimy, dirt-encrusted segment disintegrated into small pieces. She could not retrieve the rope. There was no place and no one to atone to for her father's desecration. No Talaba to come back to. But she would not give up. She decided to search for Baramusu.

****

She began her search at the Waterloo Transit and Refugee Camp, twenty miles from Freetown. Traffic congestion, potholes, and interminable checkpoints turned the 30-mile journey into a two-hour ordeal she endured only because finding her grandmother had become something like finding the Holy Grail, worthy of the physical stress on her burgeoning pregnancy.

When the driver announced they had arrived at the camp, she was surprised, for the taxi had stopped smack in the middle of a wave of pedestrians. The driver explained that the road, an undulating, muddy track packed with criss-crossing people and animals, divided the camp. Fina paid him and stepped out, as much an act of courage as of faith.

Faces, arms, legs, voices—loud, soft, and shrill—smells, animals, and vehicles surrounded her. She wobbled and for a moment considered returning to Freetown but found the strength to edge her way to what appeared like a small clearing. She stood still and surveyed the scene. As far as her eyes could see, tents, wood and cement houses, and other structures pretending to be tents, wood and cement houses extended to the horizon on one side of the road and dotted the hillside on the other. The town was indistinguishable from the camp. Sweat burned her eyes and reminded her that she could not stay in the heat for long. She stopped a man wearing a starched white shirt, with a badge tacked to his right breast pocket, and asked for directions to the registration center. He pointed to a house flying the UN flag on the coastal side of the road. She could reach it by following the muddy track around the southern end of the camp—safe but long—or she could walk straight through the camp—quicker but not a path for the squeamish.

Driven by a mix of curiosity and daring, she took the straight path. She kept the flags in sight and tried not to stare at the camp's citizenry. But out of the corners of her eyes she saw them—pockets of idle youths, forlorn women in faded wrappers and dirty blouses sitting on their heels next to boiling pots and bales of laundry, and half naked and completely naked children, indifferent to and even comfortable in their squalid circumstances. She stepped over and around mounds of decomposing food, rotting vegetables and animal entrails, stumbled into muddy potholes and rivulets, and weaved around and between tents.

Twenty minutes later, her feet and back in full revolt, she ambled into the compound of an erstwhile single-family house now functioning as an office. Out of sight but not of hearing, a portable generator spluttered electricity into the building. It was just past noon. She climbed the steps and landed on the verandah.

"Over there," a toothy young man said and pointed to an unoccupied table at the other end of the verandah. "She'll be here soon," he added when he noticed her hesitation. Reluctantly, she walked to the table and stood, like an accused person awaiting a judge's verdict. Feeling stupid for being attentive to an unoccupied table, Fina turned and faced the compound. Old men, women, and children in various stages of destitution and seeking shelter from the midday sun had etched themselves, like Egyptian papyrus drawings, into a wall. On top of it broken shards of glass stuck out like misaligned teeth—a security measure, as much a deterrent against breaking in as breaking out. The compound was silent. The only activity came from the grating metal wires that held the sign hanging from the corrugated iron eaves of the building. It read:

"GUNS AND REBELS ARE NOT THE ONLY WAYS YOU CAN BE DISPLACED; YOUR RACE, SEX, AGE, ETHNICITY, BELIEFS, AND EDUCATION ARE ALSO CAUSE ENOUGH."

"We're at lunch," a voice said, snapping Fina back to the verandah. Its owner, a fleshy, heavily made-up woman dressed in a body-hugging, ornately embroidered *temle* and *lappa*, blocked the office door. Fina wondered if she was indifferent to or unaware of the incongruity between her dress and the people and circumstances of her workplace. Fina did not like this woman and dispensed with courtesies.

"I wanna find my grandmother and the people of my village," she stated, exaggerating her American accent.

"We can help you, but you will have to come back at two o'clock," the reply came back in an impeccable West African English, followed by the sound of the closing door.

The young man kicked a chair in Fina's direction. She was grateful for the respite. A little after two o'clock, she again faced the overdressed woman. The heat and wait had taken their toll. Fina was thankful to begin the search.

"First name," the woman plunged straight into business.

"Mine?"

"No, the person you are looking for."

"Baramusu."

"Surname?"

"Er... I don't remember... I don't know." The woman raised her head and eyed Fina.

"Age?"

"Er...eighty," Fina claimed, deciding to be specific even if wrong.

231

"Height?"

"Five foot nine."

"Eye color?"

"Brown."

"Last known location?"

"I don't know."

"Name of village she last lived in?"

"Talaba."

"Do you mean Falaba?"

"No, Falaba is the town. Talaba was our village five miles to the east.

"Do you have a picture of her?"

"No."

The woman laid her pen on the table and leaned back on her chair with barely concealed exasperation.

"I was just a little girl when I last saw her," Fina offered.

"When was that?"

"Nineteen seventy-seven."

"Seventy-seven? We need the name of the last place you saw her within the past year."

"I haven't seen or heard from her in more than fifteen," Fina exhaled, recalling Cammy's words about recovering the past.

"Madam, many people have been displaced and many have also died."

"I know, but can't you help me? I *have* to find her," Fina explained, frustrated and worried by the emerging enormity of the task ahead.

"It's going to be very difficult. There are many displaced people and many camps."

"How many?"

"Ten, officially. Four big ones like this and six smaller ones. But there are many unofficial ones all over the country. Your grandma could be anywhere."

"Give me the names of the camps. I'll go to each one if I have to." Fina knotted her face.

232

The woman stared at Fina's protruding stomach. Then, without a word, she leaned to her right, opened a file cabinet, and perfunctorily flipped through its contents. "I don't have the list here. They'll have one at Tower Hill or at the refugee center, over there." She pointed in the direction of the hills. Fina's heart sank.

"It won't be easy finding your grandmother," a foreign-sounding voice arrested Fina's despair and fatigue. Its owner was Svetlana Nordstrom, a thin, black-haired white woman wearing a spaghetti-strap cotton dress that exposed her freckled shoulders. She was the Norwegian-born director of Families Reunited, a non-governmental agency specializing in rehabilitating traumatized children and reunifying families separated by the war.

Fina may have been responding to Svetlana Nordstrom's soothing voice and helpful demeanor or to the cool air rushing out of the open door of the office. Either way, she felt energized, turned, and introduced herself to Svetlana in the best American English she could summon. Her changed tone and demeanor were not lost on the overdressed woman. She hissed, popped some gum in her mouth, picked up a magazine, and devoted her attention to it.

Svetlana was traveling to Freetown to attend a meeting, so she offered Fina a ride. By the time they arrived, Fina had told Svetlana her life story with the eagerness of a sinner long cut off from a priest. Svetlana promised to help Fina find her grandmother. "But," she cautioned, "be prepared. Sometimes we end up finding out the person is dead or, worse, has disappeared without a trace. That's the hardest part. Not knowing the fate of a loved one."

Fina refused to contemplate the possibility of never being reunited with Baramusu.

Five months later, Fina gave birth to a daughter. By then, Isa and her family had returned from Guinea. To save money, they all lived in a rented house on Freetown's Circular Road. Fina worked part-time at a private nursery school. Two days before the Saturday morning naming ceremony of her five-day-old daughter, Fina received a note from Svetlana. It read:

Dear Fina,

Found an old woman who could be your grandmother in the company of an adolescent girl in the bush fifty miles north of Kono. She is near blind, known only as Mama and says very little. The girl says the woman often talks about her long lost daughter. They are not related but refused to be separated. They claim no one and no one has claimed them. Arriving F/town Friday night. Meet @ the Center 7am Saturday morning.

Svetlana

Fina frothed like freshly tapped palm wine in anticipation of her reunion with Baramusu. It would at least begin the process of appeasing an embittered past that started the night her father stepped into the *fafei*, an act she believed had unleashed the harvest of trouble that had followed her through Freetown, Koidu and the U.S. Especially now that she had reunited with Isa and her family, and had a daughter of her own, Fina saw the reunion as an opportunity to placate her grandmother and the women of Talaba, and to connect the past to the present and future. Lack of continuity, wholeness, and belonging she felt had been her undoing since that fateful night. So Fina had insisted Isa and her two girls accompany her to the Rehabilitation Center to meet their long lost grand and great grandmother. Despite the cool Harmattan breeze, she wrapped her five-day-old, unnamed baby girl and put her in a bassinet for the trip.

It was midmorning when Fina's family assembled inside the Center's receiving area, a mud floor, tarpaulin-covered enclosure adjacent to the main office. They decided on a phased reunion. Fina would break the ice. Isa would follow. Svetlana and the grandchildren would bring up the rear.

Fina shuffled toward the two figures sitting on a wooden bench, stopped a handshake away from them, and stared. The adolescent wore an ill-fitting yellow and black cotton *temle* and *lappa*. Though her hair looked as if it had not been washed in months, Fina could tell from her rounded forehead, smooth skin, full lips, and soft round nose that she was pretty. Next to her sat the old woman, leathery-faced and emaciated, and also dressed in an ill-fitting yellow and black cotton *temle* and *lappa*. Fina could not tell if she was Baramusu. A white cotton head tie covered her hair, ears and neck, and a pair of wide-framed, dark-green sunglasses obscured her eyes. On the exposed skin around the rims of the sunglasses and on her dropping jowls, Fina could make out irregular shaped white spots of skin, as if she was afflicted with vitiligo.

"Baramusu...Baramusu...it's me, Finaba."

"*Ooda?*" A somnolent voiced quizzed.

"Amadu and Nabou's daughter."

"*Oodaaaat?*"

"FEE ...NA...BA. FEE...NA...BA."

The leathery-faced woman extended two bony arms upwards. Fina grabbed them, smiled back at the others behind her, and pulled the woman up as if to embrace her. The adolescent jumped to attention, like an alert bodyguard determined to prevent an overenthusiastic fan from getting too close to his charge.

The woman's fingers traced over Fina's lips, nose, eyes, and forehead. Fina submitted to the touching like a patient to a doctor. The fingers then moved to the back of her head. There, suddenly, they became frantic, pressing, prodding, and poking. Fina winced.

"*Yu nohto mi pikin,*" the old woman howled and shoved Fina away like spoiled meat. "*Waiyoya,*" she babbled, danced around until she lost her balance. The adolescent steadied her companion with one hand and flailed at Fina with the other. One blow glanced Fina's shoulder; another landed squarely on her chest before Svetlana yanked her away. The adolescent steered the distraught, babbling woman back onto the bench. Svetlana pushed Fina and her family in the direction of her residence in a far corner of the Center's compound.

"Finda, not Fina, was the name of the woman's daughter, not granddaughter," Svetlana explained an hour later as they sat in the parlor of her residence. "Her daughter had a big scar on the back of

235

her head from a childhood injury. Discovering you were not her daughter was just too much for the old woman."

No one spoke. They settled into the silence of soldiers for a fallen comrade.

"*We behg o, we behg*," a voice desecrated the silence. They spun around to see the adolescent and the old woman standing between the kitchen door and the dining room table. "*Ar behg o, ar behg*," the old woman clapped her hands together slowly. Unable to see that the group inside the house was more surprised than unforgiving, she broke into sobs. Fina rushed and embraced her. Moments later she, too, broke down, weeping so loudly the old woman became her consoler.

"*Noh kray, noh kray ya*," she mopped Fina's eyes with her head tie until Fina calmed down. Svetlana, Isa, the girls, and the cook who had ushered the pair in stood around them.

"Yegbe. Mama Yegbe," the old woman volunteered and retied her *lappa* as if energized by the act of uttering her own name. "Mawaf," she pointed to the adolescent who was more interested in Fina's cooing baby than in Mama Yegbe's overtures for forgiveness.

Nevertheless, a round of introductions followed after which an awkward silence reasserted itself.

"Why don't you all stay here and get to know each other?" Svetlana said. "I have some paperwork to finish at the office. I'll join you for lunch."

"And then after, can we have the naming ceremony?" The others looked at Fina and each other uncertain what to make of the request. "We were going to do it today, right?" she looked at Isa.

"But a man usually does the naming," Isa said, more to be a contrarian than because she really had serious objections.

"We don't need a man. Mama Yegbe is here. She would have the honor of performing the ceremony," Fina turned to Mama Yegbe, whose head snapped back and forth in incomprehension.

"All we need is kola nuts, palm oil, some salt and half an hour," Fina clasped her hands in supplication and curtsied to Svetlana.

"I have never witnessed a naming ceremony," Svetlana warmed to the idea. "I'll make sure Cook prepares enough food for all of us and ask him to buy the kola."

"Don't bother him with that." Isa picked up her handbag and beckoned to her daughters. "They need a walk to help get rid of their pent up energy. I'll buy what we need."

Fina helped Mama Yegbe settle down into a settee and invited Mawaf to join them. The adolescent ignored the invitation. Instead, she sat in the straight back chair nearest to the bassinet and ogled at the baby.

"Take her out," Fina encouraged. Mawaf ignored Fina, who then walked over to the bassinet, picked up the baby, and handed her over to Mawaf. She cradled the child to her breasts but did not acknowledge Fina's gesture.

While Mawaf played with the baby, Fina and Mama Yegbe exchanged stories of their travails.

"But why didn't you leave when you knew the rebels were going to attack your village?" Fina quizzed as they branched to the topic of how she and Mawaf came to be together.

"Farma, my husband said he was too old to go and beg another man for cassava, so I remained with him. Isn't that what a first wife should do?"

Fina sidestepped the question. "Then what happened?"

"One morning they came. Children. '*Wi go kill ohlman! Mammy o, dadi o, pikin o. Wi noh dey lehf nohbohdi*,' they shouted. I woke Farma and told him we should run."

Mama Yegbe paused, inhaled and exhaled slowly. "Bravery is for the young. In an old man it is foolish pride."

Fina shuffled and shifted but said nothing.

"It is foolishness to hold a cutlass to fight children with guns. Keh-keh-keh-keh," Mama Yegbe cackled.

"What happened?" excitement coursed through Fina's body.

"Pow-pow, pow-pow. *Bu-dum*! He fell."

"They shot him?"

Mama Yegbe nodded. "Little boys and girls laughing and dancing in the flames. That was the last thing these eyes ever saw," she sighed.

"What do you mean?"

Mama Yegbe removed her sunglasses. Fina gasped at the bulging blue-gray pupils and the puffy-pink everted lower eyelids.

"They did this to you?"

Mama Yegbe nodded.

"How did you manage to escape?"

Mama Yegbe pushed out her pink lower lip and chin at Mawaf. "She found me and took care of me."

Though she had kept her head mostly bowed in attention to the baby, Mawaf must have heard their conversation, for Fina turned straight into her gaze. They stared at each other for a few seconds before Mawaf deferred to the older woman.

"Do you know who did this to her?"

Mawaf kept her head bowed and twiddled the baby's nose.

"Where did you find her? Were you from the same village? Are you related?"

Mawaf refused to answer. Prudence told Fina asking too many questions would be counterproductive, so she changed her approach.

"She is somebody's mother and grandmother, so thank you for taking care of her. If my grandmother is still alive, I hope she has a companion like you."

Mawaf continued to play with the baby. She did not raise her head or acknowledge Fina.

After a hearty lunch of rice and cassava leaves and a dessert of fresh mangos, they assembled in the parlor for the naming ceremony. Aside from a brief spell when Fina had taken the baby into the bedroom for a nappy-diaper change, Mawaf had been inseparable from her. Now, carrying the baby, she knelt before Mama Yegbe, who was seated on one side of the settee, a small stool to her right. On top of it was a saucer with two broad, reddish-purple kola nuts and a small mound of salt. Next to the saucer was a small bowl of palm oil. Fina, Svetlana, Isa, her two daughters, and Cook made up the rest of the party.

"You have done well," Mama Yegbe began by addressing Fina directly. "This," she reached out and collected the baby from Mawaf, "is the result when your vagina is fresh."

The girls giggled. Fina blushed. Svetlana, Isa and Cook smiled. Mawaf betrayed no emotion.

Mama Yegbe continued. "Our people say whatever name a child is given has bearing on what the child becomes. We are not *buk-buk* people who pick a name like it was a pebble on the ground. To name is to be given a destiny." Mawaf flinched. Fina, Isa, and Svetlana nodded. The girls, wide eyed, leaned forward.

Mama Yegbe picked up kola nut from the plate and held it aloft.

"Owner of the universe," Mama Yegbe's voice became louder, "thank you for this child that you have brought to preserve Fina's immortality. We are grateful. We pray for long life."

"Amen," the adults mumbled followed by the girls.

"We pray that sickness and poverty will *not* walk the same path with this child."

"Amen." This time the girls were on time, having caught on to the call and response.

"Let all who plan evil for her fall into their own traps."

"Amen."

"Let this child bring fame and glory to Fina and her family."

"I name her...Mu-su?" Mama Yebge hesitated.

"Di-mu-su-Celeste," the older of the girls interjected.

"Dimusu-Celeste," you are welcome, Mama Yegbe showed her off to the assembled group.

The girls jumped onto their feet, clapped, and rushed to greet their cousin. Isa restrained them as Mama Yebge reached for the saucer with the salt, dipped her finger in it, and pressed the salt-laced finger on Dimusu's tongue. The child suckled and a grimace rumpled her face.

"Yes, we must taste ugliness, for it is plentiful in the world."

239

Next, Mama Yegbe dipped the salted finger once more into the salt and then into the bowl of palm oil and pressed it on Dimusu-Celeste's lips. It suckled several times in succession.

"Yes," Mama Yegbe smiled. "There's balm to soothe the ugliness in the world."

****

Mawaf returned from putting Mama Yegbe to bed for her afternoon siesta to find that Dimusu-Celeste had been removed from the bassinet.

"My sister and her daughters have taken her into the bedroom to—"

Before Fina could finish her sentence, Mawaf spun around gruffly, dumped herself into the straight back chair, folded her arms under her breasts, and pouted.

"Join them," Fina spoke to her broad defiant back. Mawaf stood up and walked out of the house. Fina followed Mawaf to a small brook in the back part of the yard farthest away from the buildings. She sat beside the adolescent.

"Why don't you answer my questions or talk to me?"

Mawaf did not respond. They sat in silence for a few minutes. Then, Fina said, "Know what, you talk. I'll listen."

The tension lifted off Mawaf like a curtain on an actor about to deliver a soliloquy.

"They look alike."

"Who?" Fina's eyes lit up.

"Dimusu-Celeste reminds me of it."

"Who?"

"The child."

"Which?"

"The one I had."

"Tell me about your child." Fina inhaled deeply to stifle the one thousand questions straining to break through her lips.

"It was small. It did not live long. But I liked it. I tried to feed it, but I had no milk. So it just lay there. Its chest went up and down, up and down, quick, quick, like this." Mawaf demonstrated with a series of short, shallow breaths. "I pulled it close to me. It cried for a little bit and then it stopped. The next morning it was gone."

"What happened?"

"Captain said it died while I was asleep and he buried it so that I would not cry. But one of the soldiers told me Captain took it into the bush and he heard pow-pow-pow."

Mawaf snapped up a blade of grass, nibbled on it, and stared blankly in front of her.

"Who is Captain?"

"He took care of me."

"Was he your husband?"

"No."

"How did you get to be with him?"

Mawaf exhaled, plucked another blade of grass and started nibbling on it. "Captain was my sister's boyfriend. A gov'ment soldier. He was tall and had straight black hair. His skin was yellow. His nose was long. People said he had white-man's blood in him." Mawaf chuckled. "Captain and his men fought the rebels. One day he told us the rebels were going to attack our village and that we should leave. Some believed him and left, but many others did not. Two nights later the rebels attacked. 'Pow-pow-pow-pow... petrol... whoosh ... fire. Pow-pow-pow-pow... petrol...whoosh...fire. Children screaming, women crying, old men groaning, goats and sheep running.

"My sister dragged me through the bush because she was not able to carry me."

"What about your parents?"

Mawaf shrugged her shoulders. "When we finally stopped running, Captain and his men were standing around us, looking wild, like they were going to kill us. I began to cry.

"'Shut up,' Captain slapped me. 'Do you want the rebels to know where we are?'"

241

Mawaf plucked another blade of grass and began her routine of nibbling and spitting.

"Where did you go, what did you do?" Fina shifted closer to Mawaf.

"We went to Kono to find diamonds. Captain told us rebels, Lebanese and Nigerians soldiers were stealing our diamonds and becoming rich while we, the real Sierra Leoneans, remained poor. He told us to kill anyone who tried to stop us from becoming rich."

"Where did you live on your way to Kono?"

"In the bush."

"But where did you sleep?"

"Anywhere! But sometimes we took over villages, stayed in the houses of the villagers, and made them our slaves." Mawaf smiled, like an old soldier recalling a moment of mirth in a brutal campaign. "One time we lived in a cement house." Mawaf leaned back on her elbows and swished the blade of grassed back and forth in her mouth.

"Where were the owners?"

"They cooked for us and washed our clothes. I liked when we lived in the cement house. I had my own room and watched videos."

"Really?"

Mawaf nodded and smiled. Then she abruptly stopped and scowled like a gambler who discovers she had overestimated her hand.

"What happened there?"

Mawaf took a few deep breaths. "One night a man came into my room. I thought he wanted to kill me so I screamed. My sister ran into the room with a gun and pointed it at the man.

"'Don't shoot, don't shoot. It's me, it's me,' the man begged.

"We knew the voice. It was Captain, standing over me, not wearing his trousers and his thing sticking out. My sister slapped him. He slapped her back, and they fought and fought. He punched and kicked her. Then he dragged her into his room and beat her all night. I heard it."

Fina shuddered. Mawaf smiled and continued with her narrative.

"The next night Captain came back into my room. He said my sister was very sick and he would let me go and rub her with *ori* and Mentholatum if I let him touch me."

"And?"

Mawaf scowled. "I let him."

"*Osh ya*," Fina instinctively reached over and touched Mawaf. She recoiled. Then she reached for another blade of grass. Convinced that encouraging Mawaf to talk would be therapeutic, Fina added, "You must have felt very bad."

"I didn't care. I didn't feel anything." Mawaf everted her lower lip and raised her shoulders. "I just wanted to take care of my sister."

"You mean it did not hurt when he touched you?"

"I said I didn't care! Will you not suffer a little pain for your sister?"

Fina did not answer. "So did you get to take care of your sister?"

"Yes, but the swelling did not go down. She just lay there sleeping, refusing to wake up. Captain said she had malaria and that if she did not get well soon we would leave her behind. He said we had to be in Kono ready to dig for diamonds as soon as the rains stopped. I begged the woman whose house we lived in to help me, but the swelling on her head would not go down."

"And Captain still came to your—?"

"Every night. He said he liked coming to me because I was tight down there." Fina thought she detected a hint of pride in Mawaf's voice. "He said that if I did not remain tight he would give me to his soldiers. I did not want that."

"Why?"

"Don't you think one is better than five or ten?"

Mawaf waited for Fina to respond but getting none, she continued. "But Captain fell asleep as soon as he finished. I would push him away and go over to my sister. I begged her to wake up so that we could run away. Sometimes I slept with her till morning. Then, I began to vomit. The woman who owned the house said it was because I had *it* in my belly. I told Captain.

243

"'You stupid thing,' he slapped and then spat at me. 'You should have told me what you wanted to do.'"

"Did he still come—?"

"Yes, until my belly started to show. 'You smell. You're dirty,' he told me. 'You will never see your sister again,' he kicked me right here." Mawaf pointed to her belly. Fina winced. Mawaf smiled.

"Did you?"

"What?"

"See your sister again."

"No."

"What happened to her?"

"I don't know. One day Captain went on patrol. I begged the guard to let me see my sister. He agreed but only if I let him touch me. So I let him. Then he opened the door to my sister's room. It was empty. I cried. He laughed and laughed. I became very angry. When Captain came back, I told him what the guard had done. 'Call everyone here,' he shouted. He marched up and down, up and down until all the soldiers were gathered in the house.

"'No one,' he pointed at me, 'go near her. *Oona yehri?*'

"'Yes, sir,' some answered."

"Captain walked into his room and came out a minute later with a pistol and small plastic bag in one hand and bottles of beer in the other. He put the bottles on the table. He opened the first one with his teeth, pushed my forehead back with the pistol, and poured the beer in my mouth. I swallowed a little and coughed out the rest on him. He laughed. Everyone laughed. He pushed my head back again with the pistol and poured more beer down my mouth. This time I swallowed more beer and did not cough out as much. Captain clapped. Everyone clapped. He kept giving me beer to drink until I finished two bottles, *faim*!

"When he opened the third bottle, I began to cry. 'Shut up!' Captain said. I swallowed my cries with more beer. Then Captain shoved me onto the sofa and pushed my head back. He took some of the white powder with his two fingers and put it in my nose. 'Draw, like it was snuff,' he said. The powder stabbed inside my nose and

244

made me sneeze like I had put cayenne pepper inside. He took the pistol and pushed the remaining powder into my nose. I cried. I did not want him to shoot me by mistake. But soon I stopped crying and began to smile. Then I began to laugh and laugh. There was nothing really to laugh at and I did not want to laugh, but I could not stop laughing. And when I laughed, Captain laughed and everyone laughed back. So I laughed at them and they laughed at me and we laughed and laughed at each other. I was happy, so I sang and danced and flew around the room which was now full of blues and reds and yellows, and morning-bird sounds, and orange, lime and lemon smells."

Fina stared at Mawaf. She was leaning back on her elbows, her head slanted to one side but tilted up toward the sky, a beatific smile on her face.

"Then the colors and sounds and smells entered my body and I felt a sweetness that made between my legs wet, like sometimes happened when Captain touched me. The colors and sounds and smells made me shake and tremble with sweetness. I wanted to die."

Fina stared at Mawaf in disbelief.

"Captain waved the pistol, which was now so big I wondered how he had the strength to hold it with one hand. The soldiers stopped talking and moving, but the morning bird sounds continued to dance with greens, purples, limes, lemons, and pears.

"'This,' Captain showed everyone the big, big pistol and gave it to me, 'is for you. Shoot him!' He pointed to the guard who had touched me.

"Pow-pow-pow! I did not even close my eyes. He fell to the ground, *bu-dum!*"

"You shot him... in cold blood?"

"Yes! The blood came out *froosh*, like when the soldiers first open their beers.

'*That's* ma waf,' Captain spoke in conkey.

"Cockney?"

"Yes, conkey."

"'Welcome to the squad, ma waf.'

245

"'Welcome to the squad, ma waf,' his men repeated in conkey.

"'May she kill many rebels.'

"'Many, many rebels. Kill them dead,' they answered.

"'If someone tries to take ma waf away from me, may god give him a hernia?'

"'*Na bozin so*,' one of the boys who had attended school up to class six translated and got a roar of laughter from the squad.

"'*Big-big bozin*,' some repeated.

"'To ma waf,' Captain poured more beer all over me and gave me the pistol. 'That's for you, ma waf.'

'Ma waf, Ma waf, Mawaf, Mawaf,' the soldiers sang. From that night, everyone called me Mawaf."

"So what's your real name?"

"I don't remember."

"How can you not remember?"

"I don't want it anymore."

"But that's—"

"I like Mawaf. It shows I am one of them."

While the narration seemed to have stunned Fina, it had brought out the *yeliba* in Mawaf.

"'Now, get the water from the battery and bring some kerosene. Mawaf has a mission to complete before we she can truly become one of us.'

"The soldiers grabbed their guns and we left the house. We didn't stop till we came to a hill outside a village. We split up into small groups of five or six. Captain made owl sounds, and we waited to hear the owl sounds from the other groups. That would tell us they were ready to attack. While we waited, Captain lit a pipe and sucked two times. He sniffed and spat. He pushed the pipe into my mouth. 'Suck!' I sucked, coughed and choked.

"'Shut up!' Two more times he sucked long and deep from the pipe and closed his eyes. When he opened them, they were big like an owl's, but he looked like a crazy dog. 'Suck deep,' he told me. I sucked. I coughed a little but not as much as the first time. I opened

246

my eyes. My head turned round and round but I felt strong and powerful. I wanted to kill the nasty, evil rebels.

"'Ready? Take out your pistol and stay behind me,' Captain said when he heard the final owl signal. I removed the pistol I had tied around my waist with a head tie and followed Captain.

"'Attack!' Captain ordered. Pow-pow-pow, pow-pow-pow, pow-pow-pow.

"'*Wi go kill ohlman! Mammy o, dadi o, pikin o. Wi noh dey lehf nohbohdi.*'

"We poured kerosene on the huts. *Whoosh!* People screamed and ran. Pow-pow-pow, pow-pow-pow."

Mawaf smiled. Fina shivered.

"Then everything became quiet. The huts burned bright red, orange and yellow and the place became so hot we had to cover our faces with our hands. Soon it was over. Children, men, women and animals lay on the ground everywhere.

"'Find anything we can eat, even dead goats and sheep.'

"Then this old man came out of the redness holding a cutlass in his hand as if he wanted to fight.

"'Pow-pow,' Captain shot him. When he fell down, we saw an old woman behind him.

"Captain walked up to the old woman. 'Do you want to die like him?' he pointed to the man's bleeding body.

'*Ar behg o, mi pikin,*' the old woman said.

"'*Me noh to you pikin.* My mother and father are dead.'

"'*Ar sorry ya.*'

"'I don't want your sympathy. Did you see how he died?'

"'Yes.'

"'Liar! How can you see when you are blind? *Bring di wata!*'

"The soldiers forced the woman to her knees and yanked her head backward. One of them held a tin cup with the water. 'Mawaf, washing is a woman's job,' Captain said. 'Wash her face so that her eyes can be clean and she will not tell lies.' I made my hand into a cup by the side of the old woman's face. One of the soldiers poured the water over it, and I rubbed the water over her face with my hand. We both screamed. Captain and the soldiers laughed. The water was from the battery. It burned her eyes. It also burned my hands. See," Mawaf offered up her hands. For the first time, Fina saw the patches of keloids, shriveled, and scaly skin on her palms and fingers.

"So what happened to the woman?"

"She ran round and round like a naked child in the rain until she fell and rolled around on the ground. I wanted to help her, but Captain said I should leave her there."

Mawaf stopped speaking. Fina tried to contain her mix of rage and incomprehension.

"So you left her there to die?

Mawaf did not answer. She pointed to Svetlana's residence.

Comprehension swept over Fina.

"Mama Yegbe? Does she know?"

Mawaf shrugged.

****

"I'm not surprised," Svetlana explained after Fina told her Mawaf's story. "Many of these girls were forced to live as "wives." Terrible things were done to them. They did terrible things to others. They all blame the government."

"What kind of thinking is that?"

"She is a kid remember. She lived in the bush, was probably threatened, brainwashed, beaten and worse. You have only scratched the surface of how this war affected these kids. You need to talk to her more and then you'll see how much work needs to be done to give her and others like her a semblance of normal life."

Fina sought to do both. She arranged to meet Mama Yegbe and Mawaf at Svetlana's residence every weekend. She would arrive on Friday evenings to find the pair waiting for her. They'd open her gifts of clothes, trinkets, or hair accessories, eat, put Dimusu-Celeste to bed, and talk late into the night with Mawaf looking on, offering a monosyllable here and a shrug there. On Saturdays, Fina and Mawaf took part in team-building activities with the Center's orphan residents while Mama Yegbe looked on from the shade of a tree. On Sunday mornings they parted, Fina for Freetown; Mama Yegbe and Mawaf for their refugee camp.

Mama Yegbe and Fina found in each other a surrogate daughter and grandmother. For them, the visits were therapeutic. Their effect on Mawaf was less clear. Her aggressive demeanor disappeared, but she remained in a cocoon, lured out only by her self-imposed responsibility to Mama Yegbe and her interest in Dimusu-Celeste. Mawaf played with the baby girl when she was awake and assisted Fina with feedings and nappy-diaper changes. In such attentiveness, Fina and Svetlana caught glimpses of a tender Mawaf that held hope for her eventual rehabilitation.

As had become her practice, Mawaf waited on the steps of the verandah for Fina's Friday evening arrivals. When the vehicle rolled to a stop, Mawaf would walk up to it, grinning and peering through the windows for Dimusu-Celeste even before the engine had been turned off. However, one weekend, two months into the visits, Fina did not bring Dimusu-Celeste with her. "I just wanted a break," she explained when she saw Mawaf's fallen countenance. "I'll bring her next week."

Mawaf scowled, walked into the house, and disappeared into the room where she and Mama Yegbe slept. The next morning, after settling Mama Yegbe at the dining room table and grunting greetings to both Fina and Svetlana, she left the house without eating. Mystified, the women raised their eyebrows, but said nothing. After breakfast, Fina went to look for Mawaf and found her sitting by the brook in the back part of the yard. In this spot, Fina could hear but could not see the gurgling water. It was obscured by weeds, construction debris, and rotting garbage.

"So Mama Yegbe helped you deliver your child?" Fina began. Mawaf did not need encouragement to answer.

"Yes. She told me what leaves to eat and which to rub on myself so that I would not feel the pain when it came out."

Mawaf went on to tell how she and Mama Yegbe lived and traveled with Captain and his men until they reached Kono. Once they got there, things did not go well. There were many other groups of soldiers and rebels in the bushes around the mining areas. Each was ready to kill the other. They had no money, knew and trusted no one, so they lived in the bush, listening nightly to gunfire, the groans of dying men, the screams of women, and Captain's increasing frustration as the reality of getting a foothold in the diamond-digging business dawned on them. In the mornings, Captain and most of his men left their camp to scout and figure out when, how, and where they would establish their bridgehead to the diamonds. One soldier was left to guard and help Fina and Mama Yegbe cook. Captain and his men returned in the evening, ate and talked about what they would do the next day. On one such morning they left, but they never came back and were never heard from again. The soldier left to Mawaf and Mama Yegbe, fearing his comrades might have been captured or killed and uncertain about his own safety, disappeared during the night. Fina and Mama Yegbe wandered in the bush until they were found by ECOMOG, troops of the West African peace keeping force.

****

Later that afternoon Fina feigned fatigue and dropped out of the team-building activities to sit next to Mama Yegbe in the shade. She watched Mawaf, sometimes feeling pity, sometimes fear, sometimes admiration but mostly feeling confused. Mawaf was neither exuberant nor detached in her participation. No one cowed her, but she intimidated no one. Unlike the others who went back to their rooms at the end of the activities, Mawaf walked over to the tree where Fina and Mama Yegbe sat. Fina signaled for Mawaf not to wake Mama Yegbe and pointed to a rock on which she could sit. Fina felt a need to know Mawaf, to get into her head.

"Do you like playing with these other kids?"

Mawaf shrugged.

"Do you want to come and live here?"

"No."

"What about going to school?"

"No."

"What do you want to do then?"

"Go back to the bush."

"To do what?"

"To find Captain."

"Why would you want to be with him?"

"He took care of me. He gave me things. His soldiers did what I told them, and I didn't have to go to school. Here, people are always telling me what to do, and I have nothing."

She walked away, leaving Fina sitting in her chair, transfixed by a desire to do something and knowledge that she did not fully understand what she was dealing with or what to do if she did.

"You must help her." The voice startled Fina because she had thought Mama Yegbe had been asleep.

"How?"

"I don't know. But she cannot be left alone. Life is when we work together."

****

Fina and Svetlana watched the van taking Mama Yegbe and Mawaf back to their camp disappear. "I want to talk to you," they said simultaneously and chuckled.

"You go first," Svetlana invited as they walked back toward her residence.

"I want Mama Yegbe and Mawaf to come and live with me," Fina blurted.

Svetlana stopped at the half-open door, turned, and eyed Fina above the rim of her glasses for a few seconds. Then she turned away and walked inside.

"I'm offering them a home, a semblance of family. Do I not qualify? Do I not have enough money?" Fina's questions and statements tumbled through the door after Svetlana.

251

"That's not it. I wonder if you fully understand what you want to get into."

"Probably not. But I want to help. Mawaf is a young girl with nobody. I want to be there for her."

"And what happens to them when you find your grandmother?"

"Nothing. Honestly, I don't think I'll ever find Baramusu. But if I do, we'll all live together as a family."

"And how do you intend to support all of you?"

"I don't know. I know only that a wounded child invariably grows up to be a wounded adult."

"Good intentions are one thing, but you'll be taking on a life-long commitment with a girl who will need a lot of attention, and you have your own child."

The look of disappointment on Fina's face made Svetlana pause. "You know what, let's start with weekend visits to you in Freetown. I can arrange that. It will give you and Mawaf a chance to find out if you really want to be in each other's lives. In fact, what I wanted to talk to you about may be very helpful to you."

Fina was not particularly eager to hear what Svetlana had to say, but she pretended to be attentive.

"My deputy director is leaving at the end of the month. Are you interested in taking over his job, working here with me?"

Fina tried to contain her excitement by not answering.

"The job pays quite well," Svetlana pressed on. "It comes with the apartment you see in the back, over there. You'll oversee the rehabilitation curriculum and the day-to-day operations. I will continue to do the recruiting, placement—"

"I'll take it."

Aside from the opportunity to fulfill her dreams, Fina took the job because her relationship with Isa and Hassan had become strained. She had enjoyed living with them after they returned from Guinea. Hassan found work and contributed to the rent and food. Isa cooked, cleaned, and took care of the kids. She was particularly helpful to Fina in the months immediately before and after Dimusu-Celeste's birth. Indeed, it was because of Isa that Fina had had been able to keep her job at a nursery school within walking distance of their Circular Road residence.

Initially, the arrangement seemed made in heaven, despite the late-night noises—groans, moans, and a creaking bed—that came through the wall that divided Fina's bedroom from that of her Isa and Hassan. Fina muffled the noises, and her embarrassment, by covering her head with her pillow and was grateful that the noises stopped before being underneath the pillow became unbearable. But one night the noises did not stop. They came through the wall and penetrated the pillow covering her head. At first Fina kept her head covered, surprised, even mildly envious, that her sister and husband were not only going at it for such a long time but that they also included rough sex as part of their lovemaking repertoire. But the moans soon became screams followed by slaps and banging against the wall. Fina removed the pillow, sat up, and listened intently, even placing her ear against the wall to make sure she was hearing correctly. She heard more slaps and a woman's whimpering and crying. She banged and banged her fists against the wall until they hurt. The noises stopped.

Quietness engulfed the house after that night. Isa avoided Fina who avoided Hassan who stayed out later and later. Even the children played quietly. The quietness mounted. Svetlana's job offer provided an exit from the quietness.

Chapter 24

With Svetlana's help, Fina began the process of legally adopting Mawaf. But as a practical matter, she moved into the assistant-director's two bedroom apartment together with Mawaf and Mama Yegbe. They became, for all intents and purposes, a family. Fina did not give up the search for Baramusu, but as time passed, she revised her expectations. She hoped only for news of her death, how she died, and where she was buried. Unfortunately, all she ever heard was that a terrible carnage had taken place in Talaba. It had simply ceased to exist. Baramusu and all who might have died in it will be memorialized only in her head and the stories she would tell. There was no place to go back to, to belong to. In Fina's mind the rope would never be cut, but she decided it had to be stretched forward. She would invest her time and energy on the present and future—Mama Yegbe, Mawaf, the children of the Center and Dimusu-Celeste.

The teenager, now on the brink of womanhood, remained mostly taciturn, but Fina could see hope lay beneath her hard exterior. She helped Fina take care of Dimusu-Celeste and remained unwaveringly devoted to Mama Yegbe. In fact, her supervision of both enabled Fina to concentrate on helping the orphaned and runaway boys and girls. That help came primarily in the form of play therapy, especially the once-a-week Saturday games for which they won prizes.

Fina would shop for the prizes in the market not far away from the Center. She enjoyed haggling with the traders but even more seeing the happy faces of the boys and girls as they found out they had won a Bic pen, a used book, or even a used blouse or shirt.

"*Bo*, you are charging too much." She turned to walk away from the man she had been haggling with.

"Mama, come back, come. How much you want to pay?"

"I won't pay one cent more than five leones."

"I see you have learned how to trade for gain," a familiar voice startled her. Fina turned around. It was Sidibe Kakay!

"Oh, my gad!" she exclaimed, reached out and hugged him. Then almost immediately after, she pulled back. The hug felt right but somehow not right.

Sidibe Kakay looked older, grayer. The beer belly which had combined with his height to make him an imposing figure had disappeared. He seemed frail, undernourished, like someone who was stepping out into public for the first time after a particularly severe bout of malaria. They smiled at each other.

"You did not even tell me when you were leaving," Sidibe Kakay said.

Fina heard the accusation and explained. She was rushed. She had to return to Freetown to tell her mother and sister, make sure they would be okay in her absence, and tie up loose ends. She had started to give him a rundown of her stay in America when the trader coughed to bring them back to the business at hand. Both of them might later have denied they were happy to see each other, but the trader would have emphatically contradicted them, for from that point on Fina stopped haggling and paid whatever price he charged. Then, when Sidibe Kakay found out the reason why she was shopping, he insisted on buying a different color or style of whatever item Fina bought. The children were in for a treat.

Fina could not be sure whether she invited Sidibe Kakay to the Center or he invited himself. But sure enough, he was part of that Saturday afternoon's games, helping winners to open up their prizes and consoling losers. Fina was also not sure how, after the games, he came to be sitting in her apartment. Mama Yegbe eyed him and Mawaf served him some water. As he lifted the glass to his mouth, the wide sleeve of his kaftan slipped back far enough to reveal a six-inch, black, auspicious-looking keloid just below the crook of his elbow. Fina muffled a gasp, but it was loud enough for Sidibe Kakay to hear. He followed her stare to his scar. He rubbed one finger over it and smiled.

"Rebels," he continued rubbing the scar as if he wanted to coax the story of its origins out of it. "They wanted to cut off my hand."

"Oh, my gad!"

"Aziza, my two other wives and their children had left. But I chose to stay behind. I knew the rebels were coming. I also knew some of the young men who had worked for me were among them, but I was not going to abandon all that my father had built to children and madmen."

He pulled the sleeve down to cover the keloid.

"They ransacked the house. Took everything." Sidibe Kakay smoothed out the sleeve. "I gave them the combination to the safe. They took all my uncut stones. I thought I had made a good trade. Thousands of dollars for my life. They were satisfied, except one girl. She told them she had heard I also had a briefcase of cut and polished stones."

Sidibe Kakay stared at Fina, who held his stare knowingly for a moment, and then looked at Mama Yegbe and Mawaf. They eyed him suspiciously.

"So what happened," Fina asked.

"I told them I did not have such a briefcase, but the girl, like that one," he pointed to Mawaf with his empty glass, "she told them that the briefcase of cut stones will make them rich enough to go and live in America and not have to work for the rest of their lives. So they decided they would cut a piece of my hand every day until I told them where I hid the briefcase. During the day they went to do some mining. Every day, for nine days, she cut me open or reopened the part of the wound that had started to heal. 'You will bleed to death unless you tell us where you have hidden that briefcase,' she smiled."

"Why were you holding out?"

"Because you cannot trade with air."

"Well you're here and still have your hand, so you must have given them something."

"Not them. The white mercenaries. Their helicopter gunships destroyed my section of town. For nearly a whole day, the gunships chased and fired at the girl and her friends at the mines. I doubt any of those children survived. After the firing finished, the mercenaries and government soldiers came to town to see what was left. I retrieved my briefcase, which I had buried under the stones steps leading up to the outdoor latrine. I traded some of my diamonds for treatment and a ride to Freetown. I live here now, by myself. My wives and children? Gone! I don't know where they are."

Mama Yegbe coughed. This started preparations for her to go to bed. Sidibe Kakay left but only after he had invited Fina to lunch the next day. She wasn't sure why she agreed to go except that she sensed he was a different man—subdued and less ostentatious—from the one she had met years earlier. After their lunch, he was driving her back home along Wilkinson Road when he stopped the car, about a half-mile short of the Murray Town junction. "That's where I live," he pointed up the hill to a modest split-level house that looked out at the Atlantic Ocean.

Thereafter, he helped Fina out with the Center. Mostly, he identified carpenters, masons and other skilled workers for things that needed fixing or building. But he also referred Fina to many of his political and business contacts. Sometimes he helped her talk to the more difficult young boys. He even invited one or two of them to stay with him on weekends.

They never talked about Chip or Meredith, and he never asked her about time in America or Dimusu-Celeste's father. But every so often he would buy some baby formula. Once as he handed her a box of nappy-diapers, he said, "Just to help you because I see her she does not have a father."

He could not have been more wrong. Though Fina did not want to admit it, she thought frequently about Cammy. Soon after Dimusu-Celeste was born, she sent him some of her baby pictures and gave him her phone number. It was the right thing to do, she had told herself. Secretly, she wanted to hear his sing-song accent. Cammy had called immediately after he received the pictures and phone number. He complained she was preventing him from seeing his daughter and her grandparents from seeing their granddaughter. He wanted to fly out and see them that very week. But Fina prevailed on him to wait, explaining that she and Dimusu-Celeste were going to be returning to the U.S. in order for her to maintain her permanent resident status. Besides, she explained, she was leaving Sierra Leone the next week to attend Aman's wedding in Lagos. Cammy wanted to talk about them, to find out what happened. She told him to be patient. Both of them needed time to understand themselves and each other. He had settled for wiring money for his daughter.

As a courtesy, Fina told Sidibe Kakay the news about her planned trip to Lagos and America. They were sitting on the verandah of Svetlana's residence. The kids had dispersed after the Saturday afternoon games. Most of the young boys played soccer. One group of pre-teen girls played round after round of *akra*, kicking up dust from the furious stamping of their feet. Another, smaller group of older girls and boys gathered under the shade of a mango tree. Periodically peals of laughter rose from among them as boys and girls chased each other in pretend umbrage and fights.

"Marry me Fina," Sidibe Kakay proposed. "I still have vim and vigor and I have enough money to take care of us. When peace returns, I will be able to go back to Koidu and make even more money."

Fina's mouth remained half opened.

"And if you don't want me to go back," Sidibe Kakay rescued his proposal, "I will stay here with you, with these children, and be a father to them." Sidibe Kakay's pointer finger panned from the boys playing soccer to the young people gathered under the mango tree. "Together we will help them."

Fina remained silent. Sidibe Kakay stood up. He was ready to leave. "You know, love is like a diamond. Rough and ugly when you first find it. But if you clean and polish it, you will find beauty inside."

****

They were giddy with delight and could hardly contain themselves. It had been over a year since they last saw each other.

259

Fina's departure had been impetuous. It had foreclosed an orderly goodbye and had left Aman with a sour taste in her mouth. The reunion was all the sweeter for the chance it gave them to start over again.

"Meet my daughter," Fina said to introduce Mawaf.

"Pleased to meet you. Your mom has told me so much about you." Aman hugged Mawaf. The latter stiffened. "Uptight like your mama huh. Around me you're gonna have to loosen up, girl." Aman shook Mawaf by the arm and dragged her off. Fina looked on, smiled, picked up her carry-on bags, and followed them.

"Oh, Fina, you look so well," Aman repeated. They had been the first words out of her mouth at Murtala Mohammed airport. She had repeated them in the car, when they arrived at her house in the upscale Palmgrove Onipan residential area, and now again as they sat across from each other at the dining room table, talking and eating foo-foo and bitter leaf soup.

"You look good, too, Aman. See what life here does for you?"

"Girl, at first I was not comfortable with all this, you know." She leaned back to let her housemaid take away the used bowls and plates. "But I'm sure getting used to it."

Fina smiled.

"So is the baby looking like Cammy now?" Aman blurted out the question she had been itching to ask from the moment she saw Fina.

"I don't know. She has his complexion, but she reminds me of her namesake, Dimusu, my sister who died young."

"Oh, you should have brought her."

"No, I wanted this to be a trip for me and for her." Fina gestured with her head at Mawaf who had opted not to eat and was browsing through a magazine in the parlor. "Dimusu-Celeste is with my sister, Isa."

"And how's Cammy dealing with the separation?"

"Not sure. The same way I am, I suppose."

"I thought you guys had put the wedding incident behind you."

"Other things came up that made it impossible for us to stay together."

"Like what?"

"Hey, I'm here to celebrate your wedding. The only thing I know for sure about me and Cammy is that we needed to be apart. He needed to get to know his son and to recover fully from the kidney operation. *I* needed to come home and get my bearings. So far it has been good, fulfilling for me."

"You still love him?"

"I don't know, Aman. And that's the truth. At first, I didn't miss him, but now that my life has settled into a routine, I sometimes feel… er… can we talk about something else?"

"So, you're working at a daycare." Before Fina could answer, the maid walked back into the dining room with a bowl of water in one hand and a saucer with a bar of soap in the other. She presented both to Aman who washed her hands and mouth and wiped them dry with the towel that had been hanging over the maid's left wrist. When the kitchen door closed after the maid, Fina answered Aman's question.

"I now work with an NGO that reunites children separated from their families or places those orphaned by the war with new families."

"Do you like the work?"

"Love it."

The maid re-entered the dining room and offered Fina the soap and a bowl of clean water. As she washed and dried her hands and mouth, Aman continued with their conversation.

"I know what you mean, and I love the work here. But are you happy?"

"Thank you," Fina said to the maid before she turned to Aman. "The work makes me happy, and that's enough for now. I'm not ready yet for the happiness that comes with having a man in my life. That's what you're getting at, right?"

Aman did not answer. Instead she moved on to another topic: "So how do you rehabilitate these kids?"

Fina gave Aman a detailed explanation of the organization, funding sources, and services offered by the Center. "But we need money for everything—buildings, beds, chairs, tables, books, pens, and pencils. You name it, we need it. So," Fina chuckled, "I'm expecting a big donation from you. But enough about me. How have things been for you?"

"Can't complain, at least not when I have someone who cooks and cleans for me. Baryour stays out with friends more than I'd like, but that's about it."

"Better reel him in. How about your in-laws?"

"They're okay… except for Aunty O-nee-keh."

"Onike," Fina corrected.

"Yeah, her. 'When are you going to give me a grandchild?' is the first thing out of her mouth whenever we meet. The second is, 'You need to eat more,' as if I'm not big enough! Thank God she doesn't live nearby. I could not take her on a daily basis. She reminds me of Big Mama, my grandmother."

"What about Bayo's parents?"

"Let's just say they're not breaking out in goose bumps for me. More the quiet sort, like Baryour."

"So are you going to make Nigeria home?"

"I don't know. I'm enjoying myself for now. Life here is different, less stressful. Baryour teaches at the university and supervises the building of the clinic in his home village. After it is up and running and the rat problem has been taken care of, we'll decide if we're gonna stay or return to the States."

"Did they settle the chieftaincy business? Does Bayo want to be chief?

"Honestly don't know. But I don't think Bayo is interested in being the chief. He's too impatient. Almost every day, he comes home upset about something. If it's not somebody's incompetence, it's something that's not working or not available. I cope with these problems much better than he does. I have to keep reminding him to be patient, that he can't change everything at once. Truly, I don't think he has what it takes for the long haul of change."

Aman stopped talking as if suddenly mindful that she might have said too much. Fina sensed her hesitation and switched the topic.

"What do you do? You sounded bored in your last letter."

262

"I am a teacher's assistant and unofficial counselor at a private school. I help some of the kids with their reading, pronunciation, and writing. Can you believe that? Me, teaching English. God help those kids!" They both laughed.

"And your mom and Shantea?"

"Ma is doing okay, still going to church all day Sunday and working two jobs. She wanted to come but her arthritis is bothering her. Shantea was supposed to accompany her but, you know her; she called and said she had met Mr. Right and did not want to leave him, blah, blah, blah. Hey, let's stop talking about other people. I'm so happy you could come."

"Okay, then, let's talk about Saturday. Is everything ready?"

"I think so. Aunty O-nee-keh and some other of Baryour's relatives are coming later this afternoon. You see, my family is supposed to cook for the groom's family, but since I don't have anyone here, Baryour's family is doing everything for me. Do you know his aunts insisted that he should leave the house and go stay with his uncle until after the wedding? He was *not* pleased. Me? I'm just going with the flow."

"Good—that's the way it should be."

"Come let me show you something. Aman ushered Fina into an adjacent bedroom, where she displayed two *boubous* embroidered with elaborate gold-colored designs, along with their matching slippers and headgear. "After the reception, Baryour and I will come back here and change into these." She pointed to a matching *buba* and *sokoto*. "Mine has a story you know. It's actually the second outfit the seamstress made."

"Seamstresses," Fina groaned. "They are just like car mechanics. They never get the job done on time and never get it right the first time."

"Not quite, not quite. Mine, Miss Sidi, is a power worker. That's a person who works at the mercy of NEPA—National Electric Power Authority. She spends most of the day waiting for the electricity to be turned on. When it comes on, usually at night, she works feverishly. So power workers are skittish people. One afternoon I stopped by for our arranged fitting. Girl, she was in a bad mood. 'I'm not yet finished,' she shouted out as soon as she saw me. 'Look at what I got trying to get your dress ready.' She pointed to a lime-size knot just above her right eye. 'Know how I got it? The taxi driver who lives in the one-bedroom *adjoining* at the back parks his car outside my window and forgets to turn off his headlights. I jump up thinking the electricity had come on and rush to finish off your dress. Bam! I slam into the edge of the door.'

"'This electricity business will kill me,' continued Miss Sidi as she swung away from the light bulb dangling between us from the ceiling to sit at the sewing machine. 'My head ached all night and we've had no power most of today. It came back on about an hour ago. Come back tomorrow,' she declared, and returned to her sewing. She paused from her agitated state only to take short drags from a cigarette perched on a saucer next to my incomplete dress. The cigarette embers glowed in admiration at the *adinkra* material.

"I was about call her attention to potential for a fire when the workroom became silent. 'Damn this country!' Miss Sidi yelled, stood up, and stomped around the work room. The electricity had gone off, again.

"'How can I work? You in the rich part of town get electricity during the day. We in the poor part get it at night. But not even long enough for us to work. Is that fair?' She rubbed the knot on her forehead and stared at me. 'We don't have money, so no one listens to us anyway? What's that smell? Jesus Christ!'

"It turned out to be my material. We had to buy more and because I wanted to be sure I got it in time for the wedding, she sewed this much simpler style."

After the anecdote and related talk about fabrics and accessories, Aman and Fina returned to the sitting room where they reminisced about America, drank more soft drinks, snacked on rice *akara* cake, and discussed Cammy, Bayo, and men in general until the first in a series of women started arriving. Over the next two days, the house became a site of harmonious pandemonium—mothers, daughters, and tottering granddaughters trekked in and out; music played on the

264

radio and phones rang; instructions, directives, and conversations bounced back and forth; the women talked, cooked, ate, laughed, sang, danced, washed, slept, and sometimes even disagreed. But above all they shared. The days brought back vague memories of similar activities in Fina's childhood. She felt warm, content, and connected. Mawaf was also a source of these feelings. She was at ease with the young women, and she seemed to have taken a particular liking to Aman. Fina even felt mildly envious that in just a matter of days Aman had developed a level of familiarity with Mawaf which took her months to achieve. In fact, twice Fina had the distinct feeling her appearance caused them to break off their conspiratorial conversation.

The hustle and bustle continued into the next morning, when Aunty Onike and a group of women barged into the room and led Aman away to a purifying bath of lime juice mixed with sugar. Noticing Fina's envious glances, one of the women suggested that Fina, too, needed a bath. Grandma Onike agreed, and before Fina could protest, the women were stripping her. An hour of pampering followed. Both were massaged with shea butter and given a relaxing manicure and pedicure. In the early afternoon, they ate *Jollof* rice with a variety of spiced meats, after which they were ordered to take a nap so they would be well rested for the braiding. That would involve sitting for as many as seven hours or even more. They climbed into bed that night after 3:00 a.m.

"I hope you'll enjoy yourself tomorrow, Fina." Aman bade goodnight.

"I'll try, but remember that tomorrow is *your* day."

"I know, but just promise me no matter what happens you'll also enjoy yourself."

"Just being here is enjoyment enough."

"I know, but promise me."

"Will you stop it? You make it sound like I'll go crazy if I see another wedding. I can handle it."

And handle it Fina did. Though long, she enjoyed the church service and laughed heartily at the humorous speeches and toasts of the reception, particularly Bayo's exaggerated account of his wooing of Aman. When Aman and Bayo first entered Fela Anikulakpo Kuti hall, Fina was amidst the throng of people who plastered them with naira bills and sprinkled clayey water on them to ward off evil spirits. She cheered when they cut their wedding cake and joined in the good natured teasing when they performed their first dance. She was also among the group of women who jostled for the bride's bouquet, which Mawaf won and then promptly threw away to the consternation of many. Fina made several trips to the buffet tables and bar.

Twice Aman left the high table, joined Fina and the other aunts at their table. On both occasions, Fina had yanked Aman into the middle of the dance floor. The presence of the bride on the dance floor always energized the celebrants. They surrounded her in a twenty-minute dancing orgy. After the second such excursion, Fina walked to the bar for a drink. When she returned, she saw that two men, dressed in resplendent blue *agbadas* with matching *bubas*, *sokotos*, and *filas* were seated at her table. For a moment, Fina thought she might have been heading to the wrong table, but as she moved closer, she recognized Mawaf and noticed that Bayo and Aman were talking to the two men. Irritation crawled over her. She guessed that Aman was matchmaking for her and Mawaf. She walked up behind the men and waited.

As if on a signal, the two men turned around and beamed at Fina. Cammy and Glen in turn stood to hug and to kiss Fina, who, in startled and embarrassed confusion, promptly spilled some of her drink.

It took a couple of minutes of dragging and shifting chairs to accommodate Fina and several of the aunts who had conspired in the surprise. Aman's exhortations for her to enjoy herself and the conspiratorial conversations between her and Mawaf made sense now. Everybody except her seemed to have been in on the surprise. Bayo winked at Fina, shook Cammy's hand, patted Glen on the back, and left. Aman planted a kiss on Fina's cheek and whispered, "Promise me you'll enjoy yourself." Fina nodded as another group of guests whisked Aman and Bayo onto the dance floor. Silence fell on the table. Aunty Onike and the many aunts stared at Fina and Cammy. Their daughters, granddaughters and surrounding women made plans for Glen.

Fina and Cammy were just getting uncomfortable with their goldfish-in-a-bowl status when the lights went out. Groans of disgust rumbled through the hall. Fina explained to Cammy that power outages were common but that since the eventuality had been anticipated, drummers were on hand to keep the party going. She pointed to a lantern at the center of the table, "Just in case the blackout continues into the night."

The distraction created by the power outage gave Fina and Cammy an opportunity to whisper that they were happy to see each other and to exchange surreptitious kisses under the guise of whispering to each other. Fina was surprised at how comfortable and natural it felt to be with Cammy again, almost as if they had never been separated. He looked thinner, probably the after-effects of the surgery, but he was still charming. He was disappointed that she had not brought Dimusu-Celeste but was willing to fly to Freetown to see his daughter, so he fired off a series of questions about her eating and sleeping habits. Fina answered his questions in detail and with the pride of a mother.

Cammy reached forward and let his lips land lightly on hers. "Don't you have questions for me?" he said apologetically. Like an eager defense attorney, Fina began her cross-examination:

"Why did you cut your dreadlocks?"

"Took a look at myself in the mirror one morning and decided ah wanted a different look."

"Look, yes, but have you changed?"

"What, you think ah can't change? Let me tell you, losing a body part alters the way you look at life." He paused. Both reflected for a moment. "Ah don't take anything for granted now." He looked at her, grabbed her hands, and rubbed them for a few seconds and released them. "Ah also less impatient."

"Good! What else?"

267

"Ah've become a good listener."

"Let me put that to the test because I want to tell you about my second daughter."

"You have another daughter?"

"See, you're already interrupting. Sit back and listen."

Fina beckoned Mawaf over and introduced her to Cammy and Glen. Then she told Cammy Mawaf's story. "I'm in the process of adopting her."

"Absolutely not!" A loud, angry voice startled them. Both swiveled around to see an animated Bayo surrounded by a crowd of people. From the concerned look on Aman's face, Fina knew something was wrong. She grabbed Cammy's hand and dragged him toward the high table. They could not get close to their friends but could hear the conversation.

"Rather than give you money, let the party end right now," Bayo fumed.

"*Jos small tin, masta, and I go make sure de 'lectric kam back,*" said a thin, wrinkled-face man. He was the object of Bayo's ire. Fina recognized him as the hall's caretaker. The day before, he had appeared at Aman's house to assure her that everything was ready for the reception and party. Aunty Onike had reached into her handbag. "So we will have no problems." She had handed him a handful of bills, and he had assured her there will be no problems.

Now he was appealing to Aunty Onike who stood next to Bayo. "*Na foh give dem small tin, Mama.*"

"Are you deaf?" Bayo barked. "I will not give you or anyone else one more kobo. Move out of my way, *ojare.*" Bayo pushed the caretaker aside with one hand, grabbed Aman with the other, and pulled her behind him. He worked his way to the edge of the stage and looked out into the audience, particularly at the group already dancing in front of the drummers.

"Ladies and gentlemen," he shouted. His voice was drowned by the drums, which had risen up to a frenetic pace in an effort to fill the vacuum left by the silent stereo system. Bayo called out several times before the message was relayed to the drummers and a semblance of quiet took hold. "I'm sorry to announce that the party is over." The audience looked at him in disbelief. "This man wants me to give him some money so we can get the electricity back. I won't, and I don't want anyone to give him one single kobo. The party *don-don*. Thank you for coming."

Bayo intensified his grip on Aman and pulled her after him. They pummeled through the host of uncles and aunts. Some of them voiced their displeasure at the utter ridiculousness of a bride and groom telling family and guests to go home and, even worse, walking out of their own wedding party. "Is this what they teach you in America?" one of Bayo's aunts said, hissed loudly, and then took a swig of her Guinness stout.

As soon as Bayo and Aman left the hall, a group of angry uncles and aunts escorted the caretaker to a secluded part of the hall.

Cammy chuckled. "Looks like a good old-fashion shake down? Why is Bayo flipping?"

"I don't know. This is terrible."

"Yeah, for the guy they took over to the corner. We'll get power soon. Let's take a walk on the beach. It looks gorgeous."

"I'm just sorry for Aman. She has no family here."

"She'll be okay. She's with her husband." Fina was not reassured by this, but moments later Aunty Onike and the entourage that had left with the caretaker returned. They looked pleased with themselves and the caretaker seemed chastened. Bayo's uncle had gone to bring back the bride and groom. Everything would soon be back to normal. A little more comfortable with the evolving situation, Fina agreed to take the walk. Cammy turned around to check on Glen. He was sitting amid a group of young women.

They strolled onto a tranquil, sunset-draped Victoria Island beach. A cool, slight breeze frisked their faces. To their right, about a hundred yards off-shore, canoes with solitary fishermen frolicked on the Atlantic. Beyond them, three miniature ships lined the crimson-gold horizon. Onshore, to their left, the weeds and palm trees inclined with the breeze. They were too near the ocean to see the road, but they could still hear its traffic—the purposeful, accelerating urgency of cars, buses, and trucks on their way into mainland Lagos. But as they walked farther along, the beach curved away from the road, leaving behind the noise of the vehicles and exposing them to a deserted, open expanse of sand, a space that at once spoke of unlimited possibilities even as it revealed an inevitable, powerful, ubiquitous sameness. Neither spoke. They absorbed the setting, understood its somber paradox, and knew they had arrived at a crucial time in their relationship. They had strolled several hundred yards before Cammy began talking, explaining that he tracked her down through Aman and that they both agreed the wedding was the best time for him to come.

"So you're fully recovered now?"

"Yes and the outlook for Glen is excellent. But I have missed you so much, Fina." He had not planned to say that. It had just come out. Fina's heart skipped. She desperately wanted to know how he felt because throughout the flight to Lagos she could not get Sidibe Kakay's words out of her head. More, more, the voice in her head screamed. Fall on your knees, confess your undying love, ask..., no, beg... for my forgiveness. But she kept her composure and asked:

"Did you talk to Edna?"

"Yep. Called and told her when I was leaving. 'Have a safe flight,' was all she said.

"That's it?"

"Afraid so."

Fina bowed her head and looked at the sand.

"You have to find a way to set things right between you and Edna," Cammy said. An awkward silence followed.

He picked up a pebble and tried to skip it on the water. Fina watched him make several unsuccessful attempts and then left him to his own devices. She took off her slippers and made footprints in the sand. Then she stepped back and watched the waves erase them.

"What are you doing?"

"Seeing how long it takes before the waves wash away my footprints."

"Why?"

"Because you cannot follow footprints in the water."

"And you need an experiment to understand that?"

"Oh, hush. You're so literal. It shows we should travel tried and tested paths so we don't get lost."

"Yeah, but you can't make progress like that. It's only when I get lost that I learn my way around. You have to take risks."

"Yeah, but they can be costly. Remember a couple of years ago how we ended up not going to your friend's Christmas party? 'It runs parallel to the interstate,' you said. 'We'll get there faster.' But we never did."

"True but remember the payoff in that 14th Street motel?"

"I can't believe I let you take me to that seedy place." Fina smiled and skipped away to make another footprint. Cammy ran up to her side, took off his shoes and socks, and made his footprint beside hers. They stepped back and watched them deform and disappear.

Thirty minutes after they left the hall, they had reached the end of the useable section of the beach and were in an area marked with tufts of grass, seaweed, and granite boulders. Some were buried in the sand. Others stood in isolation. The white surf sprinted onto the beach, tickled their feet, and fizzled into the sand.

Cammy helped Fina sit up on one of the boulders, and they perched their shoes next to her. The boulder was not wide enough for the two of them, so Cammy leaned on it with his shoulder, his body half turned toward Fina and half toward the ocean. They both looked into the distance and saw the approaching darkness. As if jolted by the realization that danger lay coiled in it, Cammy abandoned all previous thoughts of being tactful.

"Why did yuh leave me without so much as an explanation? What happened?" The pain of the question only slightly quelled the anger it contained. Fina hesitated and tried several times to tell Cammy they should leave the past behind them, but Cammy argued he deserved an explanation, especially since she had left with his child.

"I needed a break, Cammy. *We* needed to step back."

"I understand that, but yuh just left, Fina—no phone call, explanation, nothing!"

271

"You're right, I should have told you. For that I'm sorry. But I'm not sorry I left."

"I thought we had something better than for yuh to treat me like that."

"Cammy, I don't say this to be hurtful, but that's exactly what I thought when you left me in the vestry. Now, you understand how I feel."

Cammy threw his head back, closed his eyes and choked back his resentment. "Ah guess we're even then." He let out a sigh, eased off the boulder, and picked up a pebble. Then he sprinted toward the ocean and threw the pebble as far as he could. He stood with his back to Fina and looked out into the Atlantic. Its waves raced up the sand and soaked the hem of his *sokoto* pants.

Fina walked up to his side and inserted her arms into his.

"I didn't leave to get even."

She rested her chin on his shoulder.

"Why did you leave then?"

"Because of the accident."

Cammy turned toward her. "What are yuh saying? The white dude recovered. He told the police what happened. I didn't have to lie."

"That's true, but you were ready to...," Fina started, then changed course. "That's not the accident I meant anyway."

When her meaning dawned on him, Cammy said. "What did you expect me to do, Fina?"

"I'm not blaming you, Cammy. But the whole thing—how the accident happened, the way the police, the lawyer, and your dad made the matter go away, and the blackmail business with Scraps. These things reopened some old wounds for me."

"Well, it so happens I now know I was not the driver."

"Really?"

"Yes, really. Scraps told Anushka that Chaplin, one of the boys I was with that night, was the driver. And yes, I know that does not excuse the fact that I was part of the accident, but at least I was not the driver."

272

"But at the time, you and your parents believed you were."

"What did yuh want us to do, Fina?" Cammy was now visibly irritated.

"Nothing. But when you told me what happened and the way you dismissed the possibility of Kizzy going to jail, all of that just reminded me of my foster brother, Ade."

"Yuh felt sorry for Kizzy after what he did to yuh?"

"I guess so. I'd certainly like to see him punished for what he did to me, but I don't want to know that he got punished for something he did not do. Anyway, I was more surprised and concerned about you. You became like Ade—people protected from the worst consequences of their own actions, able to get away with... mur...a lot. As a young girl, I swore I'd avoid such people if I couldn't fight them."

"Lemme get this straight. Yuh holding against me an accident that happened when ah was a teen, that ah know now wasn't my fault? Yuh holding it against me because my father used his position to help me? What was he supposed to do? Yuh wanted my father not to help me? Good gad! Which is it, class envy or hate? There's not much hope for us, Fina."

Cammy took a couple of steps forward as if to emphasize the gap between them. Fina remained standing in the same place. The Atlantic waves rushed through the gap between them and wiped away Cammy's footprints.

"I don't hold anything against you, Cammy. I'm just trying to get you to understand why I left. But, as usual, you don't want to listen. You ask for an explanation and yet you don't want to hear it."

"Fina, ah fed up, just fed up with your issues." Cammy exhaled, walked back, and leaned against the boulder. Fina followed and leaned next to him. They remained silent. Neither wanted to be the first to leave nor the first to restart the conversation, so they watched the waves race onto the shore and the sun collapse into the horizon. The breeze sharpened and the beach darkened. The Atlantic suddenly became a menacing presence.

"It has not been particularly good to us, has it?" Fina mused.

273

"What?"

"It." Fina stared at the ocean.

"What do you mean?" Cammy asked, relieved that the conversation had turned away from his accident.

"The Atlantic has not been kind to us."

"Who?"

"Black people."

"I guess," Cammy replied, perplexed.

"I mean many of us are buried in it. Many suffered because of it. And now it separates us."

"Maybe" Cammy said, seeming to catch up to Fina's meaning. "But *yuh* put it between us. *Yuh* left *me* and came over here!"

"True, but I came back to where I belong. You belong over *there*. And what's between us?"

"More than the Atlantic separates us, Fina. We're so different."

"Exactly! For all your M.D., you're not very bright sometimes," she said playfully and smiled, quelling Cammy's irritation. "Yes, we're worlds apart."

"Maybe, but does that mean we can't overcome our differences? Why do you think ah come here? Ah can see in your eyes and voice that you're happy ah come. Ah even see yuh want me right now."

"Look at you," Fina smiled.

"Seriously, we belong together. Ah know it. Yuh know it. Ah not going to let you walk away. Ah don't care about culture, experience, and the Atlantic. We belong together."

Fina basked in the warmth of his convictions but said nothing. They remained in a silent, ambivalent tension.

"Fina, come back and live with me in the States. Let's give ourselves another chance and give Dimusu-Celeste all that America, life, can offer."

"Oh, Cammy, please don't ask me to leave my work. The kids need me. Mawaf and Mama Yegbe need me. They all need someone who'll love and protect them, be there for them."

"I understand what yuh saying believe me, but what about us? Yuh can do the same kind of work in the States. There are needy kids all over America too. They deserve yuh help too."

"It's not the same, Cammy. I love the work I'm doing. It's important to *me*."

"Look at Aman. She could be helping kids in America but she's here. Whether yuh here or in America, the important thing is yuh'll be helping kids somewhere."

"Come on, Cammy. Working in Sierra Leone, helping my people is satisfying in a way that can't happen in America. Besides, the need is greater and more urgent."

"And what about Dimusu-Celeste?"

"What about her?"

"Doesn't she deserve to grow up with both her parents?"

"Yes, then *you* come and live with us."

Cammy paused, but he knew he could not think too long on Fina's proposal. "Permanently?"

"Permanently, temporarily. Does it matter? The real question is, are you willing to?"

"Sure, Fina, but—"

"But what? Your practice, the money, the inconvenience, what?"

"Frankly, all those things. Ah have a lot of money invested, and we'll be giving up a lot."

"No, Cammy, *you'll* be giving up a lot. But it will be for us—you, me, Dimusu-Celeste."

"Come on, Fina, yuh asking me to leave a profitable, well-established practice. I kyant—"

"Set aside your needs for me and your daughter?"

Cammy locked his hands together and exhaled through the gap between his thumbs as if he was whistling.

"Yuh asking a heck of a lot."

"I wish you hadn't said that. It's okay for you to ask me to leave everything I'm doing here, but it's not okay for me to ask the same of you?" Fina choked back the disappointment threatening to erupt into fighting words. "Just know that I feel the same sense of commitment, drive, and desire to follow my path as you do."

Again Cammy and Fina stopped talking and stared at the ocean, which had blended with the horizon into a seamless blackness, an open space full of uncertainty and peril made all the more so by the swaggering waves descending on the shore. Both felt suddenly vulnerable, away from the familiarity of the hall, which, from where they were, was now a distant speck. They decided to return but on the walk back, each searched for a way to keep the dialogue going, to accommodate the other's needs, to cross the interposing Atlantic.

"But what about schools, health care…and… you don't even live in a city." The words limped out of Cammy as they approached the hall, which was now well lit. Fina stopped, locked her arm with his under the *agbada*, and snuggled close to him so that their walk became slower and unsteady on the shifting sands.

"Weren't you the one who once said you wanted to be bigger than one place or culture? Well, here's your opportunity. Where's the man who wants to take risks so he can grow?" Cammy recalled his words and wondered about the chasm between an uttered ideal and an executed reality.

"Doctors in Africa are very comfortable too, you know. And the schools are quite good. Besides, we're talking about learning the alphabet. If we were talking about going to college, there's CC, remember."

But as Fina's mind went to her unfinished degree and Kizzy, she determined that Dimusu-Celeste would never attend CC. She looked at Cammy and was sure he was thinking the same. She changed the subject. "Life where I work is not easy. At times it's downright tough, but I want the satisfaction of knowing that I gave it my best shot. I'm just asking you to hold my hand and be by my side. I need your strength. Can you give it to me?" Cammy basked in the role in which he was being cast, but he was also aware that he was not quite in control of the situation, and he did not like it.

"I don't know, Fina, I don't know," he repeated.

"You know, Cammy, love is like a diamond. Rough and ugly when you first find it. But if you work at it, clean and polish it, its beauty will shine through."

"How about if we alternate visits first, take turns washing and cleaning this rough diamond?" Cammy proposed as he held open the door leading to the lobby of the hall.

"That might work."

"Does she have a U.S. passport?" Cammy asked.

"Who?"

"Dimusu-Celeste."

"No."

"You better get one soon."

"Yes, I thought of that too, but it also makes me sad that even as I try to make life better for the kids I work with, I'm planning to make sure my own gets all the advantages of being American."

"That's life, Fina. Like my dad, yuh doing what's in the best interest of yuh kid."

"True, but only people born with a silver spoon in their mouth and have had parents to protect and pursue their interests can afford to be satisfied with that."

"Yuh know what?" Cammy stopped just inside the door and addressed Fina. "Let's forget all of this for now. Yuh can change the world after ah gone."

"Oh, there's one more thing you should know," Fina exclaimed, restraining Cammy.

"Good gad, Fina, ah hope it's not something else that happened—"

"No, no, but I wanted you to know that I am a practicing Muslim."

"Weren't yuh always?"

"Yes, but I was not a true believer. Now I am."

"You mean yuh a born-again Muslim?"

"See, you treat everything like a joke"

"Ah do not. Look, yuh being Muslim is fine with me. Just don't ask me to become one."

"No, but it means I pray five times a day, and I will live by the teaching of the Qur'an."

"Will you have more than one husband?"

"You see—"

"Okay, okay. Ah jus' kidding."

"But it means that we cannot do anything tonight because you're not my husband."

Cammy stopped and stared at Fina. He wanted to say he would later put that born-again resolve to the test but simply said, "Let's jus' go and dance, okay?"

Hand in hand, they walked into the hall. The music was loud to the point of being searing. Men, women, and children danced as medleys of up-tempo music blasted through speakers stationed in the four corners of the hall. Cammy and Fina walked up to the high table. Fina pulled Aman aside and left Cammy to talk to Bayo.

"I just wanted to say thank you for always having my back. You have been the sister to me that I have not always been to you."

"What was it you once told me about neighbors and family?"

"Niya nehba behteh pass fawey fambul?"

"Yes, there's a lot of wisdom in that. Like everything else families must learn to grow if they are to survive. Let's build ours."

They hugged and rejoined Cammy and Bayo. Aman explained Bayo had agreed to return to the hall only after he had been assured no money changed hands and a mechanical breakdown had caused the blackout.

"We've got to stop this kind of thing," Bayo made his case to Cammy. "We'll only be able to change this country when we either hold somebody accountable or forgo something we want."

"True, but yuh gotta keep yuh cool, man. The way ah see you vex, yuh could easily have a heart attack, man. Ah seen it happen."

"That's what I keep telling him," Aman echoed.

"Hey, don't worry about me. Go and enjoy yourselves."

And so Fina and Cammy danced—hot, extemporaneous, and independent at first. The up-tempo mix of highlife, salsa, calypso, funk and pop dictated hip and torso modulations, body segmentations, wild arm gestures and quick leg work. But as the party settled into the small hours, the melodies changed to older, more mid-tempo tunes that demanded greater cooperation, accommodation. So they sensed each other's movements, following and being followed, moving and being moved, falling and rising, turning arm under arm and over head, rolling into and incorporating each other. By dawn, as Bayo and Aman said their goodbyes, Cammy and Fina, barefoot, had become a duet—turning, rolling, and surrendering themselves to each other. Time stopped, the air between them disappeared, and their heartbeats merged as they danced in the beachfront hall in that coastal West African city. Outside, the night emerged into day, bearing the still mighty but now placid Atlantic.

****

He wanted to see Dimusu-Celeste, so they had all flown back to Freetown, and he held her in his arms, squeezed, and kissed her cheeks. His heart swelled and he brimmed with love for this bundle of joy that had Celeste Priddy's sharp stare but Judge Priddy's quiet demeanor. Fina gave him a tour of the Center and showed him, first, the kids with the mangled limbs and mangled minds. Then she showed him the ones without limbs and without minds. She introduced him to Mama Yegbe, to the girls, to the ones who belonged but who also could benefit from his surgical skills.

She took him to Talaba and pointed to the burnt out village, to where the compound once stood, to the forest, now stripped and weary, within which was the *fafei*. On their way back, the road with the tall grass on either side reminded him of the one they had taken on the drive to the beachlime. On the drive back from the beachlime, he knew now that he had not been driving and so had not seen the little girl, but he imagined how she might have run out from the tall grass and the thud as the car had slammed against her body. And he was sad. He wondered if she might have been saved if there had been a doctor in the area.

Yet they had lives that had to be lived and futures that had to be planned. East or westward, the Atlantic was not a sea one traversed lightly or without thought. Yet, the goodbye at Lungi International Airport was hopeful. She said only that she wanted his support for the path that she walked. When he and Glen turned back to wave one last time before they disappeared into the airplane, he saw the mother of his daughter, the woman with whom he had danced those calypso songs, and he knew he would come back, for this was a path he could not let die.

Epilogue

A s had been their ritual over three years living in Sierra Leone, Mawaf, Cammy, or Fina took turns to tuck Dimusu-Celeste into bed. Some nights she slept immediately. On other nights she would complain or ask questions. On still other nights, she would get a talking to about why her behavior earlier in the day was wrong and unacceptable. On those nights, especially if the talking to had come from Fina, she would say, "Mommy, tell me the story of the women of Musudugu." It was one of Dimusu-Celeste's favorites. She had heard it many times. Indeed, over the years, Fina had embellished many parts of the story, but it always ended with Kumba Kargbo's dirge. And the effect on Dimusu-Celeste was almost always the same. She would feel sad and would promise her mom that she would never leave her and never destroy their home.

But one night after hearing the dirge, Dimusu-Celeste asked, "Mommy, does Kumba Kargbo ever stop singing that sad song?"

"I don't know, honey, that's where the story ends."

Dimusu-Celeste said nothing but appeared deep in thought. Fina noticed.

"Why do you ask?"

"Because it's too sad."

"So you want a happy ending?"

Dimusu-nodded.

"Well, tell me how you would want the story to end."

Dimusu-Celeste sat upright and thought for a minute. "Like this. And when the women, men, and animals from the outside heard Kumba Kargbo's song," she adopted a storyteller's tone, "they all came to Musudugu."

"'Why are you crying,' they asked.

"'Because I have destroyed Musudugu.'

"They laughed.

"'Why are you laughing?' Kumba Kargbo asked them.

281

"'Because we can build a new Musudugu,' they answered.

"And so Kumba Kargbo stopped crying and the women and the men worked together to build a new Musudugu and lived together happily ever after. The End."

Fina kissed Dimusu-Celeste goodnight. She walked into her bedroom, picked up the phone, snuggled next to Cammy who was reading a newspaper and dialed. "Edna," she began after a few seconds. Cammy set aside the newspaper, put his hand around her, and listened.

CPSIA information can be obtained at www.ICGtesting.com
Printed in the USA
BVOW05s0920170915

418392BV00005B/7/P

9 789956 727377